TRADEWINDS

THERE'S A SCHOONER IN THE OFFING,
HER TOPS'L'S SHOT WITH FIRE.
MY HEART HAS GONE ABOARD HER,
TO THE ISLE OF MY DESIRE.

C.E. Bowman

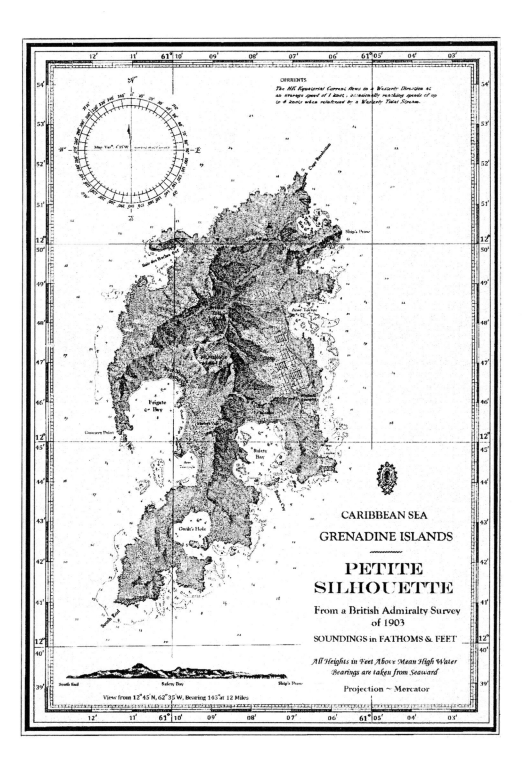

CURRENTS
The NE Equatorial Current flows in a Westerly Direction at
an average speed of 1 knot, occasionally reaching speeds of up
to 4 knots when reinforced by a Westerly Tidal Stream.

Mag. Varⁿ. 65°W

CARIBBEAN SEA

GRENADINE ISLANDS

PETITE
SILHOUETTE

From a British Admiralty Survey
of 1903

SOUNDINGS in FATHOMS & FEET

*All Heights in Feet Above Mean High Water
Bearings are taken from Seaward*

Projection ~ Mercator

View from 12° 45' N, 62° 35' W, Bearing 145° at 12 Miles

South End   Safety Bay   Ship's Prow

TRADEWINDS

A Tale of the Caribbean

C.E. BOWMAN

Copyright © 2014 C.E. Bowman

Published by Tradewind Publishing
www.tradewindpublishing.com

National Library of Australia Cataloguing-in-Publication entry
Author: Bowman, C. E., author.
Title: Tradewinds : a tale of the Caribbean / C. E. Bowman.
ISBN: 978-0-9942-490-0-5 (paperback)
Subjects: Shipwreck survival--Caribbean Area--Fiction.
          World War, 1939-1945--Fiction.
          Suspense fiction.
Dewey Number: A823.4

All artwork by C. E. Bowman
Cover Design by C. E. Bowman
Chart of Petite Silhouette © C.E. Bowman 2014
Chart of Caribbean by C.E. Bowman
Schooner *Roulette* based on original lines drawing of schooner *Harmony* by
B.B. Crowninshield, 1903

This Book is Dedicated to

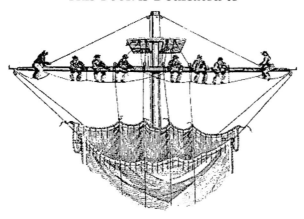

~All of the~

SHIPWRIGHTS, Sailors, *vagabonds*, **RIGGERS, rogues,** GUITAR STRUMMERS,
JACKS *of all* **TRADES, soul adventurers, SURVIVORS,** fo'c'sle philosophers,
SMUGGLERS, *Lovers of Life*, & GENTLEMEN OF FORTUNE

I've ever had the pleasure to meet.

As well as

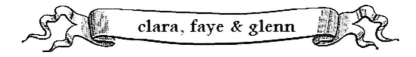

clara, faye & glenn

my three loving children.

But most of all, to my wife

VANESSA

Author's Note

*I am energized by fiction. Deep in a novel, one scarcely knows
what may surface next, let alone where it comes from. In
abandoning oneself to the free creation of something never beheld
on earth, one feels almost delirious with a strange joy.*
- Peter Mathiessen -

I first stepped ashore onto the island of Barbados in the spring of
1974, having spent thirty-eight days crossing the Atlantic Ocean
from the Canary Islands aboard a twenty-one foot sloop. It was
quite an adventure. Halfway across we lost our rudder and were
forced to steer the balance of the way with a large oar. Not long
after we found our reserve drinking water was contaminated by
diesel fuel, and for the last few days lived off raw fish when our
bottle of cooking gas ran out. Needless to say, we were happy to
reach dry land.

And what a land we found! Barbados was the epitome of the
lyrical, magical Caribbean of my youthful dreams. After repairing
our boat, we sailed west and landed on the Grenadine Island of
Bequia. Little did I know at the time how my life would eventually
become entwined with this delightful island and its people. I
would end up living there for over twelve years, working
alongside the island's shipwrights and learning to build wooden
boats on the beach by 'hand and eye', from small fishing boats to
sloops to eventually a seventy foot schooner.

The sea ran through these islanders' veins, and no craft could
be built without attracting comment from all and sundry. It was
there, under the trees, that stories and tales and histories of the
West Indies' colourful past would be told amidst the sounds of the

adze, hatchet and caulking mallet. And it was during those days I first heard tell of the death and destruction to the local schooner fleets caused by German U-boats during World War Two. These stories pricked my imagination, and stuck with me for years.

Decades later, I finally decided to sit down and attempt to weave all of that experience into a novel. Although this book is a work of fiction, I have tried to keep timelines and historical details as accurate as possible. Surprisingly little has ever been written about the German advances into the Caribbean during WWII, and I give great thanks to Gaylord T. M. Kelshall and his exhaustive treatise "The U-Boat War in the Caribbean" for so many of the facts this book has been built around.

Every Caribbean island has a different story to tell. Each has its own unique culture and heritage. The one common thread that ties these disparate people together is the sea. So to tell a West Indian story, sea water must be a part of it. The tale you are about to read, therefore, is immersed in salt spray and sea breeze and weather tide and rain squalls and sunrise landfalls and midnight rendezvous, along with local patois, creole food, and a fair lashing of rum. If you're not a 'seafaring type', unfamiliar with the Caribbean, or need some clarification on the local dialect, I have included some charts and maps to assist you, as well as a glossary of terms and an illustration of a schooner, which you will find in the back of the book.

The island of Petite Silhouette exists only in my imagination, and its people, traditions and history are of my own creation. But through the miracle of the written word, you, dear reader, can step aboard that old 'Banks schooner, and with the purple peak of Mount Majestic hovering on the distant horizon and the easterly tradewinds blowing a solid breeze over the quarter, ease the mainsheet and set a course across the sparkling Caribbean towards that alluring, enchanting isle. I sincerely hope you enjoy the sail.

C.E. Bowman
Spring, 2014

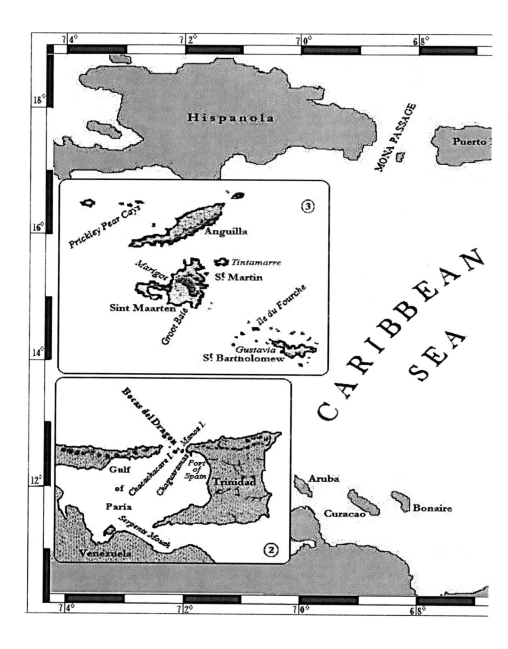

Hispanola

Puerto

MONA PASSAGE

③

Prickley Pear Cays

Anguilla

Tintamarre

Marigot

S.t Martin

Sint Maarten

Groot Baii

Ile du Fourche

Gustavia

S.t Bartholomew

C A R I B B E A N   S E A

Bocas del Dragon

Chacachacare I.

Monos I.

Port of Spain

Gulf of Paria

Chaguaramas

Trimidad

Serpens Mouth

Venezuela

Aruba

Curacao

Bonaire

②

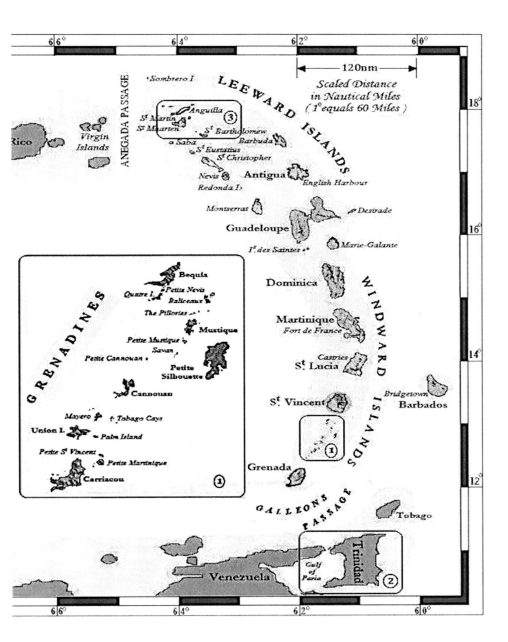

PART I

Barbados Careenage

NOVEMBER, 1941

Homeward Bound

Sunrise. Schooners rolled gently in the sheltered bay. Smoke from the galleyhouse drifted to leeward with the easterly trades. On board the *Roulette*, the crew was shaking out the cobwebs with a breakfast of fried johnny-cakes and salt fish stew they called 'bull jowl'. Good food the morning after drinking rum. A kettle of strong coffee sat atop the wood-fired stove and they helped themselves to large enamel cups of it.

Lounging about the deck, they savoured their spicy breakfast between animated jokes and laughter, the only topic of conversation being the thrilling boat race sailed the day before.

"Man – dat is what you call boat race!" said Bull, a big black man who like most of the crew had sailed with the skipper for years. "You just can't beat the Cap'n when it comes to tatics."

"An you t'ink Bequia-men easy?" joined in Kingsford. "When you does beat dem you truly know you done somethin'. But dey doesn't have a whaleboat yet to match the ol' *Antipodes!* Mon, when she does put her nose up yonder to windward dey ain't nuttin' goin' to cross her."

"Well dem fellas sure is tired seein' de King's Cup sail 'way fo' another year," called out Jono the cook from inside the galley. "I heard talk on de beach yesterday dat Blakey goin' back to de bush to build again."

"Blakey can build all de boat he wants, but we all know 'it's not boat beats boat, its man beats man'," added Gilbert with a laugh. The lively conversation continued as one by one the crew slowly stood and dropped their plates in the wash tub next to the galley door. Bare feet slid across wooden decks as they began to go about the business of preparing the schooner for the sail home.

"Ok boys – le' all we go! Remember we sailin' off de hook today fo' ol' time's sake, so stand by de peak an' throat," ordered

Zepheryn, the mate. "Dere's no profit in us sittin' around tellin' lies all day!" The men gathered around the two halyards and in silent rhythm slowly hoisted the heavy flaxen mainsail, the squeak of manila through halyard blocks echoing around the quiet bay. Once the mainsail was set, the crew put their backs into hauling up the heavy fisherman's anchor. Breaking free of the sandy bottom, it arose from the placid water and was made fast to the cat head. The stem staysail was hoisted and backed and the mainsail eased as the schooner's head fell away with the breeze. Slowly she began to gather way. The gaff foresail was raised next, then the jib. A shout rang out from an anchored vessel. Arms waved in silent tribute. The mate eased more of the mainsheet, and after weathering Middle Cay the emerald green schooner cleared out from the lee of the land. In the bright light of the early morning sun she heeled to the fresh breeze and was soon roaring along with a bone in her teeth, homeward bound for the island of Petite Silhouette, twelve miles to the southeast of Bequia in the northern part of the Grenadines.

"Hey Henry, are you done with those dishes? We've got a sweet breeze here," called the captain to his son from the wheel. "Why don't you come and take a trick at the wheel?"

The young boy came quickly aft and took hold of the wheel from his father, who pointed out the faint top of their island to him. "There's your course, mate – right at Mount Majestic. You just steer nice and steady and the boys will set the sails to suit."

The sails were trimmed and the schooner worked her way over the rocky islet of Petit Nevis. The crew could now relax, scattering themselves about the after deck, occasionally calling out advice to the young helmsman. The captain took a last look around. "I'll leave it to you, Zeph. I might put my head down for a bit. It could be I had one too many Jack Irons last night," he said with a sheepish grin as he stepped down to his cabin below.

"Dat's no problem, Cap. We does have a good man here at de helem, don't frighten. When you does win a boat race you's entitled to drink rum…even if it does mash you up next day," the mate replied.

"Hold she down Henry!" shouted Kingsford from the rail. "Den when you get de puffs le' go yo' hand an' let she swipe!"

"Fordy's right, Henry. Keep she head down low and le' de weather tide carry you up," advised the mate, standing next to the wheel. "Bull, jump a piece o' dat mainsheet gi' me," he added, turning towards the big man in the stern. Blocks squeaked as the heavy inch-and-a-quarter manila ran out a foot or two. The *Roulette* charged across the flat water in the lee of Mustique, their course taking them past the southern point of the island and to windward of the small islets of Petite Mustique and Savan.

The boy stood confidently to weather of the wheel box perched on the aft deck of the old New England fishing schooner, the end of the long main boom skimming over the deep blue of the Caribbean Sea, white water foaming off to leeward, occasionally washing through the deep bulwarks as the *Roulette* thundered through the passage and out into the open sea, the features of their island now becoming more distinct as they close reached home at over ten knots. The weathered first mate stood to leeward, keeping an eye on the young boy, every now and then gently correcting their course by reaching over and turning the wheel slightly.

"Uncle Zeph," the boy asked as he braced himself against the spokes of the cast iron wheel, "dere's somethin' dat I been wonderin' 'bout lately. Where do de Tradewinds come from? Does dey just spring out o' de sea and sky?"

A smile etched itself across the lips of the kindly black man as he stole a sideways glance at the young boy. "Well dat's a damn good question Henry – it's somethin' me never really put much t'ought into. I jus' know de Trades always was and always will be, and a good ting too, 'cause without 'em de people in dese islands would surely find it hard fo' makin' a livin'."

"I know dat, but where do dey really come from? How're dey made? Dey can't jus' come from nothin', can dey?" Henry persisted.

"Well me no know how true it is, but de old people say dat dey does spring up all de way over in Africa, which is way up yonder to windward, a few t'ousand miles away at least. It must be a hell-of-a windy place, 'cause dat's where de hurricanes does breed befo' dey does come here to gi' we hell." The mate paused as though deep in thought. "You know Henry, dat's a damn good question! Dat's why you must stop playin' de fool an' stay in school – so you can learn 'bout dem kind o' tings. I know yo' momma's real worried 'bout you."

Henry rolled his eyes and smirked. "Dat blasted place too borin', mon," the boy whispered under his breath. "It worse dan bein' in jail."

Zepheryn just gazed aloft, smiling to himself.

The captain emerged from his cabin and took a look around. They were only a mile or so off, and it was time to start trimming the sheets. "Ok Zeph, let's start hardening up," he said, walking back to stand next to his son at the wheel. Henry started to make room for his father, but he motioned for him to stay. "It's alright Henry. You've got us this far, mate. It's up to you to take her in."

The crew began to stir from their various spots and move towards their positions. First the fores'l and stays'l were hauled in tight, followed by the jib. When this was done all hands moved aft and threw themselves into trimming the long mainsheet, some pulling on the standing part, others on the tail as they slowly brought the powerful sail in. With everything strapped in tight the gaff schooner heeled to the breeze, Henry coaxing her up as close to the wind as she would go. A flock of seabirds scattered from their perches as they sailed close by Fish Rocks, crying and squawking and wheeling in the air as they passed to leeward of the guano covered outcroppings. The schooner charged into the broad expanses of Frigate Bay. The darker blue of the deep-water channel merged into aqua and then turquoise, marking the reef that lay off the opposite shore ahead.

The crew patiently waited for the call to tack as they sailed towards the quickly approaching shallows. Still Henry carried on. There were a few uneasy glances aft, but the boy resolutely held his nerve. Zepheryn cleared his throat and was about to reach for the wheel when the shout was heard.

"Ready about!" piped the red-skinned boy standing at the wheel, his shoulders barely above the top wooden spokes. With the crew in position he then mimicked the often heard words of his father and shouted, "helms-a-lee!" Turning the wheel hard to port the green schooner shot up into the breeze, sails and sheets popping and cracking like gunshots, before falling off and filling on the opposite tack.

"Good tack Henry! Dat was well done," said Zeph approvingly.

"Any closer an' he'd be cleanin' de keel-bottom wit' sand," Kingsford muttered.

"Dat boy everything like he father in truth!" Earl agreed.

They pressed on into the flat waters of the bay, the breeze now over their starboard bow, gusting down off of the green hills, showing itself in dark lines as it whistled across the opaque water and out to sea. The schooner sped towards the glittering beach ahead, keeping the grey boulders of Gunnery Point beneath them to port, the white *Roulette* pennant with green piping streaming from the masthead for all to see. At a cable's length from shore they tacked again, and as they shot through the wind the jib halyard was let go, the downhaul secured and the flapping sail quickly handed and tied down to the long bowsprit.

Without her headsail the schooner slowed markedly. One by one the balance of the sails were methodically lowered, flaked and secured. Earl slipped down below and started the engine and the boat motored slowly towards the jetty in the centre of the bay, the town of Port Victoria tucked in neatly behind it. Henry took the schooner right alongside, the lines were secured, and the engine shut down.

"Dat's what you does call sailorizing, Henry!" yelled Kingsford as he made fast a brestline. "We don't need no hogshit ol' tyres – we can use eggs fo' fenders!"

"I still want to know where de Tradewinds come from, Uncle Zepheryn," Henry said to the mate amidst the hubbub of being alongside.

"Man, you holds on like a bull shark to an ol' carcass! When you does find out you come and tell me, you hear? A man's never too old to learn," the mate replied with a feigned look of seriousness.

They were home.

The arrival of any schooner into Frigate Bay was always the cause of great interest amongst the residents of the small community of Port Victoria, but today's appearance of the *Roulette* was especially anticipated. From the moment her sails appeared from around Gunnery Point, people from all parts of the harbour began to make their way towards the main wharf. Small boys raced down the beach and onto the wooden jetty, all hoping to be the one to catch a mooring line thrown from the docking schooner.

Once alongside, the crew were quick to offload the small amount of goods from the midships hold, laughing and joking as they graphically delivered tack by tack accounts of the race to the inquisitive crowd. Six goats that had been taken on board in Bequia and tied to the foremast were carefully passed ashore. The captain stood by the main rigging keeping an eye on proceedings, accepting congratulations from various well-wishers for winning the big race yet again, as well as enjoying a joke or two with some of the old timers. He stood apart, as in most of the ports in the West Indies, as one of the only white faces in the crowd of multi-hued locals, but beyond that he was treated as if he were a native. There were enclaves of white West Indians on the various islands; descendants of English, Irish, Welsh and Scottish indentured servants who were brought out by British planters in the 17 and 1800's. Petite Silhouette had a few of these clans, as well as a number of families whose roots went back to the original French settlers of the island. The captain could easily be mistaken for a 'Bajan', as white locals were called, and often was.

"Jack McLeod! You old Aussie bastard! Don't tell me you've gone and won the Cup again!" The voice boomed over the commotion on the wharf, and Jack turned to see the familiar figure of his good friend Aubrey Kincaid making his way towards him, clad in his traditional white tropical suit and pith helmet. As he fetched up alongside, the bespeckled gentleman leaned on his walking stick and shook Jack's hand vigorously. "Well done Old Man, well done! Yet another year of bragging rights, eh what? I would love to hear all about it over a whiskey or two. By the way, this evening Edwina and I are having dinner with the new secretary to the Territory Administrator who is visiting from Barbados, along with a few others. I apologize for putting you on short notice, but we would love to have you and Jasmine join us. We do have a responsibility to maintain some sort of civility in these outposts of the Empire, wouldn't you agree?"

"Sounds good to me, mate. I'm sure Jasmine would love to come," Jack responded. Just then Zeph signaled they were done offloading. "I'd better get the ol' girl put away. We haven't had much of a chance to spend time at home lately, and I'm sure the boys would like to make the most of it. I'll see you this evening."

"Quite right, quite right. We'll look forward to seeing you for sun-downers on the veranda sometime around six, old chap."

Lines were let go and pulled aboard and the schooner backed slowly away from the wharf. A little further up the beach they picked up their moorings made fast to the coconut trees. The hatches were pushed shut, the skiff and the whaleboat were brought alongside, and after a final look around Jack and his crew dropped lightly down into the boats and pulled themselves ashore.

"Do you want Errol an' me to look after de vessel tonight, Papa?" Henry asked, trying to hide his excitement.

"Okay son, but no skylarkin', you hear? When you two are together there's nothin' but trouble. You boys can go aboard after supper."

As the skiff touched the shore two small girls in colourful dresses ran out of the shade and grabbed Jack's legs as he stepped out of the boat, their dark, curly hair plaited and tied with pink ribbons. "Daddy! Daddy! Pick me up!" they anxiously called out, holding up their arms as they jumped up and down.

"Hold on girls – hold on! Let me help pull the whaleboat up first," Jack smiled. With all of the crew grabbing on to her gunnels, the whaleboat was hauled up and chocked under the coconut trees. "I'll see you blokes tomorrow," he said, as the crew broke up, each of them moving off in a different direction towards home. Stooping down he picked the two girls up, giving them each a big kiss before walking across the white sand beach to where his wife Jasmine stood holding their youngest son in her arms. The little boy squirmed, reaching out to be held by his father, and so after putting the girls down he accepted the infant, cradling him in his arms.

"G'day Jaz," he smiled, giving her a kiss.

A smile flashed across her smooth, honey-coloured face as she reached down to take her little girl's hands. Henry sauntered over, bashfully greeting his mother. She ruffled his kinky hair, bleached almost blond by the sun.

"How was de trip Henry? You enjoy yourself?"

"It was okay," he answered with a mischievous smirk.

"Okay!?" Jack retorted. "All you did was sail aboard the boat that won the King's Cup! And then tell your mother what you did today," he urged.

"Oh yeah. I steered *Roulette* all de way back home."

"What? Well boy, you really are growin' up," she smiled, rubbing his head once again, much to his embarrassment.

And so Jack and his family made their way off of the beach, across Bay Road, and on to the narrow foot path leading up the hill to their home. The house sat on a ridge just to the south of Port Victoria; high enough to see over the tops of the coconut trees fringing the crescent shaped bay. As the family reached home the captain patiently listened as his daughters vied for his attention, each eagerly trying to explain all that had taken place in his absence. After lunch, the excitement of Jack's arrival home had run its course, and in the early afternoon he wandered out into the cool shade of the veranda. Gazing over the masts of several moored sloops and schooners, his eyes swept north across Frigate Bay, past the ruins of the ancient fort atop Gunnery Point, and on to the islands of Petite Mustique, Savan, Mustique, Baliceaux and Battowia. To leeward of them he could clearly see the blue outline of Bequia and the surrounding cays and small islets of Petit Nevis, Ile de Quatre, and Rameau. In the far distance he could even pick out the high volcanic peak of St. Vincent, almost thirty miles away. Turning south, his gaze wandered over the bird rock of Petite Cannouan to the bigger island of Cannouan, and then on to Mayreau, the Tobago Cays, Union Island, Petit St. Vincent, Petite Martinique, Carriacou and the rest of the smaller islands, reefs and cays of the lower Grenadines. At a distance of over forty-five miles, and just subtly colouring the southern horizon, lay the purple smudge which he knew to be Grenada.

Jack relaxed against a veranda post, lost in thought. He could never grow tired of the view. The ping of a few raindrops shook him from his reverie as they began to bounce off the corrugated iron roof overhead. In minutes it became a deluge as a sizeable rain squall blew down over the windward hills behind. Soon the picture window he seemed to be looking through was completely blotted from view as heavy rain and wind whipped across the harbour and away towards the western horizon. "Moon rise squall," Jack said to himself, turning to go inside. "Funny how quick the weather can change."

Plantation House

An invitation to the Kincaids' for dinner was always a welcome diversion from the daily routine of island life. These formal get-togethers didn't come along too often, and the most was made of them when they did.

After the heavy squall, their now slippery path had to be negotiated with care. Jasmine tucked the hem of her skirt into her waist, and holding her shoes in one hand and Jack's arm with the next went down the track barefoot. Even Jack was worried about splattering mud over his white trousers, so he rolled them up to his knees. Arriving at Plantation House at the stroke of six, however, the couple appeared as if they had been delivered by coach.

Wearing a white dinner jacket and perfectly creased black trousers, Aubrey Kincaid was the consummate host. "Edwina and I are so glad to have you with us this evening," he said upon welcoming them. "Come join us on the veranda."

The other guests on the broad porch stood to greet the arriving couple, and were formally introduced by Aubrey. "Jasmine, Jack, I would like you to meet Mr Reginald Bucknell and his wife Agnes, the newly appointed first secretary to His Majesty's Governor of Barbados. Of course you are well acquainted with the vigilant upholder of law and order on our fair isle, Senior Constable Peter Ballentyne, and his wife June, as well as our overworked and underpaid Headmaster Gregory Stockton and his better half Mary...leaving last but far from least my lovely wife Edwina." Greetings were made all round and orders for drinks were taken and brought by Herbert, the tall, jet black waiter dressed in an immaculate white suit.

"Cheers everyone, cheers and good health," the host said as he toasted his guests. The veranda was perched over the manicured gardens that were the Kincaid's pride and joy, and the party was blessed with a spectacular sunset over Gunnery Point as the last of the afternoon's rain squall exploded in a blaze of pastel hues and colours on the western horizon.

"I damn well have to admit I'd rather be here than in London right now, eh what!" Aubrey began. "I was listening to the wireless earlier today, and the reports out of Europe don't sound at all promising. There seems to be no stopping this Hitler chap – he damn well means business! His armies are driving deep into Russia; he has pushed right through the Balkans and marched into Athens. From the latest reports the Australians are just holding on in Tobruk, but Rommel and his Afrika Corps is cutting a swath through North Africa. If it weren't for the stubbornness of our countrymen back home, the swastika would be flying high over all of Europe."

"Yes, there seems to be no let-up in sight – especially with the Americans still neutral," agreed Bucknell, a sandy mop of curly red hair sitting over bushy blond eyebrows and a face burned too red by the tropical sun.

"I have to say, we seem to have weathered the worst of their so-called Blitz," nodded the modest and serious Ballentyne, "but their U-boats are surely raising hell on the convoys in the North Atlantic."

"What happened to the famous 'peace in our time' we were told so much about, is what I would like to know?" queried Mary Stockton.

"I should think Churchill will be the right man for it. He has given them a good taste of the bulldog tenacity, eh what? The Blitz might have destroyed London but it hasn't broken our spirit. What do you say McLeod, an old Anzac like yourself? The tide will turn and we'll give him what for, don't you think?" prodded Kincaid, the cheeks over his well-groomed moustache flushing red from his first glass of whiskey.

A long, uncomfortable silence pervaded through the room as everyone waited on a reply from Jack. He sat motionless, arms resting on his legs, staring into the depths of the amber liquid in his tumbler. Finally, as if awakening from a dream, he threw back his head and drained his glass. "You're asking the wrong person if you want an opinion about this latest calamity, mate. I'm afraid I had my patriotic stuffing knocked out of me a long time ago.

There's not much value in fighting any war, except for industrialists and their politician puppets. All that seems to come from war is suffering. And as far as I can see, there'll be a lot more before this one is finished." Standing he walked to the edge of the veranda to gaze at the last of the dying sunset.

After a moment Aubrey recovered his composure. "Hmm...er...well yes. Point taken. What say we recharge these glasses, eh Herbert? Same again all round?"

Herbert brought the drinks. "Your whiskey, sir," he said to Jack in his deep baritone, offering him a half-filled tumbler off a polished mahogany tray. He took the drink, then turned and faced the party, who were standing and seemingly waiting on some sort of sign from him. "To King George VI," he said, holding his glass high.

"Here, here! To George VI!" and the rest joined in with a hearty toast to the reigning monarch of the British Empire.

Jasmine walked over and leaned on the balustrading next to her husband, searching for further signs of his discomfort. But there were none forthcoming. He seemed to have buried it back deep down inside of himself and put a lid over it. He was good at keeping those feelings bottled up, but she knew they were still there. "Are you alright, Jackson?" she asked.

Jack took one last look at the fading sunset, then turned to face his wife. "She'll be right, Jaz. Thanks. Did I mention you look beautiful tonight?"

"Yes, but I don't mind you tellin' me so again. Now should we go and join de others? No sense you skulkin' out here playin' de part o' de rude boy."

A bell was rung and the guests moved to the table for dinner. No more was said about the war.

Jasmine was seated next to Agnes Bucknell and across from Aubrey's wife Edwina, with headmaster Stockton to her right. "And how are you adjusting to your new life in the West Indies, Agnes?" Edwina politely asked as Herbert served the starters.

"I must say I don't know if I will ever get used to it! The heat, the humidity, the mosquitos, those ghastly cockroaches – I'm honestly finding it all quite unpleasant. Not to mention the difficulties I'm having in Barbados procuring decent staff.

Patience, I must admit, has never been one of my strong points. It would seem these locals don't have much of a penchant for etiquette or social graces, although you appear to have trained your people quite well, Edwina. Did it take you long to separate the wheat from the chaff?"

Jasmine slowly turned to stare at her neighbour, a stony look of indignation enveloping her normally pleasant demeanour. Across the table, Edwina was keen to move the conversation on; Jasmine was well known for her sharp tongue and low tolerance for pretentiousness.

"Oh we've had Herbert with us for years. He's like one of the family. Yes, life here does have its challenges. I find having a good book helps pass the time," Edwina said, changing the subject. "Do you do much reading?"

"Yes, I'm an avid reader. When we return to Barbados I would like to visit the public library in Bridgetown, although my expectations are not high. I have been told it is basic at best. But then, one can't expect much more when stationed in the colonies, can one?"

"I have just read an interesting book. It's called 'Omar Khayyam'," offered Jasmine. "It was a marvellous adventure. It takes place in the Middle Ages, and tells of the great Persian city of Nisapur, and of camel trains, and tents in the desert, and the turquoise mountains, and grand bazaars. It left me dreaming of the mysteries of the ancient orient. 'Aye, we peer at the sky, but search the earth with blind eyes. If we could only know the truth!' You are welcome to borrow it if you'd like."

A stunned silence fleetingly engulfed the table. All eyes were on the secretary's wife. "Oh – yes. Why, thank you," she awkwardly replied.

"Good. I'll bring it by tomorrow," Jasmine responded. The faucet of conversation was turned on again, and dinner continued as before.

Jack struggled to hide his inward smile. *Good on ya, Jaz*, he said to himself.

After dinner the men removed themselves to the study for a cigar and a snifter of brandy, while the women took up a game of hearts. "So tell me Jack, as I'm new to this post, what your story really is," smiled the red faced Bucknell, crossing his legs as he lit a cigar and settled into his comfortable armchair. "It seems to me you are a long way off the beaten track, even for an Australian."

"That's a good question, but I don't think I have time enough to tell that tale tonight without copping a hiding from my wife. We'd be here until midnight and more than likely polish off at least one of our host's fine bottles of cognac," he replied.

"I must say it's a story I'd like to hear," chimed in Headmaster Stockton. "In the few months I have been here I have heard mention of your colourful past, but never from the horse's mouth, so to speak."

Kincaid and Ballentyne joined in the chorus so Jack had little choice but to begin.

"Alright then – but I'll have to give you the abbreviated version. I grew up in Sydney and at seventeen joined up to fight what they liked to call 'the Great War', or 'the War to End All Wars'. Well, there was nothing 'great' about it and it surely wasn't the last, as we can see today, but I won't go off onto that tack. Let's just say I was lucky enough to survive it. I was, however, badly wounded in the battle of the Somme. It took me some time to recover from my wounds in London. I read a lot of books in those days, and one of my favourites was 'Sailing Alone Around the World' by a bloke by the name of Joshua Slocum, which is a great yarn about how just before the turn of the century this fellow salvaged and re-built an oyster smack in Massachusetts and became the first man to sail single-handed around the world."

"So it was Slocum who inspired you, was it McLeod? I found his book a mesmerizing tale. The chap was so damned resourceful! I especially liked his idea of putting steel tacks on the deck at night so he wasn't surprised in his sleep by hostile natives whilst at anchor!" Kincaid interrupted.

"I think you would have no choice but to be resourceful to accomplish what Slocum did, Aubrey. At any rate, that book set me to dreaming. I was born in Tahiti on my old man's topsail schooner, but was raised in Australia. I'd always wanted to go back to Tahiti and visit the place where I was born, and since I didn't have much family to return to in Sydney, I took my release in England and decided to see if I could find a boat I could sail to the South Seas. I took the train down to the south coast to have a look around. I didn't have much money, but I knew what a good boat looked like. I spent most of my youth racing in 18ft skiffs on Sydney Harbour, and had actually started an apprenticeship as a boatbuilder to ol' Charley Dunn before joining up for the war. I was lucky enough to find a beautiful little fishing smack of a type used around the Solent, known as an Itchen Ferry. She was built sometime late in the last century, so needed a bit of work, but basically she was solid. As it happened, I met an old shipwright who helped me get her ship shape. Of course, everyone on the waterfront of the little village told me I was crazy and I would never make it as far as France, let alone across the Atlantic."

"I know this type of craft quite well," commented Bicknell. "You see many of them around Southampton. They are only what – twenty-five or thirty feet long? I might take the chance to sail to the Isle of Wight on one, but I certainly wouldn't have thought to cross the Atlantic! You really were quite bravely optimistic, weren't you?"

"Listen mate, I figured that if I could escape the hell of Passchendaele, I could do anything. Nipper and I decked her over, built a small cabin with a basic interior, caulked her up and splashed on some paint. I patched up the sails and tightened up her rig. I was close to being broke, but had a seaworthy little craft. After putting aboard some basic stores I was ready to go, and so when the local fishermen thought I'd have a run of good weather, I shoved off and scooted across the English Channel to France. I had some old charts that helped me work my way slowly south along the coasts of France, Spain, and Portugal and finally across the Straits of Gibraltar to Tangier. I continued south along the Moroccan coast and then crossed to the Canary Islands, where I spent a couple of months. From there I sailed south to the Cape Verde Islands before heading out across the Atlantic. The crossing was an interesting experience to say the least, but after twenty-four days I saw the Ship's Prow and made my landfall here at Petite Silhouette. It was love at first sight."

"That is one hell of a tale, McLeod. I can see what you mean when you say it would take us all night to hear the whole story!" said Bucknell. "It sounds like you had found yourself a seaworthy craft indeed."

"Oh the *Foam* was a little beauty. She never let me down in all the days I had her," Jack replied. "She could have taken me anywhere."

"So what happened to her and how is it you are still here?" asked Stockton.

"I hadn't been here long when the *Foam* was lost in the hurricane of twenty-one. She broke up on the bayside along with several of the island's schooners."

"Terrible one, that. Wreaked havoc on the sugar cane crop," agreed Kincaid. "Never really recovered from it, I must say."

"There was no hope of rebuilding my boat, but the people here were fantastic. They took me in and looked after me. At that point I was pretty much penniless and had to find work, so I hopped onto a deVilliars schooner and sailed to Barbados, where I found a job as a deckhand on a Gloucesterman who had come south to load rum. I spent several years working that trade between New York and Barbados with a couple of seasons of fishing the Grand Banks in between, but I always wanted to return to this place, and so when I became lucky enough to acquire my own vessel I made up my mind to come back."

"And jolly good thing you did, old man! The island wouldn't be the same without you."

"I can obviously see the many reasons why you would love this place, but if you don't mind, could I ask you just one more personal question. You didn't really, as legend has it, win your lovely schooner in some sort of game of chance did you?" asked the still curious Bucknell.

"Quite right, Bucknell! It was a game of roulette, wasn't it McLeod?" added Kincaid.

"Yes Aubrey, I'm getting to that. It turns out the schooner I was sailing on was working a very lucrative trade."

"You mean to say she was a rumrunner," the host again jovially interjected.

"Well it was a way to make some pretty good money back in those days – and totally legitimate by the way – as long as you anchored outside of the three mile limit, which we usually did. Anyway, I was on a bit of a lucky streak at the time. I was in New York in one of those prohibition 'speakeasies' and it transpired on this particular night I happened to be on a real winner at the roulette wheel. I had more than a few drinks in me, and felt as though I could never lose. Finally, I took all my winnings and placed them on 00, and what d' ya know – it came up! The House paid out and I left quick-smart before they could change their minds. There was this schooner for sale I'd had my eye on, a real beauty, a fast Gloucesterman. I paid cash and set sail for the Bahamas the next day. They say you shouldn't change the name of a ship, but I couldn't help myself, so she became the *Roulette*. I put her straight into the rum trade, but had never forgotten about Petite Silhouette. Eventually I'd had a gut-full of that ugly business, and so I decided to return to the islands and make this place my home."

"Hmmm, yes. I can see there is a bit more to you than meets the eye," said Bucknell, stubbing out his cigar. "And one final question if you don't mind, old man. That wife of yours seems a clever one, especially for an island girl. Was she educated here on Petite Silhouette?"

"My wife is a deVilliars, which I'm sure you'll soon discover is one of the leading families on the island. Her mother, who passed away not long ago, was a Crowley from Barbados, and was very well educated. Jaz had a great start to her education with old Mr Whitchurch, who was headmaster at our school for years before he retired and was replaced by our friend Mr Stockton here. Jasmine showed great promise at school, and so was sent to Barbados to live with relatives and finish her education. Besides raising our children and looking after me, she somehow finds the time to teach part-time at the school as well."

"And a jolly good teacher she is, too," said the headmaster. "I don't know what we would do without her."

"That was a most entertaining story, McLeod. And to you, Aubrey, thank you for a wonderful evening. I regrettably must call it a night. We are catching the mailboat to Barbados tomorrow and

I still have a few odds and ends to tidy up first thing in the morning." And with that the men adjourned to the parlour to join the women, who were finishing their last hand of hearts.

They walked home through the shadowy night. Hanging high in the western sky, the nearly full moon painted the island with its clear, silver light. Fireflies danced under the tall coconut trees, gently waving in the soft tradewind.

"That was an interesting evening, my dear," said Jack, giving his wife a playful poke in the ribs. "I really enjoyed watching you put that snobbish Englishwoman in her place."

"Maybe it surprised her dat a 'person of colour' like me could carry on a proper conversation, or read a book even. She been watchin' me with a lizard's eye all night. It was time fo' me to set she straight."

"You did a good job. She won't forget you in a hurry."

"What about you?" Jasmine asked, stopping to look at her husband. "It hurts me to watch you suffer, knowin' dat you got dem old war wounds still festerin' inside."

"Oh, she'll be right – don't worry. There's more to war than what you read in the newspaper or hear about on the wireless, that's all. Saying you've been through a war, and stabbing someone with a bayonet, or seeing your mates die from the effects of mustard gas, well they're different things altogether. It's a worn out saying, but it's true; there is no glory in war."

The coconut trees cast dark shadows across the path. Jasmine jumped swiftly out and closed her hands gently around a firefly. Slowly she opened them and they peeked like two children at the pulsing floresense of the little insect. "It's a beautiful magic, isn't it?" she asked, with an almost childlike fascination in her voice. "Nature's a miracle an' we so busy wit' life we don' even see it. Look at dis creature! So perfect, so balanced. Show me de man dat can make one o' dese! Yet nature does it wit' she eyes closed. Men are very good at wreckin' tings, though. I think we have a lot fo' learn." She gently blew the firefly away as if with a kiss. They watched the insect float off before drifting home in the softness of the perfumed night.

Port Victoria

After slipping out of bed and quietly dressing, Jack stepped into the cookhouse and put a match under the coal-pot. Soon the kettle was boiling and he made a cup of tea. Wandering out onto the veranda he sat down and drank it with a couple of day-old fish cakes. Before him the harbour lay calm and quiet as the first light of the morning broke over the hills behind Frigate Bay. Finishing his breakfast, he went back to the kitchen, dropped his cup in the sink, grabbed his sweat-stained felt fedora and was off down the hill into town.

Jack walked along Bay Road in the coolness of the early morning. It was a beautiful time of day on the island. The sun had just risen, but the harbour was still in shadow. The tradewinds blew over the hills and into the harbour, rustling the coconut trees and gusting across the placid surface of the bay, carrying the occasional scent of smoke from a coal-pot as someone made their morning coco-tea. The sound of a conch shell being blown from the bayside announced a fishing boat had come in and there were "fish in de market." At this early hour the island was awake; its inhabitants quietly going about their business, knowing this time was the most pleasant part of the tropical day. Passing the Anglican Church he paused to say good morning to the ancient bell ringer who was on his way from the rectory to sound the six o'clock bell.

"G'day Xavier. Beautiful morning," Jack shouted.

"Good morning, Cap'n Jack. Could have some rain later... my knee's givin' me curry," the bent up black man replied.

"It's that time of year."

"Say what?" Xavier asked, his hand held to his ear.

"I said it's that time of year!" Jack yelled.

"Oh...right. Well good luck then," he waved, carrying on towards the simple bell tower. Moments later the six o'clock chimes rang through the harbour.

The old boy is as deaf as a post, the captain thought to himself as he continued along the sandy track. *I don't think he heard a word I said.*

Jack approached the heart of Port Victoria. Double-ended fishing boats lined the shore under the trees, cotton sails tidily wrapped around their masts, bamboo sprits and booms neatly stowed, their hulls painted the traditional battleship grey. In the deep water just off the beach, a dozen or so schooners were moored, along with a few smaller sloops, their bowlines tied to the coconut trees. Two of the vessels were careened, their bottoms in various states of maintenance and repair. In the distance ahead, he could see the main wharf slowly come alive as passengers and cargo started to arrive to catch the daily passage boat to the main island of St. Vincent. Jack's attention was now drawn to a group of men gathered beneath a stand of ancient almond and fig trees, where a serious debate seemed to be raging. In front of a clutch of muted listeners a man fervently gesticulated, berated, admonished and argued, striding back and forth, his white face red with emotion. This was Elgin Salter, the island's sail maker. Jack wandered over, smiling inwardly. *I wonder what Squally is on about this morning*, he thought.

"...It's a rod dey made fo' dey own backs I tell you," he continued. "All right, yes we won de last war, but you don't have to kick a man once he's down. You don't try and squeeze blood out of a stone! Don't worry, dese Germans has been spoilin' for a fight ever since 1918!" And he was off, striding away with speed.

"Don't frighten," Uncle Simion muttered, his hands clasped over his walking stick. "He ain't done yet."

And sure enough, the words were hardly out of his mouth when the sailmaker spun on his bare heel and came charging back.

"And don't think dis goin' to end tomorrow! Dis ting's trouble I tell you! Dere's goin' to be plenty dead before dis war runs its course, mark my words!" Squally scolded, a finger held up for emphasis.

"Yes, well at least we're a long way from all o' dem far-away places Elgin," Uncle Arnold threw in. "Dat all happenin' in de outside world."

Squally snapped around. "You t'ink so Uncle? Man, dis a modern world now you know! Dis ting spreadin' like wildfire, we! You didn't hear dat dere's war in de Pacific, Africa, and now Russia? No – we's goin' to see trouble out of this in dese very islands, you jus' wait an' see!" And with that he was gone for good, striding under the trees towards home and breakfast.

"What does you t'ink of all o'dis, Cap'n Jack?" Uncle Simion asked. "You t'ink he's right?"

The tall Australian considered the questioning stares of the four old men, and then gazed over the peaceful harbour spread out like a painting before him. "Well Uncle Sim, we can only hope he's wrong," Jack finally replied. But deep down inside a knot was tightening in his stomach. As he turned and headed for the boatyard he had a feeling the sailmaker was probably more prophetic than even he suspected.

After passing through town, Jack arrived at the boatyard, where the hull of a new schooner under construction stood amongst a scattering of coconut trees. Pausing before descending down the slight hill, he stood admiring the sweep of the sheer, the sweetness of the transom, the curve of the stem as it reached out towards the waters of the bay. The yard was not much more than a flat space in an old coconut grove that had been cleared away on the edge of the bayside. Scattered about were balks of timber of various sizes and shapes, all of them displaying some sort of natural curve. Along the far side stood a rugged stone building, a remnant from the early days of the island's settlement that was now used as a warehouse for timber and other materials. Off one end underneath an extension of the roof stood the yard's prize possession, the heavy ship's bandsaw Jack had acquired on one his trips north to New England, and that he and his partner O'Neil had rigged to run off a drive belt from a diesel engine. Just off the beach a stand of almond trees surrounded two sturdy, well used work benches, where as he approached Jack could see the silhouette of Sinclair deVilliars, Jasmine's grandfather, sitting with his arms folded quietly admiring the new vessel.

"G'day Uncle 'Clairie," he said, pulling up next to him. "How's tricks?"

"Well, you know, jus' gettin' on day by day. When you young you never t'ink 'bout gettin' old, dat only happen to somebody else. But den all of a sudden it just sneaks up an' grabbles you from behind, an' dat's dat. Dey ain't no goin' back. No, mon, gettin' old ain't easy a-tall, but it's de better o' de two choices."

"I suppose I never really looked at it that way," Jack said with a grin. He leaned against the bench and joined the old shipwright in admiring yet another of his designs rising up between the coconut trees.

"Dis vessel lookin' real sweet, man," Sinclair finally said. "You surely does model a clean vessel me boy. She's not goin' to be another old cargo drogher – she goin' to just glide t'rough de watah."

"Well if she's anything like her sister, she should behave herself," Jack said. "After all, she's built off the same molds."

"Yes, mon! Dat *Theodora D*'s a fine schooner. Young Clancy says she's as stiff as a wall house, fast but still carries a good load. Dat's all a man could ever want in a vessel."

As the two sat quietly side by side, an old woman made her way through the yard filling a flour sack with some of the dry wood chips that carpeted the sandy ground. Residue from the shipwright's adze and axe lay everywhere. "Uncle 'Clairie!" she called out without looking up, "me see you dere relaxin' in the cool!"

"Yes girl – let dem boys take dey turn now. Me done my part."

"Well everyt'ing does have its time ya know," she answered as she straightened her thin angular frame, arms akimbo on her hips. "Others got to take up de slack now."

"So you still cookin' up dat sweet coo-coo an' okra, girl? You must bring some gi' me, you here?"

"All right – next week," she said with a smile. Then she called out to her grandson who was playing near the keel. "Raymond you little scamp! Come help take up this bag gi' me!" And then the two made their way out of the yard, the old woman lovingly chiding the boy as they went.

Appearing from around the stern of the new vessel, the two men were joined by the tall, wiry figure of Jack's father-in-law and partner, O'Neil deVilliars. Wearing a khaki work shirt and trousers and a weather-beaten Panama hat, a smile spread from underneath his well- trimmed grey moustache and hazel blue eyes.

"So I hear you beat dem all again, Jack," he said, extending his hand. "Well done! You just keep bringing dat cup back home, you hear?"

"Hey what's dis I hearin'? You done win again in Bequia?" Uncle Sinclair turned and asked. "Man, dem fellahs over dere ain't goin to be happy wit' dat a-tall!"

As they spoke the first of the boatyard's shipwrights began to wander down the well-worn path, walking into the yard in two's and three's. They came from various villages on the island; from Le Moulin on the windward side, from Marley's Vale, Top-o-the-World and Port Victoria itself. Soon there was close to a dozen men under the tree getting organised for the working day ahead, each in his own way prodding Jack for details of the big race.

Eventually he gave in to their questioning and told them the story. "The racing was tighter than it's ever been," he began. "There would have been close to a dozen of us that pushed off the beach at Friendship. We beat up under Baliceaux to Black Rock, which was the windward mark, and as you would know that can be a rough stretch of water. When we rounded the rock you could have thrown a seine net around the whole fleet. Our two Le Moulin boats were doing well, and so was Blakey."

"I heard it was a good day for it. I helped Orlin haul up de *Ocean Gar* yesterday when he came in and he says all o' you met some heavy seawater up over Black Rock," Cuthbert, one of the Le Moulin shipwrights said. "He said you fellahs did cut it fine. He t'ought you was goin in to pick whelks off o' de reef!"

"Yes mate, it was real hard yakka. There were some decent sized seas out there, I can tell you. My boy Henry had his work cut out down there in the bailin' hole. You know what it's like up there in a weather tide. And it was pretty tight when we passed over the rock, I have to admit. We tacked under the fleet and let the tide take us up, and we just squeezed over 'er. You could almost touch the bastard when we went 'round. That tack won us the race, because if we had to make two more we would've been gone for all money."

"One o' de boys in de *Gar* said dat two boats rolled bottom-up on de way back down," Gideon, another Le Moulin man, said.

"That was something to see!" Jack exclaimed. "Not long after the last boat went 'round, a big squall came down on us. The seawater was white in front of it, and we were all running off wing on wing. As the breeze hit, two boats just rounded up and rolled. It was all I could do to keep the *Antipodes* level, I tell you! It was a wild ride! We ran right down and went 'round Clifford's seine boat anchored just off the shore of Paget Farm."

"I bet you got plenty of advice when you tacked in to de sho'," said one of the shipwrights.

"You're right there! The shoreline was lined with people from Donovan's shop right up to the finish at Friendship, and it seemed like all of them had something to say. We went third 'round the bottom mark, behind Blakey and Hammer, but once we set out to windward it didn't take us long to work our way to the lead. Once we got ahead that was it…when we hit the beach Blakey was just rounding Middle Cay."

"Dem boy's sayin' he goin' back to de bush to build again. He say he boat too full forward, say he want to build a dart nex' time," said Cuthbert.

"Well man, he want to beat de *Antipodes* he better come here an' steal she lines," joked Gideon as he turned for the tool shed to collect his tools, "because other den dat he got two chances o' overhaulin' de Cap'n …slim an' none!"

The morning sun slowly began to climb over the hills to windward as the men now wandered off, laughing and joking as they picked up their various tools and moved towards their work. Soon, the sound of wooden caulking mallets striking metal irons rang through the harbour. Climbing up on deck of the schooner, Jack watched several caulkers feeding coils of oakum into the seams of the planked deck with the steady tapping of their long, cylindrical mallets. A young apprentice squatted on his haunches as he lit the fire under a pot of pitch, which would be paid into the seams with a ladle once they were 'made off'. Jack found O'Neil back aft by the rudder case, working with his older brother Llewellyn.

"So you outfoxed dem Bequia men again, hey Jack?" Llewellyn asked.

"It was a good win, Uncle Lew – it sure was. That *Antipodes'* still sailing as sweet as the day we first built her. There's really something special about that boat."

"Talkin' 'bout buildin' boats – when're you lookin' to begin this new schooner o' yours? It's time enough you stop buildin' fo' others and start a new vessel o' your own, isn't it?" the shipwright asked from under his broad straw hat.

"I'll make a start sometime soon, don't you worry Uncle Lew. What is it you always say – 'nothin' comes before its time'? Anyway, it won't be in the next few weeks I can tell you. We've got some freight in Barbados to collect to carry up north, and we'll be leaving tomorrow. So O'Neil, is there anything we need from St. Barths?"

"Yes man, we can use a few kegs o' spike nails an' a few mo' bales o' oakum. I know Bill wanted to talk to you 'bout pickin up some gear fo' him, too. He says he wants to launch around Christmas time, an' me don't see any reason why he can't. I got a list o' tings de yard needs up at de house. Why don't we go up an' have a look."

O'Neil and Jack climbed down off of the deck and walked through the back of the boatyard to O'Neil's house up on the hill behind. "Here's me list," he said, handing Jack a folded piece of paper. "Bill said he'd be spendin' de mornin' up at de sail loft wit Squally workin' on he sails. When we done here you might wander down and axe him what he needs."

Jack looked over the list, then refolded it and put it in his top pocket. "Good. I've got to go there anyway. Squally's been making me a couple of new sails and I should check to see if they're done."

Lost in thought on his way to the sail loft, he hardly heard his name called. "Hello McLeod! I say Jack!" The figure of Reginald Bucknell stood on the veranda of the government administration building, the Union Jack flapping in the breeze from the flagpole overhead.

Turning, he approached the waiting official. "What can I do for you Reggie?"

"Good morning, old man. Sorry to bother you. It's just a wee bit of official business and wondered if you might be able to spare a few minutes to help me out."

The two men entered the government official's temporary office. "Excuse the clutter – I've commandeered the Police Inspector's office for the few days I'm here, much to his annoyance, I'm sure. Have a seat," Bucknell said, moving around the desk and sitting beneath a portrait of King George VI. Jack sat opposite the officer as he reached into a desk drawer and pulled out a file. "As I said, just a wee bit of official paperwork and you can be on your way. I didn't want to discuss business with you last night, but as part of my new duties I am required by the War Office to register all known ex-pat subjects of the crown, especially anyone with a past military history."

"Listen, with all due respect Reggie, why would His Majesty have any interest in the likes of me?"

"I'm just dotting 'I's and crossing 'T's here, old man. I'm off for Barbados later today on the mail packet, and just wanted to finalise a few things this morning. I have here your personal details – can we just quickly go over them to make sure they're correct?" Bicknell asked, lifting an eyebrow and receiving a nod from Jack.

"Full name: Thomas Jackson McLeod. Nationality: Australian. Date of birth: December 3, 1899; Place of birth: Papeete, Tahiti. As you mentioned last night, that's another story. You wouldn't mind filling in a few blanks, would you?" Bucknell asked, looking across the desk.

"My father was from Virginia. His father – my grandfather – was a cavalry officer who fought for the Confederacy under 'Stonewall' Jackson in the War Between the States. I was named after him," Jack responded. "My old man owned a topsail schooner that he traded through the South Pacific. He married Mum in Sydney, and coaxed her to sail off with him. We were in Tahiti when I was born. I was raised on board, but when I was about five my mum had had enough of life on the sea, and took me back to Sydney. Things weren't any easier for us there, either. With my father only making the rarest of appearances, it was up to Mum to raise me, as well as try and put food in our mouths. I was ten when she died of consumption, and ended up being hand-balled on to my Auntie Kate, who did her best to raise me. When I was 17 I joined the Army and I believe you know the rest of the story."

"I have here you were with the 28th Battalion, 7th Brigade, 2nd Australian Division. So you must have been at Pozieres. I was with the Royal Warwickshire Regiment. Horrible situation. You boys certainly did yourselves proud."

"I was a green recruit then, and was thrown in at the deep end. What an introduction to war! We sure copped a hiding! It was pure hell. Something I don't really like to talk about."

"I also see you are still due the Military Cross. Any explanation?" he asked.

There was a long pause. "Later on I was wounded during the Battle of Passchendaele. My leg was shattered and then became badly infected, and so I was sent back to England to recuperate. They wanted to award me the Military Cross, but I let them keep it. I was only doing what I had to do, like the rest of us, and I didn't want any medal for it," Jack replied. "The war ended, I took my discharge overseas and I told you the rest of it last night."

"Ah – hence the slight limp. So you've been here permanently since '27. Landowner, wife and children, upstanding member of the community..." Bucknell added, flipping through the pages. "That seems to have squared everything away."

The two men stood and headed for the door.

"Thanks for taking the time to stop in. It's a mere formality, I know, but I have to do my job. Cheers Jack," Reginald Bucknell said while escorting him back outside. Hands clasped behind his back, he stood in the shade and watched the Australian disappear down the road.

The island's sailmaker worked under the red iron roof of what had once been a copra storage shed back in the days when that coconut product was in worldwide demand. Jack kicked the sand off of his bare feet and stepped up onto the worn wooden boards of the loft, walking around the jumble of new white canvas that took up most of the working space on the floor. Squally sat on a three legged stool, the sail draped across his lap as he hand stitched in an eyelet, pushing the number one gauge needle through the heavy flax with his sail palm. He was a white man, a descendent of one of the clans that habitated an area on the slopes of Mount Majestic the islanders called 'Top of the World'.

Scattered out on the floor around him was Bill deVilliars and six of his crew, busy stitching together the seams of their new mainsail with needle and palm.

"G'day Squally, Cap'n Bill – how's it all going?" Jack asked.

The sailmaker glanced up, and then back to his task. "Good. Your fores'l an' stays'l are dere – you can take dem anytime," he said, motioning with a movement of his head to the neatly folded stack of sails against the back wall.

"Hard work and steady blows, mon," Bill said as he slowly got to his feet. "Me gettin' too old fo' all o' dis. Dis schooner's de last one fo' me. I bent-up like a crab hook!"

Jack walked over and took a look at his new sails. Raindrops started to beat onto the roof overhead, within minutes turning from a smattering into an outright downpour. The rain was now thundering on to the roof and running off the open-fronted shed in sheets. Looking out through the coconut trees, the harbour was all but invisible as the rain squall blew down the hills and out over the water. Jack wandered over and stood near the edge, his arms folded over his chest, his shirtsleeves rolled up, his fedora pushed on to the back of his head. Bill deVilliars sauntered up alongside, and the two men silently watched as the rain enveloped the bay.

"O'Neil was telling me you want to launch sometime around Christmas, and you might need some gear from Antoine up in St. Barths."

"Yes, man – I want to get de vessel in de watah an' rigged fo' early in de new year," Bill replied. "Dat would be good if you could help me out. I been waitin' fo' somebody goin' up north to bring back de last set o' tings we need befo' we does launch. Wire and rope riggin', paint, anchor and chain an' some other bits an' pieces. Not to mention de rum! Can't launch a vessel dese days without dat! What time you leavin'?"

"Oh, we'll be alongside around six tomorrow morning."

"All right, I'll see you den an' we can talk."

The sail maker finished off his eyelet, pushed the sail off of his knees and stood, slowly straightening up, the constant pressure of leaning over his work obviously taking its toll on his lower back. He walked over to join the two captains.

"Those sails look good, Squally. I'll get some of the boys to come and get them after lunch. We'll bend them on this afternoon and see how they set," Jack said.

"Man, makin' dem sails was a pain in de ass! Not a soul here to help me. You t'ink handlin' dat heavy cloth me alone was easy? It's a damn good ting Bill here's takin' 'pon himself to stich he own sails. If it wasn't fo' he an' he crew who knows when we'd be done!"

Jack caught the eye of Bill deVilliars as he smiled behind the sailmaker, rolling his eyes towards the heavens. "What happened to Monroe? I thought he was working here with you."

"Mon-roe? Man, don' talk to me about Monroe! He does love de rum too damn much! He's just like de rest o' dem. Once any o' dem makes a few shillin's it's straight to de rum shop dey goin' til all de money done. Men dese days ain't studyin' hard work a-tall! An' de young ones? Well man dey's worse! I had dat boy for MacDonald here, an' he didn't last two months. One day he went home for lunch and he ain't come back yet!"

"Maybe if you took it a little more easy on de boy he'd still be here," commented one of the sailors on the floor as he casually waxed a length of thread.

That was all he needed. Red in the face, Squally turned to the man and delivered a full broadside, the rest of the men in the room struggling to hide their grins. "Easy! Take it easy you say? Man, dat's de whole problem in a nutshell! People too damn soft dese days. Did dem rough Canadian cap'ns I did sail under take it easy? No man – dey was what you call slavedrivers! Dey'd work you til you drop and den make you fight dem fo' your pay! Man – tings too easy dese days all 'round. When you is here you workin', not skylarkin'!" He charged back to his seat and took up his needle again.

The rainsquall had passed as quickly as it came, the ping on the roof of the odd droplet of rainwater falling from the coconut fronds above the last reminder. "Alright boys, I'm off for home," Jack said.

"Yes, man. Until..." Squally replied as he began to stitch a heavy manila bolt-rope onto the luff of the new sail.

The captain stepped out onto the wet sand and headed back up the road, inwardly smiling as he dodged the occasional puddle of water. *They don't call him Squally for nothin'*, he thought to himself.

The twelve o'clock bells pealed through the harbour and Jack headed home for lunch. It was a tradition on Petite Silhouette, as well as most of the other Caribbean islands, for the family to take the main meal together at midday. Jasmine would see to it that the food was prepared; the children would come home from school and join their great-grandfather Sinclair, who was there most days since the time his wife passed away. As Jack entered the kitchen it was pandemonium as usual. Children ran in and out, Jasmine playfully scolding them as she busily served up the food. Alongside her was a distant relation from Le Moulin who they called 'Little'. She was just like part of the family, taking up the slack when Jasmine was off teaching at the school.

"You children go wash your hands I tell you! You're not getting a ting 'til you do!" Jasmine admonished as her husband gave her a peck on the cheek after hanging his hat on a hook by the door.

"Afternoon Uncle 'Clairie," Jack said as he sat down. "Looks like a nice bit of grouper we have today."

"Yes man – I was on de bayside dis mornin' early on me way up to de boatyard when Baby Lou came in. He'd been doin' some bottom fishing with dis' good moon, you know. Had his boat full up with red fish and so. He says he's found a shoal where de fish almost jump inside o' de boat on dey own."

"Is dat true Poppy?" one of the twins asked, watching her grandfather intently as she sat down at the table.

"So he say. He say he jus' goes an' anchors up at his magic spot and when he whistles a special whistle de fish jus' jump into he boat like dat," he said, snapping his fingers.

"I t'ink your Great-Grandpa might be pullin' you' leg, girl," Jasmine said as she served out the plates.

"Did dat really happen, Poppy?" asked Henry sceptically.

"Well dat's de story I did hear – but you can't always believe everyt'ing someone tells you," he answered, the faintest of smiles crossing the old man's lips.

"Papa, Momma say you off fo' Barbados tomorrow," pouted Chantelle, the second twin daughter. "How come you never home?"

"It's not that I want to go, child, but in this world everyone must do something to earn a crust, and that is what I do. Anyway, I'll be home before you know it, and then it will be Christmas."

The mention of Christmas quickly diverted the children's attention, and so the meal time passed just as it did most days. Afterwards, Jack left to go aboard and help his crew prepare the *Roulette* for her upcoming trip, the children ran back to school ahead of their mother, and Uncle 'Clairie slowly made his way home for his afternoon nap.

The Careenage

It was mid-morning when the *Roulette* let go from alongside the wharf. The crew rhythmically raised the gaff foresail, three men on the peak halyard and three on the throat, their black hands meshing instinctively as the schooner slowly motored out of Frigate Bay. After gybing around Fish Rocks, Jack brought the vessel head to wind and the mainsail was hoisted; the stem staysail, jib, and flying jib quickly followed. As they cleared away from under the lee of the land, Kingsford scurried up the ratlines to the main hounds and loosed out the stops for the topsail. The sail cracked and snapped as it was hoisted, but was quickly silenced as it was clewed out and tacked down. The fore topsail was the last sail set. Sheets were hauled off and lines coiled, and all with a minimum of fuss or bother. Hardly a word was spoken throughout the whole operation. Now the long, green schooner was trimmed and on course, and with the wind in the southeast she heeled over onto a starboard tack, charging close hauled into the steep Atlantic swell, foam and spray blowing off to leeward as she left Petite Silhouette behind and climbed up over the islands of Mustique and Baliceaux and the jagged high cliffs of Battowia, and further to leeward the island of Bequia.

The crew settled into their first few hours at sea. The schooner was bound for Barbados, a ninety mile beat straight into the wind, sea and tide. The *Roulette* was a deep water schooner, and she was built for these conditions; a Gloucester Grand Banks fisherman made to take on the worst the North Atlantic could throw at her. She had been designed to sail fast, to get her cargo of cod fish quickly to market; she had spent over half of her life doing just that before Jack McLeod brought her into the West Indian cargo trade, and so it was on voyages like this when she really showed the beauty of her lineage.

"Go up girl! Go up, you ol' sow hog," Bull chanted as he settled down aft behind the wheel box. "You was born for de seawater, and dat's where we does toil fo' a livin', so up you go girl...."

Jack stood alongside the wheel, turning it effortlessly one way and then the next as the vessel knifed her way over and through the steep Atlantic swell.

"Dis vessel is too sweet fo' words, you hear," joined in Kingsford. "De Yankee-man who did draft de plan for dis was a master. He was what you call a real arch-i-tek, a scientist!"

The rest of the crew voiced their agreement, and so did Jack. When it came to designers, there weren't many better than B.B. Crowninshield. Even the famous John Alden had done his apprenticeship with the great man. As he peered forward he thought how he could never grow tired of admiring the sweep of her sheer, the proportions of her rig, or her sea-keeping qualities.

"No, you boys are right," Jack absentmindedly replied to his crew. "When it comes to schooners you don't find many much better than this. She's carried us through some serious seawater, and that's a fact."

And so the conversation moved on to Barbados, and other schooners and other men the crew had seen and met there. They talked of being alongside of the famous *Bluenose;* of the hard-driving Captain Lou Kennedy and his all steel *Sea Fox;* of the McCoy brothers and their legendary rum smuggling knockabout *Arethusa.* They argued over the best vessels they had seen and the worst; the sweetest and the crankiest, but in the end all of the crew were happy and proud to be exactly where they were.

The *Roulette* sailed on. The watch changed. Food was cooked and passed around. The sun set over St. Vincent, and night settled in. The dim, flickering shore lights of St. Lucia came and went on the leeward horizon. Rain squalls made up to windward, and blew down on them. The stars came out, and they sailed on. At sunrise, with the high peaks of Martinique just visible to leeward, they tacked onto port and hauled off south-east by south.

"Alright girl," Zeph sang as he took over his trick at the wheel, "let's go! One broadside right into de Careenage in sweet

Bridgetown. It's a long time I haven't tasted any o' yo' flying fish, coo-coo an' okra!"

Daybreak. A warm red glow spread from the east, casting a silver mantle through the crests of the oncoming waves. Crystal shards of spray washed over the port bow of the schooner as she lifted to the swell, her long stem easing into the deep troughs before rising over the next charging wave. Jono was busy in the galley house, a box-like structure built behind the foremast from which Jack emerged, making his way aft along the windward rail with two cups of hot white tea. Zepheryn stood to weather of the wheel box, coaxing the vessel to windward, working every wave, feeling for each nuance and fluctuation in the fresh steady breeze, the long main boom stretching out well over the stern and bending under its tremendous load, white foam roaring away from the rail to leeward before disappearing into the wake astern, a scar-like swath sliced through the cobalt blue sea.

Slowly the rest of the crew emerged from the fo'c'sle forward, joining the watch on deck. Gathering around the galley they accepted plates of fried fish and johnny-cakes from the busy cook. Young Dawson, his tattered cotton shirt flapping in the breeze, moved gracefully aft balancing two plates for the captain and mate while the rest of the crew spread themselves out over the deck, choosing their spots carefully so as to avoid the exploding fountains of spray blowing over the bow.

As the sun rose higher into the morning sky, a dark blue smudge began to emerge on the horizon ahead. "Land ho, Skip!" Kingsford called out from a few rungs up on the windward shrouds. "Ah boy, dat is navigation we," he said, shaking his head as he moved aft to the wheel after springing back down to the deck. "You can't do better den dat I tell you! Barbados smack on de nose! Dem extra few hours we spent carrying on over Martinique was de ticket. You see, dat is what I does call patience, eh Gilbert? When most captains would o' been hasty an' tacked we carried on. And now dis broadside is carryin' we straight 'longside de wharf. How does Uncle Llewelyn put it? 'Mo' haste, less speed'!"

The schooner smashed onward, and the low flat pancake of an island slowly began to define itself. "Jump a piece of that main for me 'Fordy," Jack said, and the crew carefully eased the sails. With that adjustment the schooner instantly began to make more speed. As they closed on the island the sheets continued to be eased until they were tearing along at over twelve knots. It was just before midday when they glided through the breakwater and tied up alongside the cobblestone wharfs inside the Barbados Careenage.

The 'U' shaped inner harbour cut into the heart of the island capital of Bridgetown was a hive of activity, where trading vessels of all types and sizes hailing from a myriad of nations jostled three and four abreast alongside its busy quays to load and discharge their cargos. Sweat-soaked stevedores lumped burlap bags of sugar off of the backs of high-stacked lorries, a chain of human muscle rhythmically passing the island's sweet produce into the deep holds of the waiting vessels. Wooden barrels of prized Barbados rum were swung on board others, wooden cargo booms easing the precious liquid down through the open hatches to waiting hands below. Casks of molasses, called the 'big sweeten', were also being loaded by their hundreds. At the same time vessels were discharging their cargos; produce from neighbouring islands, lumber and other products from North America, and highly valued essentials from war-torn Europe. Hot, humid and almost breathless, locked off from the tradewind in the lee of the island, the Careenage was, along with Queen's Wharf in Trinidad, the heart of the West Indian cargo trade. Hoisted canvas sails lay loose and limp aloft the various vessels, drying in the hot sun. Makeshift awnings strung between masts provided shade for caulkers who toiled away, methodically tapping their rolled oakum into deck seams, the ring of their wooden mallets echoing around the basin as it blended with the shouts of hawkers, the growl of donkey engines, the arguments, the laughter, and the general hubbub of nearly one hundred ships of many nations hard at work.

The yellow quarantine flag flew from the spreaders of the McLeod schooner. The captain stepped ashore, having changed and cleaned up. He moved quickly down Wharf Street, dodging between lumpers and stevedores, hustlers and grifters, seamen and shipping clerks on his way to perform his official duties of clearing in through customs and immigration. Wooden donkey carts and rattling Bedford lorries wound along the busy street. A barebacked man in tattered shorts took a green coconut from a pile on his hand cart and deftly lopped the top off with his sharp cutlass for a flat capped customer. "Hallo Cap'n Jack!" a large, jovial woman selling sweet coconut cakes from out of a glass box called in her lilting Bajan dialect, "me got some real fresh coconut cakes here today!"

"No thanks Norlina – maybe later."

"Okay darlin'. Don't forget me now…" she smiled as he edged past.

The Customs and Excise office stood at the apex of the basin, and it was a busy place. Jack moved through the crowd, exchanging greetings and asides and jokes with various people. Behind the counter, white uniformed officers moved between desks stacked high with documents while slow turning overhead fans did nothing but stir the hot, humid air into a thick soup. It took him close to an hour to get through the formalities. Next stop was the office of his shipping agent.

The agency of JP Samuels was located on Prince William Henry Street, just off of the Careenage. The captain climbed the steps to the second floor of the neat stone building, the shady interior markedly cooler than the mid-afternoon heat just steps outside the brass handled swinging doors. Inside the opaque glass door three clerks scribbled studiously at their desks. Jack waited until a bespeckled accountant looked up and motioned with his hand towards the rear of the room. "He's in his office – just knock."

"Come," a deep voice intoned from behind the polished mahogany door. Standing up from his desk, the large frame of Joshua Samuels smiled and extended his hand towards his old friend.

"Ah, Captain Jack McLeod, good afternoon! Take a seat, mon. I was just with Captain Hollis from Bequia and we were talking about you. He said you won the King's Cup again."

"Well it doesn't take long for word to spread, does it?" he replied as he sat. "There's not much goes on in these islands that you don't know about, is there Josh?"

"No Jack, there isn't. That's my job, after all."

The faintest wisp of a cooling breeze drifted through the open window where the comings and goings of the busy harbour could be seen and heard. Soon the schooner captain and his agent got down to business. They discussed the details of the loading of the *Roulette's* next cargo and other shipping concerns. Bills of lading were produced. Loading times, future cargos and freight rates deliberated. Finally their business wound to a conclusion.

The fan turned slowly overhead. Joshua Samuels' chair creaked as he turned and gazed out over the Careenage. "You know my friend, we here in Barbados are used to dodging hurricanes, but I'm afraid there is a big one brewing out there that we won't be so lucky to miss. This war is like a storm building up out yonder over the horizon. We blindly carry on with our day to day lives, pretending it's not there, but eventually it will affect us all in one way or another. We might not know it yet, but when it does arrive a lot of people are going to feel the heat."

"I agree with you, mate," Jack said, leaning back in his chair. "You can read the clouds and see the signs, but in the end there's nothing you can do to prevent it from happening."

Samuels reached into his bottom drawer, took out a bottle of whiskey and poured two glasses. "Cheers." The agent took a sip, staring pensively into the bottom of his glass. "Jack, it's my job to know people. I sit here and watch the world come and go. I was born here, and not much happens on this island that I'm not conscious of. The government is worried, mon. Bombs might be dropping on London, but that doesn't mean we've been forgotten over here. These islands are important; the oil in Trinidad and Curacao, the bauxite from the Guyanas. The Brits know this, and although they aren't officially at war, the Americans know it too. And presumably so do the Germans."

"You know me, Josh. I have a fairly jaded view of all of this. I've seen first-hand the violence and brutality men can inflict upon each other. I passed through the fire, I paid my dues and though I feel for the poor innocents who are suffering over there, I'm not going to lose any sleep over what might happen in the future. So I'm not interested in wasting time debating the global ramifications of National Socialism, or the strategic importance of these islands to the economic survival of the British Empire, because there's bugger-all I can do about it anyway. I have more immediate worries. I'm just looking for the next cargo. I just want to feed my family."

Samuels stared across the table at Jack. "I've been approached by the government to put forward a recommendation, and your name came up. I'm sorry, but you were the only person I could think of that answered all of their criteria." The agent opened his drawer and withdrew a sealed brown envelope. He passed the letter over the desk. Stencilled across the front in bold black type was written: **'On His Majesty's Service'**. "This just came this morning. I was asked to deliver it personally to you."

A long silence passed. Jack slouched into the back of his chair, slowly turning the letter over in his big hands. Finally he looked up. "Every man must do his duty for King and Country, is that it?" he asked, tossing the letter back onto the desk before draining his whiskey.

Reaching forward, the agent poured two more stiff drinks. "I don't like it any more than you, but essentially yes, that's the way it is," he replied, returning the stare.

The captain sat motionless for a few more moments before finally sitting forward. Resting his muscled forearms on the desk, he turned the envelope over several more times before tearing it open and carefully removing a crisply folded document from inside. Pushing his hat onto the back of his head, Jack read the letter intently. After reading it for a second time he glared across the desk at his agent Samuels. "So you know all about this?" he asked.

"Yes," the agent nodded slowly. "We can't escape it Jack. We are all in this thing one way or another."

"'You are hereby requested to present yourself at the earliest possible convenience to the Naval Attaché's Office, Government House, Bridgetown, to discuss a matter of urgent national importance. Signed Commander A. B. Lawrence; HMRN'," Jack read aloud. "Who is this bloke, and what the hell does he want?"

"I'm not actually authorized to discuss the matter. All I can tell you is Commander Lawrence has been recently installed as the head of naval command here. I have met him, he's a decent sort of chap. Beyond that, there's nothing more for me to say, except that the Commander is most interested in making your acquaintance. Now, why don't we have one more for the road and call it a day?"

Outside, the hustle and bustle around the careenage was beginning to wind down. Shipwrights packed up their tools. Stevedores slowly walked down Wharf Street in twos and threes, heading home to their villages of Harmony Hall and Two Mile Hill and Highgate, to Cheapside and Fontabelle and Cat's Castle. As the sun slowly canted to the west and the long shadows of the late afternoon stretched over the now-quiet harbour, Jack made his way back to his schooner. He had a lot on his mind. He wasn't exactly sure what it was that Lawrence wanted to see him about, but he had a fair idea. As much as he hated to admit it, he could see the simple, peaceful world he had come to know was changing fast. The signs were all around him; the two naval ships anchored in Carlisle Bay he noticed as they sailed in that morning, the military vehicles on the streets, the uniforms in the crowd. There was no getting away from it. As Jack stepped aboard his vessel he knew he had no choice but to take this new, unwanted challenge on and deal with it as best he could.

That afternoon, the *Roulette* was moved from the quarantine dock to the other side of the Careenage next to the large three masted Canadian schooner *Rose Ann* to wait until their cargo was ready to load. Jack hailed the vessel's skipper as they tied up alongside. "G'day Captain Ivy! How's the prettiest captain in all of the West Indies doing today?" he asked with a smile.

"Flattery will get you nowhere, Jack. I'm having a hell of a day," the woman answered as she made fast a spring line. "The fellows around here are more interested in drinking rum than anything else!"

"Welcome to Barbados, mate! You should know that by now. So how have you been? I haven't seen you since you delivered that load of fir trees to me last year." Jack smiled, reaching over the bulwarks to shake the lady captain's hand.

"I'm fine Jack. Working hard, but I'm just fine."

Captain Ivy Pearl Ackermann is one hell of a woman in any man's language, Jack thought, as he watched the sinewy Nova Scotian go back to her business of unloading the rough-sawn Canadian spruce from out of the tern schooner's hold. The woman had not only his respect, but the rest of the fleet's as well. During the depression it had been hard for anyone to earn a crust of bread, but for her to take over her father's vessel, acquire a Master's Certificate and continue to make a living was even more remarkable. Now she ran the 250 ton schooner in the tough West Indian cargo trade, bringing timber and salt fish south, and hauling rum, molasses or salt back north.

Watching on, the crew of the *Roulette* smiled with amusement as Ivy berated one of her deck hands for dropping a sling-full of boards as it was swung over the wharf. "Okay, get your ass overboard and fish those planks out! Next time you'll think a little more about how you sling 'em. And don't tell me you can't swim because I've seen you paddle like Johnny Weissmuller! Now go on!"

"Man, de rest o' de Careenage done gone home an' she still workin'? She's one hard-ass woman, you hear!" Zeph said, shaking his head in admiration.

Later that evening the two captains sat at the stern of the *Rose Ann* drinking cups of strong black coffee. Ivy was still in her khaki work clothes, but had taken some time to freshen up. Her wavy brown hair, which she normally wore tied up under an old straw sombrero, was brushed out and tied back into a pony tail. Jack could see that she had washed the dirt and grime of the day's hard work off of her face, but still showed some grease under her fingernails. The cut-off sleeves of her shirt reflected the muscles of a hard worker.

"I've got to tip my hat to you Ivy. It isn't easy for anyone to make ends meet with a vessel like this these days, let alone a woman like yourself," Jack said, then quickly added, "no disrespect intended," when she shot him a threatening glare.

"Yes, well I've got to admit there aren't many of us left any more. There's no argument…steam has taken over from sail. It's hard to compete, as simple as that. Crew's wages are higher and freights are flat – you know the story. I guess it simply boils down to the fact that I just can't see myself with a shore job."

"I understand what you're saying there. It would be hard to give up what you know for something you've never done. I mean, you've lived most of your life on the *Rose Ann*, haven't you?"

"You're right – I pretty much grew up on this vessel. When Papa died it was only natural for me to take over and keep her going. Of course, having old Archie as mate sure has helped, but he says this is his last trip. He's been hanging on the last couple of years out of sheer loyalty, that's all. I just want to see my girl through school. She only has a couple of years left. Then I suppose I might have a think about settling down. I have the house outside of Lunenburg I can always go back to, I guess. I might even have to see if I can't find myself a proper husband. And you are already taken," she joked.

"You still have the ol' girl looking good, though," Jack said, as he surveyed the wide decks forward.

"Thanks. She certainly has a few miles under her keel, so I suppose she's in pretty good nick all things considered. I've got a problem with the donkey engine at the moment, though, and I'm afraid that's one thing I need to learn more about. I've tried to fix it myself but it's still leaking oil, and since I don't really sail with an engineer I'll need to find someone ashore to fix it."

"That's an old Lister isn't it? I don't mind having a look if you want. These 'mashcanics' as they call them here will cost you an arm and a leg. It's probably only a seal. Come on – I'll show you what to do so that you can fix it yourself next time."

The two skippers went forward to have a look at the troublesome engine, and Jack crouched down and began to

42

examine it. He went back aboard to grab some tools, and soon had Ivy repairing the engine as the crew from the two cargo schooners gathered around quietly watching and helping where needed. It was sometime after nine o'clock when they had the engine reassembled and ready to start.

"Ok Miss Ivy," Jack said wiping his greasy hands on a rag. "Give her a turn and see how she goes."

Ivy slowly spun the heavy fly wheel with the crank handle until it was up to speed, then threw over the decompression leaver and the familiar putt......putt...putt, putt, putt sound of the single cylinder Lister echoed across the harbour. After starting, Jack reached down and played with the throttle, revving the engine up and then slowing it right down, before finally shutting it off.

"I think she's good now," he said, standing back up.

"Thanks for that, Jack. She's not leaking a drop of oil now. I'll know what to do next time. I really appreciate your help," Ivy said.

"Don't worry about it. That's what mates are for, isn't it?"

With the evening's excitement over the tools were cleaned up and the deck washed down before the two crews went their separate ways. Later that night, as Jack went topside before turning in, he found a bottle of whiskey on the deck next to his companionway door.

The harbour was in full swing as Jack picked his way along the crowded wharf towards Government House the following morning. In his leather satchel he carried the official letter he had received the day before. Arriving at the busy administrative centre, he was sent to a wing of the building that had recently been taken over by the Department of Defence. Soldiers dressed in khaki tropical drill uniforms were busy re-organising their new accommodations. Jack was directed upstairs where he eventually found the department of naval operations. "I'm here to see a Commander Lawrence," he said, showing a junior officer his letter. A few moments later he was shown into the cluttered office of the Chief of Operations.

As the aide closed the door behind him the officer rose from his desk and walked around to meet the *Roulette's* skipper. "Ah, Captain McLeod, it is a pleasure to meet you. Commander Archibald Lawrence. I have heard a lot of good things about you. You seem to be quite a legend in these parts," he said in a rolling Scottish lilt, shaking hands briskly. The Commander was dressed in his naval whites, baggy shorts and knee socks. He seemed to be in his early forties. Wiry and fit looking, Jack silently reckoned he would be able to hold his own in a scrap, despite his size.

"Excuse the chaos. We're in the midst of getting ourselves reorganised after moving from the broom closet we used to be in," Lawrence continued, seating himself behind his desk to face Jack. "It's taken us some time to get ourselves up and running here in the islands. I'm sure even Churchill himself would be the first to admit that this war caught us all on the back foot. The German blitz really has had us on our heels, but it looks like we may have weathered that storm…for the moment at least. But with these U boats wreaking havoc in the North Atlantic, the retreat from Greece, the defence of North Africa and the Japs sweeping through Malaya and rolling towards Singapore, our resources are being stretched to breaking point. As you could well imagine, our operation here is not at the top of the priorities list, so we must make do with what we have."

"I appreciate this war is causing great concern in many places, but this time it's not my fight, Commander Lawrence. So with all due respect sir, why exactly do you want to see me?" Jack asked with a steely edge of resolve.

"I understand you have made the acquaintance of Reg Bucknell, our Governor's busy new administrative secretary. Good man, Bucky…Army man himself. At any rate we recently had him take a run through the islands from St Lucia to Grenada and report back on logistics and personnel living and working in the area that might in future assist His Majesty in the war effort. I met with him only a couple of days ago, and I'm afraid your name has come out on the top of the list," Lawrence said. "We have also received a further recommendation from your local shipping agent. There is no getting away from a solid reputation, I'm afraid."

"And what exactly do you mean by 'assisting' in the war effort?"

"Well to be frank, Captain, at the moment we are not exactly sure. The position we have in mind is of a more general nature." Thumbing through a stack of files in front of him he removed one and opened it. "I have a copy of your war record here. Very commendable. When push comes to shove its experience like this we may need to call upon in the troubled days ahead," he said, closing the file and placing it down in front of him.

"Well that was in another lifetime, mate. I'm afraid I'm a different person these days. I've done my duty, and I've got the scars to show for it. To be honest I came in here today to tell you to bugger off, leave me alone and let me go on quietly living my life."

The Commander stirred in his chair, his sinewy muscles tensing. "Like it or not, Captain, you are still a subject of the Crown. Don't you think the people of London hiding in their air raid shelters wouldn't like to have their peaceful lives back? You owe it to me to at least listen to what I have to say."

As stubborn as he was in his resolve, Jack inwardly knew the man was right. At that moment the realization sunk in that the horrors he thought he had buried years ago had tracked him down again, even in this faraway place. He knew himself to be a man who never backed away from anything. Now it seemed as though it was time for him to stand up once again. "Okay, Commander," he heard himself saying. "I'm listening."

"As you know, since this war began we have been catching bloody hell back home. At present there is not much activity on this side of the pond, but nevertheless we have to prepare ourselves for that eventuality. Our position here in the islands would not be near the top of the list of the German High Command at the moment, but that doesn't mean this region is not relevant. The oil produced in the Dutch Islands of Curacao, Bonaire and Aruba, as well as Trinidad is extremely important to the war effort back home. If those taps were shut off our whole machine would almost certainly grind to a halt. Bauxite from the Guyanas is also crucial to our effort as it is the raw material for the aluminium we use to build our fighter planes. Most of these materials go north to the States, then across the North Atlantic in convoys to Britain. With the Yanks sitting on the fence at the moment, the supply lines from here to the States are fairly safe. Jerry wouldn't be doing anything to provoke them into becoming involved if they can help it. But of course this situation could change in the future, and I would expect that it will. Now, with the Germans in control of France through the Vichy Government, things are beginning to stir in the French territories over here. And of course, our islands are the gateway to the Panama Canal, so although we might think rum is the only product here worth fighting for, these islands are strategically very important."

"That's all well and good commander, but I still can't see what all of this has to do with me."

"Basically captain, what we need is intelligence. With your background and knowledge of the islands, you are well-positioned to inform us of any suspicious activities you might observe," the Commander said. "Your normal activities take you throughout these islands, and you have a myriad of contacts, so what we would like you to do is keep your eye out and report anything you might find suspicious – anything at all. Now, with Nazi friendly governments in the French flag colonies of Guadeloupe, Martinique, and French Guyana, enemy vessels could make their way into these waters to take on stores, make repairs and so on. This is something we would like to know about. Secondly, we know the Nazis have a very strong and well-trained espionage network. They have agents scattered across the globe, so we must assume they have some in our area. Any out-of-the-ordinary behaviour should be noted and passed on. And thirdly, there have been sightings of U-boats as far south as the Carolinas, but none have reached this far south that we know about. We have no accurate information as to their range capabilities, and have our doubts as to whether they have the capacity to get here and then make it back to Europe. We do know, however, that the Kriegsmarine has outfitted several old freighters as 'sea-raiders' as they call them, and these islands would be a perfect place for them to hide out. Are you with me so far?"

Jack silently mulled over the officer's presentation. Reluctantly he had to agree with the man. If he were sitting on the other side of the desk, he too would use whatever resources he could muster to assist him in doing his job. This was, after all, His Majesty's Navy, and this wasn't an ill-considered, flippant request. They honestly needed his help. "Yes, I understand. Of course I'll lend a hand. I don't really have much of an option, do I?"

"I was confident you would see common sense. The question is, if you do see or hear something out of the ordinary, what do you do about it? In effect, there will be a couple of ways to make contact. The first will be to let me know something directly, either in person or by message with another individual who you trust. When you are next in Trinidad, you are to report to Naval Command there and make yourself known. This is most important, as Port-of-Spain is where the centre of operations for the Eastern Caribbean is located. I will furnish you with a letter of introduction, which you can show whenever it is needed. Before I say any more, I want to make it clear that everything we discuss today is in the strictest of confidence. 'Loose lips sink ships' as they say back home. Do you agree to this?" he asked. After receiving an affirmative nod he moved on. "There's a man who I believe you are acquainted with who has been working in the islands in another capacity, but who has in fact been quietly assisting Naval Intelligence here for several years now. This man will be your main contact. His name is Harry Iverson."

At the mention of this name a look of shock and surprise came over Jack's face. "What...old Harry a government agent? I would never have believed it! So that's what he has really been doing, snooping around these islands all of these years. And he said he was an archaeologist and botanist! Well you could knock me down with a feather!"

"No, he genuinely is a scientist – and quite a renowned one at that. Let's just say he has been of assistance to us in the past, and will be even more so in the future. Harry Iverson will be, in a manner of speaking, your superior. It is very important you get together with him as soon as possible and work out the details of this assignment."

"That's all well and good, but I wouldn't have a clue how to locate that man. He is as fickle as the weather. He could be anywhere between the Amazon and Honduras as far as I know," Jack said.

"Actually he's a bit closer afield than that. His yacht the *Vagabond* is presently anchored over in Carlisle Bay," the officer smiled. "You don't need to go looking for him; he will find you. He has been briefed. You need only follow his instructions. Do you have any more questions?"

Commander Lawrence paused and waited before he continued. "Welcome aboard, Captain McLeod," the Commander said, standing and escorting his visitor slowly towards the door. "Remember, your discretion on this matter is of utmost importance."

The two shook hands once more, the door opened, and Jack took his leave. Outside in the bright sunshine he stood at the top of the steps and considered what had just taken place. He stared off across the harbour, through the maze of masts, sails and rigging towards the horizon beyond. Taking a deep breath he walked down the steps. It was not the outcome he had expected, but he was resigned to the fact that there was little he could do about it. 'Dere's plenty o' tings in dis world stronger than a man's will," is what Sinclair deVilliars had told him once. "Every man can set he course, but dat don't mean dat's where he finish up."

Jack made his way along the busy quay, lost in thought. Just as he turned the corner he was stopped short by a familiar voice.

"Where are you off to, old man?" Jack turned to see the angular frame of Harry Iverson leaning against the wall in the entrance to a shady laneway, striking a match as he lit up a cigarette.

Out of the Shadows

The captain wandered over to his friend and firmly shook his hand. "I knew I'd be catching up with you sooner or later, Harry. I just had a very interesting meeting with a Commander Lawrence, with whom I'm sure you are well acquainted. It seems you and I have become shipmates, so to speak."

"I hope there are no hard feelings, old man. These are dark days all around. How about we go somewhere and find a cold drink? This heat has given me one hell of a thirst," Iverson said with a smile.

"There's that little bar down on Easy Bay Street where you can usually find a cold beer," Jack suggested, and so the two men strolled the few blocks around to the traditional Barbadian rumshop. The hand painted sign next to the doorway read:

Inside the cool and shady establishment was a scattering of midday drinkers, some sipping beer at the bar, others sitting at tables working on 'nibs' of rum.

"Ah, now this is better," said Iverson as they entered the premises and moved towards a table near the back door, which opened onto a white sand beach. Jack nodded to several of the patrons before being spotted by the proprietor.

"Captain Jack! Good to see you back, mon!" the owner shouted from behind the bar. He was a gregarious man with skin the colour of milk chocolate, a silver head of close cropped curly hair, dark brown eyes and a sparkling smile.

"Jefferson! Good to see you too. I hope you have a couple of cold beers there," Jack answered.

"Of course I do. Two beastly cold Canadian lagers coming your way, sir!"

The two men sat down and waited for their beer. At the front of the shop, four men played dominos, loudly banging their tiles down onto the table, lambasting and goading each other in their rollicking Bajan dialect. Others sat quietly smoking at the bar, sipping on their drinks, while in an opposite corner four schooner captains were finishing a bottle of whiskey.

Jefferson brought their beers. They drank in silence, each appreciating the taste of the cold lager on such a hot day, until Jack finally broke the ice. "So tell me, my learned friend, what the hell is going on?"

Iverson lit a cigarette and puffed on it thoughtfully before answering. "I'm not sure what Lawrence has told you, but first off, let me explain that my link with the Admiralty in years gone by was only peripheral at best. When the Germans started flexing their muscles a few years ago, I was approached by an old naval friend who is high up on the intelligence side of things to simply provide them with any information I might find relevant as I went about my normal day to day business – a job not dissimilar to the one you have been asked to do. When we officially entered the war, my position was scaled up. I know the waters over here, and have a well-developed cover that can provide another set of eyes and ears on this side of the Atlantic. The Caribbean is a large area, however, and so I mentioned to my superiors that I could use some help. That is when your name came up – I hope you don't mind. I know your feelings about your experiences in the last war, but I'm afraid it's all hands to the pumps at the moment, and you are a damn good asset, whether you like it or not."

"I have to admit that I wouldn't be the first bloke to step forward and volunteer for a mission these days, but I do understand the situation, mate. I'm not one to bury my head in the sand and pretend nothing's happening either. But what exactly are we looking for? What do you think we really have to worry about? The war seems a long way away from us here at the moment," Jack said.

"It might be far away now, but it won't be if the Yanks become involved. We know the Germans are pumping out a new U-boat every week, and they are continually upgrading their designs. They are not pushing into these waters as yet, but I would be surprised if they don't eventually turn up. We also have information about several seven to ten thousand ton freighters and passenger ships that have been seen on naval dry docks in Hamburg and Bremen for unusually long periods of time, and can only assume they are being converted to clandestine raiders that would be used to operate on the open sea. In the last war they used these 'sea raiders' as they called them to great effect. It may be a vessel like this turns up in our waters to cause mischief or do repairs or look for provisioning, so that is one example of something we should look out for. Or it may be something as simple as overhearing a conversation or seeing something on the waterfront that doesn't seem quite kosher to you."

"So what you're saying is we don't know what we're looking for but we should look out for it anyway. From my experience that sounds exactly like what the military would put someone up to do," Jack said, draining his beer.

Iverson waited for Jefferson to deliver another round before remarking on Jack's irreverent statement. "Listen old friend, I know it sounds like a waste of time, but if you look at how the war is going at present, we really should be worried. The Krauts have most of Europe under their control, and large swathes of North Africa. They are halfway to Moscow and have formed an alliance with the Japs, who are doing just as much damage in the Far East. I'm sure these islands are to be found somewhere on one of Hitler's 'to do' lists; it is just that he hasn't gotten there yet. When he finally does, I'm not sure what the two of us will be able to do about it, but I at least feel we should help where we can."

"Okay, Harry, you've got me on board. So tell me, mate – where do you want me to start?"

"The first thing you can do, old chap, is to see if you can help find a crew for me," Harry said. "With my new responsibilities I feel my wife Val and I could use another hand on board. It is not an easy position to fill, as I'm sure you could imagine. I'm not looking for simply a deckhand. I need someone I can count on in a tricky situation, who wouldn't be afraid to stick his neck out if need be. In other words, someone who could assist me in my – how should I say – 'special' work. I know it's a big ask, but is there anyone you can think of who might fit the bill?"

Jack sipped his beer, mulling over his friend's request. "Well, there are a couple of boys in my crew that would be great from the sailing side of things, but I don't know how much they could help you in other ways. Then there are some local schooner captains, but..." and then he stopped short as something came to mind. "I know someone who might be just the person you are looking for – if he's here in Barbados. And if he's still alive. Have you ever heard of 'Rabbit' Haynes?"

"Can't say that I have. What's his story?"

"Where do I start? His real name is Carlisle Bartholomew Haynes, but I don't think many people would know him by that. There isn't a local around the Careenage, however, who wouldn't know who 'Rabbit' was. He is a sort of legend in his own way. I spent some time with him up in Havana several years ago, and got to know him quite well."

"A legend? How old is this fellow, and what has he done to be so noteworthy?" Iverson asked as he stubbed out his cigarette.

"What hasn't he done, is more to the point. He's been sailing on schooners since his early teens, and I'd think he's in his mid-thirties by now. Lord only knows what he's done with the money he would have made over the years. I know he likes his rum – and his women! He has at least one woman here and others scattered throughout the Caribbean. But he's a damn fine sailor, an excellent navigator, and knows these islands like the back of his hand. I don't think there's a cove or harbour between here and the Mosquito Coast he hasn't been into at some time or other. I remember the first time I met him years ago up in the Turks and Caicos. He was the mate on one of those big Canadian three masters at the time. The captain was a hopeless drunk. They were sailing north for the States loaded with Barbados rum, forty thousand cases of 'em. They caught the tail end of a hurricane and lost their rudder. The captain gave up and went to his cabin and drank himself senseless, but somehow Rabbit got that vessel into Cockburn Town using the sails alone to steer with, then made a new rudder on the beach, hung it and continued on his way!" Jack said, shaking his head in admiration. "He's certainly smuggled his share of rum over the years. When I ran into him in Havana, he was running guns into the Dominican Republic."

"This fellow sounds quite resourceful – someone you'd like to have on board when clawing off of a lee shore in a gale," Harry said.

"Rabbit is that, and when he's sober, he's as fine a fellow as you could ever want to meet. He speaks Spanish fluently from his days in Cuba and on the South American coast, as well as French Patois and who knows what else. Rumour has it he has a wife on the remote French island of Marie Gallant from when he was shipwrecked there. He has his wild side, but putting that aside, I think he could be your man."

"Well we all have our foibles, I suppose. It sounds like he's someone I should talk to at the very least. How would we go about finding him?" Iverson asked.

"I expect we could start here with Jefferson," Jack said, standing and approaching the genial barman.

"Rabbit? I haven't seen de man fo' months. I know he does have a small place down in Christchurch somewhere. I've heard tell he's been trying to do de right ting by he wife dese days and he's laying off de grog. Hey Desmond!" he called over to one of the men playing dominos, "does you know where Rabbit might be?"

The four men muttered between themselves for a moment before Desmond looked up and answered. "I heard he's got a little sloop hauled out dat he's workin' on. Not far – just down de bayside a piece."

The bright red sloop was chocked under a coconut tree a half of a mile or so down the beach from Jefferson's rum shop. Though roughly built, she had sweet lines. The words *Sea Queen* were scrawled across the stern. On board, a figure sat caulking the deck, the acrid smell of boiling pitch filling the air. Jack stepped up onto a rusty oil drum and rested his arms on the low bulwarks, the scars from countless fishing lines etched into the worn wooden rail. "G'day Rabbit – how's it going?" he asked casually.

The caulker stopped and turned towards his visitor. "Cap'n Jack McLeod – I knew you was about de place. I saw de vessel sail in a few days ago," he said, turning back to his work and knocking a few more inches of oakum into the seam, his longish blonde hair hanging from underneath a battered straw hat, the collar of his cotton shirt turned up against the rays of the afternoon sun.

"Nice little sloop you got here. She built in Carriacou?"

"Yes mon. You has a good eye," he replied, putting his iron and mallet down and leaning back onto his two hands. "I decided a while back I needed to change me ways. De kids are getting big and me don' hardly know dem. De oldest boy say he wants to turn he hand to fishin', so I went down and bought dis sloop from a fella in Union Island. Dere's good money in fish dese days you know. I've put dem wild times behind me."

Jack peered into a set of mischievous blue eyes that seemed to tell stories on their own. A scraggle of blond whiskers covered a suntanned face. Snaggled white teeth flashed an infectious smile. "I'll believe that when I see it," he said with a grin.

"So what brings you fellows down to this part of the beach? Just a social visit to check up on de ol' Rabbit?" he asked, returning back to his caulking.

"No – it's a bit of business actually. Do you think you can spare a few minutes to talk?"

"Le' me just pay off dis seam and den we can chat," Rabbit replied. Finishing off the caulking, he climbed agilely to his feet, and dipping a tarry ladle into the bubbling pitch pot squatted on his haunches and carefully tipped a fine stream of the hot liquid into the seams between the deck planks.

Stepping down onto the sand, Jack watched as Rabbit sprung lightly to the ground. After brief introductions, the two men followed the Bajan around the bow of the sloop to a rough planked work-bench nailed to a couple of sea grape trees. From underneath the bench, amidst wood chips and shavings and grown crooks of timber, Rabbit pulled out a bunch of orange-skinned coconuts from which he clipped off three with his sharp hatchet, expertly chopping the tops off and then handing one each to his guests. "These waternuts are sweet, you hear. De old man over yonder sends he grandson down wit' dem fo' me. Once I set to fishin I'll send up a fish or two gi' him," he said. They tipped their heads back and quickly drank the sweet water, after which Rabbit split the three nuts perfectly, the men spooning out the white jelly with off-cuts from the outside husk. "Now what's dis ting you wanted to talk about?"

Jack settled back onto the bench, crossed his arms and began. "You may have seen my friend Harry here around the place over the years, or at least his yacht the *Vagabond,* which is anchored at the moment out in Carlisle Bay."

"Oh yes mon, you mean dat nice little double-ended yawl? I've noticed her a few times over the years. She has de looks of a smart sailor."

"Yes, well Harry and his wife have been cruising her about the Caribbean for the past few years, and have been able to manage the boat quite well – up to now at least. I suppose I should let Harry take over, and let him explain the situation."

"Jack and I were chatting earlier today, and I asked him if he could recommend someone who might be interested in joining my wife and me as crew, and your name came up. First off I must say that the job could prove to be dangerous, but I can tell you that you would be adequately compensated for this. You could be away for a year or more, but it can be arranged that your wife draw your wages to keep your family going. Before I go into any further detail, can I ask if you are even remotely interested?"

Rabbit put his hand to his chin, thoughtfully squinting off to the distant horizon. "I've really been looking forward to takin' me boy an' de ol' *Sea Queen* fishin', but I've always made it a policy to at least listen when someone's offerin' me money. I got one question…why me? I'm sure dere's plenty of other sailors 'round de place dat could do de job."

"Actually we're looking for a bit more than just a sailor. I require someone with a certain set of skills. Jack here tells me that you are indeed a person of diverse talents."

Rabbit glanced from one man to the other. "Having de Cap'n here with you says a lot. He and I go back a long way. He wouldn't be here if you was just skylarkin'. Go ahead – I'm interested. And if I turn you down you don't have fo' frighten, what you say won't go past me and my little boat here."

Harry went ahead and explained the situation to Rabbit, sparing no detail. The Bajan listened intently, asked a few questions, and finally when Harry was finished leaned silently against the workbench for several minutes, lost in thought. "When would you want me to start?" he finally asked.

"I'm planning to leave for Martinique within the next few days. I know its short notice, but it would be jolly good if you could be aboard," Harry said.

"I'd have to say dat I'm interested. If I could have a couple o' days to square tings away here wit' my vessel, an' let de ol' woman know what's happenin', den I might say yes to de offer. I'm sure de wife wouldn't mind havin' some steady money comin' in for a change," Rabbit said with a smile.

By week's end the *Roulette* had loaded her cargo, and early on a Saturday morning her mooring lines were dropped off and the deep-laden schooner motored slowly out of the Careenage. "See you next time, Ivy!" Jack called across the water as they glided past the *Rose Ann*.

"All the best, Jack," Ivy returned as she leaned over the high bulwarks. "I'll see you next year."

"Right-o – if God spare life!" he shouted back with a wave.

And then the sound of rope through sheaves could be heard as the mainsail began to be hoisted, and one by one the sails were raised and set and the schooner cleared out from the heads, setting a northerly course for the small island of Saint Barthélemy with two cargo holds full of Barbados rum.

Martinique

The breeze came down in bullets as the *Vagabond* tacked her way into the broad bay of Fort-de-France in Martinique, the gaff yawl slicing through the small chop as it heeled and lifted into the gusts. In the early morning light, the island's high volcanic mountains were painted a deep purple against the pink and amber of the sunrise sky behind. On the shore a few lights still flickered, remnants of the fleeting night. The smell of the land blew over the water and across the deck of the *Vagabond;* an earthen, richly tropical scent blended with the salt-laden morning breeze and the smoky stench of the city.

Val Iverson appeared from the galley below with three steaming mugs of coffee, handing her husband one and Rabbit the other. She stood in the hatchway and sipped her hot drink as she surveyed the early morning scene, a white woollen sweater thrown on against the chill of the morning, her dark wavy hair windblown and ruffled from the night's passage at sea.

A few large schooners and several steel freighters lay at anchor as Iverson sailed into the anchorage, expertly bringing his yacht in under the lee of the Napoleonic Fort Saint Louis which sat atop a rocky bluff that jutted out into the bay. One by one the two headsails came down. The anchor splashed and the chain rattled out as Rabbit worked the fore deck, the boat's bow snatching around head to wind as the anchor held. The gaff mainsail was lowered next as the two halyards were eased in unison, the cotton sail flaking itself into the lazy jacks as it came down. The three sailors quietly moved from job to job as they furled the mainsail, coiled lines and tidied up the boat after its overnight sail from Barbados.

"How about I whip up some bacon and eggs?" Harry said when they were done, rubbing his hands together as he entered the yacht's galley. "Nothing like a good cooked breakfast after a hard night of sailing, eh what!"

With breakfast over with, Iverson cleaned himself up, shaved and then climbed into the dinghy and rowed ashore, the ship's papers and Barbados clearance tucked away into his leather satchel resting on the after seat. Tying his dinghy up to the small wooden wharf, Iverson strode into town and the Gendarmerie. He knew Fort-de-France well. He and Val loved this exotic port; from its colonial architecture to its mixture of French and Creole culture, Martinique had always been a pleasant and enjoyable place to spend time. The situation now, of course, was different. A war was on, and France was controlled by a pro-German military Vichy government. As a British subject, Iverson had no idea how he would be treated this time around. It was a risk he was taking, coming here, and he knew it. He was counting on the fact that he had been to Martinique many times before and was on good terms with the authorities. In the confusion of the current politics he hoped he would be able to talk his way through any potential problems.

Capitaine Lacroix was the officer in charge of customs and immigration. Normally he was jovial and easy to deal with. He had a good memory and rarely forgot the face or name of anyone who passed through his office. In previous visits his attitude was always professional, yet polite. Today, however, was a different story. As Iverson entered the Gendarmerie, the looks from the attending officers were very grim indeed. There were some new faces he hadn't seen before, and as he approached the counter the attitude was hostile and officious. Iverson was half expecting this sort of treatment, and in his best French deflected the aggression thrown at him with diplomatic flair. Soon the door marked Bureau de Chef opened and Lacroix walked over to the desk. Silently examining the ship's papers, he slowly turned them over page by page, and then again, as if he had never seen them before.

"Anglais? C'est un problème, monsieur le Capitaine," he said with a stern face. Returning the stare, Iverson noted the hard set of the officer's jaw. There was no joviality on this occasion, no friendly conversation in English. There was, however, a certain look that gave him some hope. "Monsieur, accompagnez-moi à mon bureau, s'il vous plaît," he said. Iverson followed the uniformed officer, shutting the door behind him.

Once inside his office, Lacroix became another man. Opening a box on the table he offered his guest a cigarette, and striking a match the two men lit up. "I apologize, monsieur, for my manner outside, but these are difficult times. Many things have changed. Our government here is being reorganised, and no one knows what will happen. You don't know who is working next to you. I may not even have a job tomorrow," he said in English.

"I understand. The whole world is changing, not just Martinique. My wife and I enjoy this island so much that we thought we would visit one more time before the situation becomes too awkward. I hope we are not too late. As you know, I'm a botanist and there are a few of your native plants I have not finished identifying."

Lacroix drew on his cigarette and regarded Iverson through his exhaled smoke. "At the moment the Germans are in Paris. Marshal Petain has formed a government in the south of the country, in Vichy, and for now is maintaining the pretence of independence. We all know, however, who is pulling the strings. Admiral Robert is in charge of the French West Indian Territories, which means the Navy is running the government here. The Sécurité Nationale is becoming very powerful. Certain citizens are being detained – there is a question of loyalties. General de Gaulle is living in exile in London and asking us all to fight for a Free France. It is not easy, monsieur, being a Frenchman these days."

"Damn rotten situation all around, old man. There's no telling what the future will bring. I just hope that we aren't all going to end up speaking German, if you know what I mean," Iverson said.

"I could think of nothing worse, Capitaine. As far as your visit here is concerned, I can use my authority to allow you to stay for one week, at which time you must apply for an extension. Your movements must be confined to Fort-de-France, and you must avoid the naval dockyards. We are most protective of the island's defences at the moment," Lacroix said. "Now, Monsieur, let us get your papers in order." The two men stood and went outside, where Lacroix ordered his officers to issue Captain Iverson his clearance.

The bells of the Cathédrale Saint Louis chimed six o'clock as the crew of the *Vagabond* rowed ashore. The town of Fort-de-France spread out from the water's edge, eventually rolling up the sides of the high green mountains behind. The hustle and bustle of the business day was winding down. Shop owners were putting away their wares and gradually locking up as the three yachtsmen made their way through the narrow cobblestone streets overlooked by the ornate wrought iron balconies and brightly painted shutters of upstairs residences. Turning onto Rue du Grand Caribe, they entered an open doorway and ascended the worn wooden stairs to their favourite portside bar and restaurant, Chez Francine.

"Bonjour Max," Iverson said to the bartender, who turned and greeted his three guests with a warm smile.

"Bonjour! How are you? It's quite some time since I've seen you here. What can I get you?" he asked.

"A white wine for Madam, and I think we'll have a couple of Petit Punches, eh Carlisle?" Harry ordered.

"Very good my friend – two punches and a vin blanc. Monsieur Philippe has just stepped out. He should be back soon," the barman said as he mixed the drinks.

"Thanks Max. We'll be sitting outside on the balcony."

Sipping their drinks, they surveyed the harbour that spread out before them, the colours of the setting sun reflecting off of the stone walls of Fort Saint Louis as schooners and steel freighters lay at anchor beneath. Across the broad bay, the southern end of the island could be seen tumbling off into the distance.

The bar was filling up with patrons when the threesome were joined by Philippe Javert, the bar's gregarious owner. "Ah, what a pleasant surprise! It's so good to see you again! Valerie, you are looking splendid as usual. Max – three more drinks for my friends!" he called, as he joined the table, giving Valerie the mandatory kiss on each cheek.

"Great to see you too, old man. Let me introduce you to our new crew member, Mr Carlisle Haynes from the good island of Barbados," Harry said, gesturing for Philippe to take a seat.

"Glad to meet you, mon. Harry likes to call me by my Christian name, mais la plupart des gens m'appellent Rabbit."

"Oh, so you speak French, Mr Haynes, or rather Rabbit? Plaisir de faire votre Guigou," Philippe said as they shook hands.

"So how is life treating you, my old friend?" Harry asked.

The Frenchman shrugged and frowned. "What can I say? The world is becoming a very confused place. No one knows which way to turn. I'm just a simple fellow trying to make my way through life as well as I can. At the moment here in Martinique, things are not good. There are many rumours, and you must be careful what you say. You don't know who is listening. No one knows what will happen next."

"It must be very uncomfortable," Val said. "Men are such silly beasts. If it were left to us women, there would be no wars at all."

"With this I completely agree, Valerie." Philippe said, his broad face expressing genuine good humour. "Now if you will excuse me, I must see to some things." The charismatic Frenchman excused himself, another round of drinks came, and soon the tables at Chez Francine were filled with happily drinking customers. Food was ordered, along with wine. A Creole band took to the bandstand and soon a pulsating meringue was drifting out of the doors and over the streets below.

Later in the evening Harry excused himself from the table, leaving his wife for the moment with their charming new crew member. After finding the café owner, the two slipped away to his downstairs office. "I need to speak to you concerning a very delicate matter, my friend, which must be kept in the strictest confidence," Harry said as the two sat down. The proprietor poured two glasses of Pastis.

"Santé," they said, clinking glasses.

"I consider you a friend I can trust, and I also believe we are both on the same side of this war," he continued, offering Philippe a cigarette.

"We have known each other for a long time, Harry. Anything we discuss in private will never leave this room," the Frenchman replied.

Harry took a pull on his Gitan and began. "Firstly, I should let you know that amongst other things I perform certain – shall I say 'services' for my government, as well as our neutral neighbours to the north."

"You are an even more astonishing man than I thought, Harry Iverson," Philippe said with admiration.

"I'm here because both governments are very concerned with the situation in Martinique. Over the past year, the messages coming out of Fort-de-France have been mixed indeed. We are more concerned than ever with the leanings of your leader here, Admiral Robert."

"When Admiral Georges Robert arrived here as High Commissioner of the Republic to the Antilles, he proclaimed his intention of fighting for a free France," Philippe began. "I almost remember his words exactly. 'We will fight to the death to support the Motherland in this terrible test', he said. It didn't take him long to change his tune." Philippe uncorked the Pastis and refilled their glasses.

"I remember the situation well," said Harry. "Val and I were here when Robert launched his 'National Revolution', as he called it. His measures were extremely draconian, indeed."

"Almost overnight the bastard became the staunchest of Vichy supporters. He even arrogantly called himself the 'Pétain of the Antilles'. That is when all newspapers were shut down and replaced with his mouthpiece 'Le Journal Officiel de la Martinique'. Foreign broadcasts were officially deemed propaganda and prohibited, with harsh penalties if anyone was discovered listening to them. And now, through the Sécurité Nationale, he is tightening his grip. His latest effort is to eliminate the exodus of people fleeing to St. Lucia and Dominica by using patrol boats in the north and south to try and stop them. The man is now regarded by most of us as a fascist and almost universally hated."

"So you believe that some sort of underground resistance movement would be popularly supported?" Harry asked, lighting up another cigarette.

"Absolutely!" Philippe exclaimed. "I could find recruits in the blink of an eye!"

"Good. Now to another point. Robert still maintains control of the remains of the French Navy here in the West Indies. He has at his disposal an aircraft carrier with over one hundred planes, a cruiser and two destroyers. Despite the agreement he signed with Washington a few months ago promising to disarm his fleet, the Americans are still taking this threat very seriously, and a bombardment and invasion of the island continues to be a possibility. With the growing strength of the German submarine fleet and their easy access to the Atlantic through French ports, as well as the Kriegsmarine's effective use of sea raiders in the Atlantic, my government is more curious than ever as to his true intentions. Will Robert in fact allow the Nazis secret access to the ports in the French West Indies? Could he even go so far as to allow them use of his navy here? These are questions that are seriously being asked at the highest of levels."

"Yes, before the accord with Roosevelt was signed, things here were very tense," agreed Philippe. "Rumours were running wild. Everyone was expecting American troops to be landing on our shores at any moment. With newspapers under government control, no one knows what the truth really is."

"That is the point; no one knows what the real truth is. This Robert is a cagey character. He says one thing, yet does another. He has placated the Americans, and yet he is a staunch Vichy supporter. Is he going to remain neutral? And is he really going to keep his word? The reason I'm telling you this is that we are looking for people here who we can trust to provide us with reliable information. That is what I am asking you to do. It's dangerous work. If you get caught you could be shot. I would understand if you say no. Can you help?"

For a few moments the only sound to be heard was the muffled beat of the band upstairs. The two men sipped on their Pastis. "You've come to the right man, my friend. I'm no supporter of Pétain and his Vichy cronies. Like the vast majority of my people here, I dream of a free France. Just tell me what you want me to do."

"What you need to do is keep your eyes and ears open. We know the Nazis are spreading their influence everywhere. This island could prove to be very valuable to them in the future. It could provide them with a foothold in this hemisphere. So we need to know what they are getting up to here, as well as on the other French Islands. You will need to set up a small network of trusted comrades – fishermen, lorry drivers, taxi drivers – four or five people you can really trust, who will keep their mouths shut if and when things take a turn for the worst. Like I said, this will be dangerous work. But these are dangerous times."

"All this I can do. I have the contacts. I will set it up. You can count on me."

"That's exactly what I wanted to hear. I'm now on my way to Trinidad. Someone will be contacting you quite soon. It could be me, or maybe someone else." Harry stood and shook hands with Philippe. "Good to have you on board, old man."

For the next couple of days the crew of the *Vagabond* played the part of visiting yachtsmen. Iverson and his wife made several forays to the botanical gardens, where they diligently made notes on the tremendous variety of tropical plant life there.

For his part, Rabbit spent his mornings doing maintenance on board the yacht before going ashore in the afternoons and mixing amongst the town's mariners, dockers and fishermen, which generally led on to late evenings drinking rum in one or another of the taverns scattered around the port. He spoke the island patois fluently and was easily mistaken for a white local. Harry had given him the task of gauging the true feelings of the local population, as well as uncovering any other useful tid-bits of information he might overhear.

Early one sunny morning, the crew were sitting in the cockpit having a cup of tea. Harry and Val were getting ready to go ashore to the church on the hill known as l'Église Montmartre de Balata.

"I didn't hear you come back aboard last night, Carlisle," Harry said. "Where were you drinking your rum this time?"

"In a waterside bar called L'Ancre. Its de same place I been goin' de las' couple o' nights. I met someone dere I enjoy talkin' to. An' there was a band playin' dat didn't finish up til late."

"Anything interesting to report?"

"There was somethin' dat I did spot, yes. Every night I been there me been especially keepin' me eye on dese three sea farin' types who mostly jus' sit in de corner an' drink, like dey waitin' on somethin' or someone. Dey looks to be a rough sort o' crew, an' one o' dem, most likely he's de Cap'n, is missin' one eye. Over de last couple o' days I been watchin' out to see which vessel dey was on, an' I noticed dat dey was aboard a little freighter anchored just outside o' we here. Anyways, last night a couple a strangers turned up wit' a local fellah. Dey stood out 'cause o' de kind of suits dey was wearin'. I don' know – dey jus' looked to be foreigners. Dem fellahs had one drink an' den dey was gone. I followed 'em outside, but dey got in a car an' drove away. De funny thing is, dis mornin' dat vessel is gone."

"That is a curious story indeed, Carlisle. As to this freighter, was there any remarkable about her?"

"She looks like one o' dem small European coasters. Black, an' flyin' a foreign flag. I think she could o' been Dutch. I certain sure I seen de same vessel alongside in de Careenage in Barbados not dat long ago."

"I say, that is an interesting tale. There's not much we can do other than take note of it, but it does prick one's interest. Well done, Mr Haynes. Now I suppose we should make a start before the morning gets away from us."

They finished their tea, climbed into the dinghy, and Rabbit rowed them ashore. He brought the tender alongside the wharf and the couple jumped out. Rabbit pushed off, preparing to row back aboard. "And what is your friend's name?" Val asked, smiling from the edge of the dock.

"Which friend is dat?" Rabbit asked with a shy grin. "You mean last night at de bar? Yvette. Me friend's name is Yvette."

Harry and Val took their time hiking to up to the famous church, which was a miniature replica of the Basilica of Montmartre in Paris. Climbing the hill, they took notes of the flora and fauna along the way. It was not really the church or the surrounding plant life that they were interested in, however, but the view over the bay which it commanded. From just outside the walls of the cathedral, Iverson and his wife had a beautiful view of the approaches to the port from the west. On their left, across the broad Baie du Fort-de-France, the island cascaded away to the south past the monolithic Diamond Rock, the high mountains of the British island of St. Lucia faintly visible across the Martinique Channel on the distant horizon. Below them the city of Fort-de-France could be seen clearly; beyond sat the high walls of Fort Saint Louis. On the other side of the old fort the inner harbour containing the still active dockyard built by Napoleon's navy could be clearly observed. Opposite, alongside the southern wharfs, laid the massive grey flat topped aircraft carrier *Be'am*, along with a cruiser and two smaller destroyers. This is what Harry really wanted to see. "This splendid view surly makes the hike up here worth the effort," he said.

It wasn't long before the sound of a motorcar could be heard approaching. They watched a cream coloured Citroen pull up and park. The front doors opened and two men in white linen suits and Panama hats nonchalantly made their way to the railing.

"These gentlemen don't look like tourists to me, dear," Val said.

"No, they don't. I believe I've seen one of them around town. Perhaps we should think about wandering back." Slowly they began to pack up their bag.

"Pardon monsieur," one of the men said, walking towards the pair. "I am with the Sécurité Nationale."

"Bonjour," Harry answered with a smile. "How can we help?"

The man's ill-fitting suit hung loosely over a bony frame. A wide brimmed hat shaded his gaunt face; a thin black moustache was etched over lips that now turned up into a condescending smile. "You are far from the centre of town, monsieur. I presume you would not object to me examining your bag?"

"But of course. Help yourself," Iverson replied with as much courtesy as possible.

With his hulking partner holding open the bag, the man began to search through it. Pulling out their sketchbook, he slowly leafed through the pages. After examining several sketches of various plants he looked up, scrutinizing Iverson through beady eyes. "You are very fond of plants, monsieur." He continued to look through the sketchbook, occasionally pausing to examine more closely one drawing or another, now and then commenting in Creole to his partner. Closing the book, he handed it to Iverson before rifling through the balance of the bag. He was ponderously slow, but eventually was convinced there was nothing suspicious and returned the bag. "Thank you for your patience, monsieur. Enjoy your stay in Martinique." With a slight tip of his hat he walked back to the vehicle, climbing into the passenger's side. The car wheeled around, its red taillights disappearing slowly from view as it wound back down the hill.

The pair began their walk back to town. "That was interesting. I'm glad they didn't find this," Harry remarked, pulling the sketch of the harbour with the position of the warships out of his hip pocket.

The following day, Harry and Val went ashore to do some shopping at the colourful central markets. As they navigated their way along the busy waterfront, Harry noticed the same Citroen with the two men from the day before parked up a side street. Just as they rounded the corner a young boy grabbed hold of his hand. "Venez ici, monsieur! Come, come!" Letting go, the young boy darted into an alleyway, where he stood waiting.

"You go on Val. I'll be along soon and meet you there." Iverson gave his wife a peck on the cheek and then quickly ducked in to the alley. Half way down the narrow passage the boy opened a door and motioned for him to enter. Harry stepped inside and the door was closed behind.

An elderly Creole woman with a silver head of hair sitting in an easy chair slowly stood when he entered. A crucifix hung on the wall opposite. Holding up a finger she said some words in patois before departing from the room. Not sure what was actually happening, Harry patiently stared into a glass cabinet which stood against the whitewashed wall containing several old photos, fine china statuettes and other ornaments. A few minutes later the portly frame of Philippe Javert came through the door, his white jacket drenched in perspiration; beads of sweat rolling out from under his hat.

"I'm sorry for such theatre, Harry, but it is necessary," Philippe said, motioning to a chair at a table in the middle of the room. "This is the home of the mother of my barman Max. Gerard, the boy who brought you here, is his son. He has been patiently waiting all morning for you to come ashore. We needed to warn you. Things are changing quickly."

"It's funny you are here. Val and I were on our way to the markets and were going to drop in to Chez Francine for lunch. So tell me – what's going on?" Iverson asked, crossing his legs as he struck a match to light their cigarettes.

"This morning I received a message from a friend at the Gendarmerie that there are certain people in the government that have become aware of your presence and could be planning to make trouble for you. If you stay here much longer we think it could be dangerous. My advice is to wait until night and then quietly depart."

"I see. It's funny, but I've had a bit of an uneasy feeling myself. Yesterday we were searched by a couple of goons up at the Montmartre de Balata and I believe that they've been watching us since. No use taking any unnecessary chances. The interior design of Fort St. Louis is not that appealing to me. I'll take your advice and leave tonight. Thanks for the warning, my friend. Now on another subject – I take it that the airport here in Martinique is still operating?"

"Yes, flights do occasionally come in and out."

"So if, for instance, an agent wanted to fly here from Germany, how do you suppose he would do it?"

"I have heard of people flying from here to Europe and back by going through Cayenne to Brazil, and then across the Atlantic to

Casablanca. It takes several days with a few stops, but it is possible. Why?" Philippe asked.

"Carlisle noticed something last night that sounded curious, that's all," Harry said. He then went on to explain what his crewmember had seen at L'Ancre. "It may amount to nothing, but these days it seems like anything could be possible."

"Don't worry, I will look into it. And I will also keep an eye out for this Dutch freighter."

"That would be excellent, but be careful. Do what you can to gather information, but try and keep a low profile. Someone will be in touch with you very soon."

"Okay Harry, I'll do my best to take your advice, and try not to end up inside Fort Saint Louis myself! We'll get through this, comrade. One day this will be over, and life in Martinique and Chez Francine will be back to normal. Let's have a drink to that." The Frenchman poured two stiff shots of clear white rum from the bottle on the table. They touched glasses. "Liberté!"

"Liberté!" The two men tipped back their glasses. And after a hearty handshake and hug they were gone, leaving through opposite doors.

Just after midnight under the cover of a heavy rainsquall the *Vagabond* slipped quietly out of Fort-de-France. By the time the squall had passed the yawl was well to leeward of Diamond Rock, running under a press of canvas with no lights. Nearby, but unseen in the darkness, two of His Majesty's Royal Navy destroyers were taking up station in the blockade of Martinique.

Saint Barthélemy

Daybreak was bright and clear. The sea to windward quivered as the eastern horizon lit up with the colours of dawn. The *Roulette* rolled and surged forward, wallowing in the light breeze, her heavy booms and gaffs occasionally slamming from side to side as long blue swells from the open Atlantic swept past, disappearing into the broad waters of the Caribbean Sea to the west.

"Dere she be Cap, St. Barths just off de starboard bow," Zepheryn said as Jack poked his head out of the companionway hatch after a few hours' sleep.

Ahead, on the distant horizon, stood the faint outline of the jagged peaks of the small island. To port, the high green island of St. Kitts dropped slowly astern. The captain blew out the compass lamp and climbed up on to the deck.

As the schooner pressed on, the island's features slowly began to appear before them, the morning sun reflecting shades of red and pink off the saw-toothed jumble of rocks and brown hills. Off on the leeward horizon Sint Eustacious stretched out to the north, beyond stood the dramatic, volcanic cone of Saba, clouds banking around her lofty peak.

As the island grew near, their course became more and more downwind. Soon the forward sails flapped listlessly, blanketed by the giant mainsail which was eased right out to the end of its sheet. Jack went forward, standing to windward of the towering tree of a mainmast, looking aloft.

"Tide is workin' sou 'east, Skip," Kingsford said, moving in alongside of him.

"I think you're right, Fordy. Let's gybe the fores'l," the skipper said. Grabbing the slack sheet, the two men threw the sail across to the starboard side, where it filled immediately. The mate at the wheel altered his course slightly, and soon they were surging along in the rising breeze.

Kingsford moved aft with the skipper. "You readin' both pages now, Zeph!" he called out to the mate with a satisfied smile.

As the sun climbed higher into the eastern sky the breeze grew in strength, and so did the schooner's speed. By mid-morning they were abreast of the island, and just before noon the one inch anchor chain was rattling through the hawse pipe and the *Roulette* was anchored in the calm outer harbour of Gustavia amongst a small fleet of schooners and sloops. The ship's boat was unlashed off of the midships cargo hatch, swung over and tied alongside. Not long afterwards Dawson jumped into the boat, followed by the captain, and taking up the oars the young crewman rowed the skipper ashore.

The port of Gustavia quietly basked in the heat of the midday sun. Ashore not much was moving as the flat calm water lapped against the low stone wharves framing the rectangular inner harbour. In the shade of a giant fig tree, four solitary figures observed the approaching skiff with interest. A scattering of neatly painted weatherboard houses edged the peaceful waterfront, their shutters closed to the outside world. At the head of the harbour stood a white-washed church and steeple; coconut trees waved their branches as the odd gust found its way over the dry hills and skittled across the water.

Dawson pulled the skiff at a good clip, the long oars chaffing against the wooden thole pins. A few small fishing boats lay idly about the shoreline. Although barely a soul could be seen about in the quivering heat, Jack knew his arrival had not been unnoticed. He could almost feel the curious, unseen eyes upon him. From the stern sheets the captain pointed his oarsman towards the head of the harbour, where he slowed and spun the small boat alongside. The two sailors climbed ashore; Jack tied the bowline to an iron ring set into the stonework. They crossed the road and entered through the open doors of a small white house. Inside was cool and dark, and filled with a jumble of everyday necessities. Open burlap bags of sugar and rice mixed with boxes of potatoes and garlic and bales of oakum. Basic hardware lined the wooden shelves along with tools and paint and shackles and tins of sardines. The place smelled of salt fish, cooking butter and Stockholm tar.

"Bonjour! Hello!" Jack called out as he approached the worn wooden counter, his eyes gradually adjusting to the dim light.

A voice drifted from out back. "Oui, oui...un moment, monsieur." Eventually a heavy-set man wearing a khaki work-shirt and trousers and a straw fisherman's hat rolled to the counter with a stiff, bow-legged gait. "Ah, it's you Captain McLeod! A long time since you've been here! Welcome back!" he said, smiling and pumping Jack's hand in his calloused, vice-like grip.

"Yes, it's been a while Captain Gastonay. Maybe close to a year since we were here last."

"Well it is good to see you again," the old man smiled, showing a flash of gold-filled teeth. "So are you here to collect a cargo or discharge one?"

"Both actually. We've some Barbados rum aboard for Emile Darraux, and we'll be taking on a bit ourselves."

"Very good, my friend, very good. So now, just to keep the record straight, let's fill out the book." The captain opened a dog-eared ledger and painstakingly wrote in the date, name of the vessel, and port from whence it came. Technically, St. Barths was a free port and clearances just a formality, visiting captains obliging more out of courtesy than for any other reason. As he had done many times before, Jack put his initials in the Honorary Port Captain of Gustavia's shipping record, and took his leave. "By the way, is my friend Sean O'Loughlin still about the place? I didn't notice the *Lady Luck* in the harbour," he asked from the doorway.

"Yes, he's still on the island. My nephew Luc is working for him. I think he said they gone to St. Martin* for the day. He should be back later."

---

*The island of St. Martin / St. Maarten is unique in that one half of it is French and one half of it is Dutch, with each side of the island differentiated by its own way of spelling. For simplicity's sake the French spelling is used throughout this book.

As Jack strolled around the sleeping harbour, past the scattering of black, moss-covered remnants of the island's once grand warehouses, he tried to imagine St. Barthélemy as it would have been during the romantic, swashbuckling times of the late 1600's when the infamous buccaneer 'Montbars the Exterminator' made the island his home; or during the Napoleonic Wars when as a protectorate of neutral Sweden as many as 2,000 ships a year were passing through the busy Free Port of Gustavia. *Those were the days. Now it's just a quiet little fishing village*, he thought facetiously, knowing full well that in present times it was the number one destination of contraband smugglers in the Caribbean; a haven where schooners and sloops from the highly taxed British West Indies came to fill their holds with cheap, duty-free alcohol and cigarettes before sailing home and discharging their goods in the dead of night in one of the many isolated coves and bays scattered throughout the islands.

The warehouse was located a few minutes' walk around the quay. Reaching the unobtrusive sign above the heavy wooden doors which read Darraux et Fils, Jack ventured into the cool, whitewashed interior. Amongst neatly stacked wooden cases of Scotch whiskey, Kentucky bourbon, English gin and French cognac, as well as West Indian rum, he found the proprietor seated as usual behind his large desk. Looking up from an accounts ledger, he smiled at seeing the approaching captain. Standing, he greeted him warmly.

"Captain Jack of la *Roulette*! You are looking well my friend!" the short, grey haired merchant said.

"Good afternoon Emile. And you're looking as young as ever," was the reply.

At the sound of voices two large, well-muscled men emerged from the back of the warehouse, where barrels of rum and casks of wine were stored. Smiling, they sheepishly greeted Jack. He had known Emile's 'boys' for years, since the days when they were teenagers and had just started working for their father.

"You'll be happy to know I've got a load of Barbados rum for you," Jack said with his infectious smile.

"Good news, Captain, good news. The wharf is clear today. You can come alongside this afternoon and we can offload you tomorrow."

"That's fine with me. I'll be looking to take a few cases of whiskey and wine back home with me as well."

"That won't be a problem. There might be a war on, but we are never short on product!" old Darraux joked.

"You're not wrong there, mate. So we're set then, Emile. I'll look out for your boys first thing in the morning."

Late afternoon, and the *Roulette* motored slowly into the inner harbour, tying up alongside the ancient stone wharf. The shoreline was now alive with activity. Along the main street that ran through the centre of town, a few small shops were open. Groups gathered in various places discussing the day's events. A clutch of men sat under the fig tree next to their boats, chatting with each other in their rambling, melodic creole as they watched two fishermen repair their nets. Outside a simple stone building perched on the water's edge, a queue of people waited and watched as a cow was butchered, blood running red into the harbour. An island sloop tacked in through the light, fluky breeze, her patched sails flapping listlessly as she slowly glided over the calm water. And then, from off in the distance, a low rumble of engines could be heard. Jack and his crew turned from tidying up the deck to see the *Lady Luck* roar past the sloop and motor into the harbour.

The shoreside activity slowly came to a standstill. All eyes were on the shiny motor yacht. As the craft came closer she slowed her speed as she altered course and headed for the dock and the long green schooner alongside it. Jack moved to the rail as the powerboat drifted to a stop. "Good afternoon, Captain McLeod! You're a sight for sore eyes!" her skipper called out, appearing on to the stern deck from out of the varnished mahogany wheelhouse, his voice tinted in a deep Irish brogue.

"G'day Sean – you're looking well!" Jack shouted over the noise of the idling engines.

"Let me put the old girl away and I'll come around to see you," he called back.

Disappearing inside he threw the motorboat into ahead, and with a fishtail of a flourish spun her wheel and the *Lady Luck* shot across the harbour, a vision of gleaming white paint, sparkling varnish and polished chrome.

At that moment, the flapping of sails attracted the attention of the fixated crew. Looking astern they watched the jib and main of the small sloop lower to the deck. Quietly she glided in alongside the wharf, tying up just astern of the schooner.

The western sky was ablaze with shades of ochre as twilight slipped over the harbour. Jack stood on the wharf talking to his friend Antoine Degras, a businessman who owned the local ship's chandlery.

"So Captain Jack, what's the news from down south?" Antoine asked, his sharp black eyes staring up at the schooner captain from beneath a sporty white flat cap.

"Hard work and steady blows, as usual mate. How are things with you?"

"Oh, business is business. We had some excitement not long ago, though. Guadeloupe sent some bureaucrats to St. Martin to set up a department of their Vichy government. When they then tried to come over and do the same thing here we chased 'em back on to the mailboat and ran 'em of off the island. They might put up with all o' that over in Marigot or down in Guadeloupe, but dere's no way we gonna let it happen here."

"Good on ya, mate. You folks certainly don't stand for any rubbish, that's for sure!" Jack said with a smile. "And you still find time to do some fishin'?"

"Yes, yes – I still get out on my boat and pull my pots. Life goes on as usual."

As they talked, Jack noticed a maroon convertible negotiate its way around the edge of the harbour. People stopped to watch it pass, tooting its horn as it proceeded. Driving on to the dock, the car came to a halt alongside of the schooner. The driver's door opened and Sean O'Loughlin jumped out onto the wharf, greeting Antoine warmly before heartily shaking the captain's hand.

"Jackson McLeod – it's been a while! How's the wife and family?" he queried in his deep Irish brogue.

"The family is all well, thank you, Lockie. So I see you're up to the same ol' hijinks. You'll never change, will you? Where'd you get the vehicle?"

"Oh, I found it down in Guadeloupe and had it brought here on the deck of a schooner. It's just an old Renault. Not the latest model, mind you, but perfect for here. At least now I've got my own wheels," O'Loughlin said, casting an admiring eye over his car.

"Well you must keep it busy carrying all that wine and champagne across the island to your joint."

"She comes in handy indeed. We have to get the ice out there somehow! Wouldn't think of drinking warm champagne, now would we?"

"I've gotta go, boys," announced Antoine. "The butcher's got some beef waiting for me. I'll catch up with you fellows later on."

"Okay mate, I'll drop in and see you tomorrow. There are a few things I need to collect for down south," said Jack as Antoine departed, continuing his stroll down the wharf.

"So as far as I can see, Captain McLeod, the sun is well over the yard arm. Do you fancy a wee drink?"

Jack shrugged his shoulders. "Why not, mate? Let's have one for old time's sake." After saying a few words to the first mate on deck, Jack sauntered off of the wharf alongside his Irish friend. Stepping on to the cobblestoned street, they walked a few yards to the corner where they found Le Corsaire, the island's main rum shop. Seated at the simple wooden counter were a handful of locals who turned and glanced at the entering strangers before returning to their subdued conversations.

The two men were greeted with a smile and friendly hello from the barman and owner of the shop, Thierry Deslisle.

"Deux Petit Punches, s'il vous plaît, Thierry," Sean ordered.

The bar tender placed two small glasses on the counter and half-filled them with clear white rum, followed by a dash of thick sugar cane syrup and a quarter of a bright green lime, which he squeezed before dropping into the glass.

"Cheers my friend," Sean said and the two drank.

The powerful, high–octane rum burned its way down Jack's throat, making his eyes water, sending a rush of heat to his head and a tingle out to the ends of his fingertips. He closed his eyes and shook his head. "The first one is always the hardest. After that it's all downhill," he croaked.

Sean laughed and ordered another round. They sat down at a table by the door. A local man entered the shop and after greeting the men at the bar turned and said hello. "Good evening Sean! How is the fishing my friend?"

Sean rose from his stool and reached across the table to shake the man's hand. "Bon soir, Martin! I'm sure you know my friend Jack McLeod, captain of the schooner *Roulette*. Why don't you join us?"

The man turned and asked the barman for three petit punches and then sat down. "Jack and I are well acquainted. After all, who doesn't know the famous Captain McLeod?" he said with a rather forced smile.

"And you can't do business in St. Barths without coming across Martin Lefèvre," Jack answered, tipping his hat. "Martin and I go all the way back to the first time I came to St. Barths. Must be close to fifteen years ago, wouldn't you say?"

"Something like that. It would be quite a few years now, anyway," Lefèvre answered. The three men sipped their rum, engaging in a polite, if short, conversation. They finished their drinks and then he stood to go. "Anyway, when I saw your car on the wharf I figured you two would be here so I just dropped in to say hello. Good to see you, Jack. If you would excuse us, I'd like to have a private word with Sean." The two men went out through the door and into the street, where they had a brief discussion.

A few minutes later the Irishman returned and sat back down at the table. "I never knew you had dealings with Lefèvre. Obviously the two of you share a bit of history," Sean said.

"It's old news really," Jack replied, draining his glass and ordering two more. "We had a slight difference of opinion once, but as I said, it was years ago. Water under the bridge. I prefer to do business with Emile Darraux these days, but I've got nothing against Martin. I take it you two have something going on."

"Oh, it's nothing concrete – just something that might come up in the future," Sean said cagily.

"So tell me Lockie, do you miss the excitement of the ol' bootlegging days?"

"Oh not really. I couldn't do now what I did then, boy-o. It was good while it lasted, but I was glad to get out of the business when I did. There was just too much money and too many desperate people involved in the end. But the ol' *Vamoose* was one hell of a vessel, wasn't she? She surely hauled some booze in her day! Yes," Sean added, a hint of nostalgia in his voice, "those were good times. Wild times. But things change, and time moves on..."

"And so now you're living out your retirement here on St. Barths, which is perfect, because this always was a pirate island!"

"I'll drink to that! Here's to pirates," said Sean with a chuckle.

"So how's Mercedes coping with island life? It must be far different for her here than it was in Havana."

"It's a great woman I found myself there, Jackie boy! So far she has taken it all in her stride. She's a real sport, and loves the fishing. Jesus we've caught some beauties! Blue marlin, swordfish, wahoo – you couldn't even count the tuna. And then when we need some real excitement there's always the sea plane. The lagoon over in St. Martin's a perfect place to keep her. I've leased a piece of land where I've built some concrete ramps so I can keep her on shore. We get away to Cuba or Key West whenever we feel like it. It's a shame you didn't get here a day or two earlier. We could have done some fishing together. As it is we're leaving the day after tomorrow to fly back to Cuba for Christmas, and we've got to get the house squared away. That's where I was today – over in St. Martin fuelling the Dolphin up and getting her ready to go."

"I've been wondering how the plane was working out. It's only you who'd be so lucky as to end up with something like that!" Jack said, shaking his head.

"I believe luck's played a bit of a hand with us all, if you don't mind me sayin'. But that Douglas Dolphin's a hell of an aircraft. You could live aboard if you had to – she's a real flying yacht! And her range is great. I once made the trip from St. Martin to Key West in seven and a half hours of flying time, with only one stop in the Turks and Caicos to refuel. If we leave here at sunrise we can be in Florida before dark. And I can get a couple of hundred cases of scotch whiskey on board her without any trouble at all."

"You really are still an old smuggler at heart, aren't you Sean? Landed tax free in Florida that still has to be worth a few dollars."

"It pays for the fuel, and a few nights out on the town, if that's what you mean. You know an old dog like me still has to keep his hand in," Sean said with a mischievous laugh. "Aye, it was a great day when I acquired that plane. God bless the New York Stock Exchange and all who went broke on it! I know I've been promising to do it for a while, but one day we will fly down to Petite Silhouette and pay you a visit."

It wasn't long before the crew of the *Roulette* turned up, and more rum was consumed. Sean O'Loughlin eventually took his leave, but the others didn't, and it was early in the morning before the crew finally made their way back aboard the schooner.

The Black Ship

The morning was quiet and still. *My mouth's fouler than the bottom of a cockie's cage,* thought Jack, staring at the underside of the ivory painted deck overhead as he lay in his bunk. *That last bottle of rum wasn't such a good idea after all.*

Outside on the wharf he heard voices. Rolling off his bunk and onto his feet, he made his way up the companionway stairs, and resting his arms on the hatch slide gazed groggily over the quay. The crew of the little sloop astern were busy in the morning half-light. The night before they had placed most of their ballast stones on the wharf, and now they were setting about careening their vessel. Jack pushed himself up the hatch and wandered back to the stern of his schooner, putting on his shirt as he did so. Resting down on the lazorette hatch he yawned and watched on with interest. On the dock, several locals had curtailed their morning stroll, observing the proceedings with silent curiosity.

As the captain sat watching, he was handed a hot cup of coffee. Looking up he accepted it from Zepheryn, who was now standing next to him, sipping from his own cup.

"I been speaking to Macklin last evening an' he sayin' dat dey hit some bad weather off Dominica on de way north an' sprung a leak," the mate said. "Dat ol' bamboo pump earned her keep getting' dem here – now dey heavin' out to see if dey can't caulk her up. He said it's a good ting it didn't happen goin' south 'cause de seawater could have spoiled de cargo, 'specially de cigarettes."

The two looked on as the sloop's captain made the end of the peak halyard fast to a bollard on the wharf, and once that was done he and his two crewmen began hauling on the rope, which had the effect of pulling the vessel over on her side. They continued to pull until half her deck was underwater and the whole of the sloop's bottom was exposed, including the keel. Pulling around in their skiff they began to inspect the bottom. It didn't take them long to find what they were looking for, and before long they began caulking the offending leak.

"I wish it was as easy to heave this vessel out," Jack said as he rose and stretched. "I need another cup of coffee and something to eat."

"It's like you fellas gone a bit off course last night, Cap," the mate said with a smile.

Jack beheld the mate with raised eyebrows. "I ended up putting on a bit of the wobbly boot, that's for certain. You were the smart one staying aboard. Now let me see what Jono's got cooking in the galley this morning. I need something good and greasy."

At seven o'clock sharp, the young Darraux brothers turned up alongside in their ancient lorry and the unloading of the rum began. The first to be discharged were the wooden cases of bottled rum, the crew forming a human chain passing one case out at a time until the truck was loaded, when the lorry would return to the warehouse where it was then discharged. It would take the crew a full day to offload this portion of the cargo; the wooden 'hogsheads' or casks containing exactly fifty-two and a half imperial gallons of rum each, which were stowed in the after hold, would be dealt with the following day.

It was late afternoon, and work for the day was almost done. The number one cargo hatch was covered down, and as seawater was being bucketed over the rail and the decks were being scrubbed clean, Jack watched a rugged looking steel freighter enter the harbour. The vessel was of a type known as a 'coaster', hundreds of which were built for the European in-shore cargo trade. He guessed her to be about 100 feet long, with a capacity to carry maybe 200 tons of general cargo. The vessel motored slowly in and dropped anchor in the middle of the empty inner harbour. The whole operation was done professionally, and quietly. Although Jack could see some activity on the foredeck and in the wheelhouse, he had no chance to have a good look at either captain or crew. Once the anchor was set, the slow turning main engine was shut down and no more movement could be seen aboard.

The *Roulette's* crew had all decided to walk to a small beach not far from the harbour for a sea bath. As the crew jumped over the bulwarks onto the wharf, Jono came out of the galley. "All o' you don't tarry too long, you hear?" the cook yelled out as they sauntered off the wharf. "I got curry goat an' dumplin' cookin' here, an' me ain't goin' to wait on all you to serve it up! When she done she done!"

"You don' frighten, mon," called back Kingsford. "You don' have fo' tell me twice. After all dat bull work today me alone could eat half dat goat! I'll be back quick smart, don't worry." As the crew continued to walk around the bayside Jack could hear the quips and jokes drift across the water, until they disappeared around the corner house of Captain Gastonay.

Jack was curious about this new vessel. It wasn't often a ship such as this was seen around these islands. Not long after sunset, as the day descended into twilight, he noticed some action aboard the freighter. On deck a donkey engine was started up, and soon the cargo boom could be seen lifting the ship's boat over the starboard side and into the water. Once that was done the cargo boom was put back into place and the deck engine was shut down. Darkness fell.

Jono served up the much awaited meal, dishing out heaping platefuls of black-eyed peas and rice covered with a hot curry of stewed goat with heavy flour dumplings. Jack thought the three sailors from the little sloop astern could use a solid meal, so he asked them to join them for supper. Macklin Dupree and his two teenage sons hailed from the small Grenadine island of Petite Martinique. The two boys were quiet and very shy, uttering barely a word despite Kingsford's good natured prodding, but their father was far more forthcoming and joked and carried on with the crew. As they ate he was encouraged to recount his latest trip north and their narrow escape from sinking.

"Yes mon, we was somewhere out in de channel north of Domineek, an' it was plenty rough. We did fall off de back of an ugly lump of a wave an' de nex' ting de boy says de bilge full o' watah. You seen de ol' bamboo pump we does have? Well we was pumpin' for all we was worth – each man goin' til he couldn't go no further, den de next man takin' over. We was well to le'ward – Guadeloupe a way up yonder to windward, and so I hauled off fo' Montserrat, where we did anchor in de lee fo' de night. Alwynn went over de side an' shoved some oakum in dat seam, an' dat stopped de leak long enough fo' we to sleep. Next mornin' we set off fo' over Nevis. De patch held up good, an' de leak didn't trouble we much, even in de rough watah over St. Kitts an' dem. She should be as good as gold after heavin' out today. But you know, on de way up we did see somethin' I never seen befo'. You see dat vessel anchored over yonder?" Macklin asked, motioning towards the freighter with his head. "As we passed under dat rock dey does call Redonda, just to de south o' Nevis, we saw a small little steam boat anchored right up dere in de lee. I didn't even know dere was anchorage there, but even so, why would anyone want to stop? I heard tell dat way back in de las' century a Yankee Company did mine guano or some kind-of-o'-ting out dere, but its years an' years since it did close down. Later on in de day de same ship passed to weather o' we headin' north. An' dere she be. Dat was funny – real funny I tell you."

"So you're sure that vessel over there is the same one you saw anchored under Redonda?" Jack asked.

"Certain sure, man, certain sure. Dey isn't many vessels like dat 'round here. I'm sure dat's de same one."

Jack finished his supper, quietly lost in thought. This mysterious development had him puzzled. Here was a cargo vessel obviously not hauling cargo. If they were, they would have come alongside to discharge or load. As Macklin so rightly asked, why would anyone anchor underneath that desolate bird rock in the middle of nowhere? And where have they been since he saw them? This was a very curious turn of events indeed.

The night was still and hot, and Jack wasn't sleeping well. Lying in his bunk, he could hear the mooring lines stretch and the topsides of the vessel bump up against the wharf as a small swell gently rolled into the harbour. He had no idea what time it was when he decided to go on deck for some air. Climbing up the companionway steps, he paused as he reached the top. The sleeping harbourside was silent and still. There was no movement, not a sign of life. And then he saw it; the amber glow of a cigarette coming from the wheelhouse railing of the anchored freighter. The cigarette pulsed occasionally through the black void. A different sound then reached his ears. It was the engine of a motorcar faintly echoing through the backstreets of the town behind him. Moments later, headlights could be seen swinging around the corner at the head of the bay. The motorcar drove past the house of Captain Gastonay, made another turn at the far corner of the harbour, and pulled up astern of the *Lady Luck*. The headlights now pointed straight across the harbour, shining into Jack's eyes. They flashed once, and then were extinguished. The cigarette arched through the air into the tar-like sea.

Jack was now fully awake. He heard a low mumbling of voices coming from the freighter, followed by the bang of an oar. Climbing up on deck he moved to the rigging, untied the lifeboat made fast alongside and quietly slipped over the bulwark and into the skiff. Letting go the sternline, he pushed off and drifted slowly towards the middle of the harbour. Standing up in the boat, he carefully pushed an oar through a scallop cut out in the transom and began to skull towards the opposite shore. Passing well astern of the anchored freighter, he could just make out the name of the vessel and her port of call embossed into the steel plating. *Tor* it said, and underneath, *Hamburg*. A soot-covered Dutch flag hung limply from a flagstaff above. Sitting now, he glided slowly across the water, and through the darkness could just make out the lifeboat of the *Tor* containing the indistinguishable forms of several people land on the opposite side of the harbour.

Finding shore himself, Jack quickly tied the skiff off and crept towards a shadowy group of people standing near the stern of the *Lady Luck*. Crouching next to an old shingled house near the water's edge, he settled in between fish traps and other fishing gear. He couldn't get any closer without being spotted. He couldn't hear what was being said, but he could see that a discussion was going on. The conversation ended, and he watched as four shapes climbed aboard Sean's motor boat. Several bags followed. The remaining person dropped into the tender and rowed back to the *Tor*. It wasn't long afterwards when the engines of the *Lady Luck* started up, and Jack watched from the shadows as O'Loughlin's boat motored out of the harbour.

What the hell was that all about? Jack asked himself. Walking back to his skiff, he couldn't help but wonder what strange business Sean O'Loughlin and this black ship were involved in. An hour or so later, as the first hints of sunrise edged into the eastern sky, the main engine of the *Tor* was fired up, and after hauling up the anchor spun around, and with its heavy two cylinder diesel thumping away, proceeded to power its way out of the harbour.

Later that afternoon, the balance of the cargo was discharged, and the few cases of wine, whiskey and rum for Christmas and the launching put aboard. While purchasing the materials for Bill deVilliars' new schooner, Jack asked Antoine Degras what he knew about the mysterious freighter. "I don't really know what they're up to," Antoine replied as the two men sorted out Bill's order. "The ship's been in the harbour a couple of times before, but usually doesn't spend too long. I don't know what kind of work they're doing, because I've never seen 'em take on or discharge any cargo, either. The crew's very quiet and keep to themselves. I did meet the captain once. He's a curious fellow...only has one eye, which is something you don't forget. I've noticed them take a drink over at Thierry's bar once or twice, but they don't mix much with anyone else."

"So you haven't seen Sean O'Loughlin mixing with them at all?" Jack asked.

"Not that I can recall. Now that you mention it, though, I did notice Martin Lefèvre sharing a drink with them once. But I never really put too much thought into it."

As for O'Loughlin, he and Mercedes had in fact left the island. Luc Gastonay, their young deckhand, confirmed as much when Jack spoke to him as he prepared to return Sean's motorcar back to the house in St. Jean. "He an' the lady gone to Cuba for Christmas. Dey left early this mornin'," was all Jack could get out of him. He wondered who and what else had flown there with him.

The *Roulette* left St. Barths and sailed for home. Just at sunset, Jack steered close in under the lonely rock of Redonda. Seabirds screeched and railed as the schooner sailed past the jagged, surf-lashed islet; hardly inviting for even a brief stopover. It didn't take long for the solitary outcropping to drop astern and be quickly lost from sight. In the fading daylight Jack shook his head and muttered to himself as he continued to search for a plausible answer to this riddle.

His gaze turned back to the compass, which was now glowing brightly in the gathering darkness. A rainsquall was making up to windward. The wind was growing stronger, the sea becoming more confused and angry by the minute. The captain donned his oilskins, preparing himself for a tumultuous night ahead. His attention was now refocused on the rising breeze, the breaking waves, the sails aloft, and the boat which surged beneath him.

It was early December and the *Roulette* would not move again until after Christmas. The crew would spend the rest of the month at home doing maintenance on the vessel. Tons of stone and iron ballast would be painstakingly manhandled out of the bilge so she could be careened and the bottom cleaned, caulked and painted. The sails would be removed and the masts slushed with grease and Stockholm tar. Any other minor repairs would also be done at this time, all in preparation for a busy work year which would start in early January. The first mate would supervise this work while Jack was occupied in the boatyard helping get Bill deVilliars' new schooner ready to launch.

And it was in the boatyard where Aubrey Kincaid burst in with the news. The Japanese had attacked Pearl Harbour. Germany and Italy had declared war on the United States. He stopped working and observed the men standing silently around him, knowing none of them, not even O'Neil, really understood the significance of the message. But he knew. The outside world had just taken a step closer to Petite Silhouette.

It now was truly a World War.

PART II

Freiwillig zur
KRIEGSMARINE

JANUARY, 1942

Westward Ho!

The meeting took place inside the Keroman Submarine Base, a fortress-like structure built at the junction of the Blauet and Scorff Rivers, near the famous French naval city of Lorient in Brittany. With the fall of France, the German Navy, or Kriegsmarine, was given the much desired advantage of direct entrance to the Atlantic Ocean from this well-located ancient French port, and they were quick to take advantage of the opportunity. Admiral Carl Donitz had chosen the location for the home of his beloved U-boat submarine fleet well; the position afforded a safe, well protected harbour that had easy access to the Bay of Biscay and the open Atlantic Ocean. Just a few miles north, around the Isle d'Ouessant, lay the southern entrance to the English Channel. The facility that the German Navy had built was virtually impregnable; the roof alone was a massive seven metres thick construction of steel-reinforced concrete, and there were pens for up to thirty submarines. Attending this historic meeting were five carefully selected U-boat captains. As they sat down around the polished teak table they chatted amiably about their latest missions. It was January 15, 1942, and the war was going very well for the Reich, the submarine war in particular. The five captains were flush with success, and all exuded a detectable air of confidence.

The door opened and everyone stood to rigid attention as a phalanx of high ranking naval officers burst through the door. The salute of "Heil Hitler" rang through the room. "Good morning, gentlemen – you may sit. As you all would most probably know, I am Korvettenkapitan Helmut Kandler, and I will be the flotilla commander for your upcoming mission. You gentlemen have been chosen not only for your previous successes against the enemy in the North Atlantic, but also for your mutual experiences in the area that will become your next theatre of operation. To be more specific, you all have at one time or another spent time in the Caribbean Sea. This will be your next hunting ground."

The five officers searched out each other amidst raised eyebrows, slight nods of recognition, smiles of approval, and genuine surprise.

"Admiral Donitz has been highly encouraged by the early success of our current 'Operation Drumbeat', which has led to the sinking of more than five ships a day off of the east coast of our latest enemy, the United States of America. He is therefore anxious to expedite phase two of our push to the west with what is to be called 'Operation Neuland'. Each of you has been chosen for your past experience in the West Indies. Three of you served as officers aboard merchant ships there, one of you served your time as a cadet in the same service, and one – Kapitanleutnant Albrecht – spent several years in those waters running his own small ship. Your familiarity with the area should prove to be highly useful.

"Gentlemen, we currently have Great Britain on her knees. Our information tells us that they need a supply of a minimum of four oil tankers every day to support their war effort. The bulk of their oil comes to them from the coast of South America, specifically the Dutch refineries on the islands of Aruba and Curacao, as well as Trinidad, where the Pointe-a-Pierre oil refinery is the largest in the British Empire. Oil tankers have been freely sailing from their Caribbean ports up the east coast of the formerly neutral United States before joining the convoys across the North Atlantic, of which I am sure you all are familiar. Now that the United States is in the war, the waters of the Caribbean have become strategically very important.

"At this point I would like to turn this meeting over to Kapitans Kestrel and Stieg, who some of you may be familiar with. Both of these gentlemen spent many years between them in charge of Hamburg/America Lines ships trading in this region. They have tremendous first-hand knowledge of the area, and they will be refreshing your memories as to the lights, harbours, reefs, rocks, currents and sea conditions of the Caribbean. They also will detail shipping routes, and the general habits of the merchant shipping. Afterwards we will discuss your individual missions and targets. Kapitans…"

The morning wore on with the five skippers attentively listening and taking notes, the two former merchant captains going into great detail in their breakdown of the islands, ports, channels and hazards, pointing out their various locations on several detailed charts suspended behind them. Many questions were asked at the conclusion of the presentation, at which time one of the young aids thanked the two experts and adjourned the meeting until after lunch.

In the mess hall, the group of captains sat down to their meal together and formally introduced each other. The senior officer was Kapitanleutnant Karl-Freidrich Heine of U-156, who, at thirty-nine, was the eldest of the group and had the most missions under his belt. The bearded Kapitanleutnant Nils Albrecht of U-112 was in his mid-thirties, and as the men ate described his days as a freighter captain in the West Indies, a time which he seemingly enjoyed very much. Rolf Bauer ran U-502 and was the youngest member, having done his time as a cadet on a Hamburg/American ship, and in fact had by chance served under Kapitan Kestrel for one voyage. The other two captains, Werner Von Forsner from U-67 and U-129's Klaus Shute, had both worked as junior officers on ships of the Bremerhaven Line and made visits to several of the Caribbean ports.

"It won't be a holiday, but I know where I would rather be in the middle of January," said Albrecht as the group made their way back to the briefing room. "A week ago I was off of the north coast of Scotland in a force nine gale. At least the weather in the Caribbean is a little more pleasant at this time of year."

As the men took their seats, the Flotilla Commander re-entered the briefing room followed by his phalanx of aids and quickly began the second phase of the meeting. He discussed attack areas, describing the different specific quadrants and their strategic values. He also covered communication. This group would all be carrying the new four rotor Enigma code machine through which they would send and decode their cyphers. Their radio schedules were set, and all final details worked out. An aide now passed out a file to each of the captains, on the front of which was written the number of each U-boat.

"Gentlemen, these files contain your individual, specific orders. Please take a few minutes to digest the information."

The men each intently read their orders. Heine would be targeting the port of San Nicholas on the Dutch island of Aruba and the refinery there. U-67 under Von Forsner would attack the shipping around Curacao; Bauer would hunt ships off of Lake Maracaibo and the Venezuelan coast. Klaus Shute would patrol the waters to the east of Trinidad seeking out bauxite ships bound north from British Guyana, and Nils Albrecht was given the waters around Trinidad and the southern part of the Windward Islands, an area he knew very well. The men drank coffee while several more questions were asked.

The meeting began to wind down, and as it did a junior officer quietly left the room. A few moments later he returned, accompanied by none other than Admiral Carl Donitz himself. The captains all jumped quickly to attention, each returning the Nazi salute to the second highest ranking officer in the German navy.

"At ease, men – at ease. And so now, gentlemen, you have been briefed, you have your orders, and in a few days we will have you provisioned and you will be off hunting in new waters, leading the vanguard for the Fatherland. I believe the Korvettenkapitan has updated you on the progress of 'Operation Drumbeat'. So far over 50,000 tons of enemy shipping has been sunk in three days! Compared to what you have been facing in the North Atlantic it has been easy pickings. The Americans are completely disorganised. No blackouts, their harbours lit up like Christmas trees, navigation lights blinking, no serious anti-submarine defences in place – a perfect scenario for inflicting maximum damage." The Admiral was an intense, humourless man who had dedicated his life to submarines. He had skippered one himself during WWI; had been captured and interned by the British in 1918, and while imprisoned dreamed up the concept of hunting in groups, which he later developed into the feared 'wolfpack'. Now the Great Man stood before them, all spit and polish, not a hair out of place, the Special-Grade U-boat War badge with diamonds and the Iron Cross First Class, along with numerous other medals, displayed proudly on his chest. He stood, hands clasped behind his back, his immaculate dress uniform in sharp contrast to the cavalier submariners attired simply in their operational boilersuits casually sitting around the table.

"The logistics of this enterprise are impressive. The distances are at the far end of our operational capabilities. And yet the rewards are well worth the risk. By executing this plan we will not only be cutting off valuable enemy supplies at the source, we will also be forcing them to deploy their scant recourses in an unexpected direction. With the reliable intelligence we are receiving from the different islands, we know the enemy is completely unprepared for what is about to hit them. So that is it! You have your orders, your ships are in top condition; you will be well supplied and well supported. Go to it! Give them hell! Heil Hitler!"

The five captains all stood in unison and answered the Admiral. "Heil Hitler!"

The skippers made their way back to their vessels. Albrecht and Heine trailed behind the three other excited captains. The two senior officers of the group were a little more tempered than their comrades; not quite so impressed about being addressed by the Admiral himself.

"That was quite a pep-talk from the old man, wasn't it?" commented Albrecht as he lit the two men's cigarettes. "This must be something quite special for him to actually make a personal appearance."

"Yes, well, you know the man and his attention to detail. I wouldn't be surprised if he can recall off the top of his head how many rolls of toilet paper my ship went through on our last voyage," replied Heine.

"I will credit him one thing – he knows his job. He has been there and done it all. He at least knows what it is like to have depth charges exploding on top of his head. Not like that asshole Goering, parading around in his funny white suit."

"You mean the ice cream vendor? We are lucky he likes to play with planes and not boats. Otherwise we would be in real trouble!"

answered Heine with a smile. "Anyway, maybe we can catch up this evening for a beer or two. I'll see you later my friend."

The two were now down in the brightly lit bowels of Keroman Number One. The five subs had been typically well organised and placed in pens next to each other, which were all abuzz with activity as maintenance crews crawled over the deadly war machines.

Nils Albrecht stepped aboard U-112, elbowing his way past engineers, electricians and greasy mechanics. Welders were busily occupied repairing a damaged plate where they had experienced a narrow escape with a depth charge. On the conning tower he was met by his trusty first mate Jost Weiss, who broke off a heated discussion with the bosun to greet the captain.

"Any problems Jost?" the skipper asked as the red faced bosun made his way back down below.

"No – just the normal thing. Trying to fit ten litres into a five-litre jug. This must be one hell of a long voyage because the stores keep rolling in. Horst was just letting me know in his diplomatic way that he doesn't know 'where the hell he is supposed to store all this shit', as he put it."

"You're correct in guessing we're not being stocked up for a routine patrol of the Channel. We're off to one of our old stomping grounds – the West Indies," Albrecht said.

"That answers some questions. I was guessing West Africa with all of the tropical gear coming aboard, but the West Indies sounds even better."

"It was really quite interesting at today's meeting. We even had a talking-to from Ol' Man Donitz himself. All very inspiring. And our flotilla commander is Kandler, who I have a lot of confidence in."

"So the West Indies, hey? That does sound interesting. Which part?" Weiss asked.

"Trinidad. Get the lads together. There will be a briefing in the ward room at 18:00 hours."

Over the span of several days, the five U-boats slipped one by one out of the bunker complex of the Keroman Submarine Base and headed west, downstream past the scenic coastal town of Lamore Plage and the headquarters of the Kriegsmarine, the nerve centre for all German naval operations, and out into the Bay of Biscay. It was a blustery, cold and ugly mid-winter's day as U-112 churned through the steep waves at fourteen knots, the first watch settling down to the familiar routine of life at sea. For once they were not turning to starboard and heading north towards the British Isles or the North Atlantic, nor were they bound south for the Straits of Gibraltar and the Mediterranean. Instead, this voyage was taking them south-west to the warm waters of the Caribbean Sea, a place where Nils Albrecht had spent some of the most enjoyable days of his life. Since receiving his orders, he could not help but think of the many friends he had made in the islands in those sunny days before the war. As the U-boat captain stood on the conning tower, his gaze took him over the oncoming white crested waves and beyond the gloomy sunset to his memories of one particular island far away. *I wonder how my old mate McLeod is doing*, he asked himself as he turned and dropped back down into the crowded and noisy confines below deck, where his wandering mind was immediately refocused on the job at hand.

"Traffic from HQ has just come in for you sir," said the radio operator as the captain removed his heavy black oilskins.

"Thanks. Give me a minute and I'll take a look at it." The rosy, frangipani-scented memories were gone now. That was all a lifetime away. It was back to reality. It was back to war.

The Dragon's Mouth

In the early hours of the morning, U-112 entered the channel between the islands of Grenada and Trinidad known as the Galleons Passage. In broad daylight, the submarine boldly dashed south across the ninety miles of open water towards the Bocas del Dragon, or Dragon's Mouth, the entrance to the Gulf of Paria and gateway to Port-of-Spain, the biggest commercial harbour in the Caribbean. They travelled on the surface because it was far quicker and they knew they were not expected. German intelligence was certain the defenders of their targeted destination did not believe that enemy submarines could ever pose a threat. The Kreigsmarine had many eyes and ears on the ground and on the water in the Caribbean, and Albrecht trusted his information. There were minimal patrols by air and sea; the enemy was for the most part was underprepared and complacent. As his submarine charged across the channel, Nils Albrecht was supremely confident he would have a free run to the Bocas.

U-112 had enjoyed an easy crossing of the Atlantic, and for the last week the crew were happy to discard their heavy winter gear for nothing but a short pair of pants. Kapitanleutnant Albrecht had been in constant radio communication with submarine headquarters in Lorient, and had heard of the successful attacks by U-156 on Aruba and U-67 on Curacao, as well as the sinking of two tankers by Bauer on U-502 off the coast of Venezuela, all of which had taken place one day previously. Albrecht did not want to be upstaged, and had devised a brazen plan that would hit the enemy hard, in a place they would least expect. His assigned area of operations was the waters around Trinidad, and he wanted to make his mark.

The submarine approached the Bocas around midday. These three passages, divided by small islands, allowed access into the broad Gulf of Paria, which separated the large British island of

Trinidad from Venezuela and the South American continent. On the conning tower, four pairs of powerful binoculars searched the horizon in every direction for any sign of enemy activity. The captain had his own pair trained on the channel of the second Bocas. He knew there were gun emplacements on Chacachacare Island which guarded the centre passage, as well as the high cliffs of Gaspar Grande which formed the western end of Trinidad. These heavy guns watched over the entrance to the Gulf of Paria, but Albrecht was counting on the gunner's complacency today, confident that it would be safer to enter in broad daylight rather than at night, when they perhaps would be more vigilant.

"There she is, Mr Weiss – beautiful Trinidad. We had some good times there, didn't we?"

"Yes sir, we did. Looking at her feels almost like we are coming home," the mate replied.

"Unfortunately times have changed, and there will be no rum-drinking and womanizing this time around. The cargo we will be offloading will be a little bit different as well. Let's prepare to dive and proceed at periscope depth."

The mate gave the order. The decks were cleared, the hatches secured, and slowly the U-boat slipped beneath the surface of the blue Caribbean.

With his white skipper's hat turned back to front, Nils Albrecht peered through the periscope. He knew this was an audacious plan. His adrenaline was pumping, but he counted on the odds being with him. There was a chance his periscope could be seen as it cut through the surface above, but he was confident that chance was a slim one. Passing through the narrow Bocas would be the most dangerous part of the plan, at least in its first phase. His escape strategy was only partially developed, but like so many times before in his life, he would cross that bridge when he came to it.

All was quiet aboard the submarine as Albrecht conned his way through the narrow passage, the electric drive powered by the ship's batteries pushing them close to their maximum submerged speed of six knots. Slowly they sneaked past the guns on Chacachacare and skirted Los Huevos, the rocks that lay in the middle of the channel; in a few hundred yards they would be clear. There was tension inside the sub as all ears were straining to hear the expected sounds of exploding shells around them, but Albrecht and his crew were professionals. They had been under fire many times before, and though it was never easy, they knew how to handle the pressure.

And then they were through. Gazing through the periscope, the Gulf of Paria opened out before him. After consulting the charts and his navigation officer he issued his orders. "Down periscope but remain at periscope depth – turn to port and steer a course of one-two-five degrees." The orders were repeated, the periscope slowly sunk beneath the calm surface of the sea above, and the U-boat stealthily crept towards her target.

At a little after three in the afternoon Albrecht slowed his boat and raised the 'scope to check his position before coming to a full stop. At a depth of twenty meters he gave the order to fill the ballast tanks and descend until the underbelly of the submarine softly nestled onto the bottom. "Tell the men to take a nap, Mr Weiss. I want absolute silence – not even a sneeze, ok? We will park ourselves here until after dark and hope nobody stumbles across us in the meantime."

The last flicker of daylight had long departed from the evening sky when U-112 ascended from the floor of the Gulf of Paria to periscope depth. The sub had been submerged for close to eight hours and Albrecht was aware he had to surface to replenish his oxygen supply and charge the ship's batteries before making his attack. Through the periscope he could see the lights of Port-of-Spain less than ten miles away; a sight which gave him confidence. If the enemy was worried about any type of attack, they would be observing a night-time black-out. After taking a three-sixty degree look around he issued his orders. The periscope came down and the two hundred and fifty foot long ship slowly broke through the mirror-like surface. When it was clear, the hatches were opened and fresh air rushed in and circulated through the foul interior.

"All ahead one-third," Albrecht ordered. There was virtually no military traffic at this distance from shore; the only activity the four lookouts could pick up was a scattering of local fishermen who drifted in their small pirogues illuminated by dim oil lamps.

Slowly they approached the outer anchorages of Port-of-Spain, where thousands of tons of shipping lay peacefully at anchor. Inshore, the constant flow of launches running back and forth between the docks at Queen's Wharf and the new American naval base under construction at Chaguaramas that had been described to him in his intelligence briefing could easily be seen. "Once we set this place alight all hell is going to break loose, Mr Weiss. We need to know our exit strategy before we shake things up," Albrecht said, putting down his binoculars. "So what are our options?"

"We can't escape by diving – the basin is far too shallow. We are getting only twenty meters under us at the moment," the mate answered. "And closer to shore the depths on the chart show even less."

"Yes, and out in the Gulf where it is deeper is where they will be looking for us. They will have every ship with ASDIC sonar out there pinging for us. No, I think I have an idea that might just work…" He described his escape plan to his first officer, who took another look through his binoculars.

"I've always said you are a crazy bastard," he smiled, shaking his head. "It's not something you would find in a standard Kreigsmarine textbook, but I think it will work. No one will be expecting it at least."

U-112 proceeded towards the targets, which were clearly highlighted against the bright lights of the city behind. They chose the two largest ships closest to the western end of the anchorage; the end nearest to their planned escape route. It was at 23:35 when Kapitanleutnant Nils Albrecht lined up the 7,400 ton American general cargo ship *Mokihana* and fired his first torpedo. With the first fish on its way he ordered the sub to turn ten degrees and fire on his second target, the oil tanker *British Consul*. The second torpedo was hardly on its way when the captain issued his next order. "Hard to port, submerge five meters and go ahead at three quarter speed," he said. "And turn on the running lights."

The first torpedo hit its target. A huge explosion echoed across the water, followed shortly after by a second massive blast as the

British tanker burst into flames. There was a cheer from below decks as the crew heard the result of their handiwork. In the wake of the quickly escaping U-boat, more explosions rocked the formerly tranquil anchorage as the spreading fires aboard the two ships reached fuel tanks. Albrecht watched through his binoculars as a secondary blast of massive proportions sent shockwaves across the water as the fire reached the gaseous empty hold of the oil tanker, sending flames and smoke soaring into the midnight sky. "I should think our presence has been well and truly announced now, sir," the mate commented from alongside the captain.

"Yes, I should think so. Now let's see about getting the hell out of here," Albrecht stated, turning his back to the flames with his thoughts now focused on their brazen escape.

A few minutes later the partially submerged U-112 melted into the outbound traffic of launches and small ships making their way around the western promontory of Diego Island, the land mass that separated Port-of-Spain from the Bay of Chaguaramas. The captain and the four lookouts watched as several high speed craft motored past in the opposite direction towards the explosions. Albrecht had slowed their speed down. They were traveling through the dark night at not much over seven knots, their running lights blending in with the normal flow of traffic. With only half of their conning tower showing above the surface, he hoped they would appear from a distance to be just another motor vessel leaving Port-of-Spain. It was a nerve-wracking exploit. Several times it seemed like they were being approached by an enemy ship, only for the speeding military vessel to carry on without so much as a glance, obviously distracted by the burning ships ahead.

"Mr Scherer, until we are in deeper water where we can dive we need to be able to take on any attack with our deck guns, so make sure the gun crew is standing by if we have to surface. Until then we simply have to hold our nerve," the captain ordered calmly. "And make sure Mr Klausterman is ready to give me full throttle on his engines if we need it."

"This guy has balls of steel, I'll credit him that," chief gunnery officer Scherer whispered to a fellow sailor as they stood at the bottom of the hatchway ladder, ready to scramble on deck to the deck cannon if need be. "He surely had to be a Viking in a past life!"

"Mr Pobanz, I need to know when we are off this inner bank and into deeper water," Albrecht ordered down the hatch to his navigation officer. "Please let me know the moment we can dive."

Astern, the sky was alight with flames as the two ships burned. There were several more explosions from the tanker as the fire reached more storage tanks. Both ships were now listing heavily to their port sides where the torpedos had struck, and were most likely settled onto the shallow, muddy bottom of the basin. It was well after midnight and more than an hour after the attack when the lights ashore were finally blacked out. They were travelling so close to shore they could see the headlights and hear the horns of military vehicles as they rushed up and down along the oceanfront.

"We have really stirred up a hornet's nest here, haven't we sir?" Weiss asked ruefully.

"Sir, vessel approaching at flank speed from directly ahead," one of the lookouts suddenly called out.

"Mr Pobanz – can we dive yet?"

"No sir. We are only in 15 meters of water."

"Very well. Gun crew stand by. Be ready to surface at my command," the captain ordered.

The vessel was motoring towards them at what appeared to be full speed. The white wake could be clearly seen under the boat's bow, its red and green running lights shining brightly, indicating that they were on a collision course.

"Stand by," Albrecht commanded as the vessel drew near.

All binoculars on the bridge were trained on what was now clearly an American anti-submarine PT boat. The roar of her twin sixteen cylinder Stirling Viking petrol engines could now be heard as it approached at over twenty knots.

"He is coming directly at us, sir," nervously remarked a lookout.

"Hold on lads – steady as she goes," was the composed answer, the captain's glasses sharply focused on the oncoming danger.

For the men on the bridge everything seemed to be moving in slow motion. First the bow of the boat came abreast of the U-boat's conning tower, followed by the large white letters P 105 stencilled on its side. The red port navigation light glowed through the darkness. Finally the bright stern light gleamed at them as the patrol boat flew past, the smooth surface of the ink-black water churned white by her props.

A collective sigh of relief passed through the crew. "Hey…what's that I smell? Is that you Heinz? Did you shit your pants?" a lookout jokingly queried from one of his partners.

"It's not me! It must be Karl!" the lookout quipped back. The banter continued until the captain put his foot down.

"Okay! Okay! We are not through this yet. Pay attention you two!" he sternly ordered.

Slowly they rounded Diego Island and headed across Chaguaramas Bay towards the imposing cliffs of Gasper Grande on the far side with their heavy gun emplacements. Soon they were motoring directly under the massive guns, only a few hundred meters from shore. Albrecht had driven this same route many times before during his freighter days, and knew they were now in deep water with no obstructions. Slowly they left the cliffs behind. Off to starboard lay the entrance to the First Bocas, a very narrow and treacherous passage which could only be negotiated in broad daylight. As they approached Manos Island and the Second Bocas, the navigation light on Chacachacare Island was their only guide through the pitch black night.

"We will go out the same way we came in, Mr Weiss. We will make the turn around Huevos and keep to the surface until we are through the passage and out into the open waters on the other side. The possibility to dive is there if need be, but I'm certain they will be operating a sonar gate which could set off an alarm once we submerge. It's better that we stay on the surface until we are either through or they figure us out and start shooting."

Passing the two rocky islets of Huevos they made a hard turn to starboard and steered due north, the guns and navigation light of Chacachacare to port and the dark shape of Manos Island on their right hand. The visibility was murky after the passing of a squall which was still spitting raindrops when one of the lookouts called out sharply, "Sir, sailing vessel dead ahead at two hundred meters!"

The captain swung his glasses ahead. "It's a schooner running in before the wind. Helm hard to starboard, then straighten on my order," he directed.

As they turned the schooner gybed over its mainsail and the two vessels crossed, passing within meters from each other. The sailors on the tower gazed down upon the crew of the schooner standing on deck near the wheel box, who in turn gawked at the mysterious ship passing in the night, almost near enough to touch.

"That was close. Their running lights must have been obscured by their sails," Albrecht said in passing. "Right – running lights out and prepare to dive. I think we've had enough excitement for one night."

Within minutes U-112 disappeared beneath the surface and remained submerged for exactly two hours. When no sign of the enemy appeared, the ship was brought back to the surface and proceeded to power north at flank speed, hoping to put as much distance between themselves and the British Crown Colony of Trinidad and Tobago as possible before daylight.

Trinidad

Christmas and New Year had come and gone, Bill de Villiars' new schooner *Arabella D* had been launched, the *Roulette* had been careened and her yearly maintenance completed, and now after taking on a load of arrowroot in Kingstown, St. Vincent, she was bound for Port-of Spain, Trinidad. It was just after sunset and the Point Saline light on the south-west corner of Grenada was flashing brightly. The watch had changed at six, Kingsford was at the wheel, and the schooner was sailing with every piece of canvas up. As Jack plotted their position on his coffee-stained chart, he reckoned that with her two topsails, fisherman's staysail, and flying jib set they were making a solid twelve knots, which would get them across the ninety mile Galleons Passage to the Bocas sometime early on Wednesday morning. He noted their position and speed in his logbook, as well as a brief notation on the conditions and the weather. Finished, he put down his pencil and climbed the few steps up the companionway to the deck.

"Jono's got some hot coco-tea in the galley if you want, Skip," Zepheryn said, standing to windward of the wheelbox, the glow of the oil-burning compass light illuminating him and the helmsman.

"No, but thanks anyway. I think I'll put my head down for a bit of a kip. I'll get some rest before we go through the Bocas," the captain said. "How's she steering, 'Fordy?"

"Steer? Man you don't hardly need to touch de helem – she steerin' sheself! Look at dat water to le'ward! She's foamin' I tell you! Man, when dis here schooner's loaded down wit cargo dey ain't nothin' to stop 'er. With dem trees fo' masts and all dem proper fittings and solid rigging and dat sweet bottom underneath she's a freight train! An' don't worry 'bout she age. After all o' dat bull work you an' Uncle O'Neil did on her – well she'll live another hundred years. She's solid I tell you! 'What she can't carry aloft she'll drag astern' is how de old schooner-men would put it.

Wha' d'ya say Zepheryn? You ever get tired of sailing on dis here vessel?"

"No mon, I never get tired of it a-tall! She's good. Real good," the quietly spoken mate replied with an inward chuckle.

"Good? Is dat all you can say? Man dis vessel's eight notches above good," Kingsford stated incredulously.

"All right boys – call me if you need me," Jack said, climbing back down the stairs and entering his cabin, closing the door behind him. Above the roar and rush of the waves and normal creaking of the rig he could still hear Kingsford carrying on. Jack smiled and shook his head, and then closed his eyes for the next couple of hours.

The *Roulette* neared the entrance to the Dragon's Mouth just before two in the morning, their course taking them through the Second Bocas. The watch on deck had noted that there was no scattering of shore lights on the windward side of Trinidad for some reason, but the navigation light on the small island of Chachachcare flashed rhythmically off to starboard. The crew had all been through these channels many times before, and knew the hazards, but it still didn't make it any easier. The beacon shone brightly only a few miles away; Jack steered towards the eastern side of the passage as the dark, unlit shape of Manos Island loomed up to port. The wind began to drop lighter now, and the captain ordered the fore topsail and flying jib re-set after they had been dropped during a rainsquall encountered mid-channel.

"It's a good thing we've got the tide with us tonight, Zeph. It isn't easy getting through here without an engine when she's running against you. I sure hope we can get that fuel pump repaired. I feel much more comfortable going through the Bocas with the engine working," Jack said. The conditions were a stark contrast to what they had been facing at the height of the squall only an hour earlier. Now they were reaching into the channel on a falling breeze and diminished sea. A low scattering of clouds still spitting rain hung overhead. It was eerily quiet, the creaking of the gaff jaws and the occasional rush of the water under the bows the only sounds to be heard.

"Running lights ahead Skip. A vessel's turning into the channel," Gilbert called from forward, and all eyes were now locked onto the navigation lights of the oncoming ship.

"It looks to be an outbound motor vessel," commented Jack. "I hope they can see our nav lights." The schooner had her port and starboard lights on, but they were simple oil burning lamps and not as bright as modern electric ones.

"Red and green now, Skip…maybe a mile and a half ahead. Dey's headin' straight for we, an' dey's makin' some speed. Dey really coming on fast," said Zeph as he returned to the wheel from the forward shrouds.

"Yep, I got them. We're between a rock and a hard spot here," Jack said. "If I pull away any more we'll have to gybe and there's not a lot of room to starboard, but I don't want to head up much more because of the rocks and shoals off of Manos. And in this light breeze we don't have much speed to manoeuvre anyway. Let's just hope he sees us."

The two vessels continued on towards each other on what was close to a collision course. Then, when they were only a few hundred yards apart Jack made his decision. "Okay let's gybe! Bull, get that main across!" The skipper turned the wheel hard to starboard, and amid the banging of slack sheets the huge sail slammed over onto the port side. The crew moved quickly and busily trimmed the forward sails. The oncoming ship was now blocked from view by the sails, but they could all hear the oncoming rush of water and the hum of diesel engines. A few moments later the ship appeared out from behind the mainsail and passed close astern, the iridescent red of the port running light glowing brightly less than twenty yards away.

"What kind o' ship does she be, Skip?" Zeph asked, confusion in his voice.

It was a strange looking ship at that. All that could be seen behind the bright red running light was the silhouette of a rectangular tower that was moving rapidly through the water. Just then, as they all were watching, the running lights went off, and slowly the silhouette began to submerge beneath the black surface of the sea. Within a few minutes it had disappeared altogether. What they had seen moments earlier had simply vanished before their eyes. There was a stunned silence as the crew of the schooner continued to look at the spot where the ship had once been.

"What de hell I seein' here a-tall...?" Kingsford finally muttered, breaking the stunned silence. The captain soon recovered and gave the orders to gybe back on to their previous course, struggling himself to believe what he had just seen.

Becalmed. The red sun edged into the eastern sky as the schooner sat motionless in the flat, still waters of the Gulf of Paria. The lifeless sails drooped like curtains from their lofty spars, the typical Trinidad morning haze saturating them as it hung like a shroud over the comatose sea. A few miles ahead and off to port, the emerald green foliage of Trinidad began to emerge as the heat from the rising sun slowly burned off the dewy mist. The sea may have been calm, but today there was more activity on the water than Jack or any of his crew had ever seen. As visibility improved, high speed vessels could be observed off in the distance hurtling about the broad bay of Chaguaramas. The sound of airplanes could be heard passing low overhead. When the final wisps of mist were blown away by the morning breeze, a large black pall of smoke rose from the waters far ahead in the distance. To the crew of the *Roulette* it could only be one thing. Port-of-Spain was burning!

The sun climbed higher into the morning sky and the breeze slowly grew in strength until they were soon sailing. By late morning the schooner approached the anchorage outside Port-of-Spain. What the crew saw that morning was something none but Jack had ever witnessed before; the devastation of war. Before them, two large ships lay on their sides, partially submerged and burning. Oil lay thick on the surface of the water. Military vessels circled the area, and the antiquated harbour fire boat was making a hopeless attempt to put out the blaze on the biggest ship.

The schooner was worked inshore and eventually anchored amongst the island cargo fleet that lay off of Queen's Wharf. The skiff was slung into the lifting tackles and hoisted off the deck into the water. Jack jumped into the boat with Dawson, who took up the oars and rowed the captain ashore to clear the vessel in through customs and immigration.

"You could be waiting here for a while Dawson," Jack said as he climbed up onto the old wooden wharf. "I think it might be a bit chaotic in there this morning."

"No problem, Skip," the smiling young crewman answered, joining the captain on the wharf. "I'll be here."

Inside the Customs shed there was a buzz of excitement. White shirted officials talked animatedly amongst themselves as they went from desk to desk and out onto the wharf and back in what was obviously a state of confusion. *I've never seen so much activity in this place in all of my years coming here*, Jack thought to himself. Finally he attracted the attention of an officer to come to the counter to attend to him.

"I just sailed in this morning, mate. So what's going on?" Jack asked innocently.

"Man, it's nothing but confusion in Trinidad today. Nobody really knows what happened. Some say it was an air attack, some say a German military ship. Some say it was done by spies planting bombs. All we know is those two freighters are somehow burning in the harbour. Nobody knows what's coming next," the officer answered.

"Do you know the name of the man in charge of *HMS Benbow*?" the captain asked, motioning towards the British naval station further down the wharf.

"I think his name is Captain Stafford," the official replied as he finished signing off the clearance documents and pushing the papers across to Jack. "Just see immigration and quarantine now and you're right."

It was the same story with the other departments. The officers were so distracted they didn't have the interest to be as painfully officious as was their norm. Outside on the wharf, Jack joined the animated crowd of curious onlookers who stood fascinated by the shocking scene on the harbour before them. Breaking away, he found Dawson squatting in the shade of the building talking to another waiting crewman. "All done, Skip? Dat was quick," he stated brightly as he stood.

"Those blokes had their minds on other things. Look, I have to do a bit of business now, but you can go back out and tell Zeph he can take down the quarantine flag. I should be ready to go aboard after lunch. I'll meet you here around two o'clock."

Jack stood on the wharf and watched his young crewman jump lightly into the heavy wooden skiff, shove off from the wharf and row strongly back towards the vessel. To his left began Queen's Wharf, where the largest fleet of island schooners in the Caribbean tangled three and four abreast in a chaotic dogfight of loading and discharging their myriad of cargos. Jack's gaze roamed over his rowing crewman to his schooner, anchored in the roads with a colourful mixture of other vessels, before carrying on to the outer anchorage and the burning hulks of the two large freighters, black smoke spewing into the blue Caribbean sky. What would have been just another busy Wednesday in Port-of-Spain would now be remembered forever as the day war came to Trinidad.

Jack turned and walked onto the busy street. After a few hundred yards he came to a gate guarded by military sentries. "I'm here to see Captain Stafford. It's urgent," he said to the soldier. It took some time and some wrangling, and he had to show the letter he carried from Commander Lawrence in Barbados to several different officers, but eventually he found his way inside.

Jack sat outside of Captain Stafford's office for close to an hour. The scene inside the small naval operations centre was frantic. Phones were ringing. Men were running from one desk to another. Motorcycle dispatch riders rushed in and out. Outside on the wooden dock an old sailing yacht manned by British naval personnel motored slowly in and tied up alongside. Eventually Jack was shown into the captain's office. The officer stood beside his desk, hanging up the phone as he entered. In his hand was his official letter from Naval Command in Barbados.

"Captain McLeod is it? Captain Warwick Stafford. I note with interest your letter here from Commander Lawrence in Barbados. It says you are assisting His Majesty's Government in certain confidential areas, which has in fact got you into my office on this rather hectic day. My aide informs me you claim to know who sunk the two ships last night. I hope you don't mind getting straight to the point, because as you can see I am quite busy," the captain said, returning the document to Jack.

"Last night, as I sailed through the Second Bocas, my schooner was almost run down by what could only have been a submarine motoring at high speed and bound north. Unless you have a submarine operating in this area, I would take it to be German."

The captain regarded Jack for a moment, walked around his deck and sat down. "Take a seat, Captain, and tell me all about it," Stafford said, offering a cigarette.

After listening to the description of the early morning incident, the officer thought for a few moments, as if trying to visualise the scene. "So you say that you saw what at first appeared to be a motor vessel enter the channel from the direction of Port-of-Spain, and as it drew near, this ship appeared to be nothing more than a moving tower. As it passed astern of you their running lights went out and it submerged. Did you see a deck gun? What about the hull? It all sounds rather peculiar."

"I agree – it was odd. We saw no deck gun at any stage. I understand what a submarine looks like under way, and it wasn't that. It was if they were travelling three-quarters submerged. I have to say that until they were up close it just seemed like any other motor vessel under power."

The captain sat back in his chair and gazed at the fan turning slowly overhead before shifting his gaze onto his visitor. "Well the cheeky bugger. If you were in charge of a sub in that situation, what would be the safest way out? It is night time, you have just made the first strike in an area that you know is unprepared, there is chaos all around, you can't dive because it's too shallow. Why not disguise yourself as just another motor vessel? He would have simply merged into the flow of general traffic and slipped away unnoticed. Very clever. And extremely brave."

"That's exactly how I see it. But there's something else about this business that has been bothering me. I'd wager money this bloke has been here before. No one goes through the Bocas at night at that speed without knowing the place well. He knew exactly what he was doing and precisely where he was going,"

Jack added. "You have to give him credit. If it was confusion, fear and mayhem he wanted to cause, then he's done a bloody good job of it!"

"This is not quite on a par with what the Americans had to deal with at Pearl Harbour, but nevertheless it is still quite a wake-up call. You've seen our yacht out there, the *Dorothy Duke?* The sole representative of His Majesty's anti-submarine fleet here in Trinidad, with her one depth charge mounted on the stern? Well this week we have had a rude awakening. To say we were not prepared for any of this would be an understatement!"

The phone rang and the officer spoke a few words before hanging up. "Listen McLeod, it's chaos out there and I'm wanted at about three different places at once. Thank you for reporting this. Your information will be passed on to my superiors. I'm sure there will be further questions that will want to be asked, so don't stray too far. We'll be in touch."

"By the way, do you know of an English yacht anchored anywhere around here? She's called the *Vagabond,*" Jack asked as he stood to leave.

"Yes, I know it well. She's anchored down off Diego Island, I believe."

They shook hands and Jack left the office. *I've got to find Harry,* he thought as he walked out onto the busy street, turning towards Queen's Wharf.

Out on the water, black smoke continued to spew into the midday sky.

Despite the early morning excitement out in the harbour, it was business as usual on Queen's Wharf. The early afternoon sun beat down onto the tangle of trucks and carts, stevedores and dockers, shipping agents and their runners, captains and crews, as the rugged island schooners loaded and discharged their cargos. It was hot and still. Not a breath of wind stirred the humid kaleidoscope of sweat and fumes and dust amid the shouts and arguments, engine roar and general chaos of a typical day alongside the busiest wharf in the West Indies. The captain of the *Roulette*

blended into the fray, looking for a familiar face. With an hour or so to kill before he was to return aboard, he thought he might find someone with whom to discuss the day's dramatic events.

Jack edged along the wharf, noting the various vessels, most of which he knew in some way or another. Variously rigged as a schooner or sloop, each craft was as unique in design, shape and construction as the island or country from which it came. His practiced eye could discern if a schooner was built in Grenada, Guyana, Venezuela, Carriacou or Bequia, his own island or North America. These vessels were all jammed in alongside each other, packed in as closely as was physically possible in rows up to three and four deep. As he moved along he nodded and said hello to many familiar faces, answering the traditional "good day, Skip," with a smile or a word or two, until finally he noticed a schooner in the second row he knew well. Jumping aboard a large Guyanese sloop discharging timber, he crossed the deck and climbed over the bulwarks, stepping aboard the schooner *Guiding Star,* skippered by his friend Augustus McClelland from Petite Martinique.

"Ahoy there Cap! Permission to come aboard," Jack called out. The captain stood next to the main mast of the roughly hewn schooner wearing his ever-present white English flat cap, checking over several sheets of documentation with his shipping agent's clerk. He glanced up, a broad smile spreading across his amiable face.

"Yes man, come aboard! Come aboard! Hang on a minute an' le' me finish dis ting, and den we can talk." A few minutes later he had completed his business and stepped over to greet his friend. "It's a long time I haven't seen you, Cap," he said, pumping Jack's hand. "Come man, come – let's get out o' dis hot sun an' take one for de appetite, what d'you say?"

The two captains adjourned to the cabin aft and went below. The layout was typical of the island vessels of the southern Caribbean. It was extremely simple, yet neat, clean and ship shape. The mate and the captain shared the cabin, the rest of the crew slept forward in the fo'c'sle. There was no chart table because all navigation was done purely by dead reckoning, and there was no engine. "It's good to see you Cap'n Jack! But what a mornin' to sail in! What's happenin'? It's like de whole damn world's turnin' upsidie-down!" Augustus said. Pulling up the mattress of his bunk he fumbled around underneath until he brought out a bottle of scotch. Then after ceremoniously cleaning two glasses he poured two neat shots of whiskey.

"Yes, Gus, the times are changing and that's a fact. Who knows where it's all going to end."

"Anyway – here's to good luck," Gus toasted, pouring first some whiskey from his glass onto the cabin floor in tribute to 'the old people dead and gone' before tipping the amber fluid down in one shot, with his guest following suit.

"You seem to have a good load of cargo in. The old girl's right down to her sheer plank. What do you have in?" Jack asked as he put the empty glass back down onto the small table.

"We has in a load o' cement for St. Kitts. I want to leave dis afternoon to catch de tide out t'rough de Bocas. I been hearin' a rumour dat dey does want to hold back shipping 'cause o' dis sinkin' business out yonder. Up to now nobody knows who or what even done de deed, but in any case me don't t'ink any damned German would want to waste he ammunition on an ol' pile-o'-wood like dis anyway. I has me clearance already and want to make a move," he said, pouring two more shots.

Jack wanted to tell his friend about what he had seen that morning, but knew it was not his place to do so. A rumour of submarines lurking in local waters would pass through the fleet like a fire through dry timber. "She'll be right, mate. Like you say, nobody would want to trouble the likes of us."

Augustus offered his friend one more, but it was politely declined, and the bottle was put away. Their talk drifted to other things – freights being offered and other business. Soon afterwards Jack wished his friend a safe voyage. He went ashore and found Dawson waiting for him and they rowed back aboard. Later on that day he watched the *Guiding Star* push out from the wharf and hoist her old patched sails. She was well and truly loaded down, with only a couple of planks of her blue topsides showing below her white bulwarks. Jack lifted his arm in farewell, and received one in return from the white-capped skipper at the wheel. The main sheet was eased, and with a nice following breeze the schooner sailed out of Port-of-Spain for the Bocas, leaving the two still smouldering wrecks behind.

Outside World

The anchor light hanging from the forestay shone its tawny glow and the last of the red sunset faded into a purple sky over Venezuela. Dawson stood at the shrouds and joked with the crew as they cheerily climbed into the skiff, pushed away and rowed for shore, leaving him on watch. They were all dressed neatly in their best shore clothes, ready for a night out in the bustling port city, and pity the poor oarsman for the abuse he would receive if he happened to splash anyone with seawater. Once ashore, the group moved off slowly towards town until they separated, with the captain and mate turning in one direction while the crew headed off towards the cinema.

To Jack, Trinidad was resonant with her own special magic; a mixing pot of cultures and language and music and food. It was a Caribbean island, but the continent of South America was only a stone's throw away, and although British, had originally been claimed for Spain by Columbus, and had remained wild and unpopulated for over two hundred years. In the 1700's, French planters migrated from nearby islands to take advantage of the island's perfect conditions for growing sugar cane, and African slaves were brought in by the boatload to work the land. In 1797, Nelson's navy sailed into Port-of-Spain with eighteen warships and took control of the island away from the Spanish, claiming it for Britain. With the British abolition of slavery in 1833, a new source of cheap labour was needed, and so Portuguese were imported from the island of Madeira. Labourers from China soon followed, until finally, during the middle part of the nineteenth century, the first of thousands of indentured servants began to arrive from British East India. Later, Venezuelan farmers were encouraged to come and grow the lucrative cocoa bean, and so settled their own areas of the island and were even given the descriptive name of 'Cocoa Panyols'. Even the island's locales sounded exotic; places like San Fernando and Plaisance and Cocorite and California; Maraval and Montserrat, El Sirocco and Felicity. One common thread brought the people of Trinidad together, and that was the annual Carnival.

Jack and Zepheryn headed towards Woodbrook, an area of Port-of-Spain known for its drinking establishments and nightlife frequented by the crews of not only the local inter-island traders but also those off of the much bigger steel freighters and tankers that came from all points on the compass. Jack and his first mate entered the Victory Bar, made their way to the counter and ordered two cold beers. At this time of year, the streets and drinking establishments would normally be alive with music and excitement in the lead up to Carnival, which was only a few weeks away, but tonight the mood was sombre and muted, as if the smoke from the two still-smouldering ships had cast a pall over the whole town. The first and most obvious sign of this was the blackout that now engulfed the island. The street lamps were switched off, and no other electric lights were allowed.

"Man, tings is all haywire now," said the barman as he passed across the two beers. "We gone back to de old time days of oil lamps an' block ice."

"War's not good business for anyone except those that're selling the guns," Jack said.

"True sayin', mon, dat is true sayin'," responded the barman.

At the bar, the only topic of conversation concerned the attack in the harbour, and what it would mean to these men who made their living on the sea. Arguments and heated discussions, wild theories and unfounded rumours, bold statements and nervous talk circulated around the room. Everyone had an opinion. One thing was for certain; the torpedos that sped through the dark waters on that early morning had not only accomplished their task, but had thrown all of these men's lives into turmoil, as well as the thousands of residents of Trinidad.

"So I've heard the Navy has advised all shipping to hold off on departing until what they call "the immediate threat" is over – and they won't even tell us what that threat is!" a strapping Norwegian captain exclaimed.

"They're running around like a bunch of headless chickens as far as I can see," answered another seaman, hunched over his drink.

"Well to me it can only be one thing, and that is U-boats. All this other talk is rubbish. It's not saboteurs and it's not a sea raider. It was a U-boat, plain and simple. I've heard over the marine radio they attacked Curacao, they attacked Aruba, and now Trinidad. The authorities want to pretend it can't happen, that the submarines can't make it this far, but I've seen U-boats in the North Atlantic, and now we're seeing them in the Caribbean. Today I heard talk of 'unescorted convoys' being organised. Well my view is you are safer on your own. I have a ship full of oil out there and damned if I'm waiting on these idiots to tell me when it's safe!" the Norwegian continued. "Barman...more rum all 'round."

And so the conversations went. There was bravado, and there was nervous laughter, but one thing was for certain; things had changed in the West Indies. After a couple of more beers Jack felt like moving on, and so he and Zeph wandered out to the street. As they stood at the doorway overlooking the night time scene, he noticed a familiar shape moving up the road with a laughing local girl on his arm. "Ahoy there Rabbit! Hove to and prepare to repel boarders!" he hailed as the Barbajan was passing.

"Evening, Skip!" Rabbit smiled as Jack and Zeph joined the couple on the road. "Dis is Rosie."

"Good night, gentlemen," she said, coyly shaking the sailor's hands. She was a striking Creole girl, with copper coloured skin and dark, sparkling eyes.

"So where you two fellahs off to?" Rabbit asked.

"No place special," replied Jack.

"Well man, tings is low key tonight! Dem Germans surely know how to quiet down a party! Last night dis place was tick with Yankees drinkin' rum. Attila-the-Hun had a descent crowd down at he tent singin' Calypso – but tonight wit' de blackout it's like nothin' happenin' a-tall. Where's de rest of de crew?"

"They've all gone to see a 'Tarzan' movie down at the Astor," answered Jack. "Word is they are still showing movies. The power is still on, just no lights."

"Hey Rosie! I see you still wit dat Bajan man. When you goin' to come around to yo' senses?" one of a group of boys called out in passing.

"When all-o'-you stop bein' rude boys an' start learnin' some manners, dat's when!" she answered back. "Where's it you goin' at such a speed?"

"Man, we heard de Mighty Crusader just comin' out wit' he new calypso fo' Carnival. We headin' down Tragarete Road to he tent to check it out."

"Dat sounds good – but what happen to Roaring Lion? I thought you boys was playin' pans in he band," Rosie chatted back.

"We is, but you still must know 'bout de opposition, isn't it?" the pan man answered as he and his mates rounded the corner.

"What do you say Skip? You feel like catchin' some music? It's only down de road in Town," Rabbit asked with a smile.

The captain shrugged his shoulders, looked at his mate, and then said, "Why not? Nothing else is goin' on. We might even catch the boys as they come out of the cinema."

The four stepped out onto the road and started walking through the soft Trinidadian night, thick with the scents of smoke and flowers and dust and curry. There were far fewer people out on the street than normal. It seemed to be a night to relax. The glow of kerosene lamps replaced the normal electric lights, giving the street a rich, velveteen feel. Men sat on steps smoking, women chatted on porches. A steel pan's melodic tone sung through the night as it was methodically tuned, each skilled tap of the hammer bringing it closer to its perfect pitch.

As they walked the dark street the group discussed the day's events. "I heard a rumour this evening that de government talkin' 'bout stoppin' Carnival because of de attack," Rabbit offhandedly remarked.

"Well man, dey can try, but dey won't never succeed!" Rosie answered, stopping and facing the others angrily. "Dey've tried dis ting befo' you know! It's like tryin' to put a ban on hurricanes or de rainy season! Carnival's more than just some music wit' costumes an' dancin'. It runs like blood t'rough we veins, and I can tell you now dat Carnival will go on – war or no war, ban or no bans! Dey'd have fo' jail all o' we first!"

The group strolled on until they came to the Astor Cinema, which was just emptying out as they arrived. Jack caught sight of Kingsford, Gilbert, Bull, Earl and Jono, all of whom decided to join them to go and listen to the Mighty Crusader's new calypso.

The Calypsonian's tent was only a couple of blocks from the cinema; when they turned the corner they could see the dim glow of lamplight escaping from inside. There seemed to be quite a crowd milling about, even on such a quiet night. "Man, it seems de word is out," noted Kingsford. "Crusader does usually hit de mark."

Inside the canvas tent the crowd was thick, and there was an excited buzz that had the place humming. Though he was always popular, it had had been several years since Mighty Crusader had produced a winning calypso, and people were eager to hear what he had come up with. On the small stage a band played, a sextet made up of drums, string bass and horns. It wasn't long before some whistles and clapping near the front marked the Calypsonian's entrance. He joked and chatted with the audience for a few minutes before he picked up the mike.

"Well I is a black mon, so in dis dim light most all-you probably can't even see me, but at least we got sound!" he joked amidst laughter and cat calls. "And I know all o' you love calypso like I do, and want to hear something new and hot off de press. Well, dis ting so hot she smokin'! De boys and I just finished it a few hours ago. And look at all o' you here already! It's like dey say – if a pin drops in Cocorite you does hear about it in Gonzales five minutes later! So without further ado here's we latest ting. I does call it "Outside Worl'".

The band struck up a traditional Calypso rhythm, the crowd began to jump, and the Mighty Crusader came in right on cue.

War now come to Trinidad,
Tings is goin' from good to bad;
Bombin' and killin' not so nice,
Wha' happen to all-we paradise?

Outside worl' is comin' fast,
Old-time ways ain't goin fo' last;
Me no know where dis will end,
De good ol' days won't come again!

Boats an' planes 'rive every day,
Where it stops well I can't say.
Big ships explodin' late at night,
Ha'ba' on fire give me a fright!

Outside worl' is comin' fast,
Old-time ways ain' goin' fo' last;
Me no know where dis will end,
De good ol' days won't come again.

We fightin' fo' freedom's what dey preach,
Den Yankee-mon go close de beach,
Tings ain't gettin' no bettah a-tall,
Now dey stoppin' we Car-ni-val!

Outside world is comin' fast,
Old-time ways ain' goin fo' last;
Me no know where dis will end,
De good ol' days won't come again!

After the last refrain, the audience cheered and laughed and yelled good-natured comments back towards the stage. Moments later the band started up and Crusader sang his new song again, and several more times after that, and the crowd roared its approval more loudly each time. Finally Jack and his crew edged their way out of the packed tent, laughing and joking about how quickly the astute Calypsonian had put the news of the day into song. Rabbit and Rosie came with them, and as the schooner's crew turned for the docks the Bajan and his lady friend looked to go in another direction.

"When you next see Harry just mention I'm here, will you mate?" Jack asked Rabbit as they parted.

"Yes mon – I'll pass on de message," the Bajan replied. And with Rosie on his arm, the couple strolled up the road past the Queen's Park Savannah to her momma's house snuggled in the Belmont Hills.

Square Rigger

Midday and Jono had just served up some pig-tail and breadfuit, one of his specialities, when Fiji came alongside in his bum boat. "Ahoy Cap'n o' de schooner *Roulette,* ahoy!" came the familiar cry. Fiji, his boat, and especially his white captain's hat, were well known fixtures around the waterfront of Port-of-Spain. For as long as anyone could remember, he and his beloved *Josephine* had provided a vital service rowing captains, agents and crews between cargo vessels anchored in the stream and Queen's Wharf.

"G'day, Fiji. What can I do for you?" Jack queried, resting down his plate on the cabin top and leaning over the bulwark.

"Dey's a white mon asho' who axe me to gi' you a message. He say he'll be at de Sea Breeze Bar at two o'clock. You know where dat place be?"

"No, mate, I'm not really sure."

"It's on de corner o' St. Vincent an' Park Streets, upstairs above de ol' Plaza Restaurant. You can catch de number twenty-t'ree tram from de square. She's just a few blocks up de road."

"Okay Fiji, thanks. That should be easy to find." Jack said. He moved to sit back down and finish his meal, but Fiji remained alongside, standing in his ancient row boat with his large black hands still hooked onto the rail. Jack searched the old man's face, waiting.

"Jus' a shillin' fo' dat, Skip," Fiji said with a cagey grin.

Jack returned the smile, reached into his baggy dungarees and handed the boatman a coin. "Cheers, cobber," the captain said, wondering how much Iverson had given him to deliver the message in the first place.

The open electric tram slowed at the Tragarete Road junction, and Jack jumped out. Walking through the corner restaurant, he found the stairway leading to the upstairs bar. Iverson sat next to an open window, a beer on the table in front of him. Ceiling fans turned slowly overhead. A slight breeze drifted through the window, the room shady and cool. Pulling up a chair, Jack took off his hat and sat down. "G'day, Harry. How's tricks?"

A waiter approached, and Jack ordered a Lion Beer. "A bit of chaos out on the water, eh what? I've been informed you might have seen the culprit on your way through the Bocas."

"I'm sure it was a submarine, if that's what you mean."

"That is the only story that makes any sense. It's good you are in Trinidad at the moment, old man. This latest development has changed the dynamics of what will be happening here in the islands for the foreseeable future. I think it's time we compared notes," Harry said. He lit up a cigarette, the beer was delivered, and Jack described his experience in the middle of the channel of the Dragon's Mouth.

"You should know that I had a brief meeting with Captain Stafford this morning, and your story has gone a long way towards settling the argument about what actually sunk those ships out there the other night. Before your evidence, the most popular cause was German 'agent provoquers' planting bombs. I'm sure we'll hear more about this in the coming days."

"Listen, speaking of German agents, there's something else I want to tell you about. It's been on my mind for a couple of months now. It's not something I would bother Commander Lawrence with yet, but I think it's important enough to tell you about it." Jack now described to Harry the curious incident with the black ship he witnessed in St. Barths.

"So you saw a small freighter anchor in Gustavia and later ferry two passengers ashore in the middle of the night, who then left aboard your friend O'Loughlin's speedboat for St. Martin. Interesting story indeed. From the sounds of it, this could be the same freighter Carlisle noticed in Martinique. There can't be many vessels of that description in the Caribbean flying the Dutch flag. Now, you say this Irishman has a seaplane parked up there somewhere?"

"Yes, he's got one of those old Douglas flying boats he keeps on the Simpsonbai Lagoon. He told me he was flying with his wife to Cuba to spend Christmas. He didn't say anything about taking along any special passengers."

"According to Carlisle's description, these passengers taken aboard this mysterious freighter were distinctly foreign types, and when I looked into it I discovered that there are flight connections between Martinique and Europe through South America, so it is well within the realms of possibilities these could have been German agents. And it is only a short hop from Cuba to the US mainland. The question is, would your old associate actually involve himself in something like this?"

"Look, mate, when it comes to Sean O'Loughlin, anything is possible. I can honestly say he's a close friend, and when he gives you his word you can rest assured he will keep it, but he steers by a different moral compass than the rest of us. His younger brother was an associate of Michael Collins, and was beaten to death by the Black and Tans in the aftermath of Bloody Sunday. Needless to say, Sean is not a great lover of the British Empire. During Prohibition he owned the *Vamoose*, a specially built rumrunner the Coast Guard never came close to catching. He made himself a small fortune in those days, but for some reason he had to leave the States in a hurry. Some say it was to escape the taxman, another story contends he had a run-in with the mob, but whatever the cause he upped stakes and headed south. He told me he visits Florida every now and then, but I'm sure it's not with the full permission of the US authorities. So Harry, to answer your question, would Sean O'Loughlin smuggle Nazi agents into the United States? If the money was right, I surely wouldn't put it past him."

"As interesting as all of that might be, I think we might have to let that information simmer on the back burner for a while. With these U-boats now threatening the Caribbean, I think our skills might be required in other areas," Iverson hinted obliquely.

"And what skills might those be, Harry?" Jack asked.

"Oh it is only something that came up in conversation this morning. If anything comes of it, you'll be the first to know." Try as he may Jack couldn't get anything more out of the secretive Englishman.

Several beers later they left the Sea Breeze Bar. Once outside, they jumped onto a tram and rode it down St. Vincent Street, which deposited them at Marine Square. "Look, Jack, I'm going to have to let things cool down for a couple of days. I'll send a message to let you know when our next meeting might be." The two men shook hands and walked off through the crowd in different directions.

Over the next several days the *Roulette* lay at anchor, waiting for space alongside to discharge her cargo. While the crew spent their time doing maintenance on the vessel, Jack was ashore working all his contacts trying to obtain another load once their hold was empty, which was difficult following the confusion caused by the two sinkings a week earlier. Late one afternoon as he approached the docks he was met by Rabbit, who had been waiting for him in the shadow of the Queen's Wharf lighthouse.

"Wha' happenin', Skip?" the Bajan called out as he was passing. Jack walked over and stepped into the shade. "I been waitin' to see you, mon. Harry been busy de las' few days, but says he'll meet you tomorrow mornin' at 9:45 alongside Marine Square at de corner of Frederick Street. I don't know much more 'cept to say dat its important dat you're dere on time."

"No worries, Rabbit. Tell Harry I'll be there."

Jack was waiting at the edge of the square at the appointed hour the following morning when a military staff car pulled up, a door opened and Harry said, "Hop in, old chap."

"This is very official, Harry. Where are we off to?" he asked as he slid in next to the Englishman.

"We're going to the residence of Admiral Sir Michael Hodges, head of British military operations here in Trinidad," Iverson answered casually as he lit up a cigarette. "It just so happens he's an old acquaintance of mine."

Jack took a moment to digest this piece of information. "There's no messing about with you, is there mate. How the hell do you know the bloke?"

"The Admiral and I met years ago through a common interest in botany and ornithology. He's a Navy man through and through – a very experienced campaigner who cut his teeth during the Boer War, commanded battleships in the Great War, and at one time was actually Secretary of the Navy, before retiring ten years ago to his estate in Hampshire to grow orchids in his greenhouse. When this war came along His Majesty re-employed him as flag officer-in-charge of Trinidad, which was not a bad posting until the other day when a German U-boat had the audacity to actually bring the hostilities into his back garden."

"I'm sure it's an honour, Harry, but I don't quite understand why I'm so privileged."

"Just wait and see, my friend…just wait and see."

The Admiral's residency was located in the leafy suburb of St. Claire. The staff car passed through the gates and pulled up in front of the doors of the spacious manor, where the two visitors were ceremoniously escorted through the broad entryway into a well-appointed drawing room. Present were Admiral Hodges, Captain Warwick Stafford from the Benbow naval station, and Lieutenant-Commander Ainslie Blackwell from British Naval Intelligence.

"Good afternoon gentlemen," began Captain Stafford after everyone had been introduced and had taken a seat. "As you could well imagine, the last few days have been quite hectic. Jerry has certainly taken us by surprise, which I feel safe in saying is no military secret, and we are doing our best to try and steady the ship. You must be curious as to why you are here, Captain McLeod, but I should hope all your questions will be answered before we adjourn this afternoon. Sir Michael, I believe you would like to say a few words?"

Admiral Sir Michael Hodges did not appear to be anything like Jack imagined him to be. He was not a big man, nor did his presence demand attention. Rather, he had the demeanour more associated with an academic of some kind, perhaps a university professor. As Jack inspected the luxuriously appointed room and the manicured grounds, he understood what Harry had been talking about. This present development of the war had disrupted what would have been quite a comfortable existence in an out-of-the-way backwater of the Empire.

"Yes, thank you Warwick," Sir Michael began. "I would also like to thank Commander Iverson for organising this meeting. Harry and I go back a long way, and when he makes a recommendation it is generally worth considering. I must say, Captain McLeod, he has given you high marks indeed. It is not every day the Navy is in need of assistance from civilians, but these are not ordinary days. It is obvious the Caribbean has now become a new theatre in the quickly expanding German war effort, and we clearly were caught with our pants down. What we need to do now is to learn how serious this threat is. We need to understand what the enemy's strengths are, and what we can do to counter them. And we need to do it quickly. In other words, gentlemen, what we need is intelligence. We obviously have our sources in Europe, but at the moment we are quite thin on the ground here in the islands. And that, in a nutshell, is why we all are here today. I now would like to turn the meeting over to Lieutenant-Commander Blackwell to explain precisely what we have in mind."

"Thank you, Admiral Hodges. I'm not sure what you two gentlemen would know about the military command situation here in Trinidad, or the Caribbean in general for that matter, so let me take a moment to present you with a little bit of background. Close to a year ago, our Prime Minister Mr Churchill signed over nine British military leases we held here on various Caribbean islands to the Americans in exchange for fifty mothballed destroyers, which the Royal Navy desperately needed for escorting our North Atlantic convoys. Now that the Americans are in the war, they are fully committed to building up their presence at these nine locations. Trinidad is probably their number one priority, where, as I am sure you are aware, military air strips and naval bases are frantically being constructed. Their commander is Major-General Pratt, who since his arrival here has made his presence felt, to put it mildly. It has always been his conviction that the most probable form of attack on Trinidad would come by air from German paratroopers based deep in the Amazon, a contentious theory of which there is little or no evidence. At any rate he has been hell bent on developing our air defences in preparation for such an assault, at the cost of everything else. There have been only token resources allotted towards any U-boat threat, simply because no one thought Jerry could get here. Interestingly, less than two months ago, German U-boats made a concerted attack on the east coast of the United States, where thousands of tons of commercial shipping was sunk. So it's obvious their Wolf Packs are ranging much further afield than just the North Atlantic convoy routes they were previously associated with. We now know they do indeed have the range to reach these waters.

"What I am going to tell you next must be held in the strictest of confidence. Allied military command wants none of the following information released to the public for fear of starting a panic. Captain McLeod, your report confirms German U-boats are now in Caribbean waters. Not only has there been the attack here in Port-of-Spain, but there also were raids on the refineries on Curacao and Aruba at about the same time. Four oil tankers were sunk there as well as two others in route from Venezuela to Curacao, and all on the same day. This is an obvious indication we are dealing with not just one U-boat, but several. As a result, all shipping of crude oil has now been suspended between Lake Maracaibo, the Venezuelan mainland and the refineries on those Dutch islands. Since then, several more ships have been sunk. A fully loaded Norwegian tanker, whose captain ignored our warnings, was sunk just two days ago off of Point Galera, and there has been another harbour raid – this time in St. Lucia. Obviously the U-boat Jerry is now building has a far greater range than we previously thought possible, which makes commercial shipping in these waters highly vulnerable.

"This foray by Admiral Donitz and his submarines has not only taken us completely unawares, but thrown our previous strategy for the defence of the Caribbean Basin into complete disarray. London sees this development as a serious attempt by the enemy to cut our supply lines off at the source, and is hastening us to do what we can to limit the damage, but as I am sure Sir Michael would confirm, Britain's hands are tied at the moment. We simply do not have the resources. The Americans, however, are fully committed to the defence of what they see as 'their' hemisphere, and we are just starting to see the beginning of what I am sure will become a huge investment from them in men and materials over the next few months and years as they throw everything they can at the Germans. This does not mean we sit back and wait to act. Our resources may be limited here in the islands, but they are well positioned. It is imperative we make use of whatever small advantages we do have, and that we get the most out of them. That, gentlemen, is the purpose of this meeting."

The Lt. Commander got up from the table and approached a large map of the Caribbean. "On this map I have designated the known attacks and sinkings that have occurred in the last ten days. As you can see from the widespread locations, we are dealing with at least five different U-boats. For them it must be like knocking over ducks at a shooting gallery. And even better, from Jerry's point of view, there is very little to worry about. There is minimal air-borne resistance, and only a token naval presence for them to fear. This would be most encouraging to the Kreigsmarine back in France. From an intelligence point of view, we know that since the sinking of the *Bismarck*, the German Navy has curtailed their building of battleships and cruisers. Instead, they are putting their full effort into the construction of U-boats, which their shipyards in Hamburg and Bremen are launching at the impressive speed of almost one a week. In other words, we believe these attacks are only the beginning of what could become a full-out, concentrated assault on shipping between South America and the southern coast of the United States. The fact is, gentlemen, oil from Trinidad, Venezuela and the Dutch Islands is crucial to our national survival, and the Germans are conscious of the fact. I am therefore not overstating the situation. If the enemy succeeds in turning off the taps here in the Caribbean, it could bring Britain literally to her knees.

"Commander Iverson, Captain McLeod, the War Office is most concerned that with the success of this bold campaign, Jerry will look at taking the next logical step and attempt to establish some sort of base here in the Caribbean for the resupply of their submarines. This is something we cannot allow to happen. The last thing we need is a nest of U-boats based here wreaking havoc on Allied shipping. So, from a German point of view, where would the most logical location for a site be? Obviously, due to the Nazi occupation of France, the French Territories would head the list. Martinique stands out as an ideal location from which to operate, and for a number of reasons. Politically they are subservient to Berlin through the Vichy Government. The island has a well-developed infrastructure, and logistically it is well positioned with the harbour in Forte-de-France being one of the best in the West Indies. There is easy access to fuel, food and water. The dry-dock, although antiquated, could easily accommodate at least two submarines at a time. There are quayside facilities for doing maintenance and repairs, and the island also has a large airport. We know Admiral Robert, who is in charge there, recently signed an agreement with the Americans to confine the four naval vessels under his command to Martinique, and that he is professing neutrality. This move has held off an American invasion of the island, but it does not mean he isn't facilitating the Germans in other ways. We therefore believe we must begin our intelligence gathering in Martinique. We do have some recent information about the island courtesy of Commander Iverson, but we need to know more concerning the situation there."

Captain Stafford now waded in to the conversation. "This brings us around to you, Captain McLeod. To put it bluntly – His Majesty's Royal Navy is in further need of you and your vessel's services."

At this Jack slowly lifted his gaze. "Explain 'in further need of my services'," he said warily.

"We understand your arrangement with Commander Lawrence in Barbados, Captain McLeod, which until now entailed a rather passive commitment. Obviously things have changed dramatically since then. We are groping in the dark at the moment, and we need information quickly. You present us with a ready-made answer to at least a portion of our problems. We therefore are asking you to further volunteer your services, taking on a far more active role."

Jack stared across the table at Harry. He knew immediately his friend had full knowledge of what was transpiring. "What's going on here, mate? What are you blokes roping me into?"

Harry calmly lit a cigarette. "I know it sounds bad, old man, but listen to what Captain Stafford has to say first before you get yourself too worked up."

"As I said, all of us here at this table understand what it is we are asking of you, but I'm afraid you and your vessel present too good an opportunity for us to pass up. Your credentials are without reproach. You move between the islands with impunity, and your first-hand knowledge of the area is second to none. And you are a subject of the Crown."

Jack returned the stare of the others who all were intently watching him. "I understand there's a war on, but I do have a business to run. I have a crew who are depending on me to help them feed their families. Unfortunately, I'm not a man of such means as to simply give my business away for the defence of the Empire. I think I need to hear a few more details before I become too excited."

"We would hope very little, if anything at all, changes in your day to day activities. In fact, we may even expedite cargos for you so as to maintain your cover. The last thing we would want is to draw any attention to our association," assured Captain Stafford.

"And my crew – what happens to them? They'll need to be given the option as to whether they want to be part of all of this. I assume there'll be risks involved. Will they be properly compensated?"

"Obviously you will be required to take some chances, for which you and your crew will be duly remunerated," Blackwell interjected. "Your crew plays an integral part in this operation. We must assume the Germans have established an espionage network on this side of the Atlantic. We don't want you to attract any attention. The Admiralty will therefore commit to paying you an equitable sum which should more than cover your daily expenses, including the wages of your crew. You can regard this as a sort of extraordinary commission. Any monies you make from your normal day to day business such as freights and cargos are yours to keep. So from a financial perspective you really have nothing to lose. Are there any other questions?"

Jack sat forward and reached towards his friend across the table. "You mind giving me one of those smokes, 'Commander'?"

Harry passed him the cigarette packet and matches. The captain sat back and lit up before replying. "You don't really present me with a lot of options here, do you? Harry, I'm going to have to have some serious words with you once we're done. I've been shanghaied and there doesn't seem to be much I can do about it. There are a couple of minor problems, though. I have a cargo on board, and I'm not going anywhere until I get it offloaded. My agent told me yesterday it could be another week at least before I can get space alongside to discharge. And the fuel pump on my engine is stuffed and I can't find a replacement."

"Actually your first problem has been taken care of already. You will find there is space for you and you can start offloading your cargo as of tomorrow morning," Stafford said with a smile. "As to your second point, we are hoping Sir Michael will be able to have a word with our American friends and work out a solution for you as early as this afternoon. So do we take it you agree with our terms?"

"Like I said, I don't have much choice. So yes, I agree."

"That is what we all were hoping to hear," said Stafford. "What I am about to tell you is only in its formative stages, but this operation will be called 'Square Rigger'. It will take place in Martinique, and you are at the centre of it. For the moment, at least, that is all you need to know. I'm sure you would like to discuss this matter further, Captain McLeod, but Sir Michael has an engagement with Major-General Pratt he must attend to. Sir Michael, is there anything you would like to add?"

"Captain McLeod, I realize all of this must come as a shock to you. Commander Iverson has described you as a man of integrity and courage. I'm sure once you have let the idea sink in, you will see that your contribution to the war effort could prove to be highly valuable."

At that moment there was a knock on the door and an aide entered. "Excuse the interruption Admiral, but your car is here, sir," he said.

"Oh yes...quite! Thank you Hendricks. Excuse me gentlemen, but duty calls. I will leave you in the safe hands of Captain Stafford to finish up," the Admiral said as the men all stood at his departure. "As you were, men, as you were."

A few minutes later Jack and Harry were stepping out onto the gravel drive. "Let's go have a drink, Harry – or is it Commander?" Jack said as they ducked into the waiting car. "You have some explaining to do. And it's your shout, mate."

Over the next few days Jack slowly came around to the realities of his situation. He had several meetings with Lieutenant-Commander Blackwell and Harry Iverson, when the details of how things would work became clearer. His most difficult task was breaking the news to his crew. At first they stared at him like stunned fish, not fully comprehending what it would mean to their futures. The next reaction, by some at least, was something close to anger as they pushed out their lips and sucked their teeth and muttered under their breath. "Wha' de ass me hearin' here a-tall?" Gilbert exclaimed.

Their captain explained it was not something they had to do. He made them understand it was purely a voluntary mission, but once they accepted the terms there was no turning back. Some jumped at the idea, like young Dawson and Earl. Zepheryn and Jono were far more pensive and thoughtful, while Kingsford, Bull and Gilbert were visibly annoyed with the Admiralty for putting their captain and themselves in such a position. "Man, dey can haul their muddah's ass! Me in de Navy? Me ain't no fightin' man!" cursed Kingsford.

Bull sucked his teeth and agreed. "We is all catchin' we ass now – you t'ink it easy? What if dey starts shootin' at we? How de hell we goin fo fight back? T'row ballast stones?"

The captain gave the crew twenty-four hours to consider the offer. "Look, this is a serious decision. I'll go along with whatever it is you decide. So you all think about it and tell me what you want to do tomorrow."

When the time came all of his crew decided to stay on, although some did reluctantly. "I must be a lunatic fo' doin' dis, but one in all in," muttered Kingsford, a scowl crossing his face as dark as a rain squall in hurricane season.

Early morning and the *Roulette* pushed her way out of the tangle alongside Queen's Wharf after spending the previous few days discharging their cargo, and in a light breeze sailed the short distance around Diego Island into the broad bay of Chaguaramas. With Gaspar Grande and several small cays helping protect it on one side and the high mountains of Trinidad on the other, it was a perfect natural harbour, and it was obvious to Jack why the US was so determined to develop it as a major naval base.

According to Harry, it was also the chief cause of the ongoing battle between the Trinidadian Governor Sir Hubert Young and the American's top man, Major-General H. C. Pratt. "So what's this fight going on between the Governor and the Yanks all about?" Jack had asked one night over drinks. "I thought they were supposed to be allies."

"It seems Governor Young has painted himself into quite a tight little corner, and I can't see him finding a way out. He is of the opinion that he is in charge of Trinidad, and the Americans are merely interlopers. Unfortunately, that is not how it is working out. The argument started when Sir Hubert tried to direct the Yanks to clean out the mosquito-infested Caroni Swamps and build their new naval base there. The Americans were not remotely interested. They wanted Chaguaramas and weren't going to discuss anything else. The Governor lost that fight. When you go out there you'll see the work they are starting to do. As you know, Chaguaramas has been a traditional beach-going area for Trinidadians for years and years. The first thing the Americans did was to evict all the locals and fence off the beaches with barbed wire, another move vehemently objected to by Governor Young."

"Good on the Governor for standing up for the locals, but you can't blame the Yanks for wanting Chaguaramas. It has to be one of the best deep water harbours in all of the West Indies."

"It is, and you know how the Yanks are. They don't do things by half measures. They're now going at it full speed ahead. You'll see huge changes since the last time you were there."

As Harry spoke, two smiling ladies of the night approached their table. "Evening gentlemen. You boys looking for someone to keep you company tonight?" one of them coyly asked.

"No thank you, girls. I'm afraid we're already taken," Jack casually replied.

"Okay then," they smiled, waving as they moved on.

"That's another thing the Yanks are doing their best to take over," Harry revealed. "Their enlisted men are throwing their dollars around, and the female population is making the most of it. Some bad feeling is brewing amongst the local men, who are paupers by comparison, and I'm sure it won't be long before that too bubbles to the surface."

Chaguaramas

The schooner rounded Diego Island, and in the light breeze slowly made her way across the well-protected, calm bay, eventually picking up a mooring near the mouth of the harbour.

"Our good friend Sir Michael had a quiet word in General Pratt's ear the other day," Captain Stafford had said to Jack at a meeting at *HMAS Benbow* a few days earlier. "The General seems to be enthralled with the concept of Square Rigger. He has basically given us carte blanche and affirmed that the Yanks will do whatever they can to help. So despite the public rows we're reading about in the papers, at a more practical level the two sides are actually starting to cooperate. Once you have discharged your cargo you are to move your vessel to Chaguaramas, where the American Navy will send some mechanics aboard to repair your engine."

Now they were hanging on to a mooring in the midst of a hive of military activity.

"Man, dis place like it goin' crazy!" the awestricken mate muttered to Jack. "I never seen nothin' like dis in all me life."

"You're right Zeph, the Yanks aren't messing about," the captain replied.

And indeed they were not. Bulldozers belched black smoke in the air as they cleared the land behind the bay's pristine beaches. The sound of pile drivers echoed across the water as they rammed in the foundations for what would obviously become an enormous wharf area. Sheds were going up, Quonset Huts were being assembled, and jeeps and other military vehicles scurried about in every direction. Even on the crystal clear waters of the bay the pace was frenetic, as tugs towing barges laden with a variety of vehicles and materials joined the procession of other vessels in a steady stream running to and from Port-of-Spain. The crew's heads turned to watch a twin engine aircraft thunder in low over the hills and land on the flat waters of the bay, its nose, tail and top bristling with armaments. As the seaplane manoeuvred its way on to its mooring, another three planes swept into the bay one after another and followed suit. The schooner's crew stood on and watched in dumbstruck silence. "What de hell I seein' here?" Kingsford finally exclaimed. "It's a fleet o' flying boats!"

"That's exactly what they are – flying boats," muttered Jack, inwardly impressed with the physical enormity of the seaplanes.

"How de ass a ting like dat can fly?" Earl wondered.

"Horsepower. Lots and lots of horsepower," the captain quietly replied.

It wasn't long before a small open launch came alongside with four sailors dressed in greasy work uniforms. "You Captain McLeod?" one of them shouted up to Jack.

"Yes mate, that's me," he answered.

"We're here to tow you alongside the work jetty," the sailor shouted back. Lines were rigged, the mooring let go, and slowly the grey launch manoeuvred the schooner in towards shore, where they were brought carefully alongside the wharf and secured between two large navy supply vessels. It wasn't long before a British military jeep pulled up and Captain Stafford climbed out and walked over to where the schooner was now made fast. "Would you like to come along with me, McLeod? There is someone here I need to introduce you to."

As the jeep sped around the dirt road of the busy base, the Englishman explained that they were going to see a Captain Sumner, who was the American officer in charge of naval operations at Chaguaramas. After being ushered into his office, Sumner contemptuously studied the documents presented by Captain Stafford several times before saying anything. "First off I was ordered to give you space alongside, and now you hand me this? So McLeod, let me get this straight. You've got a schooner that has a broken down Ruston engine in it, and somehow you've obtained an order here from Major-General Pratt directing me to repair it. I'm to not only get this work done immediately, but give you any other engineering assistance you may need without question. Is that it?" he asked, putting his stump of a cigar to his lips and squinting across the desk at his two visitors.

"I believe that is precisely what the order says," smiled Captain Stafford.

The American officer puffed on his cigar and turned slowly back to the requisition in his hands. "Well you know yourself all hell has broken loose around here the last couple of weeks, and I've got vessels up the yin-yang that are screaming to get work done. I've got a construction schedule the Lord Almighty would have trouble keeping to, and now I'm told your cargo schooner is top priority? Listen, the earliest I could even think about getting around to you is in two or three weeks, and you would be lucky even then," he said with a shake of his head.

"I'm afraid that won't do, old chap," Stafford calmly replied. "The schooner must be ready to go no later than Monday. I don't want to become the proverbial pain in your backside, but I am afraid I must insist. I would think the last thing you need is a phone call from General Pratt himself."

There was an awkward silence in the office while Sumner examined his orders again. Finally he glared up at the British officer. "I don't know what's going on here, but I've got too much on my plate to start making waves. I'll have somebody come down to have a look first thing in the morning."

The men all stood. "That will just have to do then," Captain Stafford said. The Englishman smartly saluted his counterpart, which was returned in a most casual manner, and tucking his swagger stick under his arm turned smartly on his heel for the door, with Jack a step behind.

Jono had the fire in the galley started early, so that at 06:00 sharp when the military jeep pulled up alongside, Jack and his crew were all ready to go. Three men jumped out of the vehicle and approached Jack, who had stepped on to the wharf to meet them.

"Captain McLeod? Good morning. I'm Chief Petty Officer Hartman. This here is Seaman Boyer and Seaman Padbury, who I have brought here to give you a hand. I've been told we have an engine to get going and its top priority, so let's get started."

Sometime after midday Jack was below in the engine room with his two American helpers when he heard a shout from above and saw the face of Captain Stafford peering down at him through the engine hatch. "Afternoon McLeod," the Englishman called down to him. "All going well so far, old chap?"

"Yes, well we've made a start," he answered as he made his way up to meet the British captain dressed in his khaki drills, his ever-present swagger stick held tightly under his arm.

"Listen Jack, things are starting to come together at rather a rapid pace. I think we should be using every spare minute we can find to prepare ourselves for your upcoming mission," Stafford said as Jack wiped his hands on a greasy rag. "Let's go for a bit of a wander, shall we. I have a few things to discuss with you."

"Sure, I can get away for a few minutes. The boys should be right." And so the two men stepped ashore and strolled along the wharf. It was hot, sunny and humid, the lofty green peaks of the lush interior of Trinidad peacefully overlooking the smoke and dust and noise of Chaguaramas. The Englishman walked slowly, as if he were out for a stroll back home in Derbyshire.

"Ah, it's hard to imagine what this place actually was like only a few months ago," Stafford said, turning to look back across the bay. "The Royal Navy had a small facility here, but it was surrounded by the most beautiful, unspoiled bay you could imagine. On weekends and holidays families from Port-of-Spain and all parts of the interior would come here and enjoy themselves. It really was a little piece of paradise. But you wouldn't know that now. The whole area is surrounded by razor wire. You can understand why the locals are upset."

"Yes, we used to anchor in here sometimes to wait for the tide to change before going through the Bocas. The little fishing village down there at the far end was a beaut little spot. You could always get fish, conch, and lobster, whatever you wanted. But not anymore. The Yanks have chased all the locals out. I guess you could say it's just another side effect of this war."

"Call it what you may, it's here to stay. That's not what I've come here to discuss, however. As I mentioned, there are many details we need to work out. Commander Blackwell has worked up a brief, along with a schedule, and has asked me to organise a meeting for tonight. How does that suit you?"

"Sounds fine to me, mate. We'll most likely finish here around six this evening. Then I'll need to clean myself up, so any time after seven would be okay."

"Jolly good – we'll leave it at that then. My driver will be here to pick you up at 19:30. I've commandeered a house not far from here at the British Officer's quarters. I'll leave you to get back to your work." The two returned slowly to the schooner. "I am now off to do some more liaison work with our good friend Captain Sumner, which is not a meeting I'm looking forward to, but duty is duty I'm afraid. We'll see you this evening."

With a wave Jack climbed back aboard and disappeared once again into the bowels of the engine room as Stafford's jeep merged into the busy traffic of the dusty road.

That night, at the first of what would be several nocturnal intelligence meetings, the logistical plan for Operation Square Rigger was developed. "The goal of Square Rigger is to lay the groundwork for a resistance organisation that will not only be able to supply us with reliable information, but hopefully over time become a thorn in the side of the Vichy governments of the French territories," began Lieutenant-Commander Blackwell. "Several months ago, Commander Iverson made contact with a well-placed individual in Fort-de-France, who we believe can put together the backbone of an underground movement on the island of Martinique. It is important for us to re-connect with him and cultivate the relationship. We have given this individual the code-name 'Fauconnier'. We are proposing to supply Fauconnier with short wave radio capabilities, as well as other equipment, much like we are doing to assist the resistance movement in France. We are hoping that Fauconnier and the group that he eventually co-ordinates will operate on two distinct fronts: firstly to provide us with information as to German activities in Martinique and other parts of the French Caribbean, and secondly to undermine the rule of the pro-Vichy regime being run by Admiral Robert. Towards that end our friends in the US Navy have volunteered to assist us by supplying the radio equipment needed, as well as the training to go along with it. Captain McLeod, your job will be to smuggle this equipment into Martinique."

It was then that the plan of how the team would make their landings in Martinique was developed. The bays and coves of the island were examined for their ease of approach as well as proximity to the main town of Fort-de-France. The nearby British island of St. Lucia would be used as a base from which to launch the mission. There were several protected anchorages on that island's north-west coast that would be suitable, and each was carefully considered.

At this point, Square Rigger encountered a major stumbling block. It was crucial to the success of the operation that a French-speaking operative be found who could make contact and liaise with Fauconnier. He must be able to blend in to the local surrounds of Martinique, and preferably be familiar with the island and know the lay of the land. Harry conducted several interviews, but none were acceptable. It was Rabbit who surprised everyone when he volunteered to be the person put ashore in Martinique.

"Listen mon – what you need is someone who even dem Martiniquais wouldn't suspect, and dere ain't no one else around fo' dat at de moment but me," he said one morning to Harry when he heard of their problem. "Not many people does know dis 'bout me, but back a few years when I was in me early twenties I was sailin as mate 'board a Canadian schooner dat went ashore in de middle a de night on de French island of Marie-Galante. How dat happen is a long story, but de vessel was mash-up an' I washed ashore half drowned wit' me leg broken, an' it was some locals who did take me in an' look after me. I always had a bit of a gift at pickin' up different lingos, an' it didn't take me long to learn de island patois. Dey's a whole set of white people on Marie-Galante, their people been there for hundreds o' years, and I fit right in wit' dem, 'specially wit a certain girl who took a liking to me. Dere's three rum distilleries on de island, an' Monique's family owned one o' dem. Tings was real good fo' a while, til it all got a bit too serious. Dere was even talk o' marriage! Ol' man Debussy was even lookin' to line me up to take over de business. It all got to be too much fo' de ol' Rabbit. As good as it all appeared I could never see meself swallowin' de anchor an' leavin' de sea to settle down on de land wit' a proper job. I found passage one night 'board a schooner bound fo' Martinique, an' dat was dat. Me never been back. But I can still speak patois as good as a local. So you all can teach me how to use dat radio, and den smuggle me ashore and I'll make sure your man Philippe, I mean 'Fauconnier', knows how to use it."

The meeting the following night was joined by a Lieutenant Briggs from the US naval station. "Lieutenant-Commander Blackwell, Captain Stafford, gentlemen...I've been ordered by Captain Sumner to give as much assistance as possible to you; if there is anything you need from us don't hesitate to ask. The main items on my agenda are to supply you with a couple of radios and train your operators in how to use them. We have just the radio for you. It is what we call a T-47/ART-13 transmitter which operates in continuous wave or 'CW' for code work, as well as modulated continuous wave or 'MCW' and AM for voice transmissions. This radio can cover low, medium, and high frequencies up to 18.1 mega-hertz, and has ten auto-tuned VFO channels which can be preset. Power output is one hundred watts and it has a range of up to one thousand miles. It is the radio our Navy flyers use, and it is compact and easy to store. Does this sound acceptable to you?"

"Bloody marvellous, old chap," Harry Iverson said.

"Me can't say I understand all your technical talk at de moment mon, but give me some time and I'll figure it out. Otherwise it all sounds good to me," Rabbit agreed.

The *Vagabond* was anchored in a quiet little cove off of Diego Island, well removed from the hustle and bustle of Port-of-Spain. Harry and Val were up early for their morning swim, and as they climbed back on board they met Rabbit sitting in the cockpit with a cup of tea.

"Good morning, Carlisle," Harry said as he dried himself with a towel. "How was your night off? I must say it was well deserved after all of the training you have been going through."

"Oh it was quiet. Rosy was busy workin' on she costume fo' carnival, so I just had a bit of a wander and a couple o' quiet rums on me own. But I did happen to come across someone who you might be interested to meet. He says he's from St. Barths and has been away from there for a long time, but he wants to go back home. Now dis put me to thinkin'. Dis fellah don't much like what's happening on de French islands and I t'ink he could be talked into joinin' we in Martinique. I didn't tell him too much, but from what he did say I reckon we could work together. It's a big job an' we could cover more ground wit' two o' we. He could be jus' de fella."

"I'm interested, Carlisle. How do we make contact?"

"I told him dat we were getting ready to sail back nort' soon, and dat we may be able to gi' he a ride in dat direction. De man was keen, so I said I'd meet him at ten dis morning in town to talk 'bout it."

Harry mulled this over for a few moments, lost in thought. "Hmmm…yes, well it sounds like this chap could prove to be quite useful. I wouldn't mind sounding him out at the very least."

After breakfast the three crew members of the *Vagabond* rowed ashore and pulled their dinghy high up onto the beach. A footpath led through the coconut trees to the main road, where they caught a crowded electric trolley bus into Port-of-Spain. "I'll meet you at the markets in an hour or so," Harry said to his wife, giving her a peck on the cheek as they parted in the crowded main square. "Maybe we'll get a spot of lunch somewhere afterwards."

"Ok darling, see you soon," Val smiled as she disappeared into the crowd, canvas shopping bags slung over her shoulder.

Rabbit led Harry up Frederick Street before turning into a series of narrow backstreets. Finally they came to a small rumshop. Inside were a few roughly made tables and chairs, where two men sat quietly drinking rum. At a table near the propped open window sat a diminutive young creole man; his longish hair was tied back in a ponytail and he sported a neatly trimmed moustache and goatee.

"Harry, dis is Gregoire Deslisle," Rabbit said as they shook hands and took a seat. Rabbit then wandered over to the bar. Soon he returned with a tray carrying a small pitcher of water, three glasses, and a tiny bottle of clear white rum. Harry gave his crewman a quick questioning look. "It's just an 'open eye', Skip," he said with a roguish grin.

Rabbit poured three shots; the glasses were held high, and amid the uttered words of "cheers" and "santé", the clear liquid was thrown down.

"So Gregoire, Carlisle here tells me you are from St. Barths and are hoping to make your way back home. Tell me a bit about yourself."

"Yes, that's right. Do you know Saint Barthélemy?" he asked.

"Yes I do. It has to be one of my favourite islands in the Caribbean. It's like a slice of the Mediterranean."

"Yes, it's beautiful, but it isn't easy to make a living there. It is quite a few years since I left and went to live with my uncle in St. Thomas, where I learned to speak English. Many people from St. Barths live over there in Frenchtown. My uncle owns a small shop where I was working, but I'm no shopkeeper, so I took to the sea. I made my way to Cayenne, where I tried a few different things. I tried to make my fortune looking for gold, but only caught malaria. It's a rough country that can swallow the best of men whole. Then the war came, and with it this new Vichy government, and very quickly the rules changed. It was follow orders or else! I got in trouble in Cayenne because I couldn't keep my mouth shut, so I made my way to Demerara and then found a schooner coming here. The jails in Cayenne are one way only. You go in but don't come out, like a lobster trap!"

Harry lit up a cigarette, drawing on it pensively, squinting through the smoke at Gregoire. "What have you been doing here in Trinidad?" he asked.

"At first I found some work cutting cane. Then I did construction for one of these big American companies. But my heart's not in this place. I'd like to get back to the French islands and see what's happening. Maybe there's something I could do to help. I don't mind speaking English, but I refuse to learn German," Gregoire said with a determined smile.

Harry took a final drag on his cigarette before dropping it to the floor and rubbing it out. "Well perhaps we can interest you in a little project we are about to embark on. It's dangerous, but probably no more so than you are used to. Have you ever heard of 'Les Maquis' in France?"

"But of course. The French Resistance is famous."

"How would you like to become a member in, let us say, the Caribbean division?" Harry asked.

"I think you're joking now, Harry."

"He ain't joking – de man's dead serious," countered Rabbit.

Gregoire looked from one man to another. "It's an interesting proposal, but I'll have to hear more. I'd like to do what I can for my people, but I need to know who I'm working with."

"Let me just say there is more to us than meets the eye," Harry said. "Now Gregoire, at the moment we have a slight concern with time. I realise you have just met us, and you know nothing about us, but all I can say is you can trust we are who we say we are, and what we are talking about is for real. Our program is set, the wheels are in motion. What I can tell you is we represent only part of a group that is well organised and serious in its intent. What you need to tell me before we leave this table is if you are interested in becoming part of our team or not. If you say no, then we will have another drink and that will be the end of it. But if you say yes, then we can move on to the next step."

Gregoire Deslisle mulled over this offer, silently looking from one man to the next before responding. "In the past I have been told I am an impetuous person, but I am a great believer in first impressions. If you are as well connected as you say you are then I am interested. I like the sound of 'Les Maquis Caraïbes'. Tell me how we take the next step."

A few nights later the *Vagabond* sailed quietly into Chaguaramas Bay and tied up alongside the *Roulette*. All was in readiness for what needed to be a quick operation. A radio would be installed aboard the yacht that night, and the work had to finish before daylight so as not to attract any attention. A crane had been brought into position, and it wasn't long before the *Vagabond* was lifted out of the water and set down on the wharf where a squad of Navy shipwrights and technicians were waiting. As one team attached the large copper earth plate onto the bottom of the boat, another set to work inside the yacht fitting the radio. Electricians ran cables and mounted an antenna onto the mizzen mast; a carpenter built a mahogany cabinet that hid the radio away perfectly. As all of this was going on, the crew of the *Roulette* helped Rabbit clean the boat's bottom and apply a new coat of anti-fouling.

"I must admit, I like how these Yanks go about their business," Harry said to Jack at one point during the night. "Once the order is given they surely don't mess about, do they?"

"It's impressive Harry, and that's a fact. From what I've seen in my short stay here, these blokes are getting straight to the point. I know Germans are renowned for their efficiency, but if what I've seen around here is any indication of the US war effort, it won't be long before the Krauts will have their hands full."

The work was finished on schedule and the yacht was put back into the water just before first light. After a final test to make sure the instillation was in order the *Vagabond* pushed off, hoisted her sails and set a course for the Bocas and St. Lucia, with the *Roulette* soon to follow.

The Shooting Gallery

U-112 broke through the surface of the Galleons Passage and powered north, leaving the Bocas and Trinidad behind. Moments later, a radio message was sent by Morse code to Admiral Donitz and the Kreigsmarine in Lorient. "Extensive damage done in Port-of-Spain. Attack achieved in complete surprise. Two ships sunk. Steering N by NW. Awaiting further orders."

The reply came quickly. "Operational area is now between 12 and 20 degrees north; 60 to 65 degrees west until further notice. Target all enemy shipping. Congratulations."

The messages were decoded through the newly updated four rotor Enigma enciphering machine. Because the German High Command considered it virtually impossible for the Allies to decipher their transmissions, Donitz demanded all U-boats keep in daily communication, with the Admiral himself in personal control of the movements of every one of his submarines.

Kapitanleutnant Nils Albrecht stood examining a chart spread out on the navigation table, with the first mate alongside of him. "Mr Weiss, I believe the crew deserves a break. Steer for Union Island in the Grenadines. Do you see this little bay on the west side? As I remember it is completely deserted. I think it will be a safe place to spend a few hours and let the men stretch their legs. After all, we are in the Caribbean. Oh – and don't worry about telling Old Man Donitz about it. What he doesn't know won't hurt him," the captain added facetiously before retiring to his bunk for a well-earned few hours of sleep.

At midday the faint blue outline of the distinct cone-shaped peak of Union Island hove into view. The submarine had been on the surface since early morning motoring towards their destination. Union was the most leeward island in the Grenadines. It was remote, sparsely populated and easily approached from the depths of the Caribbean Sea to the west. Nils Albrecht knew there to be a well-protected, isolated bay on the lee side of the island from his days as a freighter captain, and although he had never anchored there, his chart showed it to be deep right up to the shore. It was a perfect spot for his crew to relax, if only for a few hours.

As they approached the anchorage, the lookouts scoured the shore for a sign of life. "There's not a soul to be seen," the mate commented as he peered through his binoculars. "It looks to be an ideal spot. Easy in and easy out."

The grey war machine slowly entered the bay and glided towards the crescent shaped beach, until its belly grounded onto the sandy bottom. The captain knew there was no tide here to go out and leave them stranded. There were no air patrols that could spot them, and no sea patrols for them to worry about. For the few hours his ship would be there, he knew they would be completely safe. "Okay, let's go you bilge rats! Move! Over the side and into the water," the captain shouted down the open circular hatchway. Some of the fifty-two crew members were on deck already, but the remainder streamed out from down below with smiles on their faces. Some wore old shorts, some underwear, others nothing at all, which only amplified the paleness of their white northern skin. The ones that could swim went straight over the side, the more cautious crew members went forward along the deck to the bow before they jumped over and splashed their way to the beach. Most of the men went ashore, but not all. A gun crew was posted just in case, as well as a lookout. And then there was Leitender Ingenieur Kreigal, the stubborn second engineer who came up on deck in his greasy overalls and undershirt, smoking his foul-smelling Russian cigarettes, and who was not in the least bit interested in getting wet.

Weiss had to be virtually ordered to take his swim first, which he did reluctantly, but returned quickly so the skipper himself could have a decent spell ashore. Diving over the side, Nils Albrecht drifted under the surface, suspended in the warm, translucent water, and for just a few brief moments allowed himself to forget where he was and what he was doing. He swam the few meters towards shore, and finding the bottom with his feet, floated in the shallows. He watched his crew ashore, running and laughing and diving and splashing like teenagers, which in fact many of them were. He waded ashore and walked down the beach, feeling the warm sand between his toes, until at the far end he sat down next to Klausterman, the chief engineer. "I don't think you will find this exercise described in the 'Submariner's Handbook'," the captain said, "but it's good for the men to have a break."

"Yes sir. After a month inside the old tin can it's good to be able to get out in the fresh air away from the farts and sauerkraut and diesel fumes and feel the sun and stretch the legs. You can see the men are enjoying the break, sir."

The captain lay back in the warm sand, closed his eyes and let the sun's soothing rays wash over him. He let his mind float away to that soft, peaceful void where there was nothing but tranquillity. "You know, Stefan, I think I'll just stay here for the rest of the war like a castaway. You all can take the ship. Just leave me some beans and potatoes, like a maroon. I'll live off the sea. Perhaps you could give me a gun and a few bullets so I could shoot a goat or two. And when the war is over you can just come back and pick me up. What do you think?"

"It's a good idea, sir, but I don't know how the high command might take it. They may look at it in a slightly different light than you. With all due respect, sir," Klausterman said in mock seriousness.

"Yes, I suppose you are right," he sighed. "Those fellows in charge are fairly rigid in their world view." His mind drifted off towards a nearby island, and his old friend who lived there. He wondered how this war might be affecting him.

"Well it's been nice to be able to take a few hours off anyway sir. I'm sure the men appreciate it."

Albrecht propped himself up on his elbows. The sun was canting into the western sky. It was time to return to the ship. "I guess it's time we get back to the real world, Obermachinist Klausterman," he said, eventually pushing himself up onto his feet. "Round up the rest of those fellows and let's get back on board."

He watched the blonde, muscular engineer jog down the beach and begin to relay the order. By ones and two's the men slowly dove back into the water and swam back to the waiting submarine, followed at last by the Kapitanleutnant.

U-112 slipped out of the bay and turned north. The captain and the mate joined the navigator at his small chart table. "Plot a course ten miles to the west of St. Vincent, Mr Pobanz," the captain ordered his navigator. "The plan is to concentrate on blocks of areas and slowly work our way north. We don't have much to worry about from the British or the Americans, so we just need to be smart, find the richest shipping lanes and inflict maximum damage. Our job is to sink enemy shipping, and I don't care where we do it. We have twenty fish left on board, and by the time we return home I want our quiver to be empty."

It didn't take them long to find what they were looking for. It was close to ten o'clock that night, and U-112 steamed slowly north. The water was glassy calm in the lee of St. Vincent. It was a balmy, starry night with no moon. A pod of dolphins could be heard blowing next to the ship as they played in its phosphorescent wake. To windward, a few lights glimmered faintly from the sleeping island of St. Vincent. And then they picked out a ship on the horizon.

"Lights sir, off the port bow, bearing three-five-zero degrees and steering south," one of the lookouts said.

On the bridge all glasses turned in that direction. The captain quickly issued orders to intercept. An air of excitement shot through the crew as the call to battle stations was given. Their speed was increased. In the dark water alongside, the fluorescent tracks of the darting dolphins disappeared as quickly as they had come, as if through some sixth sense they perceived what was to follow. Below decks the crew moved smoothly to their allotted positions. Range and bearings were continually called out. Torpedo tubes were flooded and loaded. A firing solution was calculated. Within minutes the well-oiled war machine was fully armed and locked on to its target.

The *Golden Orb*, a ship of eight thousand tons, sailed unwittingly south, bound for Trinidad. On board the crew were peacefully following their normal routine. The off watch were sleeping in their bunks. The chief engineer was in the engine room monitoring his dials and gauges and temperatures. The mate had just made himself a cup of coffee and relieved the captain of his watch. No one saw the track of the deadly torpedo. It was a perfect shot and caught the ship dead amidships.

On board U-112 six pairs of binoculars were trained on their target. Albrecht anxiously checked his stop watch as he timed the torpedo, but no one was ready for what happened next. The missile penetrated through the hull and exploded, and as it did so set off a second almighty explosion, the shockwave from which almost knocked Albrecht and his men over as they watched. The submarine was more than eight hundred meters away, and yet if felt as if they were only fifty. The tanker was fully loaded with a cargo of aviation fuel. The crew on board were instantly incinerated, and in a matter of moments the *Golden Orb* had all but disappeared. Except for some burning flames on the water, there was no evidence the ship had ever existed.

Aboard U-112 there was stunned silence. "I don't think we need to look for any survivors...they would have heard that explosion in Barbados!" Albrecht finally said, lowering his glasses. "Turn hard to starboard and steer zero-six-zero degrees, Mr Weiss. I want to split the channel here in half and see what is out to windward."

"Aye, sir; altering course to zero-six-zero degrees," answered the mate.

The course change was made and U-112 carried out through the St. Lucia Channel into the open Atlantic Ocean and the shipping lanes running between Trinidad and Barbados. Kapitanleutnant Nils Albrecht knew where he was going. Even though several years had passed since he had last been in the West Indies, it was as if he had never left.

The following morning, just before sunrise, the navigator was on the bridge with his sextant. After noting the altitude of his five stars and the exact time the shots were taken, Karl Pobanz carefully clambered down through the circular hatchway. He made his way to his chart station, put his sextant away, and began the methodical procedure of calculations that would eventually determine their position.

The watch changed at six, and as captain Albrecht passed his navigator he peaked over his shoulder as he plotted the second of his lines of position. "So, where are we, Carl?" he asked as he sipped a cup of coffee.

"I haven't plotted all of my sights, but we are roughly here, about thirty miles southwest of Barbados, sir," the navigator answered, pointing out a small cross on the chart.

"Good. Let's see what Lady Luck brings our way today." It was decided they would proceed in a south-easterly direction, altering their course every three hours to starboard so as to turn a rough circle in twenty four hours.

The day passed without the sign of a ship anywhere. After sunset their new position was plotted and the submarine was fifty miles to windward of the island of Grenada. Here they began the northerly arc of their patrol. Again the night passed without sighting a ship. Sunrise found the captain on the bridge with the four lookouts, along with Scherer, the second mate. As the sun rose, the faint outlines of islands to the west could be seen. "Those are the Grenadines are down there, Tomasz. You saw a little piece of the place the other day when we went for a swim. It is a place I would love to go back to one day."

"So you obviously have spent some time there, sir," the mate said.

"Yes, in a past life," he said, pausing as if he were momentarily transported back to those golden days. "Weiss and I ran a small freighter through these islands for several years. What a time we had! Savannah, Key West, New Orleans, Havana, Kingston, San Juan...we saw them all, from the Gulf of Mexico to South America and almost every island in between. But you want to know my favourite spot? It's a little island not far from here. We might even catch sight of it this morning. It's called Petite Silhouette. There's an Australian chap who I met in Puerto Rico who lives there. Builds and owns trading schooners. Quite a fellow. He was even a rum runner back in the old days. I pulled him off the reef once after a hurricane. Now there's a story I could tell you one day!" Albrecht raised his glasses to his eyes and searched the horizon to the west. "Yes! There it is! You can just make out the shape of what they call the 'Ship's Prow'. It's a shame we couldn't just drop in and say hello."

"Somehow I don't think that would be advisable sir," Scherer said half seriously. Nothing this man did would surprise him. "We have other fish to fry, so to speak."

"Yes, Tomasz, unfortunately you are right. Nostalgia is an impractical emotion, isn't it?"

That afternoon, U-112 steamed in a northerly direction, and at sunset turned back to the west through the St. Lucia channel, having had no success in their patrol to windward. Just before nightfall the jagged, towering peaks of the Pitons could be spotted on the southwest corner of St. Lucia. Knowing the waters inshore to be miles deep, Albrecht rounded the corner close to shore as his ship turned north again, until at around ten o'clock the lights of a freighter were picked up. On the bridge binoculars focused intently on this potential target.

"She is bound east, Kapitan, towards the land," first mate Weiss commented. "She must be entering Castries Harbour."

"Yes, it seems so. I don't think we can get there before she slips inside. But that gives me an idea," the captain replied, dropping his glasses. "As you would recall, we went into Castries several times on the *Kate*. I know it's a tricky entrance, and there's not a large amount of area inside in which to turn around, but we could do some damage if we worked our way inside," he smiled.

The pair trained their glasses back on to the well-lit tanker and watched as she disappeared into the narrow entrance of the harbour. "I agree it is not without risk, but it certainly would cause a few more headaches for our English friends," Weiss said. "If Trinidad was not ready for us, I doubt St. Lucia would be either."

"Good – make preparations! It will be yet another daring raid by the Vikings of U-112!"

It was after midnight when the U-boat stealthily entered Castries Harbour on the British island of St. Lucia. They entered on the surface, slowly following the flashing channel markers which lead them through the narrow, winding passage into the broad basin of the brightly lit harbour, where two ships were berthed alongside the commercial wharf. From their position on the bridge, the German raiders could read the name *Lady Nelson* on the bow of the tanker and *Umtata* on the smaller cargo freighter. "We will target the tanker first with our bow tubes, then fire at the freighter with our stern tubes as we leave," Albrecht advised the mate.

Slowly the U-boat was turned until it had the British tanker in its sights. "Fire number one! Fire number two! Turn hard to port!" The torpedos sped on their way and the submarine turned a wide arc until its stern was pointing directly at the smaller of the two ships. The first torpedo struck its target, followed quickly after by the report of the second. The explosions reverberated across the water and up the hillside of the sleepy harbour, followed by a massive fireball and numerous other detonations as the fire reached the storage tanks filled with oil aboard the tanker. The crew on the bridge paused a moment, caught up in their handiwork, before the captain refocused. The stern was now pointed directly at the freighter astern of them. "Fire three and four!" he ordered, and the next two fish were on their way. It did not take long for them to reach their target, and the *Umtata* was instantaneously turned into a towering inferno.

"All ahead one third! Steer two-eight-five degrees!" the captain ordered.

The ship began to pick up speed, their rolling bow wave disrupting the black mirror-like surface of the calm harbour which reflected the flames and explosions of the ships behind. And then, without warning, U-112 came to a shuddering halt. Men were thrown forward. Utensiles flew off shelves. Pots and pans tumbled from the galley stove. They were aground! "Full astern!" the captain ordered to the engine room. "Give her all you have Mr Klausterman!"

Just at that moment a shell whistled over their heads and exploded in the water, followed soon after by another. A shoreside gun had picked them out and was firing upon them. Water streamed past the sides of the sub as the two propellers churned at full revolutions in an effort to pull them loose. Another plume shot into the air, this time much closer as the gunners began to find their range. "We're sitting ducks here! We need to get off, and fast!" Albrecht shouted to the mate. "Turn hard to port, then hard to starboard! Hard to port...and again to starboard!"

This manoeuvre slowly began to have an effect. The stern began to slew one way and then the other. Another shell burst alongside. Gradually the ship began to move backwards, and then with a sudden release she broke free of the bottom. "Rudders amidships! Astern one half!" Another fountain of water exploded ahead, this time right in the spot where they just had been.

Looking forward, the mate picked out the channel, pointing out the passage. Going ahead, they slowly skirted the edge of the bar they had struck. Another shot landed harmlessly behind. Calmly the captain and mate navigated the submarine out of the harbour. One last vain attempt was made by the gunners ashore, but the shot landed well short of the escaping sub. Astern was a scene of utter devastation as the two ships burned and sank alongside the wharf. The whole of the port of Castries seemed to be on fire. U-112 navigated the balance of the twisting channel perfectly, and once clear of the rocky entrance accelerated to flank speed, heading for the open sea.

The Rendezvous

"Decoded communication for you sir," the radio operator reported, as the captain sat eating breakfast in the wood panelled officer's mess. He accepted the paper, scratching his beard as he read his new orders. After re-reading them he put them down and addressed his waiting subordinates. "Grand Admiral Donitz continues to congratulate us on our successes. It seems we have new orders. We are to enter the port of St. Pierre on the island of Martinique, approaching from the north. At exactly 02:00 hours we should receive a coded signal from the shore. We will reply, and shortly thereafter we will be met by a fishing boat who will deliver a person to us. This person will then give us our next orders." Albrecht raised his eyebrows, surveying his crew. "All very exciting, wouldn't you agree. I suppose we should look at a chart."

Martinique lay twenty miles north of St. Lucia. Albrecht was aware two patrolling British warships were blockading surface vessels from entering or leaving Fort-de-France, but did not believe they were fitted with ASDIC capabilities and therefore wouldn't be hunting submarines. At any rate, he had to be careful. The day was spent making a wide loop to the west and then north, skirting around the patrolling frigates. Studying the chart, it was noted this open, unprotected port sat in a bay on the north-west corner of Martinique. Albrecht knew St. Pierre to be the island's second biggest city, a place made famous at the turn of the century by the devastating volcanic eruption of Mount Pele that wiped out the entire population of that bustling port but for one man, who survived only because he was locked up in jail. The approaches were extremely deep right up to the shore. They would be able to easily enter the wide open bay submerged, surfacing only when it was needed to make their signal.

U-112 slipped into the island's waters from the Dominica Channel to the north at periscope depth. At 01:00 Albrecht brought his U-boat to the surface with the scattered lights of St. Pierre roughly a kilometre away. The sea was glassy and unsettled, a confused surface of black quicksilver. Low dark clouds hung over the small port. A drizzle of rain fell. At exactly 02:00 a bright light flashed seaward from the shore and U-112 sent their quick reply. Not long afterwards, the sound of a single cylinder diesel engine echoed across the water, and an open wooden fishing boat was soon alongside. A solitary figure in civilian clothing awkwardly passed a suitcase over to a seaman waiting on deck, and then climbed aboard. Moments later the man was standing before the submarine's captain. "Kapitan-Zur-See Hienrik Scheck reporting, Herr Kapitan! Heil Hitler!" he saluted enthusiastically.

"Heil Hitler," Albrecht replied with slightly less exuberance. The submarine quietly departed the bay, setting a northerly course.

Kapitanleutnant Albrecht stood on the conning tower with binoculars hanging from his neck, taking the sunrise watch, when joined by his latest crew member. "Ah, it is good to put to sea again! It's such a pleasure to get out from behind a desk and become part of the real war, if even for a short time," Scheck said as he strolled forward to peer over the handrail, taking in a deep breath of the early morning air. His uniform was freshly starched and crisp, his hat like new. "This is the life, isn't it Kapitan? Charging through the waves on the hunt for the enemy! What a life you lead! You and your men just take all of this for granted, but let me assure you, every deskbound Kreigsmarine officer would trade places with you in an instant! What an honour to be here, leading the vanguard of our Fuhrer's expedition into the New World!"

U-112 ploughed through the Caribbean swell, traveling north at its cruising speed of fourteen knots. The lookouts scanned the horizon for any sign of shipping, as well as the off chance of attack from allied warplanes. Earlier that morning, Albrecht had received his orders. They were to proceed to the island of St. Martin, where Scheck was to connect with a local agent. "The Kreigsmarine wants to assess the potential of establishing a re-supply base in these islands. We don't believe Martinique, or any of the French territories for that matter, is a possibility because of the taciturn nature of Admiral Robert, the islands' leader. He is under pressure from the Americans, who have threatened invasion and occupation if he is seen to be accommodating us. On the other hand, he has been given instruction from France to extend diplomatic courtesies to the Reich. The Americans have been allowed to post an observer on the island, and our government has been permitted the most basic of official representation. We believe in the long run, however, that this situation in Martinique can be used to our own advantage. If we can make the Allies think we are trying to establish ourselves on the island, it might distract them while we in fact are busy somewhere else. Our overseas network has uncovered a certain Austrian national, who is a leading businessman on the Dutch side of St. Martin. This man maintains he has the wherewithal to manage a clandestine base in that area. I have been given the task of liaising with him and determining if this is indeed a possibility. Your orders are to deliver me to this meeting."

The submarine continued northward, passing to leeward of the islands of Dominica and Guadeloupe, whose dark silhouettes stood out against the sparkling sea and blue morning sky. The watches changed, but Herr Scheck remained on deck. He himself had commandeered a pair of binoculars, and was in constant search of enemy shipping. He was eager to see some action. "Where are they, Kapitan? Since I was handed my orders I have been looking forward to this moment! I may not have the chance to see action again, and now this plethora of targets you previously had before you has chosen to go into hiding. I must have the good fortune to at least be a part of one successful attack!"

Albrecht stared quietly at his over-zealous guest. "Take the con, Mr Weiss," Albrecht said, turning to the first mate. "I'm going below for a cup of coffee."

The captain was followed down the steel ladder into the control room by the second mate, Mr Scherer. "Wait until he gets a few depth charges up his arse, and then ask him what he thinks," Scherer muttered quietly, and they both shared a chuckle.

Towards midday the captain was back on deck, still accompanied by Scheck, who was becoming more frustrated with the passing of every hour, when the shout rang out.

"Sails ho, bearing zero-two-zero degrees!"

Albrecht raised his binoculars from around his neck and trained them on the smudge of white on the horizon. "It looks to be a local schooner," he uttered eventually, lowering his glasses. He said nothing further and they continued on their course, which would take them well to the west of the sailing vessel.

Scheck dropped his glasses. His face lit up with excitement, and for several awkward minutes he waited anxiously for the captain to give the order to alter his course. At last he could take it no longer. "Excuse my asking, Kapitan, but what is your intention? Are you not going to attack this enemy ship?"

Albrecht stared at Scheck for several moments before answering. "No, I'm not. We will continue on our present course. That schooner represents no threat to the Fatherland."

"I'm sorry Kapitan, but with respect I must most strenuously disagree!" Scheck replied vehemently. "As you would well know, your orders are to attack all enemy shipping where possible. This is an easy target. It is your duty to alter your course and destroy the enemy."

"I should point out you, Herr Scheck, that I am in charge of this vessel, and it is my decision to maintain our present course. I do not wish to discuss the matter further."

"I do not deny you are Kapitan of this vessel, Albrecht, but I would like to emphasize that my rank is superior to yours in every other way. I cannot command you to attack, but it is my duty to point out your refusal to do so is in blatant disregard to your standing orders and a gross dereliction of duty. Your failure to engage the enemy will be reported to the highest authority. You have a good record, Kapitan Albrecht. Do not allow this oversight to spoil it."

Deep down Nils Albrecht knew Scheck was correct, and if this incident was reported there would be serious repercussions. As much as he wanted to stand his ground and ignore this harmless craft, he knew he had no alternative but to attack. "Steer to the new heading of zero-two-zero degrees," the captain ordered. "Mr

Scherer, summon your crew and prepare the deck guns for action." The orders were passed on, and within minutes the submarine had altered its course and was bearing down on the hapless sailing vessel. What happened next was something the captain of U-112 would never be proud of. As the submarine ranged up alongside, the order was given to fire shots across the bow of the old schooner. After dropping her worn and heavily patched headsails, the rag-tag West Indian crew stood innocently at the rail facing the fearsome war machine, the captain watching on from alongside his wheel. On board the submarine, Albrecht stared at these wretched souls, waiting like deer caught in a vehicle's headlights. These hard working men had struggles enough with life. *They did not deserve this*, Albrecht thought. He probably even had met some of them in years gone by.

The gun crew waited for the order to fire. The lookouts watched their captain out of the corners of their eyes. And still he hesitated. The moment dragged on, and still there was no order. "What are you waiting for, Kapitan?" Scheck prodded. "Give the order!"

Another long moment passed before the captain finally gave in. Nils Albrecht took a deep breath. Taking up the bullhorn he addressed the helpless crew in his best English. "Kapitan, you and your crew have five minutes to leave your ship. Then we open fire!"

The message was understood. The crew frantically threw their lifeboat over the side and climbed into it – all except the white-capped captain who remained steadfastly at the helm. The men in the lifeboat hung on alongside, obviously attempting to get the old man to join them.

"I advise you to leave your ship, Kapitan! We will begin firing in one minute!" Albrecht warned. Still the man refused to leave the wheel. "Stupid bastard! Why won't he abandon ship?" Albrecht cursed aloud. He tried once more but the result was the same. Finally, he commanded the crew in the lifeboat to let go and clear away from the vessel. They followed orders and began to drift swiftly away from her.

Nils Albrecht took a deep breath. "Commence firing, Mr Scherer." The 105mm forward mounted deck cannon roared, its deadly shells tearing apart the defenceless schooner. In a matter of minutes the simple wooden vessel was blown to pieces. Scherer called a halt to the destruction as the heavily laden schooner disappeared rapidly from view, leaving only debris floating where moments earlier there had been a living ship. The wooden lifeboat, with six men in it, was soon lost in the large swell as it drifted rapidly away to the west.

"Resume your previous heading, Mr Weiss," Albrecht ordered. "You will find me in my cabin if you need me."

At precisely 22:00 hours, a signal light flashed through the darkness, and from the bridge of the U-boat a response was sent back. The submarine was hove-to in the lee of the island of St. Martin, a half mile off shore. Through coded messages sent back to their base in Lorient, this meeting had been set up between U-112 and the small cargo ship *Tor*. Slowly the two ships drew closer to each other. The freighter's boat was brought alongside and rowed across to the sub, where Albrecht and Scheck clambered aboard and were shunted back to the *Tor*.

The two men were met on deck by the freighter's captain. "Welcome aboard my humble ship, gentlemen," he said; "Kapitan Gunther Marstrom, at your service. May I introduce you to Herr Wolfgang Kruger, our local agent here in St. Martin?" Marstrom then led them through the wheelhouse to the small wardroom aft, where the men sat down around the captain's table.

Marstrom was tall and wiry, with curly dark hair and a scruffy black beard. His mechanic's hands were greasy to the quick of his broken fingernails. His most distinguishing feature, however, was he only had one functioning eye. The other stared off in a fixed, oblique direction; a milky veil bleaching it of all colour. Kruger was a stocky, barrel-chested bear of a man with powerful, tattooed forearms, a bushy red beard and an aggressive, loud nature. Albrecht had met men such as these many times before, and it didn't take long for him to work them out; one an opportunist who lived off the scraps the world threw out, the other a taker of as much as he could get his hands on, with no loyalty to anything other than himself. These were hungry men. Useful perhaps, but also dangerous.

The meeting went on into the early hours of the morning. Scheck pressed his specifications upon the shifty Kruger, who countered with confidence that he and his confederate could be relied upon to supply the Kriegsmarine with whatever they desired, for the right price that is. To Albrecht's great relief, it was decided that Scheck would leave the submarine and stay on with the ruffian Kruger. Albrecht smiled to himself as he pondered how the officious Nazi would find doing business with these two desperados, and visa-versa.

"Everything go well, sir?" Weiss asked as the captain climbed back aboard.

"It all went perfectly. We couldn't have left our friend Herr Scheck in the hands of two better people. He might just get this supply base up and running. That is, if those two pirates don't kill him first!"

The Mission

On a typically calm, humid Trinidadian morning, the *Roulette* motored north through the Bocas and set sail, loaded down with a cargo of building materials for the new US airbase being constructed in St. Lucia. Harry Iverson and the *Vagabond* had sailed the day before with an additional crew member - Gregoire Deslisle. They were sailing straight to St. Lucia, where they would wait for the schooner at the hidden hurricane hole of Marigot Bay.

On the way north, the *Roulette* had to detour to Petite Silhouette to pick up the whaleboat *Antipodes*, which would be needed for the operation in Martinique. Jack pushed the schooner hard, and twenty-two hours after leaving the Bocas they were tying up alongside the wharf in Frigate Bay. While the crew dragged the whaleboat out from under the trees and launched her into the harbour, Jack went home.

"Well dis is surely a surprise, Jackson McLeod. I wasn't expecting you home for a few weeks yet," Jasmine said, watching her husband walk up the hill to the house with Dawson and Earl in tow.

"Normally we wouldn't have stopped at all, but we needed to pick up the whaleboat." Turning to his two crew members, he directed them to the back of the house where the whaleboat's rigging and sails were stowed. "We have a good cargo on board for the US Navy in St. Lucia, but they are in a hurry for it so we aren't staying long. In fact we'll be leaving within the hour."

"So you don't even have time to stop an' see de children at lunchtime?"

"No Jaz, I'm sorry. It's the same for all of the crew. We're pushin' on." He gave his wife a quick hug and a kiss. "I'll see you in a couple of weeks."

"Okay, you go on den. I know dere's more to dis story than you're lettin' on. I can just tell. I wasn't born yesterday, you know. But all-you go on an' do what you have fo' do!"

"Don't worry – I'll see you soon." Jack waved and jogged back down the hill behind his two crewmen, who trotted ahead with the boat's rig over their shoulders. Not long afterwards, the schooner rounded Gunnery Point, hoisted her sails and set off north again, towing the faithful *Antipodes* behind.

Castries Harbour was still in chaos weeks after the German submarine attack. As the *Roulette* motored slowly through the winding channel, the crew stood on deck and gawked in awe at the wreckage, having just left a similar scene behind in Trinidad. The basin of Castries was a much smaller area than the vastness of the Gulf of Paria, and the two sunken ships and the small tugs and barges attending to them seemed to occupy a large majority of it.

Local trading vessels had been shunted to one end of the commercial dock, and Jack manoeuvred his schooner to that area, tying up alongside a rugged Bequia schooner. The *Endurance* was well known throughout the islands. She was a beamy, heavily built vessel, renowned for her cargo-carrying capacity. She was owned, built and run by the three Sims brothers, who all had reputations as extremely hard workers. Jack had always liked this vessel and her crew, and got along well with the brothers, especially Lincoln Sims, who served as her master.

"Good afternoon, Lincoln," Jack said as they tied up alongside their new neighbour. "And I thought Trinidad was a mess!"

"Yes, mon – it's hard to know if anyting safe anymore. I've heard dat ships're bein' sunk all about de place. And it's not just steamboats dem Germans is sinkin' now! Did you hear about ol' Augustus an' de *Guiding Star?*" Captain Sims asked.

"No, I didn't. What happened? I saw him in Trinidad not long ago."

"Yes, man – it's terrible news. Seems like he was caught up by a submarine under Montserrat on his way to St. Kitts. A Carriacou sloop found one o' he crew floatin' in dey lifeboat. All de rest o' dem is gone, even Gus himself. Dem boys sailed in here a little over a week ago an' dropped de boy off. Dey couldn't stay as dey had a load of bubal in, so you'd understand why dey didn't want to be talkin' wit' any police. De boy was three quarters dead an' was taken up to de hospital. Me an' Edwin went up to see him two days ago. It looks like he's goin' to be in dere for some time, but he'll be alright." The crew of the *Roulette* had gathered around near the two captains and were all muttering oaths of disbelief as they listened to the news. "We didn't get much out o' him, but what he did say didn't sound good. De boy say de submarine just motor up and shot dem to pieces with de deck gun. Dey did barely gi' dem de chance to climb into de lifeboat. Word is ol' Gus wouldn't leave he vessel an' went down wit' her. He did love dat ol' schooner in truth. It was he life's blood!"

There was a stunned silence as Jack and his crew took in this information. Augustus McClelland was a humble, good natured man who was liked by everyone in the trade. "That sure puts a new light on things," Jack finally said. "As if this trade weren't hard enough! Now we have to worry about submarines! It's like swimming with sharks in the water – you never know when one might come up to tear your guts out!"

The Bequia captain silently stared over the bulwarks, shaking his head. "Man, most o' dese fellahs don't even know where Germany be, let alone have any idea why dey would want to do somethin' like dis!" the skipper said, gesturing to the destruction surrounding them. "Dis ting don' make no sense! Good seamanship, a brave conscience and a little bit o' luck will get a person t'rough most tings, even a hurricane. Dis ain't have no rhyme or reason to it a-tall."

Because the *Roulette* was carrying a military consignment, they were directed to another area of the wharf where her shipment was to be discharged straight away. The US Army quartermaster there filled Jack in on the details of the attack on Castries harbour. Again he concluded that the captain of the attacking sub must have been into the harbour before. But was it the same U-boat that attacked Trinidad? Looking at the time frame it well could have been. And what about the tragic sinking of his old friend's schooner? How many of these subs were actually in these waters, and if this were only the beginning, what would it be like in days ahead?

There wasn't much time to ponder these questions because they were working to Army time now. Jack and his crew began discharging their cargo straightaway, and it was well past midnight before they were finished. At first light after a quick cup of tea they were off, letting go their lines and motoring out of the channel in the midst of a rain squall, the heavy grey clouds hanging low over the island's mountainous interior. Their destination was the natural hurricane hole of Marigot Bay, five miles to the south of Castries. Local legend told of how the bay was once the hideout of buccaneers as the anchorage was completely obscured from seaward, and how one wily pirate escaped from the British frigates hunting him by using coconut fronds to camouflage his masts as palm trees.

The *Roulette* motored through the narrow channel to find the *Vagabond* anchored near a sandy spit of land dividing the bay in two, the yacht's topsides reflecting a singular solitary white against the calm, murky dimness of the water and the muddy green of the mangrove lined shore. There was not another soul in sight. The schooner turned and dropped her anchor, the splash sending a flock of white egrets soaring off low across the water, and it wasn't long before the two boats were nestled alongside each other.

"Come aboard, Captain! You're right on time!" Harry Iverson said as he welcomed the skipper aboard. "How did everything go in Castries? We were there two days ago and saw what damage the Germans inflicted. It will take months to get the harbour back to normal. Jerry surely has made his mark!"

"We got our cargo off quick enough, despite the confusion inside of there. And what a mess!" Jack replied. "I found out yesterday the swine are even targeting local schooners! An old friend of mine was sunk off of Montserrat. And the most worrying part about it is that they're just getting started!"

"We really will be up against it if they decide to come here in force," Harry said. "Anyway, there is no use getting worked up about things that are out of our control. Let's see if we can rustle up a cup of tea and sit down and work through exactly what it is we have to do."

Val brought the tea and they sat down around the polished mahogany table and got to work.

While Jack and Harry sorted out the final details, the rest of the crew was busy getting the whaleboat ready, as well as making final preparations to the wooden crate containing the radio, weapons, and explosives they were to deliver to 'Fauconnier' and the Martinique resistance. At midday, Jono had cooked up one of his typically hearty meals, and so just after lunch the *Roulette* motored out of Marigot Bay.

Sailing along the St. Lucia shore into the late afternoon, Martinique stood clearly visible across the channel to the north. The sunset quickly faded into darkness. Jack gave the order to ease sheets and the schooner reached off toward the mountainous island twenty miles away. For the nervous crew, it seemed to take forever to sail the few miles to their drop-off point mid-channel. "At least you got a solid breeze to sail in wit'," Zeph said, as he turned the schooner's wheel.

"Yes, the breeze looks good. Let's just hope it holds up under the land," Jack said, checking his pocket watch. The crew were sitting in close proximity to the wheel, and all were watching the captain. "Okay Zeph, that's it. Bring her up into the wind. Let's get the jib and fores'l off her, and prepare to hove-to."

The crew moved quickly into action, and within minutes the sails were down and secured. Zeph spun the wheel and she turned briskly as her mainsail was hauled in, and when the staysail was backed, the schooner stopped all forward momentum and was now drifting quietly, stemming the lumpy oncoming seas as the whaleboat was hauled up alongside from astern. "Listen, you know what to do," Jack said, turning to his mate. "You wait for us in Marigot Bay as we discussed, and if for some reason we don't turn up, you follow Harry's lead. God spare life, we'll see you sometime tomorrow afternoon."

Zeph reached out and gripped the captain's hand. "Good luck, Skip," he said solemnly. "We'll see you tomorrow, certain sure." The *Antipodes* waited on the lee side of the schooner as her crew – comprised of Earl, Gilbert and Dawson, as well as Rabbit, Gregoire and Jack, – jumped lightly aboard. The trickiest part was passing across the heavy wooden crate in the lumpy, mid-channel swell. When they were all in and settled, the bowline was cast off and the whaleboat drifted quickly away. The mast was stepped, the rudder hung, and within minutes the sails were set and trimmed and they were off, sailing into the darkness. Glancing astern, they watched the *Roulette* disappear into the gloomy night.

Jumping aboard the open, twenty-six foot, double-ended *Antipodes* in the middle of the Martinique channel at night in a strong lee tide was a challenge, but for Jack and his crew it was done without a second thought. Since Gregoire and Rabbit were unfamiliar with the boat, they stayed out of harm's way as the others went about their business of getting her rigged and sailing. Once they were under way, everyone settled themselves onto the windward rail. Gilbert took hold of the mainsheet and Earl the jib. The seas, which were hardly noticed from the stable deck of the schooner, seemed much larger now. The wind and swell forced the waves into steep, ugly pyramids and deep troughs. Every now and then foam from a breaking wave would roar towards them, and Jack would have to do his best to steer the small boat around the rolling white-water. After a hectic hour of negotiating these difficult conditions, they began to fall into the lee of the island. Gradually they worked their way out of the channel and were soon sailing in the much flatter, protected waters underneath the land.

There was no moon and the shadow of Martinique loomed ahead. They sailed on into the darkness, every pair of eyes on the lookout for the slightest sign of a patrol boat. Before long they were reaching along below the island's low rocky bluffs, skirting a series of small bays and inlets. Ahead the three hundred foot monolithic spire of Diamond Rock seemed to spring from out of the darkness, disappearing astern just as quickly as they slipped quietly between the towering rock and the mainland a half mile away.

The breeze along the shore was light and fluky and they had to work hard trimming the sails through the shifts, but soon enough the broad Baie du Fort-de-France appeared before them, and with it came a much stronger wind, sometimes in violent gusts, as it funnelled down between the island's lofty interior mountains. Once into the steady breeze, the whaleboat heeled over and bounded away, a streak of phosphorescence trailing astern. The waves were not large, but they were short and choppy, and every now and then one would slap against the side, showering the crew with spray, which was greeted with muted curses.

Lights on the far shore shone like stars in the night, the largest collection being the town itself tucked up in the top corner of the bay. The whaleboat sailed towards the western extremity, where no lights were visible at all. As they drew near, the breeze came more from behind and whipped them around the corner. Within moments, the wind died almost completely as it was blocked off by the towering mountains above, and soon they were coasting across flat water as calm as a millpond. Without a word being said, the crew sprang into action. Dawson darted forward and rolled up the jib, Gilbert and Earl dropped the bamboo sprit and tied up the mainsail, the rigging was let go and the mast was unstepped and laid down in the boat. The oars were silently extended, and with Rabbit in the bow as a guide, Jack quietly steered them into the rocky cove.

While in Martinique a few months previously on the *Vagabond,* Rabbit had used his time to survey the shoreline in the proximity of Fort-de-France, and in doing so had come across this little cove, known locally as Petite Anse. "One thing I know is a smuggler's cove when I does see one, and man, dis one's as good as dey come," he had told Harry at the time. "Dere's a small little beach at the head of de bay where dey does haul up dey fishin' boats, an' dey's nothin' but rocks on de two sides leading in. Dere ain't so much as a fisherman's shack anywhere around. De main road is about a quarter mile away, and dere's only a narrow little track dat leads up through de rocks to it. It's quiet and out o' de way, but close enough to town to be handy."

As the bow of the whaleboat touched the sand, Rabbit jumped over into the knee deep water, followed by Gregoire. The oars were quietly shipped and the rest of the crew were quickly over the side, hauling the boat partially up onto the sand. At this point each man knew what they had to do. Rabbit and Gregoire jogged off the beach and up into the rocks to find a suitable place to bury the crate. Dawson moved down the beach in one direction and Gilbert the other to act as lookouts. When the pair of them whistled the okay, Earl and Jack pulled the wooden crate out of the boat. Gripping the rope handles, they carried the box across the sand and into the rocks. Following a faint whistle they found Rabbit and Gregoire digging a hole in the sand between the boulders. They lowered the crate into the hole and covered it up, then placed a couple of large rocks on top and did their best to clean up the spot and make it look undisturbed.

"Okay lads, you are on your own now," Jack whispered to the pair. "You know where you're going and what you have to do. If we don't hear from you over the radio to the contrary, we'll be back here at this same time a week from now. Good luck."

They all shook hands and moved off in opposite directions; Gregoire and Rabbit up the track towards town, and the others back across the beach. Shoving the whaleboat into the calm water the crew took up the oars and rowed silently out of the cove, and once clear stood up the rig, set the sails and catching the steady breeze disappeared as silently as they had come.

171

Les Maquis Caraïbes

The street was bustling with mid-morning shoppers as Philippe Javert inserted the key into the front door of Chez Francine. As he pulled it open he was approached by a bespeckled businessman typically attired in white tropical suit and hat. "Pardon monsieur – are you open for business, or am I too early?" the gentleman inquired in his regional patois. "On such a bloody hot morning it might just be about time for a petit punch."

As the stranger spoke Philippe tried to identify the accent. Where was it from? Isles des Saints? Guadeloupe? The man had the looks and the bearing of a planter from another of the French Islands, but he just couldn't put his finger on which one. In some way he seemed familiar. "It may take a few moments to open the bar, but you're more than welcome to come in and get out of the sun."

"You're most hospitable, monsieur. Perhaps I'll step across to the tobacconist for some cigarillos first." And so with a tip of his hat the white stranger crossed the road and entered the store opposite. Philippe watched him for a moment before turning into his shady doorway and starting up the worn wooden steps. Half way up he stopped, shaking his head in a perplexed way. He was sure he had met this man before, but where or when he just could not recall.

Philippe and his staff were busy with their normal routine of preparing the restaurant for their hectic lunchtime trade when the stranger came up the stairs and rested himself down on a stool at the varnished mahogany bar. Max stopped polishing glasses and turned to him with his warm smile. "Good morning, monsieur. And what can I get you today?"

"A petit punch, if you please," he said, taking off his wire rimmed glasses and cleaning them with a handkerchief. "It's been a while since I've visited Martinique, and your 'rhum' has always been a favourite of mine."

"Yes... the 'Trois Rivières' is one of our best," the barman said as he poured the man's drink. "And which island is it you come from?"

"Marie-Galante. I own a small distillery there, so I know a little something about rhum."

"In that case, make it on the house, Max," Philippe said, joining them at the bar. "We have our island's reputation to uphold. Did I overhear you are from Marie-Galante?"

"That's correct, monsieur. Here's my card," the stranger replied, removing his wallet from his inside coat pocket. '*Marc Debussy ~ Distiller of Quality Rhum*' it read.

"Interesting...so you are here in Martinique on business I assume, Monsieur Debussy?" Philippe asked, looking again at the card.

"Yes, I'm here to promote my product on your island. We make 'Rhum de l'Alize'. I don't know if you've heard of it. I'd be happy to discuss what I have to offer, if you're interested," he said, sipping his drink like a connoisseur.

"I'm not familiar with your product but I'm always curious to know what is being produced on other islands. If you'd like, we can step into my office to discuss it."

"But of course. I commend you on your punch, my friend," the gentleman said, and after finishing his drink and tipping his hat to the bartender, he collected his battered leather satchel and followed Philippe down the back stairs and through the cool storeroom to his office.

"I have to applaud you on your creole, 'M. Debussy'. You speak it like a native. It's funny, but after all of these years I never knew French Creole was spoken in Barbados," Philippe said with a coy smile as he sat down behind his desk.

"So you see, you does learn somethin' new every day! Care for a cigarillo?" Rabbit retorted in his Bajan accentuated English.

"Merci," Philippe replied as he accepted a smoke and a light. "I must say, your disguise is very good as well, Monsieur Haynes. I was wracking my brain to remember where I'd seen your face before. And then as I watched you at the bar it suddenly came to me. You certainly took me in. One day you have to tell me how it is you come to speak patois so well. But to more immediate questions – you obviously are not on the island to sell rhum. So how long are you here for, and what news do you have from my friend Iverson?"

"I'm here for only one week," Rabbit said, switching back to creole. "When we were here last on the *Vagabond* you said you were willing to help gather information for us. I'm here now to take you up on this offer – if it still stands."

"I gave my word to Harry then, and will reaffirm it now," Philippe asserted with conviction. "This is a time when all real Frenchmen must stand up for the cause, and I'm more than ready to do whatever it takes to help us regain our freedom."

"That's good news indeed. We were counting on you to say that. Much has happened since I was last here with the *Vagabond*, and things are moving quickly. Firstly, you should know that we will be setting you up to communicate by radio directly with Harry, who in turn will pass the information on to British Intelligence. You have also been given the code name 'Fauconnier' to protect your identity. As you would know, the Germans have made a big push into the Caribbean in the last couple of months with their submarines, and the fear is they will try to establish a base somewhere in the islands, perhaps even here. We also presume they're using their mission in Fort-de-France as a centre for their espionage activities in the West Indies. We're hoping you can help put together a team that will become our eyes and ears in Martinique."

"This is what I've been waiting for! I told Harry he could rely on me, and I meant it!" Philippe exclaimed. He lowered his voice and leaned across his desk, a serious look having now come across his usually jovial face. "I've been busy over the last few months, and have found several people in positions that could prove to be very helpful in providing important information."

"It's encouraging that you've started already. I've also come here with an associate whose task will be to establish a small network to work in parallel to your own. We're hoping to instigate an effective resistance movement here in Martinique along the lines of what is happening in France. We're calling this movement 'Les Maquis Caraïbes'."

Philippe smiled. "The more you tell me, the more I like what I am hearing!"

"Good! Now the first thing we need to do is collect this radio I have brought for you…" For the next few minutes the two men discussed the details of the night's operation. It was decided Rabbit would meet Philippe at the back door to his restaurant just after midnight.

"As for accommodation, you can go to the Hotel St. Louis. Just mention my name to the proprietor, Monsieur Doulcet," Philippe said as they walked through the storeroom to the back entrance. They shook hands, Rabbit slipped out the door and walked down the narrow alleyway. Emerging onto the busy Rue Victor Hugo he paused and lit a cheroot, and after a casual look around made his way through the morning shoppers towards the hotel, located just around the corner from the Cathédrale Saint Louis.

"Papa, Papa, look who's here! It's Gregoire!" the girl exclaimed after opening the door and seeing her distant cousin standing at the bottom of the steps.

The girl's father came to the door, a welcoming smile on his face. "Now this is a surprise! Don't just stand there like a beggar – come in my, boy come in."

This was the home of a fisherman. The small, brightly painted wooden house was modest but well kept. Chickens pecked the ground around the cleanly-swept yard; a pair of oars was propped into the crook of a gnarled tamarind tree, to which a goat was also tethered. It had been several years since Gregoire had paid his relations a visit, and they all were glad to see him. Ascending the few steps up to the porch, he shyly entered the house, where he was met by all of the excited family.

After the initial hullabaloo died down, Gregoire asked his Uncle Patrice if he could have a private word. Crossing the yard, they entered his small work shed. Light rushed in through the four open windows, falling upon nets and floats, as well as a work bench covered with tools and shavings. They sat down, facing each other on two roughly hewn stools.

Gregoire knew 'Patu' to be one of the hardest working and most respected figures in the small fishing village of Grand Case. What he had, he built with his own hands; his house, his boats, and his reputation. Gregoire also knew the people of this isolated coastal town to be fiercely independent, and like most fishermen throughout the islands, had little time for government interference in their affairs. If an underground movement were to be started, he reasoned, this would be a good place to begin.

"As much as I enjoy seeing you and your family again, Uncle, I want to say from the outset that I'm not simply paying a social visit. I'm here on serious business. The political situation in the French territories is changing quickly, if my experience in Cayenne is anything to go by. How are things here in Martinique?"

"Not good, my boy, not good at all," Patu said, leaning forward onto his elbows, lines of concern etched onto his dark brow. "People aren't only nervous, they're very afraid. Many village mayors have been arrested, and have yet to be charged. They have been replaced with puppets loyal to this fascist government. No one will say anything for fear of being dragged in front of the magistrate for 'promoting public discord'. Informers are everywhere – there are few people you can trust. It has gotten so bad that schoolchildren are being forced to make the Nazi salute before starting class every day. It is hard to believe these things are really happening in Martinique!"

"It was the same story in Cayenne. There were severe shortages of food, which led to street demonstrations and then riots. The Army crackdown was brutal. The Sécurité Nationale was extremely heavy-handed, arresting anyone who voiced any objection to the new government policies. I found myself on their wanted list and had to make a run for it, escaping to Trinidad just in the nick of time. It was there fortune smiled on me and I was given the chance to try and do something to make a change. Are you interested to hear what I have to say?"

"You know this village, my boy. We've always been an independent lot. In the old days even the tax collectors were afraid to come here. But this is different. There's a strong feeling in the village that something must be done, but we have no idea where to start."

"That's why I'm here, Uncle. Are you ready to take a chance to fight back against these people? And if you are, do you know a handful of others who might want to join us? Think about it and answer carefully. You could be putting not only yourself but your whole family in danger."

Patu slowly raised his wiry frame and moved to the window, where he gazed across his yard towards the sea below. "You know, Gregoire, most people don't appreciate their freedom until it's taken away from them. I don't want to live in fear of what I say or think, and I don't want my children to grow up in such a place either. I'm ready to take a stand, and I know some others who think the same way as I do. The spirit is here...all we need is a little guidance."

"That is what I was hoping to hear," Gregoire said as he stood and shook his uncle's hand. "Welcome to Les Maquis Caraïbes!"

Rabbit sat amongst the rocks surveying the deserted beach in front of him, and as he waited, thought about the training he and Gregoire had gone through in Trinidad. It had been an intensive week and they had learned many things, from the use of firearms to the basics of radio operation. Both men were natural students of their teacher's craft, and learned quickly. "It's important to keep your contact groups as small as possible, and to keep them isolated from each other," Blackwell had instructed them. "Remember, the people you are working with won't be professionals. They might have the best of intentions, but don't count on them keeping quiet if captured and the blowtorch is applied to the soles of their feet." It therefore was important for security reasons, in these early stages at least, to keep Gregoire and Philippe apart until it was absolutely necessary they meet.

For Rabbit, much of what he had been shown was basic common sense. From his point of view, the most critical ingredient in this business could not be taught at all – either a man had it or he didn't. That ingredient was nerve, or 'huevos' as the Spanish would call it. A man who could stay cool and calm and not panic in the face of adversity could work his way out of almost any situation. From what he had seen, both Gregoire and Philippe appeared to be this type of person. What they were doing was very dangerous indeed. The penalty if caught would be torture, a long prison term or even death. His mind went on to the many nights he had spent either on a boat or on the beach doing similar things. This operation was definitely a step up from rum smuggling or gun running. When you landed contraband alcohol, the locals were usually on your side; what you were doing was a benefit to them. Even the police would turn a blind eye – once they received their cut. Here the stakes were much higher, and if things did go wrong the consequences much more severe.

Movement on the water caught his eye, and as he peered into the dark night he could see the approaching shape of a boat as it rowed quietly into the bay, its four long oars pulling it methodically towards the shore until it touched the sand. He watched a dark shape jump over the bow and then push the boat away into the murky night.

Rabbit gave a low whistle. Gregoire crossed the beach to find his partner sitting amongst the rocks waiting for him. Without a word said, they rolled away boulders and scraped away sand until they found solid wood. Like two pirates uncovering hidden treasure in the night, they removed the box and put it aside before refilling the hole and covering it up again. Prying the lid open with his pen knife, Rabbit removed a heavy leather suitcase; Gregoire used a small rock to tap the lid back on. As they waited for the boat to return to shore they quietly discussed their next move.

"So far my cover is good," Gregoire stated. "The people of Grand Case are all related in one way or the other, so to them family's more important than anything else. Patu is a 'patron' of the village, and what he says goes. It seems I'll be safe, at least for the time being. How are things at your end? Does Fauconnier have any information on the Germans and what they're up to?"

"There are some developments in that direction. He has someone working inside the small mission the Nazis have set up here. We hope to get something from them soon. And what about a target? Do you have any names to give me?"

"Yes. The man's name is François Stoddard, a vicious ex-policeman who has somehow managed to become head of the Sécurité Nationale. It appears he handles all of Robert's dirty work, and is the most hated, and most feared, man on the island. The story is that he trusts no one and will do anything to enhance his own power. There is even a rumour he works voodoo, which true or not helps his reputation. I want to know where he lives, how he gets to work, where he drinks – in other words find out as much information as possible about him."

"Ok my friend, I'll ask our man to start working on it immediately. Where do we meet next?" Rabbit asked.

"There's a bar near the waterfront in the port called 'L'Ancre'. Do you know it?"

"Yes, I know it well," Rabbit replied with a smile.

"Good. I'll be there tonight after eight," Gregoire said, as Patu's boat reappeared at the water's edge. They ran the box down and put it aboard. Gregoire jumped in, Rabbit pushed off and within minutes the boat had disappeared into the darkness. As Patu and his men rowed their boat back towards Grand Case, Gregoire unpacked the wooden crate. Inside were six Sten submachine guns and ammunition, as well as a small package of explosives. In the bow of the boat was a large basket of small fish Patu had caught earlier that evening. Emptying the fish into the bottom of the boat, Gregoire placed the crate's canvas-wrapped contents into the basket and then covered them back up with the fish. He next took two large ballast stones from the bottom of the boat, placed them inside of the empty crate and lowered it over the side, where it sank quickly away. The captain then lit the kerosene fishing lamp, matching the scattering of other boats out on the water at this early hour of the morning.

Recrossing the beach, Rabbit picked up his suitcase and headed up the path to the main road. He found the roadster parked underneath a dark stand of trees, where he put the suitcase in the boot before climbing into the passenger's seat. Starting the engine, Philippe turned on his dim headlights, pulled out onto the deserted road, and headed back towards Fort-de-France. As they drove, Rabbit discussed the idea of making the feared Stoddard their first objective. "Your friend is ambitious...he certainly hasn't picked an easy target. Stoddard is a ruthless bastard and is very secretive, keeping well away from the public eye. But every man has his weakness. I'll see what I can find out."

"Yes, see what you can discover. Gregoire is keen to make a statement before we leave. And that's in only six more days."

"I'll do what I can, my friend."

The car soon entered the deserted streets of Fort-de-France. Philippe drove down the alleyway behind his restaurant and parked. He opened the delivery door and Rabbit carried the suitcase inside. After lighting a lamp, Philippe led the way, climbing the steps past the empty restaurant and up one more flight to the top floor of the building. Old tables and chairs and a clutter of other odds and ends from the restaurant filled the room. Rabbit lifted the suitcase onto a table and opened it. Taking out a revolver and ammunition he set them down next to the case. Next he removed the shortwave radio. "Incredible," Philippe said, looking from the radio back to Rabbit. "It is so small and compact!"

"Yes, we were lucky to get this. The American Navy fliers use this model. It's just about the smallest radio transmitter you can get. It has a range of one thousand miles, so you should be able to stay in touch with Iverson at all times. There's a code book, as well as a radio schedule which includes transmission frequencies. I've only been given basic training, but I'll teach you what I know. Our first schedule is tomorrow night so I can be here to help you use it for the first time."

For the next hour Rabbit went over the setup with Philippe, and when they were done they packed it away and stored it inside an old dust-covered wardrobe in the corner of the room. Rabbit picked up the revolver and handed it to Philippe, who held it gingerly in his hand for a moment before dropping it into the pocket of his coat. After locking the door behind them the two men wound their way down the stairs and stepped into the alley. A rain squall had just blown through, and the street was wet, the early morning air still and cool. Rabbit stood at one end of the alley and watched the tail lights of the roadster disappear around the far corner. Turning, he walked back to his hotel through the silent streets to try and get a few hours of sleep. Tomorrow would be another busy day.

It was late morning when Rabbit returned to the Hotel Saint Louis after a breakfast of coffee and croissants at a nearby sidewalk café. Entering the small lobby, he noticed two men lounging in the cane chairs set against the far wall. One man read a newspaper, the other leaned back and squinted at him through the smoke of his heavy French cigarette. "There are two men to see you, monsieur," the manager said warily as he handed him his key, eyes warning of approaching danger.

As Rabbit turned from the desk he found the men standing and waiting behind him. "Pardon monsieur, we are with the Sécurité Nationale," the thinner of the two said. "We would like to see your papers, please."

"But of course," Rabbit said, taking his leather wallet from his inside coat pocket and presenting it to the man. "Is there some sort of problem?"

"It is just a routine check, Monsieur...Debussy," he said with a dismissive smirk. "And what is your business here in Fort-de-France?"

"I've come here from the island of Marie-Galante to promote our fine product. Have you ever tried 'Rhum de l'Alize', monsieur?"

It was as if the thin man did not even hear the question. Slowly he scrutinized the identity papers of Marc Debussy with his ferret-like eyes as his associate took notes. "No monsieur, I can't say I have," he finally answered before folding up the wallet and handing it back.

"That's a shame. I don't mind saying that my rhum is one of the finest in the Caribbean."

"Perhaps. Now could you tell me how long you intend to be in Martinique, Monsieur Debussy?" the man asked, lighting up a cigarette and blowing the smoke into Rabbit's face.

"I hope to complete my business in the next few days. My departure depends on my luck in finding a ship back to

Guadeloupe. Movement between the islands is quite difficult these days, as I'm sure you are aware."

"Yes, these are difficult times indeed. That is why we must be forever vigilant so as to protect our island from corrupting influences. We will without doubt be paying you another visit once we verify this information. Please make sure you don't leave Fort-de-France in the meantime. Good day, monsieur." The two men turned and left, not before saying a few harsh words to the desk manager. As Rabbit climbed the steps to his room he exhaled a sigh of relief. "Always remember to believe your story. You have to live it, to become it," Blackwell had told him during his training in Trinidad. At least his papers had passed the test. He knew now he must be extremely careful, act quickly and cover his tracks. It would take the authorities at least a couple of days to get in contact with the remote island of Marie-Galante to check on his story; in the meantime he must continue to play his part and keep his cool. "Magic is the art of misdirection," Rabbit quietly said to himself as he closed the door behind him.

Le Combat de Coq

'L'Ancre' was one of several bars located in the lively waterfront district of the commercial port. The blockade of Fort-de-France set up by the patrolling British navy had virtually stopped all incoming and outgoing trade to the island, and several foreign freighters lay idly at anchor, having been trapped inside the harbour. The officers and crew from these ships mixed with sailors from the four French naval vessels of Admiral Robert's fleet as well as the regular local crowd to keep the area busy. Rabbit entered the loud, smoky saloon, surveying the scene as he pushed his way through to the bar. A four piece band played meringue from the corner bandstand. Silky women of the night laughed and smoked and mingled with the rowdy crowd. A group of European seamen argued loudly at the bar. Out of the corner of his eye he spotted Gregoire, who was sitting amongst a small group at a corner table.

Rabbit ordered rum and turned to face the band, keeping one eye on the door as he sipped his drink to see if he had been followed. It wasn't long before he was joined by a striking creole woman who asked him for a light. Her curly golden hair fell to her shoulders; her skin the colour of dark chocolate, her almond eyes sharp and piercing. "Bonsoir Yvette," he said, turning to face her. "I was hoping you'd be here tonight. My name, by the way, is Marc Debussy, at least for the moment."

"That's an interesting name," she smiled. "You can tell all me about it later. I'm so happy to see you again! I have to admit it took me some time to recognise you, but you do look cute in glasses. And I love the suit!"

"Thanks…would you like to dance?" he asked, draining his glass.

"I'd love to dance."

The music was hot. The dance floor was crowded and thick with the scent of sweat. As they spun waist to waist Rabbit whispered in her ear. "Do you see the fellow who is watching us from the table in the corner?"

"Do you mean the handsome one wearing the beret?"

"That's the one. His name is Gregoire. After this dance, I want you to take me to his table and introduce me to him as if he's an old friend of yours. Don't ask why. I'll explain later."

The song finished and Yvette smilingly took his hand and led him to the table, greeting Gregoire as if she had known him for years with two traditional pecks on each cheek. "I want you to meet a friend of mine," she said. "Gregoire, this is Marc."

"Nice to meet you," Gregoire replied, playing the game and flashing his electric smile. "Care to join us?" Two more chairs were pulled up. Yvette squeezed close to Rabbit, her hand on his knee, acting as if she had known Gregoire all her life.

"Good evening, I'm Yvette," the girl quickly said, turning towards the two others at the table.

"Oh pardon my poor manners," Gregoire interjected. "Let me introduce two friends of mine; Raul and Francis, Captain and chief engineer of the freighter *Dorado*. These two gentlemen are on an extended 'holiday' here in beautiful Fort-de-France, courtesy of the British Admiralty."

Drinks were then poured for all from the bottle of whiskey on the table, except for Yvette, who preferred champagne. Raul turned in his seat and ordered a bottle from a passing waiter, and soon a bucket with ice was brought, the cork was popped and everyone at the table smiled and cheered. After a few minutes of small talk Rabbit turned and whispered discreetly into Yvette's ear. "Do me a favour – the next song ask Raul to dance, would you?" A few minutes later the band struck up, and she did as requested, taking the tall, good natured captain's hand and leading him to the dance floor. "Excuse me gents, but nature calls," Francis said, pushing himself away from the table, and now the two accomplices had a few minutes to themselves.

"I found out today from one of Fauconnier's contacts that Stoddard never misses the cock fights on Saturday night," Rabbit said, leaning onto the table to address Gregoire. "It's about the only time he relaxes his guard, although I was told he doesn't go anywhere without at least a couple of bodyguards. Do you know the village of Colombier where the Gallodrome is?"

"Yes, I've been there once years ago to see Le Combat de Coq."

"I haven't been there, but Fauconnier thinks this is our best chance to get to Stoddard. I've been working on a plan since this afternoon, but I need to go to Colombier first to check the lay of the land. I've been told that as you enter the village there is an old rhumerie off to the left. I'll meet you there just after dark on Saturday night. Just make sure you are there with your crew and we'll finalise the details then. From Colombier we'll go straight to the beach to meet Jack. As for myself, I need to be careful. I had a visit today from two of Stoddard's thugs, and they are checking on my story. I'm guessing it will be only a matter of time before they come looking for me, so I'll be going to ground very soon. If I'm not at the rhumerie it means the authorities have grabbed me, and then you'll be on your own."

The song finished and the others returned to the table. After a few more drinks Rabbit excused himself, but not before enjoying one more dance with Yvette. "I may need a place to stay tonight. Any ideas?" he whispered.

"I thought you would never ask. Do you still remember where I live?"

"I remember," he nodded as the dance finished. "I have some business to attend to first so I won't be there until later. I hope you don't mind."

"I'll be waiting," she replied with a peck to the cheek. Flashing a smile over her shoulder Yvette sashayed her way back through the crowd to Gregoire's table. Rabbit paused for a last look before slipping out of the bar onto the dark waterfront.

Rabbit slid quietly through the back door of Chez Francine and found Philippe in his office doing some paperwork. "Good evening my friend," Philippe said, looking up over his reading glasses as Rabbit sat down in the chair across from him. "I'm studying up on this Morse Code business. It's something that will need a lot of practice."

"Yes, well the most important thing when sending and receiving is being prepared so you get through as quickly as possible. The longer you have the radio on air the more dangerous it can be. The Germans do have radio tracking devices. It's unlikely they would have one here on Martinique, but no use taking any chances. Have you been able to get any more from your man inside the German mission?"

"I met with Gerard only this afternoon. He gave me some information that might be helpful. Three weeks ago, an important person arrived by aeroplane from South America by the name of Scheck. Gerard routinely took coffee to this man's room, where one day he observed him going over a chart of St. Martin, St. Barthélemy and Anguilla. He left abruptly the following day, and hasn't been seen since. Gerard found out from the mission's driver this man was taken to St. Pierre, but we have no idea where he went to from there." Philippe took off his glasses and wiped his face with a handkerchief. "Not long after, he heard a U-boat had entered Fort-de-France briefly in the middle of the night to drop off a wounded man. The submarine was not allowed to stay, but this wounded German sailor is still in the French military hospital."

"That's excellent information. Tell Gerard to be very careful. We wouldn't want to lose him. This evening I met my comrade at 'L'Ancre'. He'll meet me at the rhumerie in Colombier on Saturday with his crew. We just have to hope Stoddard will be there as well."

"He'll be there. My source says he rarely misses a fight."

"Good. Now, I believe I have a problem. I don't think I should take a chance going back to my room at the Saint Louis. It's only a matter of time before my story will be broken. I need a place to hide out for the next couple of days, preferably somewhere in proximity to Colombier. Do you know anyone in that area who would take me in?" Rabbit asked, leaning back in his chair and lighting up a cheroot.

"Let me think," the Frenchman said, staring distractedly off into the distance. "Of course! I know a sugarcane planter whose property is only a few miles from Colombier. His name is Jean Lefroy, and is an old friend of the family. He can be a bit obstinate and difficult, but I'm sure he'll do what he can to help. We can call on him in the morning. As for tonight, you can sleep here if you have to."

"Thanks, but tonight I'll be staying with my friend Yvette." Rabbit scribbled the address down and handed it across to Philippe. "I was hoping you could pick me up there in the morning. I think my friend could be a valuable asset to you in the future, especially for gathering information around the port. She knows everyone down there. I'll work out a time and place where the two of you can meet. Now, it's getting near the scheduled hour. I think we should get this radio set up," Rabbit suggested. The two men stood and climbed the stairs to the loft above the restaurant, and later that night made their first radio transmission.

Early the following morning, the roadster weaved along the winding coastal road, leaving the port city behind. Their first attempt at using the radio had gone off without a hitch, and all of their information was sent and received. They also confirmed their pick-up time for Saturday night. Philippe had decoded Iverson's responses with only a couple of minor hiccups, and was now set to keep up a twice weekly timetable.

They followed the island's western coast before turning off onto a dirt road leading higher into the hills, eventually finding the drive that led to Jean Lefroy's plantation. At the top of a rise Philippe stopped the car and they gazed down upon an ancient stone manor house. "I think you will be safe enough here, don't you think mon ami?" he said. "Colombier is only a few kilometres down the road, and I'm sure the old man will take good care of you in the meantime."

"This looks an ideal spot," Rabbit replied. "Are you sure it will be okay with Monsieur Lefroy?"

"I'm sure Jean will be most happy to assist in the cause. He is a proud Frenchman, as well as being a lifelong friend of my father. He is like an Uncle to me. You will be in safe hands, you'll see."

It was just after sunset when Gregoire arrived at the rhumerie in Colombier. He rode in the front seat of the truck next to Patu. In the back stood four strong, young Grand Case fishermen he had chosen a few days earlier. They pulled up in front of the centuries-old stone building and the six men disembarked. Gregoire and Patu entered the dark, open doorway. In the dim light the figure of a man could be seen sitting at one of the heavy oak tables, the red glow from his cigar a pinpoint in the darkness. Otherwise the room was empty.

"Good evening friends," the voice said. "You're right on time."

"Bon soir. Les Maquis Caraïbes have arrived," Gregoire said with a grim smile. The two men sat down and introductions were made.

Rabbit took out a box of matches, lit a candle and placed it between them. Reaching into his coat pocket he removed a folded piece of paper with a rough map drawn on it. His eyes flicked from one to the other in the candlelight. "I have been doing a lot of thinking, and I believe I have come up with a plan that could have a beneficial, long term impact. There is a part of it which might sound a little surprising to you, but please hear me out before you object. Now this is what I propose to do…" Rabbit then described his plan as Gregoire and Patu listened with stern conviction.

The village of Colombier sat in the top corner of a cul-de-sac, nestled in the valley between two hills. At the end of the only road running through the small group of shops and houses was the Gallodrome, a simple, open sided building with a corrugated iron roof pitched over the enclosed dirt cockfighting pit. Attached to one end of this was a small building which housed a bar with some tables and chairs. It was also a brothel, with several small rooms tacked on out back. It was a popular location for working men who came from far and wide to gamble on the weekly fights, drink strong white rum, and if the urge presented itself spend a few francs on one of the handful of girls who attended the saloon.

Rabbit, Gregoire and his Uncle Patu found an advantageous spot in the shadows, patiently observing the dirt parking lot and the crowd as it arrived. Finally they saw what they were looking for. "That's him," is all Patu had to say. The men waited for the first fight to start, then entered the crowded building. Moving in different directions they searched for their target and his bodyguards, one of whom was the same thin man who had rousted Rabbit at the Hotel Saint Louis. The throng of close to one hundred men were working up to fever pitch as they pushed and shoved and elbowed their way in towards the central ring. Handfuls of cash were being exchanged as the two fighting birds attacked each other. The shouting built to a crescendo and then erupted as the fight suddenly ended with one bird dead; some men laughing as they collected their winnings and others scowling and arguing bitterly over their loss. The crowd eased away from the ring, with many moving to the bar while others milled about waiting for the next fight to begin. Gregoire's gaze locked on to Rabbit's, who was standing off in a dark corner of the shed. They had recognized their quarry. Now it was time to move.

Rabbit lit a cheroot and casually made his way to the edge of the cockpit, where a flamboyantly dressed black man in a blood red shirt and broad black hat adorned with a tall pink plume was taking bets on the next fight, directly in the view of Stoddard and his two minders. The crowd had begun to filter back in as the next two combatants were brought into the ring by their handlers, and Rabbit began an earnest discussion with the bookie as other men pushed in to make their wagers. Rabbit finished placing his bet and gazed deliberately across the cockpit at Stoddard, who was staring intently at him as the thin man spoke into his ear. With a nod of his head his two minders moved off, pushing their way through the crowd towards Rabbit, who casually turned and made for the door.

As this was taking place, Gregoire edged his way in behind his foe. Pushing the gun inside his pocket into Stoddard's back he spoke quietly into his ear. "Do as I say monsieur, or you are dead. Just walk to your car, and don't make a fuss."

Rabbit was now making his way quickly across the dirt car park when his pursuers emerged from the doorway. "Halt or we'll shoot!" one called. Stopping, he melodramatically put his hands in the air. Turning around he faced the two henchmen, who were walking quickly towards him with revolvers raised.

"And so we meet again 'Monsieur Debussy'," the thin one said, with a smirk. "As you can see, you cannot hide from the Sécurité Nationale. Lower your hands, monsieur. You are now under state arrest."

"Actually, my friend, it is you who are now under arrest. Please put your guns on the ground and step away from them," Rabbit said, taking one more pull of his cigar and flicking it away.

"Don't try and be funny, monsieur."

"Do as he says," Stoddard said from behind them.

Turning and seeing that they were all covered by Gregoire, the men dropped their guns and moved back a step. Rabbit bent down and collected their weapons. "Let's take a walk to your car, shall we? We're going to go for a little ride."

Rabbit sat casually next to Gregoire as he drove, chatting and waving his gun in the faces of his three prisoners in the back seat. "You know, if I were you I would be just a little bit nervous. There are a lot of people on this island who are very upset with your actions over the past year, and you are going to meet some of them tonight. I think this will be a most entertaining confrontation, don't you partner?"

"Yes, these people are extremely unhappy with your steel-fisted abuse of power," Gregoire said as he slowed the sedan and turned off of the main road, the car now lurching up a rutted dirt track. "They are armed, they are angry, and they are anxious to make your acquaintance."

The three men looked straight ahead. "You don't scare us," Stoddard said. "You will never get away with this."

Rabbit chuckled. "Whether we get away with it or not won't really matter to you three, will it! You'll be dead, and your naked bodies will be swelling in the hot sun in the Plaza Saint Louis!"

"Ah – here we are," commented Gregoire cheerfully, as he pulled the car into an empty clearing. He turned off the engine but left the lights on. Rabbit ordered them out, pushing them around to the front of the car and on to their knees, their shadows stretching eerily towards the dark bushes beyond.

As the three knelt in the bright headlights, they could hear the sound of footsteps approaching from behind. "Now, gentlemen, I would like to introduce you to Les Maquis Caraïbes," Rabbit said. "These are patriotic Frenchmen who have seen innocent citizens dragged away by you and your cronies for no valid lawful reasons other than what has conveniently been termed 'enemies of the state'. I'm telling you now that this practice will stop as of tonight. My friends…do what you wish."

At this moment, the metallic sound of three sten guns being armed could be heard, followed by a sudden burst of machinegun fire. Terrified screams escaped from the kneeling policemen, but when the firing stopped, all three continued to kneel unharmed in the headlights.

"Frightened, are you?" Gregoire now asked. "Afraid to die, monsieur Stoddard? Well we are not going to let you off so easy. Take the others into the woods, but leave me to deal with this one." At Gregoire's order, the two men were dragged to their feet and taken to opposite ends of the clearing. Nothing more happened as Stoddard continued to kneel, sobbing and shaking. Several minutes passed before two separate bursts of gunfire ripped through the still night.

"Good," Gregoire said, pushing the cold steel of his gun into the back of the security chief's neck. "That scum has been dealt with. Now it's your turn, you pig. It would give me great pleasure to simply pull this trigger, and perhaps one day I will take the opportunity, but not tonight. Unfortunately, killing you would not help our brothers who are suffering under your hand at Fort Saint Louis. So this is what you are going to do. You will go to work as usual on Monday, but in return for your worthless life you will follow my instructions exactly. Every week, you will receive a list of names who you will release from prison. If you don't do this then you and your family will pay the consequences. You will also receive instructions from time to time that you will follow to the exact letter. Don't try to find us or think you can discover who we are. We are the Maquis Caraïbes, and you are alive because we allow you to be. Tell me you understand these instructions!"

"I understand what you say! I'll do what you want – just don't kill me!"

"I said I'm not going to kill you, and I'm a man of my word. But just to make sure that you keep up your end of the bargain, I'm going to take a little something of yours. Let's call it collateral." With that Gregoire grasped the kneeling man's ear and sliced off the lobe with his sharp fisherman' knife. Blood squirted out and ran down the front of his cream jacket as the petrified man let out a terrified scream. "You have the reputation of a man who likes to dabble in the black arts, so understand me – I will take this bloody body part to an old Haitian woman who knows exactly what to do with something like this. She will only need a word from me and your life will prove to be very uncomfortable indeed. I'm sure you understand what I mean."

François Stoddard continued to kneel in the headlights with his eyes squeezed shut. He waited for something else to happen. He waited for what seemed an eternity. Finally he took a tentative peek over his shoulder. No one was there! Slowly, carefully, he got to his feet. His legs and hands were shaking. He felt nauseous. Blood continued to run down his neck and on to his suit. Cautiously he moved around to the open car door. The keys were in the ignition. He quickly climbed into the car and drove away as fast as he could.

In the dark of the night, two naked men ran mindlessly in opposite directions, crashing their way through the bush. They were following their orders as well. They were going back home to their villages as fast as their legs would take them, never to be seen working for the Sécurité Nationale again.

Patu drove his vehicle back down the hill, blending in with the rest of the traffic heading home from the Gallodrome. As the truck bumped and lurched along the pot-holed road they discussed the night's activity. "I think tonight was a great success," Gregoire yelled over the noise of the engine, "but our work is far from finished. I need more time to get things properly established, so I'm going to stay on for as long as it takes to get our network well and truly in place. And we need to make sure that bastard Stoddard does what he's told. We have planted the seed but I need to make sure the roots take hold. We've only started. Guadeloupe and the other French territories must be next."

"I thought you might say that," said Rabbit. "It will be dangerous but it makes sense you stay. Patu and his boys are going to need more training. You're going to have to recruit a few more people. You can trust Yvette. She can liaise between yourself and Fauconnier so you don't need to contact him personally. We've made a good start, but it won't mean anything if we don't build on it. When you're ready, you let Fauconnier know and we'll come in and pull you out."

It was after midnight when the truck pulled over to the side of the road near the trail leading down to Petite Anse. Rabbit and Gregoire jumped out and stood next to the open door. The two men hugged. "Good luck." Rabbit said. He turned towards the path, and then stopped. "Oh, and keep an eye on Yvette for me, will you?"

"It will be a pleasure!" Gregoire replied with a grin as he climbed back into the truck. With a grinding of gears and a belch of exhaust smoke Patu made a wide U-turn and accelerated slowly down the road towards his village of Grand Case.

Rabbit descended the path to the beach to meet Jack and his whaleboat. He didn't have to wait long, as exactly on the stroke of two, from out of the darkness came three loud whistles, which he answered from the edge of the water. Moments later, the whaleboat rowed up to the shore. Rabbit pushed off and jumped aboard. As they cleared away from the beach the sails were set and with a brisk wind behind them they were soon clear of the land and charging across the Baie de Fort-de-France.

As the sun rose and daylight slowly spread from the east, the *Antipodes* was well across the channel, and early that afternoon the small boat swept through the narrow gap that opened out into Marigot Bay. Drifting across the calm, almost breathless water the whaleboat coasted in alongside the *Roulette*, the schooner dwarfing the much smaller *Vagabond* tied up on her opposite side. The two vessels sat lifelessly in the silent lagoon, surrounded by dense mangroves and watched over by the island's towering emerald mountains peeking through the clouds.

The flickering amber light from polished brass lamps illuminated the plush mahogany panelling of the *Vagabond*'s cosy main salon as Rabbit recounted the tale of his week in Martinique. Harry glanced up from the notebook into which he had been jotting down important details. "You have missed your calling in life, old man. You really should have been a secret agent, don't you agree Jack?"

"From the sounds of it, you and Gregoire along with our associate 'Fauconnier' seem to have made up a very resourceful team. And your friend Yvette sounds as if she could prove to be quite handy in the future."

"I must admit that I'm impressed with the fact that Gregoire decided to stay on and work with his Maquis Caraïbes, and Philippe certainly has lived up to his earlier promises. So far, he has kept to the radio schedule faithfully. I'm sure he will prove to be a valuable resource. But after being there yourself, what do you think? Is there any sign of any German naval presence in Martinique?" Harry asked.

"So far there doesn't seem to be a hint of anything dat you could call long term. Dere's Germans on the island, an' dat's a fact, but dey keepin' a low profile. Philippe does have a contact who's workin' inside de mission as one of the staff. He's keepin' his eyes and ears open and pickin' up some useful information." Rabbit now described what they had learned concerning the agent who flew in by plane and his interest in the charts of the northernmost of the Leeward Islands. He also recounted Scheck's mysterious departure, as well as the arrival of the wounded sailor, all of which was well noted by Iverson.

In the early hours of the following morning, radio contact was made with Trinidad. The *Vagabond* was to sail south immediately for Port-of-Spain and deliver their report, while the *Roulette* was to proceed to Petite Silhouette and wait on further orders.

After breakfast the anchors were raised. The schooner followed the white yacht through the narrow passage and out to sea, where they hoisted their sails and turned their heads south, and once out of the calm lee of the island felt the full strength of the easterly breeze. Reaching across the channel towards the faint outline of St. Vincent, the *Roulette* gradually left her companion astern, until she was nothing more than a white speck on the horizon.

Tintamarre

U-112 entered the heavily fortified Keroman submarine base at Lorient to a hero's welcome. Kapitanleutnant Nils Albrecht and his crew were the second of the original five-boat West Indian fleet to reach home, with the others following within a day or two of each other. The crew proudly lined the deck as the submarine slowly motored up the channel leading to their undercover pen. Bands played and people on the shoreline waved flags and cheered. A few days later, Albrecht sat in the operations room alongside the other four captains, attending his debriefing.

"Good morning men, and congratulations," Flotilla Commander Helmut Kandler commended as he greeted captains Heine, Bauer, Von Forsner, Shute and Albrecht seated before him. "My compliments come from as high up as the Fuhrer himself. Operation Neuland has proved to be an outstanding success. Even as we speak, a dozen of your comrades are steaming west to replace you. You will be proud to know that in twenty-eight days of operation we have estimated from your reports that over two hundred thousand tons of enemy shipping has been sunk. This operation has been so successful, a significant amount of our North Atlantic resources are presently being redeployed to this region. As Admiral Donitz told me himself, we have to beat the iron while it's hot. So gentlemen, make sure you and your crews get well rested over the next few days, because you all will soon be on your way back. It is important for us to learn as much as we can from your experiences. Now let's get to it."

For the rest of the day, the five captains worked with the Kreigsmarine intelligence officers breaking down their reports, describing the U-boat El Dorado they had found waiting for them to the finest detail; a golden sea littered with targets, scant enemy opposition or organisation and very few operational hazards. The only negative was the distance the fleet had to travel, which limited the time the boats could spend in the area. This problem was being addressed in two ways, a subordinate officer explained. "Firstly, we will be positioning U-tankers in strategic locations in the Western Atlantic. These ships carry up to 700 tons of fuel each, which allows us the capability of sending even our older boats with less range into this arena. Even now, U-tanker 459 is located here, south east of Bermuda," the officer said, pointing to the ship's location on the chart behind him. "This gives us the ability to significantly extend each boat's time in the operational theatre. Secondly, we have, with the help of Kapitan Albrecht here, established a location where we can reprovision, re-fuel and water our fleet. We are presently working out the details and scheduling and will present more specific information to you in the next few days."

Later that night, Albrecht sat at a table sharing a meal and a bottle of wine with Karl-Freidrich Heine at a small bistro in the nearby town of Lorient; two war-weary veterans who trusted and respected each other's ability and were satisfied to savour this simple moment, this brief respite away from the all-encompassing life aboard a submarine.

"So here we are, old friend," Heine said as he re-filled the two men's glasses. "Isn't it interesting how even such simple food can taste like the finest meal you have ever eaten? Even this 'vin du table' could be mistaken for the best of Bordeaux's. It makes one wonder when the world might get back to normal."

"Normal? Do you mean taking afternoon cake and coffee in the garden with grandmother?" Albrecht asked forlornly. "Or picking fresh berries with the children on a warm summer's evening? Maybe even a night out at a beer fest singing traditional songs, eating sausage and pretzel and drinking bock beer and schnapps? Karl, when do you really think we will see those days again? It's hard to imagine what the future will bring with these lunatics at the helm."

The hardened warrior stared at a spot on the table for a frozen few moments, as if the images his friend had painted were visible there before him. "Memories, memories! I think we have no choice but to do our jobs and hope for the best. We are caught up in the tide of history, of which I am afraid we are little more than a postscript. One thing we can never do is turn back the clock."

"Yes, of course you are right," Albrecht sighed. "I suppose it could be worse. We could be forcing down battle rations and freezing our asses off in a foxhole somewhere on the eastern front. Here's to French food and red wine." The two men smiled, clinked glasses, and slowly finished their meal.

The following morning, Nils Albrecht sat outside the Flotilla Commander's office waiting for his scheduled eight o'clock meeting. He was fairly confident as to the reason for the meeting, and was prepared for the worst. He knew a man like Scheck would not overlook what he saw as a major disregard for the rules and would have more than likely filed a report concerning his reticence in sinking the old schooner under Montserrat. As he entered the room he found Kandler busily initialling documents at his desk in front of him.

"Heil Hitler Kapitan, and good morning," the Flotilla Commander said as he passed a stack of papers on to his subordinate. "Please take a seat."

Albrecht returned the Nazi salutation and sat down opposite Kandler, who opened a file before him and leafed through its pages. "I have read your report here, Albrecht," he said. "Your actions in Trinidad and Saint Lucia were brave, creative and very effective. You seem to have made very good use of your local knowledge, and from an operational point of view we could not have asked for more from one of our officers. You could be eligible for a Knight's Cross," he continued, closing the file and looking up. "But for an incident Kapitan-Zur-See Scheck detailed in his report, your actions have been exemplary. Would you care to explain yourself in relation to this event?"

"I have nothing to hide, sir. I understand what our standing orders are, but did not believe they were intended to include such simple island craft that I would think hardly deserved wasting ammunition on. I see that perhaps on this occasion I was wrong. It won't happen again sir."

An awkward silence fell between the facing officers before Kandler continued. "I have noted this minor transgression Kapitan, and will leave it at that. We have bigger fish to fry. Let's move on to Scheck's other recommendations. I want to have a firm plan for the deployment of our Caribbean Re-supply Base within the next forty-eight hours and your input could prove to be most valuable." For the balance of the day Albrecht assisted Kandler and his subordinates in developing the final plans for a clandestine submarine base, and much to his relief, no more was said of the island schooner incident.

A few weeks later, Kapitanleutnant Nils Albrecht stood on the bridge peering through his binoculars across a stormy, foam-streaked sea. "There she is Mr Weiss – U-tanker 459, exactly where she's supposed to be. Let's make preparations to go alongside." The submarine bashed its way over the surface of the rough South Atlantic towards the rugged refuelling vessel. This would not be an easy exercise in the prevalent stormy conditions, but it was important for U-112 to top up on fuel if they were to reach their ultimate destination, which were the shipping lanes in the furthest reaches of the Western Caribbean.

As Albrecht brought his ship close in under the lee off the tanker, the captain of the 459 filled the radio waves with expletives as they struggled to get the fuel hoses connected. "Kapitan Hermann isn't getting any easier in his old age, is he Mr Weiss? You would think they'd have put him out to pasture years ago."

"Who – Kapitan Otto Hermann out to pasture?" the mate yelled back into the howling wind. "You must be joking! I can't imagine the old goat ever leaving the sea!"

"Listening to him you'd think this gale is all our doing! Anyway, we will wait for a few hours and then give it one more attempt. If we can't get these hoses connected we'll just have to leave the old man to stew in his own juices. Someone is going to get killed before the day is through if this weather doesn't ease off."

In the end it was all to no avail. "There's no chance hooking up in this weather, men," Albrecht finally told his crew. He gave the order to abandon the refuelling exercise and plot a course for the Windward Passage. "We'll just have to make sure Kruger has fuel waiting for us at Tintamarre, or else we might have trouble getting home."

U-112 entered the Caribbean through the Windward Passage on the surface and at night, and even Albrecht was amazed at the lack of resistance. The following morning they had the outline of the 6,700 ton freighter *L.D. Creighton* in their sights, and two direct hits sent her to the bottom. Six hours later, another large tanker hove into view, which took three torpedos to sink. And still they continued to lurk in the southern vicinity of the Windward Passage with impunity. "I can't believe the Americans haven't done anything to defend these major passages yet," Albrecht said to Scherer as he swept the horizon with his binoculars. "It is almost too easy! We should take advantage of this good hunting because I can't see things remaining like this for much longer."

The following morning, U-112 was ordered by headquarters to continue their cruise to the southwest. North of San Andreas, an island which lay off the coast of Central America, they had more success, sinking two large freighters within an hour of each other. "This is like shooting fish in a barrel, Skipper," Klausterman said as he took some fresh air on the bridge. "If all of the other boats are having the same sort of run then the numbers will be staggering!" And still they sailed on without a sign of enemy resistance.

The attack on Port Limon, Costa Rica would be audacious, even by Albrecht's high standards. Von Forsner may have sunk more aggregated tonnage, and Bauer more individual ships, but no one came close to equalling the daring raids executed by U-112. Port Limon was a major depot on Costa Rica's Caribbean coast, bunkering and distributing oil to a large part of Central America. Normally the tricky, reef strewn entrance was only negotiated with a port pilot on board, but Albrecht had found his own way in before with the *Kate*, and after going over the charts with Weiss and Pobanz his mind was refreshed, as if he had only been there yesterday.

"In another few months I doubt there will be many virgins left around the Caribbean, gentlemen," he said at the briefing of his senior officers as they all squeezed in to the tiny officer's mess, "and Port Limon presents us with a target as good as it is ever going to get. Admittedly it is an awkward place to enter. It's a long channel with a few twists and turns, and if you miss it you could end up high and dry on the reef, so we have to have our wits about us. I don't think the local harbourmaster would be so accommodating as to send a pilot out to meet us, so we're going to have to do this by the seat of our pants. To pull this off we will need good visibility. We will enter with a high sun in broad daylight, and on the surface."

Port Limon was located on Costa Rica's mainland, and serviced mostly local trade; small freighters and schooners who worked the coast from Panama to Mexico, as well as small tonnage oil tankers that discharged their cargos into the storage tanks ashore. It was just after noon when Albrecht brought his U-boat to the surface in the deep water outside of the mouth of the channel. He had been surveying the area from periscope depth since first light, and had actually followed a medium sized freighter a partial way into the passage to visually confirm their plotted course. Now as they made their final run he had both twelve cylinder engines operating at full throttle, and in the relatively protected conditions they were making close to twenty knots. "There is no use for stealth today, my friend," he yelled to the mate as they stood at the rail of the conning tower. "Our best chance is to strike like lightning. Go in fast and leave just as quickly." Both gun crews were on the ready. The lookouts scanned the sky and horizon for any sign of enemy presence. The radar operator concentrated on his METOX equipment, which was installed just before leaving Lorient. By locking in on enemy radar, the latest piece of German technology was meant to provide an early warning of attack by air. Every member of the fifty-two man crew was at their post and focused intently on their job.

"This will be one for the history books if we pull it off, Kapitan!" Weiss shouted over the rush of water as it passed over the deck.

"Not if, Jost, but when!" Albrecht shouted back.

The sub twisted and turned down the channel, following the dark blue colour of the water, until the low laying mainland appeared ahead, its skyline profile dominated by several cylindrical oil storage tanks, crane masts and ship superstructures. As they neared the entrance to the harbour the crew focused on the ships that were berthed alongside.

"Anything on the METOX, Rudy?" the captain asked.

"No sir. All quiet," was the reply.

If anyone noticed the approaching German submarine there was no obvious sign of it. Continuing on her merry way, U-112 crossed the open water to the entrance of Port Limon, where the order was given to cut their speed. Perhaps someone in the harbourmasters tower had seen a submarine entering the port, but if they did it was far too late, because as if on cue the 8,000 ton *Jamiaquill* was being turned by two harbor tugs and was perfectly broadside on when the sub slowed to a stop. The single torpedo that hit her was perfectly aimed. It struck her right in the heart of the engine room. The ensuing blast rocked the small harbour. Alongside the wharf of the narrow harbour a discharging oil tanker suddenly exploded when a torpedo struck her amidships. "That should keep them busy for a while. There won't be many ships coming or going from Port Limon until they move that wreck. Now let's see if we can get out as easily as we got in," said Albrecht, and the order was given to turn around and head back out to sea. As the submarine made its escape a wild shot was fired from the gun emplacement at the mouth of the harbour. Several more shots were fired but none came close to threatening the escaping submarine.

A massive cloud of black smoke from burning oil filled the sky astern as U-112 charged through the channel. It was still only early afternoon. "Not a bad day's work, Kapitan. I would think that it will take them some time to get Port Limon operational again," the mate said as he lowered his glasses.

"If only it were always so easy! I think we should enjoy this moment while we can, men. I have a suspicion that we are seeing the end of an era going up in flames back there," Kapitan Albrecht said. In his heart he knew that the Americans would not stand for this sort of audacity for much longer. "Have Weller confirm our action with Lorient, Mr Weiss. Once we are clear of these reefs steer a course of zero-nine-zero degrees. We are heading back east."

"There it is Jost …Tintamarre Island. We must have passed it many times in the good old days on the *Kate* but never would have considered stopping. And yet if Scheck didn't have this little operation running, I doubt if we would have enough fuel to get back home," the captain said, turning over the periscope to the mate after picking out the low silhouette of the island in the darkness.

"Yes sir. I've examined the chart and entering seems to be straight forward enough. It's deep with no obstacles almost up to the beach," the mate replied.

"What about you, Schäfer? Any radio contact as yet?" Albrecht asked, turning to his radio man.

"I am just receiving something now, sir! Just a moment!"

After a few minutes the decoded message was handed to the captain. "To his credit, it seems as if Scheck does have the system working properly. Using Marstrom's motor vessel for our radio link was a good idea. It seems they are waiting for us. Let's surface and send the visual signal and see how they respond."

Slowly the U-boat broke the surface. Using the signal light, they flashed the coded sign of the day towards the dark island, and shortly thereafter received the appropriate response. "That's it then. Let's take her in."

Cautiously making her approach, U-112 made her final turn and entered the open bay that formed the semi-protected anchorage at Tintamarre. One makeshift range light burned ahead, and one shone astern on the island of St. Martin itself. The captain carefully lined them up and drove the sub into the anchorage until the bow edged itself up onto the sandy bottom. "This is as far as we go, I guess, Mr Weiss. Let's keep things running until we're sure everything is right. And leave the gun crew standing by, just in case."

From the conning tower the island appeared to be deserted. There were no lights to be seen anywhere. The range lights, which were nothing more than burning coconut branches, had been extinguished. After six weeks at sea, the earthy smell of the land was strong. For a few moments Albrecht lost himself in the sound of the crashing of distant surf, the feel on his face of the tradewinds blowing over the land, the clear universe of stars overhead. The peacefulness of the moment was shattered by one of the lookouts on the bridge. "Ship approaching sir, bearing one nine zero degrees."

Turning and putting his glasses to his eyes he picked up the distinctive shape of the *Tor*, and soon after could hear the thump, thump, thump of its slow turning two cylinder engine. "Oh, the good old Alpha Diesel...just like the one we had on the *Kate*. I would know that sound anywhere," the mate said.

"Yes, it's a beautiful sound, especially to a connoisseur of such things like yourself. Right, Mr Weiss, make preparations for them to come alongside. Get the chief to start rigging the take-off pump, and open the ports to tanks five and six. I believe we are to take on twenty tons of fuel, so we need to work fast if we want to finish by daylight."

The freighter rolled its way into the anchorage and her captain brought her alongside, his little coaster dwarfed by the long thin machine which was almost three times its size. The silhouette of the freighter's one-eyed captain, Gunther Marstrom, could be seen nonchalantly leaning over the railing of his wheelhouse wing deck, a cigarette glowing in the darkness as he silently watched proceedings. When all was secure he turned his gaze towards the German bridge. "I believe I have some fuel for you," he yelled, flicking the butt of his cigarette over the side.

"Yes, Kapitan, we're ready to go," Albrecht called back.

The refuelling was an awkward job, as the anchorage, though protected by the island from the main onslaught of the open Atlantic, was still affected by a rolling swell which had the *Tor* surging and jerking at her lines. And since the fuel was being discharged from forty-four gallon drums the process was slow, as only a small hose could be used.

They had taken aboard perhaps half of the fuel when the roar of another set of engines could be heard. From around the southern point of the island, the shape of a powerboat could be discerned against the night sky. It did not overly concern captain Albrecht; the boat was expected. "It looks like our wine has arrived, Mr Weiss," he said.

The craft came in quickly, banking in a wide arc, pulling up alongside the *Tor* without fuss. And now a new operation began, as cases of wine, spirits and cigarettes were passed aboard. The German captain returned the favour and handed Marstrom a briefcase full of French francs he had been given in Lorient. As the fuel continued to be transferred, Albrecht gave permission for each watch in turn to go ashore and stretch their legs. Soon the powerboat was gone, and a few hours later the small freighter had left as well. By first light the anchorage was deserted, the smouldering ashes of a small campfire ashore the only sign that anything had transpired on Tintamarre at all.

The second voyage of U-112 to the Caribbean had taken a little over nine weeks. Upon their return, Kapitanleutnant Albrecht and his crew found the Bay of Biscay a far less hospitable stretch of water. The sky seemed to be filled with British Whitley, Halifax, Sunderland, and Catalina attack aircraft, supported on the surface by fast moving Royal Navy corvettes and destroyers loaded with depth charges. By the time they finally entered the safety of their Keroman base, the nerves of even Scherer, the hardest of all the crew, were seemingly shot. As one damaged U-boat limped in after another, it was discernible to all and sundry that life as a submariner had taken on a whole new aspect. And though they didn't realize it yet, in the span of just a few short months, the tide of war had turned. The hunters had now become the hunted.

PART III

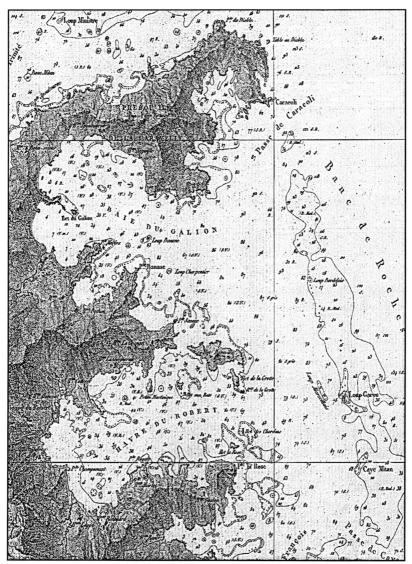

Windward Coast of Martinique

JULY, 1942

Fire on the Water

With the passing of only a handful of weeks, life on Petite Silhouette had changed. The danger of silent, invisible predators lurking in their once peaceful waters was taking its toll on island morale. One by one, the island's fleet of schooners made their way home to tie up to the coconut trees, with few skippers willing to take a chance to leave the safety of the harbour. The shops of Port Victoria were running short of essential supplies; on the main island of St. Vincent it was even worse. In the shade of the almond trees, the foremost topic of conversation was the war. Fear and trepidation had spread through the population. In the beginning the war was something happening far away in the outside world. It now had landed on their doorstep.

Early one morning on his way to the boatyard, Jack came into town to find a larger than normal group of men gathered under the trees, deep in animated discussion. Amongst the crowd were several of the island's schooner owners and captains, and even from a distance he knew Squally would be the heart of the argument. Quietly easing himself up to the outside of the group, he listened as the sailmaker worked up a head of steam.

"Man, dat's de same ting dat I been sayin' all de time! Where's de government when you does need dem? Look at de amount a vessels here in de harbour jus' sittin' around idle waiting fo' someone to tell dem wha' happenin'. I hear over in Bequia its de same damn ting! I hear you can walk across de harbour from Hamilton to Belmont without touchin' shore! Dey isn't afraid to axe fo' your port dues, but when you wants to know anything 'bout safe shipping routes dey shrug their shoulders an' acts like nothin's happenin'. Everyone knows dere's vessels goin' down, but de government ain't sayin' a word! Jayford here was lucky 'cause he made shore. What 'bout de ones dat don't?"

"Yes man, we was lucky to be to windward of Grenada, an' dat we had a good life boat," the captain agreed. "But dat German wasn't easy a-tall! Gave us five minutes to move befo' he opened up. Dem vessels is serious too...dey's all business. An' de gun? Man it's a cannon! De ol' *Lady Angelina* was nothin' but driftwood in minutes."

"My boys've been lucky so far wit our vessel, dat's all I can say," said Uncle Herman, a stout Bajan from Top-o-the World, his white skin sun-blotched from years at sea. "I was just happy to see de boys come 'round de point de other day. But dem two is ignorant, you here? Dey say dere's good money to be made out dere – 'war time rates' dey does call it. An' since most vessels is tied up waitin' to see what's goin' on dere's plenty a cargo to be had. I heard you can sail straight alongside Queen's Wharf and load de nex' day! I say it ain't worth de risk, but dem two is set on leavin' again soon as dey can find crew."

"Dat's youth fo' you," chimed in one of the old-timers seated on a root of the giant tree, his walking stick propped between his legs. "Takin' chance means nothin' to dem. But you can't spend money in Davey Jones' locker. De only currency down dere's seaweed. I was speakin' to Tanti Clara de other day an' she said she had a dream dat Bill was sailin' *Arabella D* north de other night. Dat's not a good sign a-tall."

"Man, sailin' north in a dream means only one ting in truth!" agreed another.

"But hey, Cap'n Jack might know a little somethin' more den de rest o' we," Squally said, looking straight at him with a stare he couldn't avoid.

"Well boys, I don't know if there's anything I can say that will help. These Nazis are making a big push into our waters, and that's a fact. Even though the government won't come out and admit it, the amount of damage these U-boats are doing to the freighters and tankers sailing these waters must be staggering. They've sunk ships inside the harbours of Trinidad and St. Lucia, and the Allies are battling to keep up. The Yanks are building air bases on St. Lucia and Antigua, along with Trinidad, but the Brits are really struggling and are looking to the Yanks for help. It's dangerous out there, there's no denying it, and you're rolling the dice when sailing these waters – just look what happened to ol' Gus and the *Guiding Star*. But if you're hoping for anything like gunboats out there to protect us, well I'm afraid to say I can't see that happening anytime soon. They have a lot of catching up to do before even thinking about that."

"So what do all we do, then? Just tie our vessels up an' wait for dis ting to blow over?" Squally demanded.

"I'm afraid that's about it. Otherwise make your passages at night, if you can, and just close your eyes and take your chances. And if you do, make sure you have a good lifeboat with a proper sail and plenty of provisions in it, and if you meet up with one of them pray to the Good Lord the German captain has a heart and gives you time to abandon ship, and doesn't just shoot without any kind of warning."

Jack left the group and made his way to the boatyard. What else could he say? As much as he would like to help calm their fears, there was little else he could do but tell them the truth. What was happening was like a bad dream, he thought to himself. "I just wish I could wake up and it would be over," he muttered.

In the boatyard, the same anxious feeling hung over the normally happy site like a shroud. The men were fitting the grown cedar frames to a new schooner, the skeleton of the vessel standing up like the ribs of a big beached whale in the sand. Even Jack's partner, the ever optimistic O'Neil was gloomy, his face showing the strain of worry over this unprecedented travail. "Man, in all my years I ain't never seen somethin' like dis," he said as he helped two men roll over a large log they were siding with adzes. "You don't know where dey goin' to strike or when. You can't get ready and you can't prepare fo' dem. And you can't out run 'em neither. These here is dark days, very dark days I tell you."

The weeks passed slowly, and Jack was kept busy working in the boatyard. Early one evening he had just returned home when a small boy came running breathlessly up the path. "Cap'n Jack," he panted, "I just come from Le Moulin. A steamboat's on fire to windward! Papa sent me to come get you!"

Jack was on his feet and striding to the galley for his hat within moments. "Jasmine," he called out, "a ship is burning off Le Moulin! I'm going down and see if Kincaid will drive me out there to have a look. Can you get Henry to run over to Zepheryn and ask him to get the crew together? If there are people in the water we should go and see what we can do to help."

"Yes okay! Henry shouldn't be too far away," she replied from the kitchen doorway.

Jack jogged down the path to the main road, where he turned and walked quickly into town to the house of Aubrey Kincaid. The Englishman was sitting on his porch, enjoying the sunset with his wife.

"Oh hello, I say, if it isn't McLeod! Just in time for a cocktail, eh what?" he said, standing to welcome his unexpected guest.

"I'm afraid it's not a social call this evening, Aubrey. It sounds like a freighter's been torpedoed out to windward of Le Moulin, and I was hoping we could use your car to go and get a bearing on it. I'm going to take the vessel out there to see what we can do to help, but I'd like to have a quick look to see where they are first."

"Of course old man – anything to help! Just let me grab the keys and we'll be off." Moments later he gave his wife a peck on the cheek and joined Jack. They crossed the yard and opened the garage to find a gleaming Austin Sports-Tourer, the Englishman's pride and joy. Aubrey got in and started the car up, eased off the handbrake, carefully pulled out of the garage, and soon he and Jack were bouncing down the road.

It was just after dark when they reached the small settlement of Marley's Vale, which sat in a saddle below Mount Majestic overlooking the windward side of the island. From here the road meandered down to the fishing village of Le Moulin a mile or so below them, the ruins of the ancient windmill that gave the village its name just visible in the dying light on the ridge above. Kincaid pulled up and stopped amongst a knot of people standing at the side of the road looking out to windward. In the half-light the burning ship was easy to see. The flaming freighter drifted slowly to leeward, roughly seven miles away to the south-east. Occasionally the flames grew brighter, rising higher into the night sky when a fuel tank exploded. The crowd stood in awed silence as they watched the burning ship drift across the distant horizon, only a few muted comments passing between them.

"Well there's no way back for her now," Jack said to his friend after a few moments. "It looks like the Krauts have done a proper job on her."

"Yes, quite," answered Kincaid. "What do you propose to do, old chap?"

"We'll go out there and see if there are any survivors. Hopefully the sub will be gone by the time we get there, but that's a chance we'll just have to take."

"Perhaps Edwina and I should round up some volunteers to set up a station where the injured can be looked after. The schoolhouse would be the best place for that. Mattresses, blankets, food, that sort of thing. And of course whatever first aid we might be able to muster up. I'll shake up Dr Preston-Taylor and get him on board. I'm sure he'll be willing to help," Kincaid said as they walked back to the vehicle.

"Good idea, Aubrey. And I'm sure Jasmine will help Edwina organise some women to lend a hand."

They drove back down the hill into the harbour, pulling up in front of the moored schooner, where a clutch of men had assembled in the gathering darkness.

The *Roulette* cleared out from under South End and shouldered into the easterly trades. The loom of the burning ship glowed on the horizon to starboard, just off the lee bow. It was a bright night, the moon close to full, the foam of the bow wave radiating with phosphorescence as it blew away into the blackness. The shadow of the land disappeared slowly astern as the schooner lifted and lurched into the oncoming waves.

"She's blowin' a solid bit a breeze tonight, Skip! She' be white up over Petit Cannouan," Zepheryn half shouted, his yellow oilskin flapping in the breeze as he spoked the wheel.

"Hopefully the crew got away in their lifeboats and will be somewhere close to the ship so we can see 'em. Otherwise it'll be like finding needles in a haystack," Jack replied.

They ploughed on into white-topped seas. An hour later they began to close on the stricken ship, which was now alight from stem to stern. "Looks like an oil tanker, and fully loaded, so she must've been bound north," Jack said as they approached her, keeping his vessel to windward. "Ok Zeph, I'll take the helm. Fire up the engine, get the fores'l and jib off her and then let's hove-to." He watched as the mate went forward and issued the orders, and it wasn't long before the schooner was sitting comfortably head to wind, drifting along at about the same pace as the burning tanker as they stemmed the wind and heavy sea. Slowly they edged near to the ship, searching the oily waves for any survivors. There was a shout from forward as Gilbert's keen eye spotted a human form in the water. It was difficult bringing the pitching schooner near enough to haul him aboard. Finally Kingsford jumped into the water with a rope made fast around his waist. Swimming through the treacherous swell he reached the stricken seaman, and after grasping the man under his arms waved, and the two of them were hauled back aboard. Not long after, they spotted a second person in the water, but he was lifeless. They brought the body aboard, but the sailor had obviously suffered severe trauma and had not made it. Throughout the night they continued to search the vicinity of the stricken ship for more survivors, but with no luck, until just before sunrise they picked up a third man, and though unconscious, he was still alive.

With the rising sun there was renewed hope, and with four crew perched aloft on the trestletrees they searched the foam-streaked ocean for any sign of life. They were lucky, and in the morning picked four more men out of the water, all of them suffering from exhaustion, injuries and burns. The ship continued to drift to the west, a smouldering wreck doomed to belch its black smoke onto the horizon for days to come. It was close to noon when Earl shouted from aloft that he had spotted something floating to leeward that looked like a lifeboat. Sailing down upon the drifting boat, they soon had it alongside. One by one, the survivors were helped aboard, some severely injured but all thankful of their rescue. In the late afternoon the *Roulette* was finally turned for home, towing the empty lifeboat astern.

The first man to regain his feet was the mate Harrison. "Our ship was called the *Esco Atlantic*, twelve thousand five hundred tons, loaded with crude oil from the refinery at Point-a-Pierre, Trinidad. We were bound for New York, from where we were going to go north to Halifax to join a convoy across to Southampton," he told Jack as he smoked a cigarette with his back to the windward bulwarks. "Captain Atkinson was a good man and a good skipper. I've been with him for close to four years. He was smart and he was lucky. This was our third trip out of Trinidad, and his idea of sailing close to the windward sides of the islands and staying out of the shipping lanes had worked a treat. Until yesterday, that is. It's a crapshoot whichever way you go, I guess. Since leaving Trinidad, our radio had been picking up maydays from all points of the compass, from the Mona Passage, the Windward Passage, and the coast of Venezuela right out into the South Atlantic. There are ships going down all over the place! These U-boats seem to be everywhere, but the Allies don't have enough ships or planes to protect organised convoys like in the North Atlantic, so men like us just have to take our chances and run the gauntlet. Our luck ran out yesterday."

"Was Captain Atkinson on the bridge when you were hit?"

"Yes, it was his watch. I don't think anyone up there had much of a chance. The first torpedo caught us just forward of the bridge and the second came in right behind it. I had just come off watch and was back aft in the wardroom having a cup of tea when they hit us. The bridge and everything forward of where we were went up in flames real quick. The lads you picked up out of the water were all back aft like me – cooks, stewards and a couple of AB's off of my watch. But the fire was so bad we couldn't even get to the boats, so we could only go aft and wait until the flames reached us. We had no choice but to jump for it in the end. It was the lads from the fo'c'sle who got the boat over the side and fished me and a couple more of us out of the water. Thank God for you and your crew, otherwise we'd be adrift out there and probably never be found."

The sun was disappearing behind Gunnery Point when the *Roulette* came alongside the wharf at Port Victoria. A large crowd had gathered to see how many survivors they might have collected. Aubrey Kincaid tooted his horn to make way for his vehicle as he backed through the crowd, using it as a makeshift ambulance. The worst of the injured men were carefully helped over the rail and into the waiting automobile, with Constable Ballentyne, O'Neil and several others standing by to give a hand. As Jack awaited Kincaid's return he was met by Harry Iverson, looking every bit the yachtsman in his faded blue shorts, white cotton shirt and canvas sun hat.

"Grim business, eh McLeod?" Harry commented as he edged alongside the big Australian. "I suppose these men can count themselves lucky they were hit so close to shore. Imagine the amount of crews that we don't know about who have disappeared into the wastelands of the Western Caribbean."

"G'day Harry. Yes, it's a ugly business indeed. So when did you arrive, and what brings you here?"

"We sailed in from Trinidad this morning with the express purpose of seeing you, my friend. As soon as we came ashore and found out what was happening, we went up to the school to see what we could do to help. Val was trained as a nurse in her youth, so she volunteered and has been up there with your wife making things ready since early afternoon."

"I had a feeling it might be something like that. Once we get these men safely ashore I'll be heading up to the school myself," Jack said as he jumped back aboard his vessel. "I suppose we'll need to talk."

"Right-o. I'll see you up at the school, old man."

After several trips, the injured seamen had all been moved to the temporary clinic, where a crowd of volunteers were waiting to help.

Once the rescued mariners were all ashore, the schooner was moved back to her moorings. Jack and his crew jumped out of the skiff as it touched up on shore, and all together they hauled the ship's boat to its spot up under the trees.

"Is there anything else you need we to do today, Cap?" the mate asked.

"No Zeph, you blokes have been great. I'm not sure of our next movements, but I'll get in touch as soon as I know anything. You all take a couple of days off and we'll look at going back to work on Monday – that is, if nothing comes up before then. Thanks for all of your help." The men said their goodbyes and moved off home, while Jack turned towards town and the makeshift hospital.

At the school, Dr Preston-Taylor had the situation well under control. While Jack was out in search of survivors, the retired doctor had taken up Aubrey Kincaid's request for help and come to the schoolhouse first thing the following morning. O'Neil arrived with a crew of shipwrights from the boatyard and put together a couple of rows of long benches covered with donated bedding, which made up the patients' beds. Jack met Harry at the door and watched as Val and Jasmine, headmaster Stockton, his wife Claire and others helped tend to the wounded men.

"Dr Oliver Preston-Taylor comes from an old family of planters over on St. Vincent," Jack explained to Harry. "They had a plantation here and, along with Kincaid, were the major producers of sugar cane on the island in days gone by. The family still owns a lot of land out on the windward side where he lives. He spent the early days of his youth here, but in his teens was sent away to boarding school in England, where he became a doctor. When the bottom dropped out of the sugarcane market in the 20's, his family shut the plantation down and returned to St. Vincent. The piece of land I own I actually bought from them. When Ollie retired, he decided to leave England and return here to live. His wife died several years ago, so he just lives out there on his own. He's a very fit man, does a lot of walking, and has a huge library. He's also a bird watcher, which would be of common interest to you and Val, I would think."

The doctor noticed the two men standing at the door and walked over to say hello. "Jack, what a great job you did pulling these fellows out of the drink," he said, shaking his two visitors' hands. "And I must say, Iverson, your wife is an excellent nurse, and is being ably assisted by Jasmine and our other volunteers."

"I see you've met Harry already, Doc," Jack said. "It's unfortunate the situation is so serious because I think the three of you share many of the same interests and would enjoy each other's company."

"Yes, it was quite a surprise and an unexpected honour to meet such esteemed visitors to our small island. I've actually read several of Mr Iverson's works. I was especially intrigued by an account I read of an expedition you made years ago into the upper reaches of the Congo, and in particular your views on Cryptozoology," the doctor said. "I know it's not the time or place for such a discourse, but perhaps one day we will find the time to get together to discuss this and other such fascinating subjects."

"I appreciate the compliment, Doctor. If you find that subject interesting, then I'm sure you would be intrigued by my latest work here in the New World. Unfortunately, the war has put the brakes on my research, but hopefully sanity will return at some point and my wife and I can return to what we love best."

"We can only pray for the day when all of this will be over, I suppose. Until then we must try and deal with the situation as best we can."

"And what is your assessment of these men's condition? Are there any really serious cases, Doc?" Jack asked.

"I have only had time to give each man a cursory examination. In general, all of the men have been through a lot of trauma, and most have suffered an assortment of minor injuries, with one I believe to be life-threatening. That man is unconscious with a head injury, and except for making him comfortable there is little else we can do. Another has some fairly severe burns. Unfortunately we are very short on supplies, but we are using the local remedy of applying the sap of the aloe-vera cactus on his wounds, which seems to be easing the pain," the doctor replied.

Jack and Harry continued to talk over the situation with the doctor for a while longer. It was decided since there was not much more they could do at the school they would walk back to the house. The two men had important business to discuss.

The Hurricane of Thirty-five

Halfway down the hill Jack finally asked the question that had been on his mind for the last little while. "Cryptozoology Harry? I'm no kind of scientist but I've got to admit I've never heard of that one!"

"It's a word I coined after an experience I had in Africa when I was a young man. I was making my way up the upper reaches of a tributary to the Zambezi when we were swooped by what looked like a flying dinosaur. The beast was enormous – a giant bat-like creature. From that moment on, I became fascinated by the stories, folklore and traditions of people who believe such animals exist, and I have been on a search for them ever since. So to answer your question, 'cryptozoology' literally it means 'the study of hidden animals'. In other words, it's the search for animals whose modern day presence has never been proven, or like dinosaurs are considered extinct. It also entails the examination of animals that appear in legends and myths but lack physical proof of their existence. Officially, it is not really a science, but hopefully one day I'll be able to come up with enough evidence to make it more widely accepted."

"Well you've got me interested, mate. The upper reaches of the Zambezi? Giant flying bats? There's still a lot about you I'd like to hear about. Let's get this bloody war over with and then all of us can get on with far more important things."

The light from the kerosene lamp spread out over the veranda. Harry crossed his legs and rolled a cigarette. A small, round table sat in front of the two men, a bottle of Scotch whiskey and two glasses irradiated in the lamplight. "So what's happening in Trinidad, Harry?" Jack asked, pouring the drinks.

The men touched glasses. "Cheers," Harry said. "Nice drop of malt, old man. Now where do I begin? Over the last two months, the pace in Trinidad has picked up dramatically. Quite frankly, everything is pointing to an all-out enemy assault on the Caribbean. It seems that since the first attacks back in February, Donitz has been quick to discover what easy pickings this area has on offer. What started out as a trickle of sinkings has now turned into a deluge. At last estimate U-boats are now sinking an average of 30,000 tons of shipping a day, which equates to over twenty ships a week! Nowhere seems to be safe; from the Gulf of Mexico in the north, to Panama in the west, to the South Atlantic, and the Guyanas to the east. The Kreigsmarine has turned what originally was more than likely no more than an exploratory venture into a well-orchestrated, full-blown assault. It really is rather chaotic out there at the moment. As much as a shock as those first sinkings were, they seem to pale in significance to the onslaught we are under at present. It has taken a few months for an Allied response to the German assault to start to take effect. Just in the last few weeks we've seen the reinforcements start to arrive. Five US destroyers are now based in Trinidad, and the Canadians have sent two of their smaller corvettes. The Royal Navy has a fleet of five motor torpedo boats operating from *HMS Benbow*, along with a similar fleet to be based very soon in Barbados. To their credit, the Americans have done remarkably well, considering they have only been in the war for seven months. Chaguaramas has six squadrons of flying boats stationed there, and with the Army Air flying their B-18s out of Waller Field we will finally be able to start putting some heat back onto Jerry. So the future is not all doom and gloom, Jack."

"In the meantime, the trading fleet on almost every island has gone into mothballs, and no one is being officially informed as to what the hell is going on. The islands are running out of provisions, and the people are truly afraid for probably the first time in their lives," Jack muttered.

"There isn't much I can say on that score, old chap. As you would well know, military men have never been renowned for their concerns over civilian hardship. We can only hope things will get better in the near future. On a brighter note, I've been asked to tell you that Operation Square Rigger has provided us with extremely valuable information. Discovering a U-boat had taken advantage of the facilities in Martinique has led directly to the stepping up of the blockade of Fort-de-France. There are now four US destroyers with full ASDIC capabilities operating there, and U-boats will be finding it extremely difficult to enter Fort-de-France. Our man Fauconnier is keeping to his radio schedule with me, and continues to operate beyond our expectations. The underground movement Haynes and Deslisle set up seems to be stirring up the locals and is giving the Vichy government fits. In the last two weeks alone, there has been a general strike and several food riots. Gregoire has been doing a bloody marvellous job!"

"So what brings you up here then, Harry?"

"As I said Jack, the powers that be are very impressed with the work our 'Maquis' have been doing in Martinique, and would like to get something similar started in Guadeloupe. They want us to pull Gregoire out and get him to Barbados, where he can be debriefed."

"So what are you talking about? We go in and bring him out the same way we took him in?"

"It's not quite that easy this time, I'm afraid. Fauconnier reports that since the Maquis have started making their presence felt, there has been a crackdown on security not only around Fort-de-France, but the whole lee side of the island as well. A large amount of the population is trying to escape from the island; to Dominica in the north and St. Lucia in the south. The navy has stepped up its coastal patrols trying to stop this exodus. I think we are going to have to be a little more creative this time around, Jack."

"Does Philippe have any idea about where we should take Gregoire off, then?"

"Javert suggests we take him off from the windward side, and thinks the village of Le Robert would be our best option as he has good contacts there. He wants to use the Bastille Day celebrations on the 14th of July to help cover the operation," Harry explained.

Jack gazed out over the dark harbour below them. "The windward side – that's a challenge. The place is nothing but a maze of offshore reefs. I'll need to have a good look at a chart to get a grasp on what exactly he's talking about. And with U-boats and patrol boats thrown in, it's a whole different kettle of fish this time."

"You have a think about it, old man. The 14th is still over a week away. We have some time to get ourselves organised."

The sounds of the night settled in around them. Somewhere in town a dog barked. The wind rustled through the trees. A cock crowed. Harry settled back into his seat and lit up a cigarette as two more drinks were poured. "Who would have thought that it all would have come to this?" Jack sighed. "I guess you could say I've been spoiled. I've been here off and on since '21, and things have hardly changed on the island since the day I first arrived. Life was always simple. It seemed to move at its own pace. There were marriages and births. Someone built a new house. A schooner was launched. Old people passed on. Years were remembered by their hurricanes, or how dry a rainy season was. But a war raging right here on our doorstep? I never would have seen that coming."

"You wouldn't be the only one, old chap. Once that demon is let out of its cage, there is no hope of predicting where its foul stench will appear. Six months ago, I don't think even Jerry at his arrogant best would have foreseen today's events."

"Six years ago I would have been sitting right here sharing a drink with a German mate of mine, and war would have been the furthest thing from either of our minds, I can assure you."

"A German mate? I don't recall you ever mentioning anything about that to me."

"He was a year or two before your time, I should think. His name was Nils Albrecht, and he really pulled me out of the shit after the hurricane of '35. Haven't you ever heard that story?"

"I can't say that I have old man. And there is no time better than the present. My wife is busy nursing for the night, Carlisle is over in Le Moulin, most likely drinking rum, and we have over a half a bottle of Scotland's finest in front of us. There is nothing I would rather do at the moment than to sit back and listen to one of your enthralling tales, Captain McLeod," he said enthusiastically. "So how did you meet this fellow?"

"I first came across Nils in San Juan, Puerto Rico. It must have been back in '32 or '33. He was running a small freighter in those days called the *Kate*. I remember he had just come in from Savannah with a load of Georgia pine, and the stevedores were on strike. Anyway, he was a hell-of-a good bloke, and we ended up playing a lot of chess while we waited for the strike to end. When I left, I mentioned that if he was ever passing through this part of the world he should drop in and see us, which he in fact did on several occasions."

"Sounds an interesting sort of chap," Harry said. "That would have been a fine time to be running through these islands."

"He had a very good trade going. The *Kate* was one of the few 'steamboats' around in those days, so he was kept real busy. Nils was a real favourite of the locals here, too. He was always bringing hard to find items and doing favours. He even made a special trip to Barbados to collect Aubrey Kincaid's motor vehicle. And at a schooner launching once I remember he brought ashore two wheels of Dutch cheese as his contribution towards the party. People here still talk about it, as it was the first time most of them ever tasted cheese."

"It seems as if he was almost part of the community. So you say he helped you out in a hurricane. What year was that?"

"It was towards the middle of October in 1935, and we left here with the *Roulette*, bound for Demerara to load rice. We were sailing light, just carrying a bit of stone and a couple of hundred fuel drums filled with water for ballast. As you would know, the hurricane season is supposed to be finished by then, but that year we caught a late one. We were three days out, and well to the southeast, when we saw the first signs something was coming, and so we turned around and tried to make a run for it. The wind dropped light and then started blowing strong, out of the west. We were making little headway and our engine was next to useless. The barometer was falling fast, and slowly the wind began to back 'round to the east with the occasional heavy squall. We were hoping we were far enough south to miss it, but no such luck. The wind continued to swing right around the clock, and we tried every trick we knew to avoid it. The barometer continued to plummet, and it was now a certainty that a serious hurricane was bearing down on us, and there was nothing we could do about it. I won't forget the morning it caught up with us. The day broke black and ugly, the clouds at sunrise were blood red, and the wind and rain squalls were ferocious."

"Val and I have been through two hurricanes since we've been out here, but both at anchor in a safe harbour, which was terrifying enough. I wouldn't want to have to sail through one of the blighters, especially in a schooner like yours light on ballast! So what happened next?"

"Like I say, the day started ugly, and as it went on it only got worse. The wind had been backing right around the compass, until finally it was howling from behind. We ran off with it all day, but the wind just kept growing stronger. We sailed on into the night, and by midnight we were feeling the full force of it. It was chaos. Two of our sails had blown to shreds and we had been rocked onto our beam ends and almost capsized more than once. When first light came and we thought it couldn't get any worse a shout came from forward warning of breakers ahead! Navigation had been impossible for the two previous days, and none of us had any idea where the hell we were. We couldn't turn around because we had a full strength hurricane behind us. There was nowhere else to go. Our only choice was to sail on and hope for the best. What happened next was quite remarkable. We hit that reef at full speed, and the keel was ripped clean out of the bottom of the boat. But we didn't stop! The wind and seas drove us right over the reef and into a lagoon beyond. Of course it was still very rough, but the reef did block some of the swell. We were now full right up with water, but the swell drove us on with our decks awash until we fetched up onto the beach of a small cay. The vessel was now over on her side and being pounded by the waves, but we could at least find some shelter below decks and wait for the storm to ease off. By the following morning the worst of it had passed, and we could start to have a look around and try and figure out where we were. And where do you think that was?"

"I couldn't even hazard a guess," said Harry, shaking his head in amazement.

"When the rain and wind finally cleared we couldn't believe our eyes! We had sailed clean across World's End reef and wrecked in the lagoon of the Tobago Cays! Our lifeboat was still in one piece, so along with two of my crew, I rigged the boat and set out for Petite Silhouette. We camped the first night on the beach on Cannouan. Between the sails and oars we made it back home the next day, where we found the hurricane had done a lot of damage. I got my partner O'Neil and a few others with me, and after throwing some tools and materials together, we got ready to sail back to the Cays on another vessel. It turned out Nils Albrecht and the *Kate* had ridden out the storm down in Gwilt's Hole, which as you know is very well protected. Once he heard about the shipwreck he offered his help, and so the next day he followed us south. It took us close to two weeks to do it, but we got her off the beach, and using the empty fuel drums we kept her afloat. It took a full day for Nils to tow the *Roulette* back home with his freighter. Once we got back to Frigate Bay, we ran block and tackles from our mastheads to anchors in the deep part of the harbour and turned the vessel completely upside down, and with the drums still keeping her afloat we fitted a new keel, caulked her up, flipped her back over, pumped her out and went back to work not long afterwards!"

"And that is the same schooner floating in front of me today?" Harry marvelled. "Amazing story, Jack. I'm surprised that I haven't heard it before! And this chap Albrecht, whatever happened to him?"

"He stayed on until we finished the job. Nils and his first mate helped me rebuild my engine on deck of his freighter, and while he was here was almost like part of the family. When we were done he left, looking to pick up freight out of Trinidad. By then, things were beginning to get real tough in the cargo trade. I didn't hear from Nils for months, until I finally received a letter from him saying he was heading back to Europe to try his luck over there. That was the last time I heard from him."

"Remarkable tale, old man. One thing you can say about you fellows here is you are resourceful. I wonder what your friend might be doing now."

"That's a good question. I've thought about the bloke on more than one occasion lately."

A wave of excitement spread through the village of Port Victoria the following day, when two schooners arrived alongside the main wharf within hours of each other. The first vessel to break around the point was the recently launched *Arabella D,* deep laden with steel and other building products loaded in Trinidad and consigned to Barbados. Also on board was a cargo of foodstuffs desperately needed on the island. As Jack reached alongside, bags of rice, sugar, coffee and other staple goods were being passed up out of the hold and trundled off of the wharf.

"G'day, Cap'n Bill! You look to have a good load in, mate," he shouted over the rail.

The broad face of the bull-like skipper broke into a beaming smile. "Yes man, she's deep laden in truth!" he called back. "We had to stop de trucks from comin', dey would have sunk we alongside Queen's Wharf if dey had their way! Me never seen anyting like it. Trinidad's desperate fo' vessels. It's like nobody wants to leave home a-tall!"

"Well I understand; it's with good reason. Just look what they did out to windward of us the other day!"

"Yes man, me did hear 'bout dat in truth. Dem fellahs got de whole o' de Caribbean jumpin' at shadows. I thought twice 'bout takin' on dis load meself, but in de end figured dat I couldn't jus' keep hangin' on in Port-o-Spain. Dis crew o' mine was sendin' me straight to de poorhouse! Man dem fellahs can eat! But once we drops dis load in Barbados, me done wit' dat. It's straight home and make fast to de coconut trees fo' me."

"So when are you looking at sailing, Bill?"

"Well today is full moon, so I reckon we'll let she settle in fo' a day or two, an' den try an' catch hold o' some weather tide to help carry we east."

"Okay then mate – we'll talk before then. These boys we rescued off the sinking freighter would be much better off in Barbados. You think you could make room for them aboard?"

"Yes, man. I'll do whatever I can to help."

Just then the shout went up. "Sail ho off de point! It's Clancy an' dem!" And it wasn't long before the *Theodora D* was gliding in and berthing alongside the busy wharf as well.

The Old Chart

"Nothing like the hustle and bustle of a Caribbean port, is there McLeod? The noise, the jostling, the vibrancy. The smell of sweat and smoke and Stockholm tar – it all has something magical about it, don't you agree?"

Jack smiled inwardly as he glanced out of the corner of his eye towards Iverson, who had appeared alongside of him as quiet as a ghost. "I was hooked from the moment I landed in these islands, Harry, and I hope I never live to see the day when things are any different."

"Being a scientist, I know that change is a fundamental law of the universe; it's an integral part of life. Unfortunately, things don't always change for the better."

"You can say that again, mate. There's plenty of change takin' place these days…a bit too much for my liking, I'm afraid. But then, how would you Darwinians put it, adapt or perish?"

Harry laughed. "Something like that. Anyway, to more immediate issues – have you checked in on our patients yet today?"

"I was just on my way up to the school. Bill deVilliars has offered to take the injured seamen aboard and get them to the hospital in Barbados when he goes in a couple of days. It will be interesting to see what the Doc thinks of the idea. Care to join me?"

"Absolutely, old chap. I want to drop in and check on my wife. Knowing her, I'd wager she hasn't taken a break since she started." Leaving the crowded wharf, the two men set off through the village, slowly working their way up the hill towards the schoolhouse. "Have you given the Martinique operation any more thought?"

"Yes I have. Listen Harry, the more I think about it, the more I'm convinced I'm going to need some help with this next little venture," he finally said. "I'm going to speak to O'Neil to see if he'll give us a hand."

"You do what you have to, Jack. I'll go along with whatever you decide."

"Good. I'm going to head down and have a word with him after our visit. Why don't you meet me in the boatyard around sundown?"

"Jolly good, McLeod. Carlisle and I will be there at six."

Inside the school, the volunteer nursing staff moved quietly amongst their patients, doing their best to make them comfortable. Dr Preston-Taylor was making his rounds between the thirteen injured men, speaking to each as he examined them. Eventually he approached the two visitors.

"Good day to you, gentlemen. I take it you're curious to know if there's been any improvement in our patients."

"Yes Doc, we certainly are. I saw Aubrey Kincaid on the wharf earlier and he mentioned that you feel they need to get to a proper hospital," Jack said.

"Aubrey is right. None of them are in very good shape, but two are especially critical. The first engineer has suffered extensive burns to a large portion of his body and is in severe discomfort, and unfortunately with no drugs there is very little we can do for him. The other badly injured man received a blow to the head and has failed to regain consciousness. Both of these men need proper medical attention as soon as possible. All we can do here is to try and keep their wounds clean and make them as comfortable as possible. It would be best if they were in hospital in Barbados, but getting them there is the problem."

"Bill deVilliars sailed in this morning from Trinidad on the *Arabella D* on his way to Barbados, and has offered his services. It may not be the most comfortable of rides, but at least they'd be better off once he gets them to Bridgetown. Do you think your patients are up to it? He won't be leaving for another day or two."

"It's an offer that should be considered. The passage will be hard on the badly injured, but in the long run the discomfort would be worth it. Let's see how they're doing in another twenty-four hours, shall we?"

"And how is your nursing staff handling the challenge?" Jack asked, smiling as he received a discreet wave from his wife.

"I must say all the volunteers have been absolutely wonderful. Valery is an excellent nurse, and has organised her helpers in a most admirable way. There are women cooking and making tea, washing linen, even emptying the bed pans. It's been a sterling effort by the whole community, I must say," the doctor remarked with pride.

"Okay Doc, we'll get out of your hair. You don't need any more distractions. I'll check back with you in the morning," Jack said.

"That will be fine. And don't worry about your wives! I'll make sure they are home with you tonight. They have performed beyond the call of duty and deserve a good night's sleep."

Four o'clock, and one by one the shipwrights in the boatyard packed up their tools, said goodbye and started for home. Jack and O'Neil were the last to leave. Walking past the new schooner under construction, they followed the sandy path through the coconut trees and up the hill to O'Neil's house overlooking the yard. The two men sat down in the shade of the front veranda, quietly gazing out over Frigate Bay and Gunnery Point beyond.

Jack finally broke the silence. "Listen O'Neil, something has come up, and I could use your help. Let me explain. When I was in Barbados a few months ago, I was asked to do some work for British Naval Intelligence. Basically it was simple stuff. As I travelled through the islands, I was asked to keep an eye out for anything suspicious and report it, that sort of thing. Surprisingly, my immediate superior turned out to be none other than Harry Iverson."

"Me always knew dey was somethin' more to dat fellah. Nobody can spend dat much time writin' books."

"It turns out he's been working for them on a part-time basis for several years. Then these U-boats hit the islands and suddenly things got busy. I won't go in to all the details, but one job we did was to smuggle a couple of blokes into Martinique to find out what was going on there. One of them was our Bajan friend Rabbit Haynes, who has more tricks up his sleeve than a bloody magician. We went back and brought him out a week later, and it's now time for us to go in and fetch the other fella. Our contact in Fort-de-France has said we're to take him from the windward side of the island, and as you can imagine, that won't be so easy. We'll be going in with the whaleboat, so I'll need a skipper for the *Roulette* while I'm gone. It's going to be a tricky operation, and that's why I'm here. There aren't too many people I'd trust with the job, and I was hoping you might be able to take it on."

O'Neil reclined casually in his chair, legs crossed, absentmindedly stroking his dog between the ears. The trees nearby rustled in the breeze. A man-o'-war bird glided high over the bay. Moments of silence passed. There was a slight movement of his head towards Jack. "Okay, I'll gi' all you a hand," O'Neil finally said. "When is it you'll want to be leaving?"

"We need to move within the next couple of days. The pick-up is scheduled for the 14th of the month. Our contact has told us where we'll meet, but the finer details still need to be worked out."

"That's in only a few days' time. What do you know about dis location?" O'Neil asked, leaning forward onto his knees.

"Nothing except a name. I don't know a whole lot about the windward side of Martinique full stop. We need to look at a chart and figure it all out."

"I think dere's an old chart o' Martinique 'round here somewhere. Why don't we go see what it says?"

In the storage room at the back of his house O'Neil began to rummage through a chest of drawers, and after flicking through several items seemed to find what he was looking for. Carefully he unfolded what looked to be a very old chart onto the table.

"Well O'Neil, you really are full of surprises! Where the hell did you come across this antique? It says here it was drawn in

1831, which makes it over a hundred years old!" Jack remarked, bending down to examine the chart more closely.

"Man, dis here chart been in de family fo' longer than I can remember. Me grandfather ol' Napoleon deVilliars handed it down to me father, who gave it to me. Nappy got hold of it, along wit' a lot of other gear, when a big French schooner ran up on de reef just south of Anse Tortue. He an' he two brothers sailed out dere wit' dey sloop and salvaged her. Dat's how de ol' man got started in life. He built he first schooner from everything he pulled off o' dat vessel. Dat all happen when Sinclair was a small boy, an' he goin' on eighty-eight dis year, so you can figure fo' yourself when dat was."

Jack took a moment to look over the old French chart. "This is an impressive bit of work, isn't it? The men who made this chart surly had some skill."

"Yes man, dem ol' time fellahs had patience and plenty strength. Just movin' a vessel from place to place to take all o' dese bearin's an' measurements wouldn't o' been easy. Like my brother Llewellyn would say, 'De world is gettin' wiser but weaker.' So tell me, what is it we lookin' fo'?"

With O'Neil leaning over the chart next to him, Jack explained how and where they had made their first drop-off and pick-up at Petite Anse, near Fort-de-France. "We've heard the French are patrolling the whole of the lee side, from St. Pierre in the north to Diamond Rock in the south, making the option of landing again anywhere on that side far too dangerous to consider. That's why we've chosen to take our man off from the windward side. Do you know anything about that part of the island?"

"One ting I does know 'bout de east coast o' Martinique is you does want to steer well clear, especially at night, because dese shoals run a-way out," O'Neil stated, pointing to the rocks and reefs marked on the chart.

"Our man on the island says he wants to use the village of Le Robert as the pick-up point, which we can see here on the chart. What we've got to do now is work out just how we're going to get in and out of there without being caught, stuck on a reef, or sunk by a U-boat. No worries, eh mate?"

O'Neil took a quick sidelong glance at Jack, the beginnings of a smile playing beneath his grey moustache. "Dere's not much can't be done by a man once he does put he mind to it," he finally said.

It was just after sundown when O'Neil's young grandson Errol uneasily approached Harry and Rabbit, who were leaning quietly against the workbench under the trees of the boatyard. "'Scuse me Cap, but my Grandpa O'Neil sent me to take you to he house up yonder," the boy nervously said, pointing up the hill.

"Lead the way, young man, lead the way," Harry replied, and together they followed the boy as he jogged ahead up the path.

Benjie barked at the strangers as Errol opened the gate and led them across the yard to the house. "Grandpa! De white men is here!" he shouted as he rushed through the front door.

"Show dem tru' to de back, boy!"

Entering the room, they found Jack and O'Neil busy studying the chart. "I see you've got your own chart. I didn't know so brought a couple of my own," Harry said, laying the roll he had tucked under his arm on to the table. "I say, chaps, this looks interesting," he commented after a few moments. "Tell me all about this relic!" And so the story of the old map was retold, much to the Englishman's appreciation.

"At any rate, I'm sure nothing has changed too much since this was drawn," Jack said. "We've been studying it and have a couple of ideas. Tell us what you're thinking."

They faced each other across O'Neil's rustic table, with the chart between them. "According to Fauconnier," Harry began, "Gregoire will be taken as far as the small town of Le Robert, where he has good contacts. The two of them will be there on the night of the 14th of July, which as you know is Bastille Day. This should be a helpful distraction. That night, you chaps are to land Carlisle ashore somewhere close to the village. Fauconnier will be looking out for him in the church square in Le Robert, and take him to where Gregoire will be waiting. Jack, you will then pick the two of them up at the rendezvous point and get them back aboard your vessel. The finer points of how you will do this will be left up to you to work out once you get there."

"And how do you feel about all of this Rabbit? You think it can work? After all, you're the one that'll be in the hot seat."

"Yes man, well I know a little bit 'bout dis area. When I was livin' in Marie-Galante, ol' man Debussy told me he had relations who grew sugar cane out on dat side o' Martinique. If he had a bad season, sometimes he used to buy 'cane from dem for his distillery. From Port St. Louis, dey used to sail dey schooner to windward o' Guadeloupe and come in from de north, sail round Cap Caravelle and straight in to dis place called Galion Bay. He told me about it once. Said dere were plenty o' reefs about de place, but dere were passages between 'em. Le Robert is here, just to de south o' where I'm talkin' 'bout. Once we get true de outside reefs in de whaleboat de rest should be easy. We jus' need to find a good place for me to go ashore. I still have de identity papers fo' 'Mark Debussy', so if anyone axe any questions I should be able to get by."

Jack listened intently to what the Bajan had to say, and looked carefully again at the chart himself. "What you think is easy is obviously different from what I do, mate. Do we have any information concerning any French naval presence on this side of the island?"

"As far as our man knows, there is one patrol boat based on the windward side," Harry replied. "That's about all he could tell me."

"Right. Well let's put our heads together and see if we can't figure something out, shall we?" Jack said, and over the next couple of hours the basis of a workable plan was conceived.

Three days later, just before sunset, the *Arabella D*, carrying the thirteen injured merchant seamen, sailed for Barbados. The *Roulette* was not far behind. Harry and Val would remain anchored in Frigate Bay for another day before sailing for Barbados themselves, where they planned to meet up with the *Roulette* upon their return. Jack bolstered his crew by asking Clancy deVilliars, O'Neil's youngest son, to come along. O'Neil also asked for his old first mate Selwyn McCreery, also known as Pepper, to join them as well. Clearing away from under the ruins of Gunnery Point, they caught the full strength of the tradewind, and after working the trim and adjusting to the breeze, the schooner put her nose north and was soon knifing into the oncoming seas, quickly overhauling the deep laden *Arabella* as both vessels sailed close-hauled over neighbouring Mustique. It was a clear night with a moderate breeze blowing from the south-east, and they were sailing her hard. O'Neil stood at the helm, delicately easing the long, narrow vessel along as she cut a swathe through the phosphorescent sea, all sails including fore and main tops'ls set and drawing. The *Antipodes* sat nestled on deck to starboard, as if patiently waiting for her turn to take part in the operation.

Once on course, the crew settled in around the wheel drinking hot cups of coffee while Rabbit sat in the stern next to the mainsheet with Jono and Bull, slowly working on a bottle of Jack Iron rum. The crew were wide awake. There was no thought of sleep, the excitement of their mission leaving everyone highly alert. Pepper, O'Neil's old first mate, zigzagged his way across the steeply leaning deck after checking the foresails, his tattered black oilskin jacket flapping in the breeze. An equally ancient sou'wester was pulled down tight over his head.

"Now dis is all I does ask for!" he began, to no one in particular. "You jus' gi' me sea water work, ya hear! Me fed up wit all o' dat hog-shit land work, mon! Me did born fo' de seawater. A well-found vessel, a good captain and handy crew, dat's all me does ask fo'. None o' dat hoein' an' plantin' fo' me. Me done told me ol' woman so, too! She want me stay to help she work de garden to get ready fo' planting season, and me say what – with three big children you want me to turn down a trip like dis? No mon, get dem lazy boys out in de garden, we. Me goin' wit O'Neil an' Jack, an' dat's de way it goin' fo' be!"

"Yes Pepper, me know what you is sayin'," replied Kingsford with a smile. "I does face de same ting at home all o' de time, but a man got to do what he born to do."

The Grenadines were quickly left behind, while ahead, lost in the clouds off the lee bow, lay the high volcano of St. Vincent's

Mt. Soufriere. Through the night they sailed, and sunrise found them to windward of St. Lucia, with Martinique faintly visible on the horizon beyond.

The day slowly passed as they sailed north with two men constantly on watch from the mastheads looking out for the dreaded U-boats, as well as any sign of enemy patrol boats. The balance of the crew lounged about the deck, napping in the shade of the sails as they readied themselves for the big night ahead. There was excitement around mid-morning when Gilbert hauled in a beautiful bull-headed Dorado with the fishing line he was trailing astern; the fish barely landing on deck before Jono had it cleaned and its head in the pot cooking as he quickly made up a fish broff for lunch.

Time seemed to stand still as they slowly came abreast and then passed the high purple shadow of Martinique, until finally towards late afternoon they gybed around onto port tack and began to run down towards the island, which now lay roughly twelve miles away. With Clancy and Gilbert up the mast they closed in on the land, the two best sets of eyes aloft on the lookout for the deadly shoals lying offshore, and also for the passage which would take the whaleboat through. When the shouts from the masthead did come, Jack went aloft to have a look himself, where he confirmed the course they would later take through the reefs.

Slowly daylight blended into darkness, and as it did the joking and light-heartedness ceased altogether. In the dying light, a meeting was held back around the wheelbox. As Zeph steered, Jack looked into the faces of his long-time crew which he knew so well, from the red complexioned, stormy Kingsford to the dark, solemn Bull; the anxious Gilbert to the care-free smiling young Dawson; the bright-eyed Clancy to his cousin the serious, practical Earl. Pepper stood with arms folded alongside the imposing frame of O'Neil deVilliars, whose very presence brought with it a confidence that seemed to quell all fears or anxiety. And then there was Rabbit Haynes, languidly lounging with his back to the bulwark, as if without a care in the world.

"Right – this is all straightforward enough. We've talked about it, we've looked at the chart, we can pretty much see where we have to go and now we simply need to do what we came here to do. As I mentioned before, Clancy, Gilbert, Earl and Dawson will join Rabbit and me in the whaleboat, which leaves O'Neil to run the vessel with the rest of you. If God spare life we'll be back here sometime after midnight tomorrow. Now let's get ourselves ready to go."

During the course of the day, the whaleboat had been thoroughly attended to by Pepper, who had meticulously examined every aspect of the boat and rig. He replaced worn rigging. He stitched repairs into the sails. And he had young Dawson on the hop as he harangued him over every detail. "You is de bailing hole man, isn't it?" Pepper queried. "How many bailers you does have?"

"Here it is, right here, Uncle," the smiling Dawson answered.

"One calabash? Dat's it? An' what if you fill-up an' happen to throw dat one overboard? Den what?"

"Right then Uncle Selwyn, I'll find a nex' one," the boy grinned.

"Make it two at least! You never know when you might need dem! Now let's have a look a de oars an' everything else. You don' want some hogshit oarpin breakin' jus' at de wrong time!" And so it went for most of the day, until the fiery second mate was close as possible to being satisfied.

With the treacherous Bank de Roches lurking in the darkness a mile away under their lee, and the Pointe du Diable somewhere off in the murky distance, the whaleboat was hoisted over the bulwarks on her lifting tackles, and with her sails and spars and oars all lashed securely inside, swung out over the rushing water to leeward. "Hey Dawson, you sure you got de drain-plug in? Certain-sure better den crack-sure, you know!" Pepper shouted at the last minute.

"Yes Uncle, de drain plug's in. You made me check it t'ree times!'

"Let's jus' put de blasted boat in de watah we; we'll sail clean past de island fo' Pepper be happy!" Bull exclaimed, holding a turn on the halyard.

"Alright O'Neil, bring her up slowly. Stand by to lower away!" Jack yelled back towards the helm.

Carefully the schooner was brought up on the wind. "Ease de mainsheet gi'me," O'Neil directed, and ever so slightly the schooner slowed down, until just at the right moment Jack gave the order, the halyards were eased and the whaleboat was in the water, rolling in the big swell. As soon as she touched, the crew leapt aboard, and with dexterity quickly released the tackles and pushed free. Once clear, the schooner trimmed her sails and continued on her way, sailing towards a small bay on the north coast of St. Lucia, thirty-odd miles away, where she would anchor and wait out the day before returning the following night to meet the *Antipodes*.

Le Havre du Robert

The schooner quickly melted into the night, her long main boom and rectangular mainsail a disappearing shadow in the darkness. The crew of the *Antipodes* needed no instruction, quickly springing to their tasks without a word being spoken. As Jack swung the rudder over the stern and hung it in its gudgeons, the others were stepping the mast. Dawson ran the tackline of the jib forward, the two shrouds were made fast port and starboard, the mainsail was unlashed and the bamboo sprit set. The crew jumped to their positions, the flapping sheets were trimmed, the sails filled and they were sailing. Jack pulled the tiller to him, bearing away towards the land, and the double ended whaleboat began to surf down the large, windblown waves towards the dark, forbidding shore.

Once they were on course and settled, Jack asked Rabbit to go forward and stand on the bowseat to look out for the reef ahead. "Me can jus' see some lights inside o' dere. Must be de town o' Trinite. Just steer fo' dem," he shouted into the wind. "She lookin' clear right t'rough!" With scattered breakers to port and starboard, Rabbit piloted the whaleboat past the dangers of the outer bank. "We can pull off to port now, Skip. Dere's de headland we lookin' fo'."

Trimming their sails, they hauled off for the approaching cape, which was now beginning to emerge from out of the dark silhouette of the high, mountainous island. Astern on the windward horizon, the rising moon shown through the clouds, casting an eerie light over the rugged, surf-fringed shoreline that the *Antipodes* was quickly approaching.

Soon the cape could be plainly seen jutting out into the rough Atlantic, just as Rabbit had described. The sea was becoming more confused, the waves steep and square, as the swell rebounded off of the treacherous shore, keeping the crew of the small boat busy.

The occasional sloppy wave would break over the boat, leaving two or sometimes three of them bailing. "Man it's a good ting Pepper made you find more bailers, isn't it? Otherwise we might be headin' straight to de bottom!"

Ahead lay the eastern extremity of Martinique, which was appropriately named Pointe du Diable. "Man, I can see why dey does call it Devil's Point! Dis here is worse than goin' over Ship's Prow with a weather tide!" Gilbert shouted as he again jumped down into the boat to bail out more water. With Earl working the jib and Clancy on the mainsheet, Jack weaved his way through the pyramid-like seas. The Table au Diable appeared out of the gloom; a big, rectangular, flat-topped piece of stone that sat just above the water's surface, white water draining off of it with each receding wave, only to be covered again by the next booming surge. Slowly they surfed past the black rocks and exploding waves, and as the point was gradually rounded the seas became less confused. With the steady wind and smoother water, they were now sailing far more comfortably. Rabbit continued to pilot the whaleboat from the main thwart, steadying himself against the mast. "Out dere to windward is de nex' set of shoals, an' to starboard would be Galion Bay. Down inside dere to port is Le Robert and de two islands we looking for. Should be safe to haul off and head across in dat direction now, Skip."

"Yes, I reckon you're right. We should be well inside of the Bank des Roches now," Jack agreed. "Trim the main and jib, and give me half of the centreboard, and let's see what the ol' girl can do." Protected by the shoals from the deep ocean swell, and with the wind on the beam, the crew all hiked out to windward and the *Antipodes*, now in her element, reached across the choppy, moonlit water towards Le Havre du Robert.

The two small islands that formed the end of the natural harbour Jack had marked out on the chart slowly appeared ahead of them. In the bright moonlight, the shoals and reefs could be picked out by the sign of breaking waves, and with sheets eased they rounded the outer islet and ran into the bay. In the protected lee of the twin islands they gybed, and the whaleboat was carefully worked into the junction of the two cays, where they found a shallow cove with a sandy beach at the top of it. Slowly gliding across the calm sea, the bow touched up on the sand and the crew jumped out into the knee-deep water. The sails were quickly made up, the rigging let go, and the mast laid down inside the boat. The five oars were taken out and placed cross-ways on the beach to form skids for the keel to run on. With three men aside, the boat was hauled across the sand, stopping only to retrieve the oars from behind to lay them down in front again. The last shove had the whaleboat up under a dense stand of scrubby manchineel trees. "This is perfect," Jack whispered. "She'll be well hidden under these trees. Rabbit and I'll walk up to the top of the rise and have a good look around. The rest of you spread out and see if there's any sign of life on the island."

Winding their way through the bushes, they found open ground behind the scrub-lined beach. The crew all headed off in different directions as Jack and Rabbit picked their way to the top of the rise, which formed the highest part of the island. From the peak they could see across the water to the sparkling lights of Le Robert in the top corner of the bay. "It looks like we picked out a good spot in truth, mon," said Rabbit. "What is it – a mile and a half, two miles to town? From up here we can see right 'round in every direction."

"Yes, this is a perfect spot for reconnaissance. Can you see much with the glasses?"

"It's a bit dark, but what I do see doesn't look too promisin'. Look just there, coming out o' de bay."

Jack took the glasses and quickly picked out the silhouette of a patrol boat steaming out to sea. Soon the noise of a diesel engine could be faintly heard; then the ship's profile could be discerned as it made its way out of the harbour. Passing close by the end of the outermost cay, it could be seen that the ship was a substantial vessel with a gun mounted on the foredeck. "Well there goes the theory about not having to worry about any patrol boats. It's a good thing we weren't a half hour later, isn't it? Otherwise we might have run smack dab into her!"

After one last look around they walked back down the hill to the whaleboat. One by one the others returned, all reporting they had seen no sign of life on the island. "Right then, let's get ourselves some shuteye," Jack ordered. The cotton jib was pulled out and laid over the leaf-covered sand, and the crew made themselves as comfortable as possible. One by one they dropped off to sleep, waiting for daylight.

Slap.

"Damn mosquitos!"

Jack opened one eye to see Earl get up and walk into the bush, where he could hear him urinate. Slowly pushing himself up, he sat and blearily gazed out over the bay. It was still early; the sun had not yet broken over the horizon. Rising slowly to his feet, he stretched and walked the few feet to the edge of the beach. From where he stood he could not see the village, but in his field of vision there was nothing moving; no fishing boats, and no patrol boat. Slowly the others started to rise from the various sleeping positions. Rabbit had slept inside the boat and now stuck his head over the gunnel. "All clear, Cap?" he asked.

"So far so good."

"All o' you brought a bottle of rum, isn't it?" Rabbit asked of no one in particular. Climbing over Clancy to get to the back of the boat, he began rummaging through the stern locker where their food and provisions were stored.

"Oh me muddah…what de ass you up to now?" Clancy chided. "Can't you see a man sleepin?"

"Me jus' lookin' for an openeye, mon. An' it's about time you got up anyway! French police might be coming through de bush to arrest you' ass right now! Dey might catch you sleepin, but not de ol' Rabbit!"

"Barbajans! Man, dey all de same! You must never've had milk from yo' mother's breast – she must've put you straight on de rum!"

"Listen, it's only de one me havin' just to clear out de cobwebs. Anyone else?"

"Alright fellahs, I'm going back up to the top of the hill. You boys coming?" Jack grabbed the satchel with the field glasses and the chart out of the back of the boat and headed away from the beach. Striding across the dry brown grass, he climbed up to the peak of the hill. Taking out the glasses and facing seaward, he slowly searched the waters for any sign of the patrol boat, but couldn't see it anywhere. Looking north from the top of the cay into the furthest extremes of Baie du Galion, he scanned the southern side of Cap Caravelle right out to its windward extremity. He could see where they had sailed in the night before, and could see the breaking shoals of the Bank des Roches to the east. From the top of this hill he had a three hundred and sixty degree view of the whole area. Sitting down and propping his arms on his knees he now looked shoreward, casting an eye over the surrounds with the glasses. The bay opened up directly in front of him, with two smaller cays between him and Le Robert, where a tall church spire marked the centre of the village. Except for a few small fishing boats hauled up on the shore, there were no signs of any type of vessel on the water. To his right, the small island they were camping on was separated from the mainland by a stretch of shallow water and semi-submerged reef. Removing the chart from its canvas protection, he unrolled it and laid it at his feet, comparing it to what he saw before him. To the north of the village the open shoreline soon terminated into a mangrove-lined bay formed by a hook-shaped spit that swung abruptly out to the east. At the edge of the mangroves, he detected a foot path running from the water up to the top of a ridge where there looked to be a road leading into town.

"So how does she look, Cap?" Rabbit asked as he sat down next to Jack, followed by the rest of the crew.

"I think I see what we're looking for, mate. On the other side of the bay, just to the edge of the mangroves, is a track which leads from the water to a road that seems to run along the top of the bluff. Here, have a look for yourself." Rabbit now peered through the glasses. Several minutes passed while he examined the terrain. "So what do you think, Mr Haynes?"

"Yes mon, it looks good. I think if you can get me to de bottom of dat path yonder I can find my way into town easy."

The crew of the *Antipodes* sat up on the top of the hill well into the morning, etching the details of the surrounds into their minds. To the north of their little island they also carefully examined the myriad of reefs and rocks and breaking white surf, identifying what appeared to be two meandering channels of dark blue deep water winding through the lighter turquoise of the shallows. "There's not much hope in getting through that lot except in daylight," Jack pointed out. "What do you boys think?"

Gilbert took the glasses from the captain and had a look. "Me wouldn't want to do it at night, but in good light you might find a way through, yes."

They also noted a gap through the breakers in the wild offshore Bank de Roches reef to the east. "See dat gap t'rough de outside shoals?" Rabbit asked as the group all turned to look. "I think dat passage would be good to remember."

Jack swept the glasses towards where Rabbit was pointing. "That must be what the chart here calls the 'Loupe Bordelaise'. It looks to be a narrow channel with a few twists and turns, but appears to be a clear passage out to the open ocean. It could save us from sailing all that distance back to Cap Caravelle where we came in. We should take some bearings on it, just in case."

Finally they headed back to their hideaway. From out of the stern locker Jack retrieved some of the food Jono had prepared for them. One by one each man took a piece of fried fish, johnny cake and cold cornmeal 'fungi'.

They napped off and on through the day, preparing for the night ahead. As they lay dozing in the heat of the mid-afternoon, Rabbit began to talk. "You know, ol' man Debussy knew a lot 'bout dese French islands. Dey does have some colourful history in truth! One story he told me was dat way back in de 1600's dere was dis rich count who happen to kill he cousin in a duel back in France, an' because o' dat had to run away here to Martinique. When he got here he was given a commission as an' officer in de Kings Army – dat's how it worked in dem days when you was born to de right people – and soon he made a name for heself by defeating de local Carib Indian chief in a big battle. For dat he was given a large piece o' land out dere on de end o' Cap Caravelle by de guv'nah, where he built a grand 'chateau' overlooking de bay. An' dat is de bay out yonder, jus' inside o' de point. It came to be known as Baie du Corsaire, an' all kinds o' mischief was said to go on in dat place. He had warehouses and slaves and so, grew 'cane, tobacco an' other crops, but really made he money from bubal. Dat ol' Count used de bay to harbour smugglers and notorious buccaneers who anchored inside o' dere carrying on all kinds o' wickedness with de Count's wild African slave women, while he an' de Pirate Captain would be up in de castle dressed in all their velvet finery, feastin' on whole roast pigs, drinkin' rum and turnin' beast!" The crew all let out a guffaw. "Debussy used to say dat if you went lookin', you'd find de ruins of de ol' chateau up inside o' dere somewhere still."

"Rabbit you is somethin' else, we! You sure can spin a yarn," Dawson said, with his beguiling smile.

"See what slavery did for dem ol'-time white people?" commented Gilbert. "Me can jus' picture dat castle, high up dere on de hill, all dem black slaves below tendin' sugarcane an' tobacco an' cotton! Servants waitin' on de massa hand an' foot, de overseer struttin' round wit he big bull-whip, wearin' he big white hat an' smoking a cheroot! Warehouses full o' contraband...man, dem was real plantation days in trut'!"

"An don't forget de buccaneers!" Earl chipped in. "Tradin' all dat plunder for rum an' women – man who owned dat place out dere all on he own would o' been like a real king! Wouldn't want to be a black man in dem days, dat's fo' sure!"

The approaching drone of diesel engines distracted Rabbit from his story. They all turned at the same time to see the French patrol boat slowly re-enter Le Havre du Robert. Taking up the binoculars, Jack watched the patrol boat cruise past until it disappeared behind the small islet in front of them. "I reckon we should take a hike back up to our lookout and see what they're up to, don't you?" In the long shadows of the late afternoon the crew stealthily climbed back up to the top of the hill, and keeping low they knelt down and keenly watched as the grey ship approached the crescent-shaped basin in front of the village. Slowly, it began swinging in a wide arc until its bows faced the wind blowing straight into the harbour from the east. Not long afterwards, a splash could be seen as the anchor hit the water. The enemy ship now rested less than two hundred yards from the southern end of the little islet in front of them; one which they had to pass to get Rabbit ashore.

"Well this will make it interesting," Jack said, lowering the glasses. "That boat's sitting in a bloody awkward spot, isn't it? There's no way we can pass around the south side of the little island without being seen. And to get out of here the same way we came in will be next to impossible. I think this means a change in plans, boys. We all better try and get a last look at those reefs up yonder before it gets dark, because like it or not, I think we'll most likely be making our way through them later tonight."

The peal of church bells could now be heard from the far-off cathedral. In the fading light Jack McLeod and his crew put their heads together and made their final plans. By the time they returned to their hideout, it was dark.

The whaleboat was shoved down and everyone silently found their position. They were rowing, not sailing, and the mast and sails rested on the seats inside the boat. The oarsmen extended their oars through the wooden oar pins and began to pick up the pace. The captain stood in the stern sheets and steered with a long oar they called a sweep because they would be passing over shallows, and the steering oar was much easier to manoeuvre than the rudder. Rabbit pulled the fifth oar, rowing from the most forward position. They had even borrowed the old whalermen's trick of muffling the sounds of the oars by securing canvas over the wooden oarlocks. The plan was to stay close to the western side of their island, keeping to the shadows. As they neared the northern end, Jack could see the reef ahead. It was from here they had to make their run. Turning to port, he pointed the bow towards their destination.

"Okay boys," he said, "it's now we have to get a move on. Le' all-we go!" They had close to a mile of open water to cover before they reached the cay standing between them and the mainland. The crew were pulling in perfect unison; the only sound of their passing was the rolling of their bow wave. Slowly the dark shape of the small islet grew closer, and as it did the patrol boat gradually became concealed by the headland. A few more yards and they would be out of the cutter's vision. And then the searchlight came on, wildly flashing through the darkness as it skipped over the far side of the bay and then out to sea. It swept back towards them. "Stop rowing and lay down!" Jack ordered, and everyone lay back into the boat as it continued to glide on under its own momentum. The searchlight slowly swung over their head, and continued to move on. "Don't worry boys, they're only speculating!" Jack whispered. And then the cutter was completely blocked from their vision. "That's it lads, we're safe for the moment at least. Good going!" And on they rowed.

Approaching the shore, they now slowed their rate. The whaleboat coasted towards the islet. The northern end had a shallow reef virtually connecting it to Martinique itself. Carefully they paralleled the shore, until they reached the end, where they turned towards the shoal. Rabbit stood up in the bow, and as the stem touched the reef he vaulted over the gunnel, his pantlegs rolled tightly up over his knees. The oars were shipped and one by one the crew walked forward. Sliding into the calf deep water, they dragged the whaleboat across the shallows into the deeper water on the western side, from where they could see the village of Le Robert brightly lit up across the bay. They now had to cross another half of a mile of exposed water before reaching the landing spot on the other side. Jumping into the boat they pushed off for the far shore.

Within a few strokes they were in rhythm again. Instead of steering straight for the landing spot, Jack took a more circular route, looping to the right and keeping to the shadows of the mangroves. The cutter came into view again, and they watched as the searchlight continued to slowly sweep the harbour. Then it switched off. Two hundred yards from shore and they stopped rowing. The boat glided across the calm bay. Six pairs of eyes scanned the shoreline for any sign of life. "Anyone see anything?" Jack whispered. "Gilbert – anything?"

After a long silence, "Looks okay to me, Cap. Nothin' movin' inside o' dere."

"Right, let's go in then," he ordered, and moments later they touched the muddy bayside. Rabbit jumped out. "Best of luck, cobber," Jack whispered. 'We'll anchor in that corner over there," he said pointing to a spot a couple of hundred yards away. "We'll be looking out for you. Just give a whistle and we'll be here." The Bajan pushed them off before headin up the small path and into the night. They pulled into the murky little hole, drifting into the bushy, dense mangroves. Jack reached over the stern and grabbed a limb as they backed in. Taking a spare line, he tied the boat off. They were safe and out of sight. Now all they could do was wait.

Loup Bordelaise and the Bullet

Rabbit swiftly climbed up the narrow path. Turning to his left at the top of the hill, he walked along the dusty road, which was still warm to his bare feet from the heat of the day. Dressed in khaki work trousers and shirt, unkempt blond hair hanging out from under his straw hat, chin covered with week-old stubble, and carrying a pointed cutlass sharpened on both edges, Rabbit had the appearance of a cane cutter coming out of the fields after a hard day's work. It was close to two miles to Le Robert, and soon he was at the outskirts of the town. There were plenty of people on the road, all moving in the same direction. Nobody gave him a second glance.

The road entered the main part of the clean, neatly kept town. Coconut palms and flamboyant trees with their bright red flowers grew amongst the whitewashed buildings with their red iron roofs, wrought iron balconies and shuttered windows. Following the flow of people, Rabbit continued on towards the central square. Passing the ornate Hotel De Ville, he soon came upon the Cathédrale with its white spire facing onto the town's central plaza. From the square the streets sloped down to the waterfront a few hundred yards away, where the anchor lights of the patrol boat could be seen out in the bay.

A dais had been set up at one end of the plaza draped in the red, white, and blue banners of the French Tricolour. A large crowd of townspeople mingled in the square, waiting for the ceremonies to begin. The population was an eclectic mix of colour, from white planter stock to the jet black of the Afro-Caribbean and almost every complexion in between. Rabbit remembered Debussy telling him that in the Creole patois there were over thirty words used to describe the different shades of colour of the French Caribbean, and it seemed that all of them were represented in the square that night. Everyone was well-dressed; men in neat suits and panama hats, the women in intricately laced dresses and refined headwear. The mood, however, was not celebratory. This crowd was not there for a Bastille Day fête. This was a crowd intent on far more serious business. Standing on the fringe of the square, Rabbit could hear all the comments, and he did not envy the mayor, whose speech seemed to have been rejected before he even began.

There was also a large police presence. Gendarmes dressed in their khaki uniforms lined the edges of the crowd, batons hanging from their wide black belts. Rabbit's keen eye searched the crowd for Philippe Javert, eventually spotting him on the far side of the square near the door of the church, smoking a cigarette. Slowly making his way through the crowd, he eased his way to the foot of the cathedral steps. Philippe swung his gaze around until it locked on to Rabbit's casual stare. With a slight nod of his head away from the dais, Philippe took one last pull on his cigarette, dropped it and carefully ground it out before moving towards the far end of the square. Rabbit nonchalantly moved in the same direction. Arriving at the furthest edge of the crowd, he saw Philippe standing in the shadows of a narrow laneway leading away from the plaza. Reaching into the pocket of his shirt, Rabbit took out some tobacco and rolled a cigarette. "Would you have light, monsieur?" he casually asked Philippe.

"But of course," he politely answered. "In ten minutes meet me behind that wall on the other side of the square, under the old fig tree," he whispered as he lit the cigarette.

With a tip of his hat, Rabbit melted back into the crowd. He could see that something was about to take place on the dais. The energy of the gathering began to intensify, the crowd tightening up and pushing forward. Still he waited, craning his neck as if to see the stage. Seats on the dais were now filled by persons of obvious importance. A man wearing an honorary sash got up to address the crowd, and was met with immediate derision. The louder he tried to speak the more boisterous the crowd became. The Gendarmes on the periphery began to tense their muscles. Rabbit slowly started to edge his way out of the throng, moving towards the shadows of the old stone wall. Finally he was clear. He took a last look at the agitated crowd before sidling around the end of the wall, noting out of the corner of his eye the moon rising over the eastern horizon.

A giant fig tree stood before him, casting the ground beneath in dark shadow. He had walked several paces when a voice came from behind. "Not interested in hearing the speeches? That isn't very patriotic!" He turned to see a swarthy fat man in a wide brimmed hat leaning against the wall. He recognised him instantly. He was one of the men who had fronted him at the Hotel Saint Louis when he was posing as Marc Debussy.

Rabbit conjured up a dull-witted grin and answered him in his best colloquial patois. "Of course, Brother. I just need to take a piss."

"Urinating in public is a jailable offence."

"Since when is a man put in jail for answering a call to nature? After all, when a man's got to go he's got to go!" he replied with a smile, unzipping his trousers. "Now are you just going to stand there and watch? Or do you enjoy this kind of thing?"

The man continued to look on as Rabbit did his business against the wall. He smiled a dirty smile, then took a last pull of his cigarette and flicked it away, the dying ember arcing through the air. "So what are you saying, I am some sort of queer or something?"

Rabbit was starting to get worried. Philippe would be there any second. He had to do something to get rid of him. After zipping himself back up, he turned and walked up to face him. "Not exactly, only I find it strange you should worry about someone pissing against the wall when there is a riot about to explode next door."

The man looked at Rabbit. Slowly a spark of recognition grew in his eyes. He reached into his coat. Rabbit knew he was going for a gun. He had a split second to react. In one motion he brought his razor sharp cutlass up under the man's chin, grabbing him by the shirt front with his left hand at the same time and pushing him against the wall. "Move the wrong way and I'll cut you open like a pig," he whispered through clenched teeth as he pushed the man along into the shadow of the old tree.

"I am Sécurité Nationale! Let go of me or you are dead!" the fat man gasped.

"Is that right? And what about this then?" and in one swift motion Rabbit's knee came straight up between his legs. As the fat man doubled over he caught him with his fist, this time plumb on the nose. The man's expression showed shock and surprise. His wide eyes bugged over Rabbit's right shoulder as he gasped for air, blood running from his broken nose.

At that moment a car pulled up, skidding to a stop behind him. "Get in!" a voice shouted. Rabbit threw one more punch into the man's soft midriff and then jogged around the car and jumped in next to the driver. The car was stationary for a split second longer.

The bleeding man drunkenly reached under his coat. "Who's he?" Philippe shouted from behind the wheel.

"Sécurité Nationale!"

"He's going for his gun!"

Rabbit watched as the back seat passenger pointed a Sten machine gun out of the window and fired several bursts, knocking the man back against the wall, where he slowly slumped to the ground, his gun firing harmlessly into the ground. In the square the sound of gunfire momentarily silenced the crowd before confusion erupted. Two men in suits emerged from around the wall, brandishing handguns. Tyres spun as Philippe accelerated away from the scene. "Don't fire Jacques, you'll hit the crowd behind!" he yelled as he aimed the car at the agents, forcing them to dodge out of his way.

The car sped down the narrow street with the sound of gunshots ringing out from behind. A few blocks later, Philippe made a hard left around the corner. Slamming to a stop, the door was yanked open and Gregoire jumped in next to the gunman. "Now where do we take you?" Philippe yelled.

"Just outside of town, on the road to Trinite!" Rabbit answered. "I'll tell you when to stop!"

Philippe hit the accelerator and at the top of the hill turned hard right, speeding towards the outskirts of town. Behind, the faint sound of a police siren could be heard. The burly man in the back seat pulled back the bolt on his Sten.

"Sorry Gregoire. It was supposed to be a little less exciting than this," Rabbit said.

The car sped up the road, Philippe glancing intently into the rear-view mirror. "Stop at the top o' the hill!" Rabbit ordered. "Okay Gregoire, we gotta run," he said as the car skidded to a halt. They jumped out. "Good luck and Godspeed, brother," he yelled, slamming the door behind. The sound of sirens was getting closer. The car sped off into the night and they ran down the hill. Gregoire in his white suit and two-toned patent leather shoes was right behind, until he hit a slippery patch and fell onto his backside, his hat flying off as he scrambled to his feet. As they neared the water, Rabbit began whistling loudly. "No use bein' discreet now wit' de whole o' de island's police force on our ass," he said, whistling again. "You better take dem fancy shoes off G, 'cause we may have to swim fo' it!" Looking out into the gloomy bay Rabbit impatiently whistled again. The sound of sirens grew near. Two cars went speeding past.

"I think we lost them," Gregoire said, looking over his shoulder. Just then the second car backed up and stopped at the top of the hill, its blue light flashing. "Or maybe not…"

The whaleboat appeared out of the murky mangroves, four men putting their backs into the stroke. At the top of the hill, khaki clad Gendarmes began running down the path, whistles blowing. And just at that moment the searchlight from the patrol boat flashed across the water, landing squarely on them. The bow of the whaleboat slipped into the mud of the marshy shore. "Catch us and push off hard!" Jack yelled. Stopping the momentum, Rabbit locked his leg, and then with a running push shoved the boat off. Gregoire tumbled in and Rabbit scrambled over the rail after him. "Back off hard, boys! Back off hard!" The boat rowed backwards towards the dark mangroves. The spotlight flashed across the bay. The first policeman reached the shore and stood, blowing his whistle as he removed the pistol from his holster, took aim and fired. A bullet whizzed over their heads. Several more shots were fired. The boat stern swung around. "Alright lads, go hell for leather!" Jack yelled. Rabbit jumped into his forward stroke position and pushed out his oar, catching on to the rhythm. A few more gunshots rang out from shore, but they were soon out of range.

Jack stared into the shadowy night towards the anchored patrol boat, which was still trying to find them with their light. Noticing movement alongside, he quickly realized the meaning. "I don't want to put an added incentive on this, boys, but those navy blokes have jumped into their launch and it looks like it's heading this way. We better reach that shoal before they do or we're done for."

And so now the race was on. Jack stood calmly in the stern steering his whaleboat towards the shallow that ran between the mainland and the small islet off the end of the point. They had to get there ahead of the launch. It was their only chance.

The *Antipodes* skimmed across the flat water of the bay. The French launch was nearing the middle of the cay as the searchlight attempted to keep focused on them. The whaleboat drew within one hundred yards of the shoal. "Come on girl, you never lost a race befo'! You can't start now!" Gilbert chanted from the after thwart. "Come on boys, put your backs into it!"

"Keep it up...we're going to cross them. You're doing well lads, keep it up!" They could hear the sound of the launch's diesel now, and Jack could see its bow wave. "Ten yards to go. When we hit it's all out and haul as quick as you can!" They had less than fifty yards on the launch. He only hoped it would be enough. "Stand by. We'll touch in five, four, three...okay, ship oars and all out!" The whaleboat surged onto the reef, and as the keel touched the crew were out, grabbing hold of the gunnel and running with it, dragging the boat across the shallow. The launch was very close now; they could hear the sailors' voices, a babble of excited French confusion. There were several unsteady gunshots. As they reached the other side of the shoal, the pursuing launch hit the reef hard. Jack glanced over his shoulder just in time to see its crew go tumbling forward on top of each other.

The whaleboat reached deep water and her crew leapt aboard, scrambling to their positions and shoving out their oars. Jack was the last man in. He gave a mighty push and jumped onto the stern deck. Splashing across the reef, a sailor raised his rifle to his shoulder and fired.

Standing in the stern, Jack watched the men on the reef behind straining to get their boat off. "It looks like they're stuck hard, which should buy us some time. Pull steady lads! We're almost out of range!"

The whaleboat disappeared slowly into the night. In a last gasp effort, the French sailor stood at the edge of the shallows, took aim and pulled the trigger. Then bullet hit bone, and Jack McLeod spun and tumbled back into the boat. He tried to move, but something was wrong. The world was spinning. He knew what had happened. He had been there before. "I've been king hit…" he calmly reported. Then he passed out.

There was a moment when everything on board the *Antipodes* seemed to freeze, like they were stuck in time. The crew saw the skipper fall, but it took several moments for them to comprehend the full meaning of what had just happened. Earl was first to react. "Take de hel-em Clancy!" he directed. "We got to keep movin!"

Clancy pulled in his oar and jumped aft to take hold of the long sweep.

Rabbit grabbed Gregoire and gave him his oar. "You take dis! I got to check on de Cap'n! Keep pullin' boys, otherwise we's all in de shit!" Skipping back aft, he jumped into the bilge, where he found the captain lying in a heap, blood turning the bilge water black.

"How is he, Rabbit?" Clancy worriedly asked.

"Not good, man. Shot clean true de shoulder blade. It's bad, man – dey's plenty o' blood!"

"What's goin' on wit' dem Frenchmen, Clancy?" Gilbert yelled. "Can you see anything?"

"Looks like dey got de launch off, but dey got to go right 'round dat cay to try an' catch we. It seems like de big patrol boat is pulling up their anchor, though."

"So what we goin' fo' do?" asked Earl.

"I think we put Rabbit in charge. He do de thinkin' an' we'll sail de boat, right boys?" Gilbert urged. The crew all agreed.

"We've got to take a good look at de skipper for a start! Help me pull him up an' chock 'im next to de centrecase," Rabbit ordered. Gilbert dropped down and carefully helped drag the injured captain forward, who unconsciously moaned as he was shifted into the middle of the boat. Rabbit knelt over Jack, and pulling his rigging knife out of its sheath, cut away the bloody shirt-sleeve. "At least de bullet has gone through and through, but it has taken a hell-of-a lot of meat with it. We need to stop the bleeding. We need somethin' clean," he said, looking around. Then he focused on Gregoire's white cotton shirt. "I think dat shirt has got to be it, G. You mind takin' it off gi'me?"

"Of course, of course," he replied, quickly removing his shirt. Rabbit tore it into strips. Reaching over the side, he soaked the strips in seawater. "That's good. The saltwater should help clean the wound. And pressure," Gregoire said as he rowed, "it needs plenty of pressure." Jack groaned as the Bajan placed wads of cloth on both sides of the bleeding wound and squeezed. Blood continued to run down his chest.

Slowly the captain regained consciousness as the blood-soaked rags were thrown overboard and the process repeated. "Can you hear me, Cap?" Rabbit asked.

Jack opened his eyes halfway. "Yeah – I can hear you. But I wouldn't say I'm bonza, mate. It feels like that bullet took away half me shoulder," he weakly replied, laying his head back onto the top of the case. "What's going on with the patrol boat?"

"Dey hauled up de anchor an' are motorin' out de bay. It's lookin' like de cutter goin' to take de long way 'round to try an' catch we on de nex' side, an' de launch comin' for us on dis side to stop we from doubling back," Clancy said as he stared of into the darkness astern.

"Listen Rabbit, you boys've got to get out through these reefs into open water. You can't worry too much about me. Just remember what we looked at today. O'Neil will be out there somewhere waiting. I'll hang on, don't worry," he said weakly. "If those Frenchmen get a hold of us we're finished."

"Okay, well you try and take it easy. We can't do much more for you now except to try and stop the bleedin'," Rabbit said. "We'll get out through dese reefs, don' frighten."

The whaleboat reached the shallow reef system well ahead of the pursuing launch. Astern they watched the cutter steam out of the Havre du Robert. Navigating through the shallows was not going to be easy, even with the help of the rising moon. With Clancy standing at the steering oar and Rabbit also on the lookout, they could see where the waves were breaking, but had no clue where the hidden rocks and coral heads lurked beneath the surface. Still, from their surveillance from the top of the hill earlier in the day they had a rough idea where the two channels lay, and after only a couple of false turns the whaleboat was brought in line with the narrow cuts exiting into Baie du Galion. Their route had led them into a broad basin, bordered on the north by a long rocky spit, and to the south by a jumble of reefs and breaking surf.

"Dere's where we have fo' go boys. We've got to find our way out true dat mess o' white water," Rabbit said, pointing away to the east.

All the crew were standing, looking at the route for themselves. "Yes man, we can see where it's breakin' an' where it looks like deep water," Gilbert said, pointing out the white water.

After a short discussion, everyone agreed with the decision to take the left hand exit. It was narrower but it provided a better angle on the wind. Then Rabbit gave the order to step the rig. "We're sailin' for we lives here, Kopai, if you didn't know it already. We can't afford a mistake." The oars were taken in and secured to the seats, and then the mast was stepped. The shrouds were made fast, the jib tack secured and the bamboo boom and sprit put in place. Clancy fit the rudder and took hold of the tiller. The sails were flapping in the wind as everyone found their position.

"Gregoire, you come here and look after de Cap'n. De bleedin' seems to have slowed down a bit."

"I said don't worry about me! Just sail the boat, Carlisle!" Jack said weakly with eyes closed.

Earl hauled off the jib and Gilbert pulled in the mainsheet, the centreboard was lowered halfway, and with the breeze over the starboard beam, the boat immediately picked up speed. The waves ahead flashed white in the darkness where the wide basin narrowed down to a cut passing between two low, flat slabs of rock. With Rabbit standing and giving directions, Clancy steered through the cut and then bore away to port, taking the left hand passage as a big mass of breakers loomed ahead. The channel here was slightly wider. To port was the second of the flat rocks sitting just above the surface, while to starboard breakers viciously crashed over the semi-submerged rocks. "Tide must be going out…it's ripping us along!" shouted Rabbit. "I sure hope dey ain't no shoals inside o' here! If we does hit at dis speed, we be done fo'!" With the current behind them and a full breeze pressing their eased sails, the whaleboat was moving as fast as it had ever gone, and no one had any idea what was ahead, whether hidden rock or reef. Even on the brightest of days they would have thought twice about attempting this passage, but tonight they had no choice, and so they charged into the night, flying on blind faith and educated guesswork alone.

With waves exploding on each side, they could see the open water glittering in the moonlight ahead. Not a word was spoken, each person intent on their work. To port the crashing of waves ended abruptly; to starboard they continued. And then they were through. With a last flurry the current catapulted them out of the channel and into the open waters of Galion Bay.

"Dere's de first part done with!" shouted Rabbit, looking out over his right shoulder to see if he could see the cutter. But he saw nothing. They sailed on for a half an hour, with Gilbert scanning the horizon to starboard looking for any sign of the patrol boat. With each passing minute the thought they had actually gotten away with it began to take hold. And then came Dawson's call from the bailing hole.

"You better take a look to le'ward Rabbit! I t'ink dey done pick we up again!"

Rabbit immediately squatted down to peek under the mainsail. There, perhaps a half of a mile away, was the silhouette of the French patrol boat. And it was turning onto a course straight towards them. "It looks like dey've seen us in truth. Dere's no chance of us out-running 'em, that's for certain. I think we only have one chance, an' dat's to get ourselves t'rough dat cut to windward dey call de Loup Bordelais! Haul off dat jib and main, and drop de centreboard gi' me!" Rabbit stood in the boat facing aft. The moon sat high in the eastern sky, giving a fleeting glimpse of their surroundings as it peaked through the threatening clouds overhead. "I need to find me line-up now. The peak o' de island wit de saddle 'tween de two high mountains behind Le Robert was de range mark, wasn't it?"

"Yes man, dat should lead we into de cut," agreed Gilbert, now looking aft over his shoulder. "Wha' happenin' wit de cutter, Dawson?"

"She closin' de distance quick!" he called out as he squatted in the bailing hole. "You better have a look Rabbit."

He ducked down under the mainsail again. "Well I got dem right where I want dem, boys! I'm hoping to get dem to follow us right in to dat shallow water out yonder, if we can get there quick enough. First sign of breaking water I want to hear about it, and I want to know where it is." Now that they were sailing close hauled, their speed had slowed and the cutter was drawing ever closer.

"Breakers ahead, maybe two hundred yards off to starboard!" Gilbert shouted, pointing away at sixty degrees. Rabbit took another peek under the main. The cutter was three hundred yards away to leeward.

"Ready about boys, and make dis de best tack o' your life. Everyone set? Okay Clancy, t'row she 'bout!" The helm was pushed down and the whaleboat flew up into the wind, swung through and bounded away on the port tack having hardly missed a beat. 'Good tack! Now, where's dat shoal?" In the moonlight the breaking water showed ahead, crossing their bows from north to south.

The bow of the patrol boat was directly behind them now and closing quickly. They were fifty yards from the breakers and the cutter was the same distance behind. Their heavy forward gun fired a shot and a fountain of water erupted in front of the whaleboat. A loud horn was blowing at ten second intervals. Their searchlight was bouncing over the water, trying to keep focused on the whaleboat. Now the ship was within twenty-five yards, and another shot was fired. No one said a word. "Tell me Rabbit! You got to lead me t'rough!" called Clancy from the helm as he steered the boat to the fluctuating breeze.

"You got to keep up! De shoal's underneath you. I want to put dem strait on top of it!" Another shot soared overhead. "On my word you must pull down hard, okay Clancy?"

"Got it!"

"Keep up...keep up...a little more...okay, we over de shoal! Pull away big! Ease de main, ease de main!" Another wild shot was followed by panic on the bow of the cutter as the breaking reef was suddenly spotted. Astern there was a loud roar as the cutters engines went into full astern. "Push her up now Clancy, push her up hard!"

The boat luffed and the breaking shoal swept past under the lee. "Good job, boy! We're t'rough! We can sail de boat now! Haul off de sheets. We got to figure out de nex' step," said Rabbit, a calmness now returning to his voice. Looking astern he checked on their pursuers. "Looks like dem Frenchmen backed off in time. Dey've swung their bow north an' are steamin' hard in dat direction. Dey must be headin' fo' de passage under Cap Caravelle. We'd better hope dat O'Neil ain't too far away or else dey'll run we down. How's Cap'n Jack doin', Gregoire?"

"The bleeding has stopped, but he's lost a lot of blood. He's very wet and cold. He isn't looking too good," Gregoire replied, crouching next to the skipper.

"Have you had a chance to look at the wound? What really happened?"

"The bullet came in through his left shoulder just under the joint and come out the back through the shoulder blade. It has taken a lot of bone with it. The wound where it came out is a big hole, torn and ragged. He's going to be in some pain when he comes to, that's for certain."

The boat lifted over the big ocean swells. From their spots on the rail, the crew continually glanced at the wounded captain. This was a man who had always been there, who never let them down. For the first time in a long time, doubt entered their minds. Now they knew they were on their own.

And then Rabbit broke the ice. "No time to lose concentration boys!" he urged. "Once dem Frenchmen get aroun' dat reef, it won't take dem long to get up we ass. We got to do what we can to get outside where O'Neil can track we down. An' on top o' dat it looks like we got some dirty weather comin'…jus' cast you' eyes to windward! G, you better get yo' skinny ass up here on de rail! Dat squall up yonder goin' to come down hard!"

And as if emerging from a dream, the crew all turned their eyes to the horizon in unison, where a bank of pitch-black clouds was rushing down to meet them.

Escape to Windward

Outside the Bank de Roches, the windblown swell marched in off of the open ocean. The whaleboat heeled to the clear breeze, each man on the rail throwing their weight out as far as possible. "Wind's gone round to de nor' east," yelled Clancy over the crashing of waves and whistle of the wind. "Dis goin' to be a heavy beat…oh me muddah!" he swore as the top of a breaking roller came down on them, dumping bucketloads of water into the boat.

"You must light de jib an' let she head come up!" Clancy yelled at his jib man.

"What do you think me doin'? You jus' steer de boat, mon, don't tell me 'bout de jib!" countered Earl.

Dawson feverishly scooped water out of the bottom of the boat. They pressed on. To windward the sea showed white through the pitch-like gloom of the night, the moon obscured by the rushing clouds. It was hard work; the small, open boat was sailing on the limit of what she could bear, sails having to be constantly adjusted to each heavy gust and breaking wave. Sometimes foam would roll over the bow and half-fill the boat with water; then three of them would have to bail, but not for long because their weight was needed on the rail.

"Hold steady boys while I drop down an' see how de Cap'n doin'," Rabbit shouted into the wind. Sliding off his spot on the rail behind the rigging, he squatted down next to Jack, who still sat propped with his back to the centre-case, his feet pressed against the boat ribs. He was soaking wet, like everyone else. Blood seeped through his bandaged shoulder. His normally nut-brown complexion was a pale, sickly white, his sandy hair wet and matted.

As Rabbit carefully tried to examine the wound, Jack's eyes half opened, his head lifting up off of the top of the case. "We got any water anywhere? I'm as dry as a Balmain pub on Good Friday," he croaked.

"Dat's de Cap'n we been waitin' to hear from!" Rabbit smiled. Dawson took a bottle out of the stern locker and passed it forward. Jack opened his eyes, took the water in his right hand and drank. "I've got to say, I seen you lookin' better, Skip. You look like you just came out o' that pub you was talkin' about after three days o' serious drinkin'," Rabbit finally said.

Jack's eyes flicked up to the Bajan, a slight smile playing on his lips. "Cheers, cobber. Now tell me – where the hell are we, and what happened?"

"After de bullet took you, we worked our way out o' de reefs an' thought we might be clear, but de cutter picked us up again so we took a chance and managed to find we way true de Loup Bordelaise. De Frenchmen look like dey gone north 'round de bank, so dey'll be out here lookin' for we jus' now. How's dat shoulder o' yours?"

Jack looked at his wound and grimaced. Gregoire's bandage was pushed into the hole in his shoulder and caked in blood. Turning away, he put his head back and rested it on top of the case, his brow beaded in sweat. "Let's just say I won't be playing cricket for a while. So I assume the plan is to try and reach a spot where O'Neil can find us before the Frenchmen can," he winced as a wave of white water crashed over the boat's bow.

"Yes, mon, but dat won't be easy wit' dis squall we got bearin' down. It's all we can do to jus' stay afloat, let alone outsail dem Frenchmen!"

"Dis really startin to get ugly now, boys!" Earl shouted as he looked out to windward. Holding the jib sheet with two hands, he was hiking his body as far out as he could without falling overboard. "What you t'ink, Gilbert?"

"She looks to be breakin' out o' de north," the mainsheet hand replied, standing up and calmly reading the conditions. The boat dropped and rolled and thrashed through the waves and wind. "An dere's plenty o' breeze in 'er too, don't worry!"

Jack closed his eyes in pain, trying to will himself on. Dawson squatted in the bailing hole, his curly head just under the level of the bamboo boom as he scooped out water to leeward. The squall was closing on them quickly, and the first gusts started to be felt. "She's breakin' from north in truth," yelled Earl. "At least she should lift us well on dis tack!"

The first full effects of the gale began to batter the whaleboat. "Oh me muddah…look what's comin down!" Clancy shouted. A line of wind, rain and water was avalanching towards the small boat. "Ease de mainsheet!"

"Knock out the sprit!" yelled Jack, and before the words were out of his mouth Earl was leaping for the mast, handing Rabbit the jib sheet. Using one hand, he knocked the rope becket and it slid down the mast, allowing the bamboo sprit to drop, releasing the tension on the sail. Unhooking the sprit from the end of the sail, he dropped the bamboo down inside of the boat, pushing it as far forward as he could. The mainsail was reduced in size to almost half just in time. And then the squall hit. Though they were anticipating it, the ferocity of the wind still took the crew by surprise. The boat was knocked down to the point of capsize. The rain came horizontally in sheets and visibility disappeared altogether. The wind gusted fiercely, the loose top of the mainsail flapped loudly to leeward, the mast and rigging shook violently with the sails flogging, and Clancy did all he could to simply keep the boat upright. Waves rolled over the bow and washed through the boat. The three spare men were torn between keeping their weight on the rail and bailing for all they were worth. "Keep her up Clancy! Keep her sailin!" encouraged Gilbert as he continued to work the mainsheet.

"Sail de boat Reds, don' frighten!" yelled Earl into the howling breeze. "We're lifting going up…just keep sailin de boat! Gregoire, Rabbit, come up on de rail an' t'row your weight out! Dawson you too! Leave de bailin' fo' now! Le' go your hand an' le' she go up!" And so they battled on. The whale boat was buffeted by the rain-filled wind and assaulted by the relentless white foam that rolled out of the void. It was a fight for survival. The crew of the *Antipodes* had no option but to battle the storm head on, for to take the safer option and run downwind with it would send them blindly careering towards the treacherous reef that extended for miles to leeward of them and take them away from their meeting point with the *Roulette*, as well as potentially landing them in the hands of the French authorities who were hunting for them from somewhere out of the darkness behind.

For Jack the physical exertion was taking its toll. Having initially lost so much blood, his body hadn't had time to recover, and the constant pain was wearing on what little physical reserves he had left. Every movement was agony. He struggled to keep focused on the realities of the present. His mind faded in and out of a world of surreal fantasies until a shout or a sound or a movement would bring him back into the moment.

And then as quickly as it came, the squall was gone. The last few droplets of rain fell, and all that was left was a confused, lumpy sea and very little wind. "Let's get that sprit back in befo' de new breeze reaches," Clancy ordered. Again Earl did the work, and once again they were moving under full canvas. They sailed on through the jumbled conditions. "What d' ya t'ink Rabbit, is it time to fire up one o' de flares? We've got to be at least five miles off shore by now," Clancy inquired, looking over his shoulder at the shadowy bulk of the island, which now lay under the remains of the rainsquall that was disappearing astern.

"Yes, we can give it a go. I reckon de vessel couldn't be too far away now."

Dawson dug into the stern locker and brought out a canvas bundle tied with a piece of marlin twine. Unrolling it, he found four stick flares wrapped in greased paper. Handing two of them to Rabbit he then rolled the parcel back up and put it away again. "Well here goes…"

Rabbit ignited the end of the phosphorescent flare and standing on the forward seat held it aloft, the eerie red glow flashing up on the sail and out into the night. Time seemed to stand still as all eyes in the boat searched for a reply out of the void to windward. And then the sign came. A similar flare flickered well to the north, shining bright orange on the pitch-black horizon. "He's dere!" Rabbit excitedly yelled, pointing towards the light.

Jack pulled himself up just enough to see the schooner's response from over the rail, and then eased back into his old position, as if the effort had taken all of his energy. "How far away do you boys reckon he is?" he asked after a few minutes, eyes closed as if in a trance.

"Three or four miles," answered Gilbert.

"Leave it for fifteen minutes and then we'll fire off another one." They sailed on, punching into the waves on port tack. The wind was again on the rise after the passing of the squall. New lines of menacing clouds could be seen banking up on the windward horizon. Over their shoulders the crew nervously looked behind, and into the ugliest of nights the *Antipodes* battled on with grim determination.

The second flare was lit, and again within minutes there was a reply, this time much closer. Still, in the gloomy murkiness of the stormy night, trying to get both boats at the same spot at the same time was not the easiest of tasks. They had two more flares remaining, and they had to use them judiciously. Another few minutes passed and Rabbit again stood on the main thwart with a phosphorescent flare held aloft. The schooner again replied, showing itself to be within a mile to windward. And still there was no sign of the patrol boat.

"Looks like O'Neil's coastin' down from windward. We must make sure he doesn't over-run us! We have fo' try an' get ourselves in line so as dey pass we can meet up," said Rabbit. "We've got one flare left, so we got to time it right."

"Yes man, dat is what we must do," Clancy agreed. "But we better do it quick before de nex' squall breaks, because no tellin' where all we might be after dat hits!" The *Antipodes* tracked on, with everyone on board attempting to estimate the exact spot of their intersection. Rabbit was preparing his last flare when another signal was shown by the *Roulette*. "Dey is close now – can't be more den a few hundred yards. Fire de ting now Rabbit!" Clancy ordered.

The last flare was held aloft until it burned itself out. Moments later the sails of the schooner loomed into sight. "Dere she is boys! All you keep yo' eyes 'pon she!" The crew stood and watched in excitement as the big schooner bore down on them; the surge of the water under her stem and the shake of her sails could now be heard, as well as seen. The wind was on the rise again, another rainsquall imminent as O'Neil steered the vessel past the whaleboat and rounded her up into the wind. Clancy carefully aimed the whaleboat to come alongside the surging schooner. It was just at that moment that a cry rang out from aboard the *Roulette*. "Gunshot!" was the shout, and moments later there was an eruption of water close by.

"It's de gunboat!" shouted Rabbit from the seat, pointing in the direction from which they had just come.

"Let's go Clancy! Get she alongside an' quick! Dey's really close!" yelled Earl. "Once we catch a line we must dump de rig!" The whaleboat ranged up alongside of the schooner and a line was tossed but dropped short. Another flash from behind, another near miss from the cutter, and now there was shouting and commotion coming from both vessels. Bull tossed the line again. Rabbit caught the end and made it fast around the seat and the boat was pulled up alongside.

"Get de Cap'n out first, and watch he shoulder – he hurt bad!" Rabbit yelled up to the figures above as Earl flashed around the boat, letting go the rigging. It took all the strength Jack had left in his body to lift himself up to face the vessel. Arms reached down to grab him as Gilbert took him by the belt, and with one almighty heave the captain was lifted over the bulwarks and tumbled down onto the deck while Earl frantically set about ridding the whaleboat of her mast and sails.

"Quick, hook up de lifting tackles gi' me!" Zepheryn shouted from the deck above. Another shot whistled overhead. The two blocks swung down into the boat and were hooked into place, and as they were the schooners sails were trimmed and she began to pick up speed again.

"Out o' de boat now!" cried Clancy as the tackles started to take strain, and everyone quickly clambered over the rail on to the deck. All except Earl, who stood with one foot on each side of the whaleboat's mast.

"Grab de masthead!" he shouted as he lifted, and someone did just that as the rig – sails and all – came out of the boat, over the rail and were thrown to the other side of the deck. As the boat was being hauled out of the water, the first signs of the approaching squall could be felt. And looming only a few hundred yards astern, the dark shape of the French cutter could be seen charging towards them, the red flame from its deck gun randomly blazing out of the darkness.

As part of the crew strained to haul the *Antipodes* up on deck, the rest were busily trimming sheets. "We need more sail or de Frenchman goin' to overhaul we!" yelled O'Neil as he leaned over the wheel, occasionally turning to look at the approaching cutter over his shoulder. "Loose out dem tops'ls quick smart, and get de fisherman ready to hoist!" The whaleboat was swung on board as Kingsford scurried up the after ratlines. It was Jono the cook, seeing everyone else occupied, who leapt up onto the fore rigging and quickly darted up to the fore masthead himself.

"Haul off some mainsheet gi'me!" ordered O'Neil as the two men aloft unlashed the tops'ls. The schooner was gaining speed but the patrol boat was getting closer, its searchlight now beaming through the night as it tried to lock on to the schooner. Off the windward quarter, the line of rain and wind were marching towards them. Storm clouds rushed overhead. A shout came from the main masthead, and the order was given to haul away on the topsail halyard. As the sail was hoisted, the full force of the squall hit. The topsail cracked as it whipped and shook in the heavy wind that had engulfed the vessel.

"Haul out de foot!" Zeph ordered, as Pepper simultaneously oversaw the hoisting of the fore topsail. The schooner heeled to the new pressure of wind and sail, and surged away with the heavy breeze. The cutter, white foam rolling off her bows, surfed along on a wave not one hundred yards astern, disappearing in the thundering rain that overtook them both. The fore topsail was hoisted and set, but the main topsail was still flogging in the wind. "De outhaul done wrap around de end o' de gaff!" yelled Zeph as he looked aloft, trying to see what was wrong. Shielding his eyes from the pelting rain, Kingsford spotted the problem. As the sail beat and whipped to le'ward, and as the schooner heeled wildly under this press of canvas in the breaking squall, he ran out on the gaff, acrobatically holding on to the peak halyard for support, and laying out on the end of the wildly swinging spar caught hold of the flailing outhaul and in one motion deftly undid the wrap. The outhaul was taken up, the sail was set and Kingsford slid down a halyard to the deck.

"De foretops'l done set an' de fisherman's ready to hoist, Skip!" hollered Zepheryn as O'Neil stood alongside of the wheel, white water roaring over the rail as the schooner tore away with the wind and waves, the sea foaming white as it streamed past to leeward.

"Just keep she ready to hoist – we couldn't carry it now. But as soon as dis squall starts to ease I want she up, along wit' de flying jib. If de wind drops light, we has to keep movin' or we done for!" And so the *Roulette* roared south with the rain and wind, safely obscured for the moment by the squall, her crew nervously anticipating what would happen when it eventually passed them by.

From the moment Jack was hauled on board he was in a world of agony. In trying to help him up over the rail, someone had unknowingly reached under his bullet-torn shoulder and lifted, tearing open whatever healing had taken place and making him scream with pain. Gregoire and Rabbit had found him sitting with his back to the cargo hatch, soaking wet and shivering and almost unconscious. Helping him to his feet, they had walked him aft and then below, where they carefully stretched him out on his bunk and rewrapped the wound, which had started bleeding again after its most recent trauma.

"He needs to see a doctor, and soon," Gregoire said. "If this wound gets septic he'll be in real trouble."

"Yes man, we have fo' do we best to keep it clean until we reach Barbados."

"Look, I'll keep an eye on him," Gregoire said as the pair made their way across the lurching cabin towards the companionway steps. "There isn't much I can do on deck except get in the way."

"Well I'm going up to see wha' happenin'…"

On deck, O'Neil had braced himself next to the wheelbox, two hands on the spokes and driving the *Roulette* as hard as she had ever been driven. The old captain was not steering any sort of compass course, he was going for pure speed, and for a schooner that point of sail is the broad reach. O'Neil had the howling breeze blowing over his left shoulder. The vessel's sails were trimmed to perfection, not one of them showing the slightest sign of a flutter. And then, when Bull sprung to ease the mainsheet as a huge gust began heeling them beyond what any of the crew had seen before, when green water was surging over the leeward bulwark onto the sidedeck and it seemed either the rig would go overboard or the vessel would capsize, as Bull leapt to ease the huge sail O'Neil stopped him in his tracks. "Don't touch dat mainsheet!" he bellowed, glancing over his shoulder. "Dis vessel can take all a dis an' more! You just stand by. When I tell you to ease, you ease, an' not before!"

The gust passed, the schooner straightened, and O'Neil slowly took a peek behind, as if listening to the wind. "What'd you reckon Zeph? You t'ink she 'bout done?"

The rain was still coming horizontal, the wind had hardly eased a notch, and yet somehow he felt the change. The mate stood facing the tempest, screwing up his eyes against the bullet-like pellets, observing the foam-white sea astern. He looked up at the clouds, he looked towards the horizon. He looked O'Neil in the eye. "I t'ink she got a bit more in her still, but not much. We seen de worst of it at least."

"I reckon so too. Pepper you got dat flyin' jib ready to go?"

"Yes man. Jus' say de word."

"An dat fisherman stays'l is rigged is she, Zeph?"

"She's ready to go Cap," he replied.

O'Neil took one last look to windward. There was the slightest of signs; the rain started to ease, the whiteness of the water astern began to change back to black, the wind itself might have dropped a few knots in intensity; whatever it was he felt it. "Right! Get dat flyin' jib up. An' as soon as she set, I want to see you hoist dat fisherman!"

Pepper and Zepheryn went forward with their crew, and both sails were hoisted. It took the combined muscle of all of the crew to control the flailing sheets as the sails were hoisted, but slowly they got the sails under control. In the falling breeze, the *Roulette* was sailing even faster, if possible, and when the clouds cleared and the rain stopped and the squall passed, there was no sign of the French cutter anywhere. They had outsailed them, they had outfoxed them, and now they were outrunning them. "Who wants to do a trick at de helm now?" O'Neil asked at last, taking one last look behind just to make sure. "I want to take a look at Jack."

"Gi' me de helem, Uncle," said Jono. "It's a long time since I had a chance to steer dis vessel in a good breeze like dis."

"Eh, wha' happen? Is Jono still de cook or is he done wit dat?" Kingsford inquired to no one in particular. "De way I seen him go up dem fore ratlines, de man missed he callin' in truth! Now he takin' all o' we home!"

After a few minutes a big, white-toothed smile flashed across the face of the normally quiet, self-effacing cook. "Man, what de big joke?" Kingsford asked with a chuckle. "Wha' makin' you so happy all of a sudden?'

"It's what we just did back there – takin' on a coast guard an' leavin dem fo' dead! We grandchildren goin' to be tellin' dat story to dey grandchildren one day!"

"Let me tell you somethin', Jono," Clancy interjected, shaking his head, "you ain't heard de half o' it yet!"

So with all eight sails aloft and drawing, and a solid breeze sitting on their port quarter, the schooner *Roulette* sailed away from the waters of Martinique, and with the passing of the squall, the weather cleared and soon they were reaching under an eternity of shining stars. It was then that Rabbit broke out the bottle of Jack Iron, and as the crew settled themselves around the mainsheet aft, the legend of how the *Antipodes* conquered Martinique was told for the first time, but by no means the last.

Lost in another bizarre nightmare, Jack tried to surface but couldn't. He was adrift on an endless sea and there was no way home. He had begun to panic, but the dream hung on until he wondered if it was real and not a nightmare at all. From out of the brooding sky, a dark shape flew at him and he tried to yell in fright, but the sound would not escape his mouth, and then his eyes opened and he saw O'Neil and Gregoire standing over him.

Sweat lined his brow, his shirt was soaked and his shoulder burned like fire.

"Gregoire here has been tellin' me 'bout what happen. Sounds like you fellahs had some narrow escapes de last couple o' days. To be truthful you ain't lookin' too good a-tall. He says it's a real nasty wound. We're takin' you straight to Barbados to de hospital, okay?"

"Well you know me O'Neil," Jack weakly answered, "it takes a lot to knock me down and keep me there, but this thing has really hit me for a sixer. Not that I don't trust Gregoire's obvious medical skills, but it might be a good idea to have a second opinion."

"Well you just try and take it easy. We've got a good easterly breeze touchin' to de north, so we should be there by mornin'."

Returning to the deck O'Neil lit the compass light. "Steer a course of sou'-east b' sout', Jono," he told the helmsman. "And I hope all o' you rum drinkers back dere aren't goin' to let dat Bajan lead you too far astray, because we still have work to do. You all got a sick captain down below, an' somehow me don't think you drinkin' rum is goin' to help. So while you all are there, haul off a piece o' dat mainsheet before we see about trimmin' the rest o' dese sails, because it's Barbados we bound!"

Done Wit' Dat

The ceiling fan turned slowly overhead. Gradually it came into focus. The sheets were starched and clean and crisp, and smelled of soap and fresh air. One thing Jack knew was that he was not aboard the *Roulette*. He turned his head. The pillowcase crackled in his ear. Blurred memories came rushing back, vague recollections of leaving the boat, and an ancient ambulance with a big red cross and curious black faces, and then not much more but strange dark dreams he couldn't remember. Raising himself up off the pillow he looked around to see other patients in other beds. A passing nurse noticed his movements and came over to check. "So we're finally awake, are we?" she asked in her musical Barbadian lilt, a mask of mock seriousness covering a face that Jack could read good-natured humour into.

"So which part of heaven am I in?" he croaked, his eyes smiling.

"You're not in heaven darlin', and I'm no angel neither. My name is Venus and you're in St. John of God Hospital. It's nice to see you finally wit' us now, Cap'n McLeod," she said, fussing with his sheets and placing another pillow under his head.

"How long have I been here, anyway?"

"You came in two nights ago, de doctor sedated you, and you've been sleepin' since. Now how's dat shoulder? Is it givin' you much pain? And do you t'ink you could drink a cup o' tea?"

"Oh, the shoulder. It's okay, I guess. It only hurts when I breathe. And yes, I'd love a cup of tea, or a whole pot if you can spare it."

Jack had just finished his breakfast when Nurse Venus informed him he had a visitor. As she cleared away his tray, the wiry figure of Harry Iverson appeared around the far door and proceeded to his bed by the window. "Good morning old chap! So good to see you are in the land of the living! You're looking jolly well better than you were when I first saw you! I just had a word with Doctor Garner and he says you should be over the hump now and taking the first steps on the road to recovery, which is bloody good to hear, considering at one point it was touch and go whether you would pull through at all. You had us all damn worried for some time, I can assure you. But then, you always have been a lucky chap."

"Yes, well it's better to be lucky than rich, as they say. I just saw the doctor before breakfast and he assured me the wound should mend itself, but it's going to take some time. Apparently the bullet really did some serious damage. It shattered my scapula and tore up a heap of muscles and ligaments. He said I was lucky in two respects: that it missed my left lung, which would have probably killed me, and that it didn't smash my shoulder joint, which would have pretty much handicapped me for life. Doc Garner also was surprised to see how uncontaminated the wound was considering the circumstances. The boys did a great job keeping it clean. So in all reality, things could have been much worse."

Harry lit up two cigarettes, handing one to Jack. "They say that when one suffers such a trauma one of the first things that goes is short-term memory – some sort of defence mechanism or other. Sometimes victims have no recollection of what happened at all. I'm not sure how good your memory of the event is, so let me remind you," he said with a smile and an obvious nod and a wink. "Do you recall stopping in at Baliceaux to hunt those wild goats, and the gun accidently going off, or not?"

Jack took a pull from his cigarette and gazed at Harry through the smoke. "That really is incredible! I don't remember stopping there at all. It must be my mind playing tricks on me, but I could have sworn it happened in a different way entirely."

"It just goes to show the power of the subconscious, doesn't it? And of course, it's a stiff reminder to us all that even someone as experienced as you can fall prey to misadventure. And all of this for a little bit of goat meat!"

Jack looked long and hard at Harry, a slight smile playing on his lips. "So if you are telling me that's how it happened, well then so be it. I guess it had to happen somehow. There is one person I've been worried about, though, and that's Philippe. Any word from him?"

"It seems he had a narrow escape in Le Robert, but as far as he knows, his cover wasn't blown. He has been keeping to his schedule, and so far it's business as usual."

"Well that's a relief. We aren't the only ones who had a close call!"

"At any rate, it's jolly good to see you here and in good hands, McLeod!"

"Speaking of being in good hands, I was wondering if I would see any of those blokes off of that sunken freighter we picked up off of Petite Silhouette. Are they on another ward or what?"

A dark cloud extinguished Harry's sunny expression. "Bad news on that front I'm afraid, old man. The *Arabella* never arrived in Barbados. I think we have to assume the worst."

This news hit the wounded captain hard. He sank back into his pillows and closed his eyes. "When is all this shit going to end, Harry? Has the whole word really gone that crazy? What kind of war is this, anyway?" Jack finally asked.

"Very good questions my friend. Humanity has always had its darker side, and it seems this war is bringing it out in spades. I think it would be safe to wager it will get worse before it gets any better."

"Excuse me gentlemen, but I hope you don't mind if I interrupt," Nurse Venus said as she bustled up to the side of the bed. "Now dat de Cap'n here is awake an' had he breakfast, it's time I get him up and make sure he has a good wash. He won't be long, sir, if you don' mind waitin'."

"No, no, it's quite alright." Harry stood and replaced his hat. "I just dropped in to see how our patient here was progressing. It's good to see you've come around, old man! I'll drop in tomorrow morning and check in on you then. Cheerio!"

It was three more days before Jack was released from hospital. During that time he had visits from O'Neil and the crew, Harry and Val, his agent Joshua Samuels, as well as Rabbit and Gregoire. He was looking forward to returning home and sleeping in his own bed, to seeing his wife and children again, walking through the harbour in the cool of the morning, talking to the old men under the trees, being in the boatyard and listening to the jokes, working on the plans for his new vessel, as well as simply sitting down on his veranda and reading a good book. It was not only his wounding, but the loss of Bill DeVilliars and his crew that hit him hard. Lying in his hospital bed he longed for the solitude of his island, where he could sit down on his own and just listen to the wind through the trees.

Harry Iverson appeared at nine o'clock in the morning, exactly as scheduled, to pick up Jack from the hospital. After saying goodbye to the nurses and staff, he slowly followed Harry outside and gingerly climbed into the back seat of the waiting taxi, his shoulder well bandaged with his arm in a sling. Dawson had delivered him a set of freshly washed clothes from the vessel, so he felt like he could once again face the world. Instead of driving to the careenage, however, the taxi went in the opposite direction. "So where are we off to now Harry?"

"Oh I just thought you might enjoy a spot of breakfast with some old friends of ours. Nothing to really worry about, old man. Just ironing out a few final details before you head home."

The taxi carefully made its way out of bustling Bridgetown, the road following the shady west coast as it ran parallel to the sparkling blue sea. It didn't take them long to escape the confines of the crowded city, and soon they were driving along a sandy shore lined with coconut palms. A half hour later, the driver turned through the gates of an old, well-kept estate. A uniformed soldier opened the car doors and showed them inside. After climbing a wide set of polished stone steps, they were led out onto a broad terrace overlooking a pristine beach edged by coconut trees that waved in the morning breeze. The familiar frames of two British officers stood with their hands clasped behind their backs, looking out over the sea. As their guests arrived, the officers turned to greet the new arrivals. "Ah, here we are now!" Commander Lawrence enthused. "Captain McLeod, Commander Iverson, we meet once again! You of course know Lt. Commander Blackwell from Naval Intelligence?"

"Of course," Harry answered as they all shook hands.

"Are you based in Barbados now Ainslie, or just here on vacation?" Jack asked with just a hint of sarcasm.

"Quite on the contrary, McLeod. I still have my hands full in Trinidad, but I do need to make the occasional sortie up here to keep my finger on the pulse. At any rate, it is you we are here to see this morning! We understand from our debriefing of Deslisle and Iverson's man Haynes that you all had quite an adventure in Martinique. Even took one for the team in the line of duty I see. How's the shoulder – tender as all hell I would imagine? I must tell you, everyone, from the top brass right on down, wants to congratulate you on a job extremely well done. But enough of this for now! I hope that you have a healthy appetite, because Commander Lawrence's staff has prepared what looks to be a jolly nice breakfast for us all."

"Yes gentlemen, by all means, let's take a seat and have something to eat. We wouldn't want any of this to get cold," Lawrence insisted as he guided them towards a table set up on the terrace, where they were served a traditional English breakfast.

"This certainly beats the porridge and pea soup I've been eating the last few days," Jack commented as his bacon, sausages, fried tomatoes and eggs were placed in front of him by a white-gloved waiter. Not much was said as the four men tucked into their meals, until Jack broke the ice with the question he had to ask. "I know I'm stating the bleeding obvious, but in all seriousness, gentlemen, what the hell is going on out there? These U-boats are having a bloody field day! When is the cavalry going to come charging over the hill to our rescue? Or does that really only happen in the movies?"

"I have to agree that the situation is bleak indeed, McLeod," Blackwell replied as he buttered a piece of toast. "Jerry really has turned up the pressure. This obviously has not gone unnoticed by the War Office or by Washington. The ships being sunk are crucial to our war effort, and we know we must do more to protect them. Unfortunately it takes time to build air strips, manufacture planes, and construct patrol boats, but to their credit the Yanks are making a good fist of it. Resources are being rapidly developed throughout the Caribbean, and with the recent appointment of a new Governor in Trinidad, the rift between the Allies is all but smoothed over. The airbases being built in both St. Lucia and Antigua are not far away from completion. To the north, Puerto Rico and Guantanamo Bay are both being developed as quickly as Trinidad, as are bases in Florida. And to the west, both Curacao and Panama have received massive re-enforcements. So despite the bleakness of the outlook at present, there is the slightest ray of light beginning to shine at the end of the tunnel. But as interesting and informative as all of this is, McLeod, it is not really the reason we invited you out here this morning."

"Quite right, Ainslie, quite right," Lawrence added, taking his cue as the last of their dishes were cleared from the table. "If everyone has had ample sufficiency, I suggest we adjourn to somewhere a bit more comfortable."

Leaving the table, they followed Lawrence to a smartly furnished lounge that looked out over the blue Caribbean through tall, open windows framed by massive louvered shutters. "This is quite a place you have here, Archie," Jack said as they relaxed into a set of stylish rattan easy chairs while one of the staff placed a fresh tray of coffee onto the teak table before them. "You'll be sad when the war ends and you have to move out of this place."

"Unfortunately this is not really my residence, Jack. I live in far more humble digs. This place is especially reserved to entertain dignitaries like you where – shall we say – discretion is of utmost importance."

"Well I'm honoured to be looked upon as a dignitary! What about you, Harry? I've been called a lot of things before, but never that! Anyway, something tells me you didn't bring us all the way out here just to chew the fat over breaky."

"No, you are correct there, McLeod," Blackwell agreed. "To be perfectly honest, we have brought you here as a show of gratitude and respect from His Majesty's Government for your actions that were above and beyond the call of duty. I know you are not too interested in medals, but in different circumstances you probably would be awarded one. Unfortunately, in your line of work, all you will receive is a quiet pat on the back from someone like me on a job well done. This does not mean His Majesty doesn't appreciate your work. We know your actions have been performed out of a sense of duty, despite your philosophical objections to the contrary. But I cannot stress enough how important your team's deeds have been in furthering our cause here in the Caribbean. Gregoire Deslisle has proved to be a remarkable find, and so has this fellow Haynes.

"Today, however, it is my official duty and honour to recognise you and all of your crew for the courage, determination and resourcefulness you have shown in furthering the war effort. 'Operation Square Rigger' has been a resounding success. Because of your hard work, we have been able to deter the German high command from any plans they might have entertained in establishing a base in Martinique, as well as starting a resistance movement that is spreading through the French Islands like wildfire. As a consequence of your extraordinary hard work, the risks you have taken and the serious wound you received in the line of duty, I have been ordered by His Majesty's Government to not only express our whole-hearted appreciation, but to present you with an ex-gratia payment of one thousand pounds to be divided up as you see fit between you and your men. As of today, you are also honourably discharged from all official duty to the crown, under the proviso that none of this may ever be spoken about or conveyed in any way by you or any of your crew under penalty of the Official Secrets Act, which you have previously signed and sworn to. That, Captain McLeod, is why you are here."

Riding back to town, Jack gazed out of the window as he tried to gather his thoughts. Harry leaned over the front seat and mumbled instructions to their driver. A few minutes later, they pulled over to the side of the road. "I thought we could stop for a morning 'open eye' as Carlisle would call it, and this looks as good a place as any," Harry smiled as he climbed out of the car. Jack followed the Englishman through the shade of the palms to a small ramshackle rumshop set on the edge of the beach. They sat down at a rickety table, and were soon brought a nib of rum.

"You must feel pleased about how things have worked out in the end, old man! I would think that sort of ties everything up quite tidily, wouldn't you agree?" Harry said as he poured a couple of shots.

"I have to admit, it's a good feeling to know I've done my bit, and my part in all of this is over. Maybe I wouldn't be so lucky next time."

"Quite right, quite right. At any rate, you can now sail home with a clean slate and know those chaps won't come knocking on your door again," Harry said. "One thing that does slightly concern me however, is your crew. No chance of any of the lads getting in a skinful of rum and inadvertently letting the cat out of the bag?"

Jack looked Harry for several moments, and then shook his head. "It's the last thing you need to worry about, mate. These boys have all run their fair share of contraband in the past. They know how to keep their mouths shut. And people at home know when not to ask a question. That's not to say they don't know something has been happening, but they know enough not to question the story of me hunting goats in Baliceaux. Who was it that came up with that explanation, anyway?"

"It came from someone of extremely high authority; right from the top, so to speak," Harry answered with a smiling nod. "It came from O'Neil himself."

Jack chuckled. "If that's where it came from, then I suppose it'll pass muster. So now what's on your agenda? Is this trip still on to Guadeloupe, or aren't I allowed to ask?"

"By all means, old man, you're still in the club. Guadeloupe is next on the agenda. It seems Gregoire was so successful in Martinique it's hoped he might do a similar job further north. I must say he seems to be looking forward to the challenge. From my brief discussions with him so far, it appears the 'Maquis' we started in Martinique has already formed links with their compatriots in Guadeloupe, and there is tremendous scope for organised resistance there. Because we have no way of establishing radio links with them yet, Carlisle will be the conduit between Gregoire, me, and Trinidad. I think we'll be very busy for the next few months to come at least."

"Not to mention the fact that August and the hurricane season are just around the corner. What do you propose to do about that?"

"Val and I have found a perfect hurricane hole on the island of Antigua. Have you ever been to English Harbour?"

"I've only heard rumours about the place. I've been into St. John's with cargo over the years, of course, but that spot is a bit off the beaten track. I've had no call to go there. What's it like?"

"It is an excellent anchorage. The inner harbour is completely protected, and even contains the remnants of Admiral Nelson's old naval dockyards, which, remarkably, are still in quite good nick. The last time we were there it was completely deserted, so it can be a little lonely, but it will be a perfect place for us to base ourselves over the upcoming months."

"And so from there you will be doing your runs to Guadeloupe?" Jack asked as he poured another round of rum.

"In a way, yes. For that part of the operation we'll work out of Prince Rupert Bay on the nor'west corner of Dominica. Apparently quite a large population of expat Guadeloupians are now living there, having escaped south across the channel in a bid to get away from the fascist regime that is now ruling their island. It should be a perfect place for Gregoire to start building his network."

"Well it sounds like you'll have your hands full, that's for sure. Here's to your good fortune," Jack said, raising his glass.

The two men finished their drinks and walked back to the car.

The taxi entered the outskirts of Bridgetown and was slowly moving towards the careenage when Harry asked the driver to stop. "I'll be jumping out here, old man. The periphane stove on the yacht needs a new burner and a chap told me I might find one here. Jerome will drop you alongside. Remember what the good doctor advised you! Don't overdo it! Best of luck and give my love to Jasmine. We'll catch up again sometime soon!" And after a shake of hands, Harry jumped out of the car and quickly disappeared into the crowd.

The crew of the *Roulette* wandered down Easy Bay Street towards the Blue Atlantic Bar. All were dressed neatly in their shore clothes, looking forward to the night out. "Man, dat Rabbit must have some sort of sixth sense or somethin'," Kingsford was saying. "When it comes to havin' a good time he's always in de right spot. So now he gone out an' foun' a goat to roast? De man is somethin' else, we!"

"An Gregoire sayin' he de one for cookin' goat. Man, me lookin' forward to dis!" said Bull.

"Well at least he didn't have fo' go to Baliceaux to find dis animal, an' he didn't need to shoot de Cap'n to get it neither!" Gilbert joined in. "Uncle Earl you is lucky de police hadn't been 'round to lock you up!"

"Yeah – on what charge?"

Gilbert now spoke in a deep baritone voice, sounding extremely officious. "De warrant reads, 'wrongful discharge of a firearm causing grievous bodily harm, maximum penalty ten years breaking stone as a guest of His Majesty!' You's de one shot de Cap'n, isn't it?"

"So de story goes…"

And so the jokes continued until they entered the Blue Atlantic Bar. "Man, me can smell dat ting roastin' already," Kingsford sniffed. "Where he be – out de back?" He and the others slowly made their way through the back door and out onto the beach behind, where Rabbit and Gregoire had the goat on a spit, turning it over a bed of red hot coals.

"Good night Captain Jack!" Jefferson smiled. "Good to see all o' you this evenin'! I hear you been laid up. So how's de hand?"

"Oh it's still giving me a bit of curry, but the doc gave me some tablets that help. I don't know how long I'll last tonight, but I thought since I'm still alive I might join the crew for a while."

Out the back of the rumshop, the party had well and truly started. Rabbit was in his element as he stoked the fire and ribbed the boys between drinking shots of rum and telling Gregoire how to cook the meat. Pepper had refused to come along, volunteering instead to stay aboard as night watchman, but O'Neil and Zepheryn did, and once they had a cold beer in their hands joined in the fun.

Jack had gone back to the bar to buy another round when Jefferson dropped the bombshell. "It's a terrible story about de *Rose Ann*, isn't it?"

"What story are you talking about, mate? Something didn't happen to Cap'n Ivy, did it?" Jack asked, the smile quickly evaporating from his face.

Jefferson remained quiet for some time and simply stared at Jack with his dark brown eyes. "Yes man – I t'ought you would o' heard de news already. De *Rose Ann* went down east o' de Bahamas. Seems Miss Ivy had just taken on a load o' salt from de Turks an' Caicos an' was headin' north when dey were sunk by a U-boat. De US Navy sent out planes and a cutter to search for survivors after dey received de distress call, but dey found no sign of anyone a-tall. I'm sorry to break de news to you, Cap. I know Miss Ivy was a good friend o' yours. I t'ought you did know."

Jack pursed his lips and stared at his beer but saw nothing. Slowly shaking his head he took a deep draught of the Canadian Lager. "Now that's a shock. It's a chance we all are taking, I suppose, but when it happens you still aren't ready for it. And this just after getting the news that Bill DeVilliars and his new vessel have gone missing! You'd better pour me one of those strong rums, Jefferson, and pour one for yourself. We have to drink to an amazing woman and a real gentleman, two people who would be the last on the list to deserve such a fate." The barman poured the drinks. "To Captains Ivy Pearl Ackermann, Bill DeVilliars and all the other captains and crew who have been lost in this crazy war." The two men touched glasses and downed their shots.

Stepping out back, Jack joined his crew. He thought about Ivy and how selflessly she had worked and how much she had sacrificed to see to it that her daughter had a decent education. Making a living on the sea was difficult enough. Simply running a big three-masted schooner in such a demanding trade was a challenge for even the best of mariners. But to lose her ship and her life like this was hard for Jack to fathom.

"I just heard 'bout your ol' friend Cap'n Ivy," Zepheryn said as he stepped up quietly alongside the skipper. "It's terrible news in truth. It just ain't right. Dey really is no justice in dis world. I wonder what'll happen to she daughter now. It's a damn shame I tell you."

Jack took another deep pull from his beer. "This whole bloody war is a damn shame," he said quietly.

The party carried on and Jack tried to stay in the spirit of it all. It was a fine night. The sea could be heard lapping softly onto the sands of Carlisle Bay a hundred yards away, and with no moon the sky was alive with a million stars, glittering through the waving dark shapes of the palm trees overhead. Around the fire there was plenty of good natured argument as to how the goat was cooking, but finally it was deemed ready to eat and Gregoire, with Bull's help, set about carving up the meat. Jefferson's wife had cooked a big pot of black-eyed peas and rice, and so the food was served.

It was a battle now for Jack as he was fading fast. His shoulder was throbbing with pain and the strength he had found earlier was ebbing. He had to get back to the vessel and rest. Just as he was about to slip away, Rabbit came up and sat down next to him on the battered piece of wood that formed his makeshift seat. "It looks like you ain't goin' to last much longer, Skip. De hand givin' you problems now?"

"Yes, I took another tablet but it hasn't helped much, I'm afraid. I think I'm going to have to make a move and go and put my head down, mate. It was great of you to organise all of this tucker. The boys are really enjoying themselves. The goat was an excellent idea."

"Well we been t'rough de fire, an' dat makes brothers of we all."

"You really did step up when you had to up there in Martinique, Rabbit. I, and all of the boys for that matter, truly appreciate it."

"Like I tol' you before – I only did what had to be done, just like de others. O'Neil did he part, Clancy did too. You did yours. It ain't no big ting, mon. It's one o' de tings I does base me life upon. 'Difficulties are de tings dat show what men are'."

"And who coined those sage words, if you don't mind me asking?"

"Epictetus."

Jack shook his head and smiled.

"But before you go, Skip, I got somethin' to gi' you. I been worried 'bout your shoulder an' all dat pain it'll be givin' you. It set me to thinkin' 'bout bush medicine an' de old time cures. I went to see an old Jamaican who knows 'bout all dem kind o' tings, and he gave me dis to gi' you. You can make tea out of it and drink it, or even roll it up like a cigarette an' smoke it. I use it occasionally meself. I'm certain sure it will ease de pain an' do you some good."

"Thanks for thinking of me, cobber. I'll give it a go. Now I'd better get moving before I collapse." Jack stood and said his farewells, and tucking Rabbit's packet of bush medicine roughly rolled in old newspaper under his arm headed back to the *Roulette*.

"What's dat you got there Jack?" O'Neil asked as they walked back along the dark, quiet street.

"I don't know – it's some sort of herb that Rabbit gave me. He got it from a bush doctor that said it might help with the pain."

O'Neil nodded as they walked on. "Could be a good ting," he said after a while. "Dem ol' time remedies does generally be very useful sometimes you know."

The *Roulette* loaded a cargo of much-needed foodstuffs and left for Petite Silhouette a few days later. It was a nervous run home. The news about the loss of the *Arabella D*, along with the sinking of the *Rose Ann*, had spread like wildfire through the schooner fleet moored inside the Careenage, causing more fear and consternation. There was not much of the usual cheerful banter and carelessness aboard the vessel that night as they cleared away from the breakwater and set sail across the ninety miles of treacherous water for home.

Sunrise and the islands of the Grenadines lay before them. The rosy glow of the sun's first rays reflected off of the lofty cliffs of the Ship's Prow, with Bristol Hill and the dramatic peak of Mount Majestic standing behind. Jack stood to windward, his left arm in a sling, his back to the early morning breeze.

"You can see dat sight a thousand times but it'll never grow old. It's always good to come home, isn't it?" O'Neil said from alongside the wheel.

"It's the sweetest sight in the world. Nothing could be more beautiful than that," Jack replied as the schooner lifted and rolled and surged downwind with the swell. A booby bird soared past to leeward. To the east the sea glittered as if sprinkled with gold leaf.

"So now what, Jack?" O'Neil finally asked. "Have you thought about what you're going to do with yourself an' de vessel?"

"Well, it's no use trying to swim against the tide, is it? These Germans have got everyone nervous, including me. I guess there's not much else to do but tie the ol' girl up to the trees for a while. Let the hurricane season pass and then see which way the wind's going to blow, which will be a good thing because it might give this shoulder a chance to heal properly. There's plenty I can do to keep myself busy. There could be a lot of things worse in life than having to spend a few months at home with my family."

"Yes man, no use sailin' out from safe moorin's into de eye of de storm unless you got no choice. You jus' get de hand right, dat's de most important thing. No one home goin' fo' starve, so like you say we just have fo' pull we heads in an' see wha' happen.

PART IV

U-boat under attack by a Sunderland in the Bay of Biscay

MARCH, 1943

The Last Voyage

"Stand and fight! Who's the genius who dreamt up these orders, Hans Christian Anderson? The Brothers Grimm? Do they have any idea what it's like out there these days?" Korvettenkapitan Karl Heine drunkenly shouted over the blaring cacophony of the band and the chaotic discord of a beer hall full of hard drinking sailors.

"It's like most of the ideas coming down from the top these days," agreed Kapitanleutnant Nils Albrecht as he took a deep draught of his beer. "Sometimes I think they're all away with the fairies."

"I'll tell you who are not something out of a children's fairy tale – those RAF bastards!" Heine continued. "They're turning the Bay of Biscay into a U-boat graveyard. Everyone knows we can't hope to crawl across the Bay submerged, especially with the Royal Navy on our ass, so they give us a couple more guns and tell us to stay surfaced and take the RAF on! You're damned if you do and damned if you don't! We're catching hell out there. But then, I'm sure you know all about it, Nils. Didn't you just come back from the South Atlantic somewhere?"

"Yes, we were stationed off the coast of Brazil for the last two trips, and that was no vacation I can tell you. Now it looks like we're off to the Caribbean again. What's it like over there these days?"

"The West Indies? Well, they are not the happy hunting ground that they were on our first voyage, that's for certain. Was it really only a year ago? It seems like three lifetimes at least," Heine said as he grabbed a shot glass of schnapps from a passing waitress and downed it in one motion. "You know, of the first group of us who sailed west, you and I are the last ones standing. The Americans are really tightening the screws over there. Trinidad is a fortress.

Don't even think about pulling off another stunt like you did on your first voyage! The Bocas is mined and wired with sonar, the Galleons Passage is alive with sub-chasers, torpedo boats and fast moving destroyers, and the air is filled with planes of all types and description. And up north is even worse! We got caught on the surface in the Windward Passage on our return voyage and were lucky to survive. Then the refuelling tankers we were to rendezvous with weren't there – when we reached the designated spot we found the enemy waiting for us instead! I don't know how we made it back. We must've been running on fumes!"

"Yes, Karl, it is hard to remain optimistic with the enemy lurking around every corner. Not having the milk cows out there to refuel us is going make things even more difficult, if that's possible. Accepting that we get through Biscay, I plan to dodge well north of the Azores to get around those American carrier groups skulking about in the mid-Atlantic, which will make the distance even greater. Now more than ever, refuelling in the Caribbean is imperative!"

"Yes, but how long is that going to last?" Heine asked. "Have you ever met the crazy Austrian that's running the show down there? Don't expect him to hang around for too long once the Allies get wind of what's happening."

"Yes, I've met him. He doesn't inspire a lot of confidence, I must admit. Hopefully he'll still be there once we're ready to come home," Albrecht said before downing the last of his beer. "Oh well. In the end, what we think doesn't matter anyway. I have my orders and I'll be running the gauntlet in another two days."

"I'm afraid it won't be too long before we'll be joining you. First my sub will have to be practically re-built because of the damage we sustained, but they are doing that quicker and quicker these days. Anyway, enough of this old friend. Let's not spend our time complaining when we could be drinking! Waitress, bring more beer – and don't forget the schnapps!"

On the thirteenth of March, 1943, U-112 left the Keroman complex and headed out into the Bay of Biscay. The tight-knit crew had been through a lot together, and the Kapitan knew his men well. Today he could see there was something wrong. Today they were not a happy ship.

"Is there a problem with the men Jost? I've never seen so many glum faces."

The mate shrugged. "You can give all the orders you want, but you can't stop the men from talking. Seamen everywhere are a superstitious lot, and our boys are no different. Once they think that a voyage will be unlucky, you'll never get that notion out of their heads. They are all asking why we couldn't have waited just one more day before leaving. You know what they all think of starting a voyage on a Friday."

"Well you know what those paper-pushers at HQ are like – they wouldn't think of holding back an operation because of some ancient superstition. If there's a timetable set, then we must stick to it, hell or high water," Albrecht responded.

Eight U-boats left Lorient together and were now sprinting across the Bay of Biscay as a group, hoping to be able to defend each other when the inevitable air attacks came. It was a seven hundred mile dash for the open Atlantic and safety, seven hundred miles until they were out of range of the RAF, and although pushing their engines at close to top speed would use up precious extra fuel, the subs had no choice but to get across the Bay as quickly as they could. Crashing through the rough waters at sixteen knots, their objectives were not only to escape aerial attack from the RAF planes based in the south of England, but to dodge the increasing numbers of fast-moving submarine chasers, corvettes and destroyers the Royal Navy was deploying in the English Channel and beyond. The Allies were also winning the technological war with their advancements in both radar and sonar, and the U-boats that had been so deadly only a year earlier were now fighting for their own survival every step of the way.

Low, grey clouds scudded overhead, the vision forward nothing but white foam as U-112 slammed through the heavy oncoming seas. "At least the weather is on our side!" the mate yelled over the howling wind. "I never thought I'd be so happy to see a gale on the Bay of Biscay!"

"Hopefully the weather's just as bad up the channel and those RAF bastards can't get their planes airborne," Albrecht shouted back.

The night came on and the gale worsened. By midnight, the seas were sweeping across not only the decks, but the conning tower as well, and the lookouts on the bridge had to grimly hang on to keep from being washed overboard. Yet all on board knew that as bad as the storm was, it was far preferable to the hell the Whitley, Halifax and Sunderland bombers that the Royal Air Force were flying would rain down on them if they had half a chance, not to mention the smaller but quicker PBY Catalinas.

The unrelenting tempest continued on through the second day and well into the night before it finally began to subside. Sunrise came as an eerie red smudge under sombre leaden clouds to the east. The gale had blown itself out; the pewter sea ran lumpy and confused. A fine mist of rain was falling. The eight U-boats cut a broad swath through the water. On board U-112 the atmosphere was tense. Gunners manned their stations, and as lookouts scanned the low horizon, the Metox receiver was closely monitored. As the morning passed, the cloud and rain increased and the seas flattened. By midday the ocean surface had turned to glass.

"We are three-quarters there, Jost," the captain said as he lowered his glasses. "If this weather holds we could be in luck."

But it didn't. By early afternoon, the rain had stopped and the clouds were lifting. An icy breeze had filled in from the Northwest. And with it came the first wave of planes. The starboard lookout spotted the attack first, raising the alarm. There was no warning from their Metox system and the gunners had less than one minute to swing their four-barrelled twenty millimetre cannons into action. A trail of .30 calibre machine gun bullets walked across the water towards the sub, the forward gun of the low-flying Catalina spitting fire. Both deck guns from U-112 were trained on the enemy aircraft, firing at will as it roared low overhead, dropping four depth charges as it screeched past, their violent detonations shaking the submarine from stem to stern. It was only a matter of seconds before another attacker was spotted, this one coming at them from dead ahead. And so the battle started. The tactic of the submarines staying on the surface and fighting as a group was a new one, the boats having been rearmed with a second anti-aircraft gun, which replaced their heavy foredeck cannon. Fighting as a group was thought to be of benefit, so that each quadrant of an attack could be defended while advancing at a much faster rate on the surface. But within the first two hours of the battle, Nils Albrecht could see this tactic was futile. His second mate was more direct in his appraisal.

"This is bullshit! If we sit up here much longer we'll be blown to smithereens!" shouted Chief Gunnery Officer Scherer, as a big Halifax boomed in on a pass, her bombs throwing the seawater high in the air as they detonated each side of them. Moments later, a direct hit turned U-509 – running some 200 meters astern – into a massive fireball of twisted metal, black smoke and towering flames. There was no time to look, however. Planes were now homing in on them from every direction. The gunners trained their weapons on a Catalina as it levelled off low to the water on their starboard quarter. Spent shell casings vomited out onto the deck as smoke began to issue from the attacking plane. Passing low overhead with one engine spewing flames, the stricken Catalina rolled slowly onto its side. As a wingtip clipped the ocean surface, the plane began cartwheeling across the water before it erupted into pieces. At the same moment, another vicious track of bullets snaked across the water and up the deck, hitting the forward gunners and tearing two of them to shreds before ripping across the bridge, chopping the portside lookout in half. Deafening explosions bracketed the boat as blood streamed over the steel deck.

"New orders from Central Command, sir!" a seaman screamed into the captain's ear, handing him a piece of paper. "It says we are to take evasive action and proceed individually!"

"Clear the decks!" Albrecht yelled. "Get those men off that forward gun, Mr Scherer, as quick as you can please. Diving stations! Dive! Dive!"

The bleeding gunners were dragged across the deck and handed down the hatch as the submarine prepared to crash dive. With shells and depth charges churning up the leaden sea around them, U-112 quickly descended beneath the surface.

"Hard starboard rudder and dive to one five zero metres, Mr Weiss," the captain ordered. It was chaos in the operations room. Wounded men were screaming; blood mixed with seawater coated the floor. "Get these wounded men taken care of! And someone clean up this floor. Schäfer – give me a fleet damage report!"

"U-509 is gone, sir, and so is 153. U-464 and 67 are badly damaged and are attempting to return to base, and 344 has been ordered to cover them until they can receive support. That leaves only U-156, U-614 and ourselves to continue on. Here are the new orders, sir."

At that moment the blasts from a series of depth charges could be heard, with each detonation further and further away. Albrecht sat and read the new orders, joined by the first mate.

"This new strategy didn't last too long, did it Mr Weiss? It looks like we've got to get out of this mess as best we can on our own. What's the damage?"

"Three men dead, sir, and two wounded," the mate responded. "The doc says the wounds are serious but not life-threatening."

"You get hit by a thirty calibre round and it is going to be serious, isn't it? Anyway that is some good news at least. Who were the unlucky ones?"

"Müller, Schmidt, and Schneider, sir."

"Damn fine lads, all of them. Take care of the bodies as best you can, and we'll give them a decent burial as soon as it's safe. We still have our work cut out for us to escape this death trap, but we have been here before, haven't we, old friend?"

For the next two days, U-112 played cat and mouse with their attackers, dodging airborne sorties as well as Royal Navy depth charges, surfacing only to charge batteries and take on fresh air. Finally, after three days of constant harassment, U-112 came to the point where they could travel on the surface at speed once again. A course was set, taking them in a wide arc north of the Azores and east of Bermuda, adding several hundred miles on to the voyage but hopefully keeping them away from the American sub-hunters known to be patrolling the waters of the South Atlantic.

As U-112 approached the West Indies, Nils Albrecht plotted his course to enter the Caribbean Basin through the Anegada Passage. German intelligence had briefed the Kriegsmarine as to the latest developments concerning the American deployment in the Caribbean, and from this and his past experiences, the captain knew the US had dramatically built up its resources on Puerto Rico and at Guantanamo Bay on Cuba in an effort to protect the major shipping channels of the Mona and Windward Passages. Because the Anegada Passage was rarely used by merchant shipping, he felt the chances of being detected were far less because aerial surveillance would be working in the more concentrated areas to the west.

"The cracks are getting tighter to slip through, Karl," he said to his navigator, "but they are there nonetheless."

The submarine entered the Anegada Passage late in the afternoon, having picked up visual contact of Sombrero Island, which lay at the centre of the ninety mile wide channel. Their designated area of operation was to the south of the island of Hispaniola, looking for targets heading for the two main commercial shipping passages out of the Caribbean Basin on each side of this big island. Once Albrecht's position was well south of the American island of St. Croix, he turned due west. They were heading into what was now a dangerous, well-patrolled area, but one that was thought to be busy with commercial shipping.

The 8,000 ton oil tanker *Rajasthan* was approaching Navassa Island, located in the straights between Jamaica and Haiti, when U-112 struck. The stricken ship was able to send off may-day signals for assistance, which set the seas and skies abuzz with US military planes and ships based at Guantanamo Bay searching for the German submarine. For days afterwards, Albrecht and his crew were on the run, crash diving countless times during the day as enemy planes attacked from out of the clear tropical sky. Night times became even more dangerous as the enemy attacks were coming out of the black void, unseen until the last moment. The Metox receiver randomly warned of the incoming attacks, but the Allied planes seemed to be tracking them in the darkness with ease. The crew were weary and showing the strain after being constantly on edge for over three days.

On the morning of the fourth day of their pursuit, U-112 surfaced to send and receive radio messages. As they motored through the dawn, the captain discussed their situation with his two mates and navigational officer. They had run southeast, away from their attackers, and finally seemed to have found some respite.

"It's time we send a report in, gentlemen, and I want your opinions before we do. Has the enemy developed a technique of tracking us by locking in on our Metox receiver with some sort of device, perhaps even their radar? How else can they be so accurate in their attacks at night without the use of flares or lights?" Albrecht asked his officers.

"Either it's that or they're using black magic," answered Scherer.

"It does seem uncanny how easily they are finding us at night," agreed Weiss.

After discussing the situation at length, it was unanimously decided to send a radio message back to central command stating these fears. "I'm glad you men agree. Send the following message then, Schäfer," he ordered his radioman. "'Air activity intense in designated area. Propose to move further southeast. Suspect enemy using new location device that locks in on Metox receiver. Enemy making accurate night time attacks without the use of searchlights or flares.' Get that off now and let's see what they say," he ordered.

The U-boat motored into the sunrise, and though the crew were still at full alert, there was a feeling that for the moment at least, they all could catch their breath. It seemed as though their evasive manoeuvres over the last few days had shaken off their dogged tormentors. An hour after sending the transmission, Oberfunkmiester Schäfer was on the bridge with a reply. *Proceed to location X to resupply, then to Operational Area C and confirm position,* the captain read. Handing the transmission back to his radio operator, he turned to follow him down below when a shout came from one of the lookouts. "Aircraft at zero nine zero!" Once again the order was given to crash dive.

The deck watch, gunners and officers flew down the hatch as the submarine quickly slipped below the surface. Every spare man rushed to the bows of the ship to increase the weight forward. The dive siren hooted. Men shouted. Valves were turned shut. Diesel engines were shut down and the electric motors started. The aircraft was a B-18, and on its first pass it dropped four MK-44 depth charges. The bombs landed close to the sub and everything inside the vessel shook and vibrated. The sound was deafening. The lights went out and the emergency lighting came on. By the time the big plane could turn to make a second pass, the sub had descended to over 100 meters and continued to dive and turn. For the next hour, the captain ordered evasive action. As long as there were no surface vessels in the area he felt they would be safe – for the moment at least.

But something was puzzling him, and he called his officers together in the wardroom to discuss it. "Don't you find it odd, gentlemen? We had seemingly shaken off the Americans, but the moment we initiate radio traffic they track us down again? Is it just a coincidence? That is almost an exact copy of what happened two days ago. Mr Schäfer, do you think it's possible they could be using our own radio transmissions to locate us?"

The young radio man thought about it for a moment. "I suppose in theory it could be possible. If they know what frequency we are transmitting on, and with the right equipment placed at several different locations to pick up those transmissions, then theoretically it would be conceivable for them to triangulate our position."

"But are they that well organised, sir?" Weiss asked.

"And could they really have advanced their technology that far?" queried Pobanz.

"I think we can put nothing past these Americans. From now on we must assume they are using our Metox to track us from above, as well as locking in on our radio transmissions to triangulate our position when we call home. From now on, we will use the radio judiciously, if at all. We are now like the lone wolf separated from the pack, gentlemen, using all his wits to survive. We are on our own."

It was close to midnight when U-112 surfaced one mile to windward of the island of Tintamarre. Using their powerful signal light, the submarine flashed the coded letters of the day towards the shore, and moments later received a reply. There would be no moon, which meant that for the next two nights German U-boats in the area would be entering the island's anchorage to restock on fresh provisions, and more importantly resupply with fresh water and fuel. Nils Albrecht had done this before and knew the procedure well, but tonight he was overly cautious. The situation had changed dramatically since his last voyage to the Caribbean, and he was leaving nothing to chance. Passing well to leeward of the island, he slowly turned his big vessel, and after picking up the makeshift range lights, carefully crept into the bay. Within the hour, the little steel freighter that acted as a supply vessel was tied up alongside, and soon bags of fresh tropical fruits and vegetables were being passed from its deck into the bowels of the submarine. At the same time, the engineers had opened the ship's water and fuel tanks, and began transferring several tons of fresh water and fuel oil from the freighter. As this operation was taking place, the *Lady Luck* entered the bay, and after tying up alongside, the freighter was soon passing cases of wine, spirits and cigarettes across the decks to the waiting sub.

"So tell me Marstrom, what are the latest developments here? We've only recently arrived from Europe, but it is obvious things have changed markedly since our last voyage," Albrecht inquired as he stood on the deck of the freighter, next to her skipper.

"The screws are tightening, and quickly," the one-eyed captain replied. "The naval airbase on Antigua is now operational, and they are flying Mariner and Catalina seaplanes from there. My sources tell me the US Army has nearly finished building a land airbase as well. In just the past month, American engineers along with two support vessels arrived on St. Martin and started surveying for an airstrip. With these frequent aerial patrols being flown locally, we have to be very careful. You don't want to spend more time out here than is absolutely necessary. I would advise you to be gone well before daylight."

On the beach, a small fire had been started, sending out an enticing signal from the shore as it reflected off of the stony backdrop of the cliff behind. "Permission to send the starboard watch ashore, Kapitan," the first mate requested from the submarine's bridge.

"Go ahead, Mr Weiss. Get them ashore and let them get some exercise. But inform them it will be only a short stay this time, with an hour ashore for each watch," Albrecht answered from the bridge of the freighter. The engines of the *Lady Luck* could be heard starting up, and letting go their lines, the yacht motored slowly out of the anchorage. "He doesn't seem to want to spend too much time around here either," Albrecht said.

"No...as I said, we have to be careful these days."

A few hours later the steel freighter was gone, and at first light U-112 reversed out of the small cove, turned its nose south and proceeded towards the next designated area of operation.

After leaving Tintamarre, U-112 sailed west for two hundred miles before turning south towards Trinidad. Albrecht knew Martinique was now under a full naval blockade by well-armed American warships, and so steered well clear of this area. After two days of steaming, he brought his submarine gradually to the east towards the Galleons Passage. In the fading light after sunset, the captain scanned the horizon with his binoculars for targets. It had been a very unproductive trip so far, with only the one sinking near Navassa Island to show for their efforts. Now, with the faint outline of Grenada on the horizon to port, he was approaching the busy shipping lanes near Trinidad. He knew it would be dangerous, but was still hoping for some success.

"What a difference a few months can make, eh Jost? What happened to our happy hunting grounds?"

"It's certainly a lot harder work this time around, that's for sure, sir. The enemy has become very well organised in quite a short time."

While on the surface, Albrecht had directed his radio man to listen in to the traffic between other subs in the area. There were close to fifty U-boats operating in the western Atlantic from Brazil to the Bahamas at the time, and from what they were hearing, all of them were under intense Allied pressure. "It does seem some of the lads are getting some hits in, but are paying dearly for them afterwards. These Americans really have turned up the heat, leaving very little room in which to operate."

"It unquestionably sounds like the enemy is far better equipped this time around. Now if I may suggest, sir, why don't you take a break and get a bit of sleep. It's been a long day. I'll call you if anything comes up," the first mate suggested.

"I'll take you up on your suggestion, Mr Weiss. I could use some shut-eye. Call me in an hour," Albrecht said, as he descended below to his cramped quarters. He was asleep within minutes. It seemed like the captain had hardly closed his eyes before he was awakened by the voice of his second mate, Scherer. "Sir – excuse me, sir, but we have picked up something! You need to have a look."

Albrecht was up in an instant, shoving his weathered skipper's hat on his head as he rushed through the control room and up the ladder onto the deck. "What is it men? What do you see?" he asked.

"There's a convoy ahead, Kapitan. Once your eyes have adjusted to the darkness you'll see it. It's a big one, sir," he heard Weiss say. It took a few moments, but peering through his binoculars, he gradually began to pick up the silhouettes of a long procession of ships stretching directly across their path.

"Beautiful! It looks as if we are finally in luck, doesn't it gentlemen," he said, putting down his glasses. "You can be certain this convoy will be escorted, so let's take a page out of our old North Atlantic book and get the fox inside the henhouse. We'll submerge and see if we can't work ourselves into the middle of the convoy where we can then surface fire so the escorts can't pick us out on their radar. Prepare to dive – and make sure we observe strict silence once we are below. We don't want to tip anyone off."

Within minutes, U-112 had submerged to periscope depth, and was stealthily approaching the unwitting convoy when Schäfer, sitting with the sound detection headset on, spoke out softly. "Sir, propellers approaching from the south at speed!" Turning the periscope in that direction, the captain swept the horizon until he picked up a vessel making a swift approach.

"Enemy ship at eight hundred meters! Dive! Down 'scope and dive!" he quickly ordered. Once again, the crew responded immediately and rushed to their crash dive positions as they rapidly descended.

"Their ASDIC has locked onto us, sir!" Schäfer called. Down and down they dove. Tension showed on the men's sweaty faces as they waited for the inevitable attack from above. "Splashes in the water! They have launched depth charges!" And then came the first explosion, followed by another and another, each one closer. The ship jolted and shook and reverberated as depth charges detonated all around them. They continued to dive before levelling off at their maximum designed depth of 230 meters. Still the ship was rocked by the nearby blasts. Captain Albrecht had recently learned from naval intelligence that the MK-44 depth charges the Americans were using could not exceed the depth of 250 meters before self-detonating, so to the anxiety of his crew, he ordered the submarine to continue to dive, finally levelling off at 300 meters.

The pressure on the hull was intense. Seawater burst through pipe connections. As engineers battled to stop one eruption another valve would spring a leak. The ship creaked and groaned. It was the deepest the submarine had ever gone, and every member of the crew took each breath as if it might be their last. But the tactic was working, with the depth charges discharging harmlessly overhead. And somehow the ship held together.

For the next several hours, U-112 used every trick in its arsenal to try and escape the assailants. Steering an easterly course, they headed out of the Galleons Passage towards the open Atlantic. Eventually the ASDIC pings became fainter and fainter. Albrecht kept his sub under until he had no choice but to surface. He knew it would be dangerous, but he was banking on the chance that the escorts would have lost them and returned to support the convoy. Carefully he took his sub to the top. To his relief the horizon was clear.

As U-112 powered east at their maximum surface speed of twenty knots, Kapitanleutnant Nils Albrecht stared into the open Atlantic. He knew they had been fortunate to survive the latest ordeal. He wondered how long this good luck would last.

Stand and Fight

On the bridge, Albrecht swept the horizon with his binoculars as seven other sets of glasses also searched for any sign of the enemy – air or sea borne. It was a windy day with a solid sea running. High banks of cumulus clouds drifted down from windward, bringing the occasional rainsquall with them. "I don't like the look of these clouds, Mr Weiss. It's far too easy for those Catalinas and Mariners to hide up there." The captain turned to his navigator as he came on deck to take his morning sun shot. "Mr Pobanz, I realise this cloud cover is not conducive for obtaining a good sight, but it is very important we know our position as soon as possible. I know it won't be easy, but do your best."

The navigation officer quickly prepared himself. After anxiously waiting for a break in the fast moving clouds, he finally got what he was looking for. Quickly raising his sextant to his eye, he just managed to get a fleeting sight of the sun. After recording the exact time, he then returned below decks to calculate and plot his line of position.

The submarine continued to slam into the heavy seas as they powered on in a northerly direction. The atmosphere on the bridge was increasingly tense as they waited for the inevitable attack to come. "I want you to change the lookouts every hour, Mr Weis," Albrecht ordered. "We need them to be fresh and wide awake."

"In these conditions I think that is a good idea, sir. The men are tired as well...no one has had much sleep the last few days. I'll work out a rotation right away."

"I have plotted our position, sir," Pobanz shouted up the hatch a few moments later.

Going below, the captain crossed to the navigation station and leaned over the chart. "This is our line of position," the navigator pointed out, "and with my dead reckoning I estimate we are here, roughly 20 miles southeast of Grenada."

"Good. We will proceed towards the north-east and hopefully find some targets away from Trinidadian air cover." U-112 motored through the squally weather for the rest of the day, a dirty sunset chasing them into the dark night.

There was no warning. The first sign of the incoming attack was the roar of the Mariner's engines seconds before it shrieked low overhead. Depth charges turned the water around the submarine white, the dive alarm shrieked, and the crew flew down the hatch. Inside, a mad scramble was underway as they went into yet another emergency descent.

"Where in the hell did he come from?" Scherer bawled at the radio man. "I'm taking that useless Metox machine and throwing it overboard the first chance I get!"

"We are like a sitting duck up there! What are you doing Schäfer, sleeping on watch?" yelled the first mate as he closed down one of the overhead valves.

"I'm telling you, the machine didn't make a sound!" retorted the angry Oberfunkmiester.

"Take it easy men – take it easy! It isn't Schäfer's fault! He's only doing his job like the rest of us!" the captain commanded as he moved to the chart table. "There's something they are doing with their radar that must be jamming our machine. Let's spend our energy fighting the enemy, not each other!"

The submarine spent the next several hours performing evasive underwater manoeuvres. It was close to midnight when U-112 finally resurfaced. For the moment they seemed to be safe, but now they had been located from the air it wouldn't be long before they were tracked down again. Albrecht knew their only hope was to get to the northeast and away from Trinidad as quickly as possible. Travelling on the surface was dangerous, even at night, as the cover of darkness no longer assured safety, but he knew he must roll the dice and take the chance in an effort to outrun their pursuers. The submarine slammed through the big swell, with the engines pushing close to top speed. As they surged over a large wave, the starboard lookout gave a shout. "Kapitan – I'm picking up a vessel bearing zero-seven-zero degrees. It seems to be a local sailing craft, sir, running without lights."

Albrecht swung his glasses in that direction. "I think you're right, Horst. It is probably a local schooner sailing north-west from Tobago. Keep a good eye on them. They might be just what we are looking for."

Moments later a warning was issued from below. "Metox has picked up enemy radar, sir!"

"Thank you, Mr Schäfer. Gentlemen, let's dive. Descend to periscope depth, Mr Weiss," the captain ordered.

"Well thank Christ for small favours," shouted Scherer as he hustled down the hatch. "So the bloody Metox does work after all! I just wish it could make up its bloody mind whose side it was on!"

Once below the surface, Albrecht picked up what he was looking for through the periscope, and issued his orders to suit. Changing course, he steered his ship towards the nearby schooner, the outline of its flapping sails standing out against the night time sky.

"Here, Mr Weiss – take a look. That old schooner just might be our ticket out of this jam. We'll tag along with them for a while and hide in their shadow. It just might help to shake these Americans off."

Just then, the distant sounds of depth charges rattled through the submarine. All eyes swung towards the mate as he looked through the 'scope, expecting him to give the order to commence evasive action, but all he did was smile. "The fellows on that boat can thank their lucky stars those depth charges missed the target! Hopefully the pilot will recognise his mistake." A few minutes later this theory was confirmed by a flare dropped by the aircraft. The illuminated night sky made the schooner clearly visible. Once the flare had burned out and there was no sign of a further attack, the order was given to surface.

"I think we'll be safe accompanying these boys until morning," Albrecht said. "While we hide in their shadow, we can take the time to get the air tanks full and the batteries completely charged. I have a feeling tomorrow is going to be a busy day, and we must be ready for it."

With the sunrise U-112 returned to its previous northerly course, bashing through the oncoming seas at flank speed, having left the cover of the schooner an hour earlier. The rotten weather continued, and visibility remained poor. As the hours slipped away, the feeling of desperate nervousness continued to build. It was just after midday when Albrecht was called to the radio station. "Traffic from home base, sir," said Schäfer. "They are demanding to know our position and asking for a situation report."

The skipper pushed his hand through his hair and closed his eyes, knowing this was a big decision. Moving to the chart table, he jotted down their latest position. On a scrap of paper he wrote, *N12.2 degrees; W61.2 degrees; under continuous harassment; constant attack by air makes approaches to Trinidad untenable; repeat suspicion enemy employing new tracking device on Metox receiver, as well as using Kreigsmarine radio transmissions to triangulate our position.* "My gut is telling me we should not be responding, but orders are orders. Send this message Mr Schäfer, and let's see what happens. We will know very soon if our theory is correct." The captain put his cap on and climbed back up to the bridge. "Look sharp, lads. We should have company arriving any time now," he predicted.

Once again, there was no early warning from the Metox, and because of the cloud cover, the lookouts picked up the plane one minute too late. Albrecht knew they were in trouble. He knew there was no time to dive. They had to stand and fight. "Return fire, Mr Scherer! Return fire! No time to dive!" he shouted. Moments later, the Catalina's bullets were ripping across the deck. Looking up, Albrecht could see the four well-aimed bombs flying through the air towards his ship, and as they landed four massive concussions rocked the vessel, partially lifting the one thousand five hundred ton ship out of the water. It was as close to a direct hit as U-112 had ever experienced. As the men on the bridge recovered their feet, the lookouts warned of another attack from starboard, but the gunners were ready this time and threw up a barrage of fire – too late to stop the plane from dropping its depth charges, which again rattled the submarine to its foundations as they erupted around it. The enemy plane screeched overhead, smoke trailing behind the banking aircraft. There was no time to celebrate. The next assault was upon them, and the gunners hardly had time to swing and face it.

Down below, the situation was chaotic. It took several minutes for Albrecht to receive a damage report from his first mate. "One electric motor was blown completely off its mountings," the mate shouted up the hatch, "and we have no electrical power. The starboard engine is heavily damaged. The lube oil tank has split and the bilges are full of oil. The high pressure lines are broken and water is pouring through the stern glands. Many of the men are injured but there are no fatalities."

"Can we dive?"

"I'm afraid not, sir – not at the moment, anyway! Kreigal and Klausterman are working on it and I will let you know as soon as we are able."

Over the next hour, the crew feverishly worked to repair the damage as the gun crew repelled attack after attack. The oil being pumped out of the bilges was causing a huge slick in their wake, adding to the submarine's visibility from above. The engineers battled with the heavily leaking stern gland as they tried to stop seawater from pouring into the vessel. Electricians frantically worked to get the sub's battery power back on line. During a brief respite, the captain joined his men below as they struggled to get their damaged systems up and running. With one engine down, the sub could only manage a maximum speed of nine knots. And then the next wave of attacks hit.

On deck, things were desperate. Two of the gun crew were dead and others were badly wounded. The second mate had tied a tourniquet where he had been hit by a round. Still bleeding profusely from his left leg, Scherer refused to leave the bridge as he continued to direct fire at the unrelenting swarm of planes hovering like a pack of wild dogs moving in for the kill. Down below, the crew fought desperately to keep the ship afloat. Klausterman and the other engineers were struggling to get at least one electric motor operational. Albrecht knew their only hope of escaping the onslaught was to get below the surface. Because the hydraulics were down, the sub was being steered by the manual emergency system. And to make things worse, they were running out of ammunition. The four-barrelled Turim machine guns were effective, but ate up the 20mm shells at a colossal rate.

As nightfall approached, the captain went below again to determine their status. "How is it looking down here Jost? Can we get the electric motor going? Is the hull sound enough to dive? I need to know now! We're running out of time!"

"I think the boys are about to try the motor now. They have only jury-rigged the system. I don't know how long it will go for – if it works at all." Just at that moment there was another assault from the air. Below decks the sounds were horrific. The roar of Scherer's deck guns could be heard countering the hits being made by the enemy rounds, before the inevitable deafening detonations of depth charges blasted around the ship. Once again pipes ruptured, bodies were thrown across the vessel, water and oil sprayed everywhere and pandemonium reigned as the concussion caused by the explosions shook the boat from stem to stern. Then there was silence from above.

Pulling himself up the ladder, Albrecht found the conning tower torn to shreds. The four lookouts were dead. The gunners had been blown to pieces. Scherer lay on the tower floor with a gaping hole in his chest, his dead eyes gazing blindly into space. The captain threw his head back and stared into the heavens. And as he did so, the first pellets from a howling black rainsquall began to pound his face. The rain came down in torrents, the wind turned the water white, the sun disappeared and day turned to night like a flick of a switch.

Slowly he began to regain his composure. In the driving rain he crawled over to the damaged guns. They were of no more use. The sub was defenceless now. If it were not for the rainsquall, the Americans would have had no trouble finishing them off then and there. Their only hope of survival was to get below the surface where they could not be located from the air. Looking up into the thunderstorm, the captain made his decision. They had nothing to lose. He shouted down the hatch for help and two sailors emerged from the hatchway. "Help me check all of these men and see if any are still alive, and if they are, carefully get them below decks," he ordered. Of the twelve bodies on deck, only two still showed a sign of life. After taking one last look around, Captain Albrecht said a final farewell to the souls of the brave men he had placed on the floor of the tower. He then climbed down the ladder, dogging the hatch behind him.

"Mr Weiss, do we have electric power yet?" he asked of his sweat-stained mate.

"On one engine only, sir, and I'm not sure how far it will get us," was the answer.

"Can the hull take it if we submerge to periscope depth?"

"I don't really know. There may be cracks in the pressure hull. It's a chance we are taking. We could be lucky."

The captain took a deep breath and looked around the room. "Men, this is our only hope. Either we sit on the surface and wait to be slaughtered, or we submerge and put ourselves in the hands of the gods. At the moment, this squall has temporarily saved us. Mr Pobanz, how far is it to the closest island?"

"We are approximately twenty-five miles from the nearest of the southern Grenadines, sir."

Kapitanleutnant Nils Albrecht slowly looked around the operations room, staring each man in the eye. "Fill the ballast tanks, Mr Weiss, and descend to periscope depth," he finally ordered.

As U-112 slowly slipped beneath the surface, mayhem broke out in the severely damaged interior of the warship. Seawater sprayed and leaked from a multitude of pipes and valves damaged during the hostilities of the last two days. Electricians and mechanics, able seamen and officers, engineers and cooks, stripped to the waist and covered in sweat, battled not just to keep the ship afloat and moving; they were fighting for their very lives. And the captain was everywhere, assisting with whatever he could. He knew his crew was flagging. Most of them had not slept for days, their nerves were shot from the constant strain of battle, and yet not one of them had yielded to the pressure.

As the night advanced, the crew slowly managed to contain the damage. Pipes and fittings were leaking, but not at an alarming rate. The engineers were able to keep the one electric motor running. Their estimated speed was not much more than two knots, but they were making progress. "So far so good, sir," the mate said, wiping the sweat from his brow with the back of his arm.

"We're not out of the woods yet, my friend," the skipper replied. "Although we've slowed the leaks considerably, we're still taking on a substantial amount of water and using up a lot of juice keeping the pumps running. I'm worried about our limited battery power. Eventually we will have no choice but to surface to charge our batteries, and when we do we both know what we will be facing."

"I just spoke to Hassler, and he feels that at our present rate of electrical usage we should have another four to five hours of battery life remaining," Weiss reported.

"How are Klausterman and his crew getting on with the port diesel engine?"

"They have given it away. Apparently a line burst and the engine seized from a lack of oil. It needs a major overhaul to get going again."

"Right – well let's just make sure we will have one good diesel engine when we need it, Mr Weiss. At the moment, we have one goal and one goal only, and that is to get ashore somewhere. I have seen enough men die in the past two days, and I don't want to see any more if I can help it."

Somehow they made it through the night. At midnight the submarine ascended briefly to take on much needed air and recharge the overworked batteries. The leaking stern gland had been partially repaired, and the men needed some respite, so the engine was started but not put into gear, which would undo all the engineers' hard work. The captain kept his ship floating motionless on the surface for the bare minimum of time before slipping beneath the waves yet again.

Powered by their one remaining electric motor, the U-boat crept towards the west, and the night slowly passed. Daybreak arrived, and Albrecht had no choice but to give the order to surface yet again. Out of habit the captain searched the horizon with the periscope, knowing it was a futile effort because without their guns they could not defend themselves. "It looks clear enough from here, Jost. Up we go and let's see what happens."

The submarine broke through the top, and as it did the starboard engine was fired up. The captain followed the lookouts on to the deck as he had done countless times before. He was prepared for the worst. Fortunately, an attack did not eventuate from any quadrant. For the moment at least, they seemed safe.

Below decks there were more dramas. As soon as the diesel engine was put into ahead, the temporary repair of the stern gland failed. Seawater once again began pouring in, and the pumps could not keep up. In desperation every possible solution was tried in an effort to stem the influx of water. The chief engineer plumbed the seawater intake for the engine into the bilge, and the crew formed a human chain and were manhandling buckets of water out of the boat, but it was obvious they were losing the fight. Slowly the water rose over the floor boards, and soon it was up to the men's knees.

"Alright, Pobanz, which is the closest island?" the frazzled captain asked his navigator.

"It looks to be the island of Cannouan, sir. There are others to the south, but this one seems to the easiest one for us to reach."

"Right, then. Give me a compass course towards that island. Somehow we have to get there," the captain ordered.

Seawater was now half-covering the main engine, which was overheating. The men were becoming weary with their bailing, having trouble passing the heavy, water-filled buckets out of the hatch. The time had come. "Mr Weiss, prepare the life rafts. We have little choice but to abandon ship, but will leave it until the last possible moment."

And so in a last ditch attempt to get his men as close to shore as possible, the order was given to run the struggling engine up to full revolutions. As the shaft turned faster, more water poured in. The captain ordered the crew onto the deck. The wounded men were brought up and laid out on the tower floor, and the life rafts were prepared for launching. Food and water were passed up, as well as weapons and ammunition. Nils Albrecht climbed on deck to supervise their preparation, and as the sun rose higher into the morning sky the shape of an island began to emerge on the horizon before them, roughly twelve miles away.

Unfortunately for the men on U-112, the weather had moderated, and the skies were clear.

The flight of Mariners out of Chaguaramas had been searching all night for a wounded submarine they knew was there, one which they were determined to find. The severely damaged U-boat had somehow slipped away from them close to twelve hours earlier, and they had been criss-crossing the area in a vain attempt to find it. Running low on fuel, the four planes were about to turn for home when the U-boat was spotted to the east of the island of Cannouan. Now they were moving in for the kill.

The end was brutally swift. Aboard the defenceless U-boat, no lookouts were posted and no guns were manned. As Albrecht and Weiss supervised the preparation to abandon ship, the first of the enemy planes dropped silently out of the clouds, skimming over the water from the east. It swept in low and fast, and its bullets and bombs were on target. Fifty calibre shells ripped the unprotected men to pieces. Two bombs were perfect hits, cleaving the ocean open either side of the U-boat's tower. Again and again, the four planes pummelled the defenceless sub as the crew frantically attempted to escape in their rubber rafts. Waves swept over the semi-submerged decks. At long last, the stern section filled completely with water and slowly disappeared, the trapped air inside rushing forward. The bow rose vertically into the air, a bizarre metal monolith towering over the grey surface of the sea. For the longest of moments, U-112 paused, as if to have one last look at the world above. Finally, the forces of nature overwhelmed the valiant ship, and with a rush she slipped beneath the sea, leaving the surface boiling like a hot cauldron behind.

Desperate Survival

Nils Albrecht had lost track of time. The sun was shining brightly into his eyes as he lay in the bottom of the rubber raft. There were others nearby. As he surfaced, he could feel at least one body next to him. Then he detected motion, and blocking the sun out with one hand he squinted to see movement all around him, until raising his head he understood what these men were doing. They were paddling for their lives. Sitting up, he leaned against the rubber roll in the stern of the boat and took stock. The wind was at his back, the sun baked down from above, the salt spray from the choppy waves caked his eyes and lips and hair, and eight men on either side of him kneeled and paddled Indian-style towards the high island ahead in the distance.

Slowly he came to the realization of where he was and how he might have gotten there. Besides the goose-egg on the back of his head, he concluded he was suffering from no other injuries, and so seeing one of the young sailors in front of him flagging, he pulled him aside and took his place with the paddle.

"Good to see you're okay, sir," Weiss said as he glanced across the raft as he paddled. "I've been saving this for when you woke up." The mate smiled and handed the captain his faithful old skipper's hat.

"You don't miss anything, do you, Jost?" he said as he put his hat on. "I can't remember exactly what happened. It's all a blur to me at the moment."

"The last attack did us in. I saw the direct hit that sent you flying. You hit your head on the deck as you landed. We pulled you into the raft with us, hoping you would come to. That be was a good six hours ago, and we've been paddling hard ever since. The island ahead is our only chance. We all know what'll happen if we miss it. But it doesn't seem like it's getting any closer!"

"My head is very sore. There's a pretty big bump where I must have hit the deck. Did anyone else make it? Are there any other rafts in sight?"

"We haven't seen any sir," Weiss sombrely responded. "It was chaos at the end. The bastards were savage in their attacks until the old girl went down. Once we got into the raft, the wind blew us away so fast we had no chance to paddle back to look for any other survivors. In the end we decided it was useless to use up our energy trying to go back. We can only hope some of the others found a way to save themselves."

They paddled on for the rest of the day. The steady tradewinds blew from behind and the white-capped seas pushed the rubber raft in the general direction they wanted to go. As the day passed, the singular cone-shaped peak of the island did gradually grow closer. In the back of their minds, everyone knew that if they missed it and drifted into the west they would surely die, just as if they had been wrecked in the middle of the Sahara Desert. Klausterman was the driving force behind their survival. The muscular engineer had taken it upon himself to almost singlehandedly will the nine men in the boat to get themselves to the safety of the island ahead. His energy was unrelenting, his determination unyielding as his non-stop paddling propelled them on. Reaching the island was their only hope of salvation, and he knew it.

The sun drifted into the western sky and disappeared behind the silhouette which frustratingly danced before them. Darkness came and they wearily paddled on. It was as if the island were playing some sort of bizarre game and somehow kept dancing away from them, taunting them to catch up as it stayed just out of reach.

They were into the breakers before they heard or saw them. One moment they were paddling for the nearby shore, and the next they were being lifted by a large wave and thrown onto the shallow, unseen reef. The raft was upended and the crew tumbled over the shallow coral. The unexpected shock had them gasping for breath. The sharp coral grabbed and cut and tore at them, as the relentless waves broke over their heads and rolled them violently across the shoal as the surge tried to drag them under. The raft washed away, and there were long moments of disjointed confusion and fear, but one by one the crew began to emerge out of the surf as it dissipated into a deeper lagoon on the leeward side of the reef, one hundred yards off the island's windward shore.

Quietly wading through the sandy shallows, the survivors of U-112 staggered out of the sea and flung themselves onto the sand. The men were beyond exhaustion. They had no water. They were parched, sunburnt and shell-shocked, bleeding from coral cuts and half drowned. But somehow they had made it ashore. It was only now that Nils Albrecht and his men could contemplate the events of the past days and hours.

They had survived. But the captain knew they had no time to relax. His men needed water, they needed food, and they had to keep moving. Studying what was left of his crew, he suffered mixed feelings. There was relief for the ones that had been saved from what would have been a certain death, but also immense sadness for the loss of the forty-three brave souls who did not make it. Forty-three good men! They had been like brothers to him; they had worked and lived together through thick and thin, and now they were gone. But these men were alive, and he had to figure a way to get them off this beach and off this island. But how? It was a long way from the beach of this remote island to any kind of safety.

The nine men lay on the sand, the gentle waters of the protected lagoon lapping at their feet. No one spoke for a long time. The horrors of the past days washed over them. Finally, Albrecht pushed himself up to his feet and gazed inland. Behind the beach, a small ridge ran from the southern end of the island, slowly ascending until it blended into the mountain peak standing over them to the north. He knew from his previous years travelling through the islands with the *Kate* that they had landed on the sparsely populated island of Cannouan, and that on the other side of the hill was a bay where he had seen small sloops and schooners at anchor. Slowly a plan began to form in his mind. First he had to take stock of their situation and see exactly what equipment and supplies they had been able to salvage from the upended life raft. "Right, men – let's see what we were able to save from this disaster." Kneeling down next to the others, he was able to account for only one machine gun, along with a shoulder bag containing two officers' pistols, a pair of binoculars and a handful of ammunition. There also were a couple of empty water bottles, a sausage and a bag of soggy bread. "Well this is excellent, isn't it, lads," the captain finally said, looking up with a smile at his men. "I think we have more than enough here with which to conquer the Caribbean, don't you?"

"Jost," he said to his mate standing at his side, "I don't know if you remember, but I believe there is a little village on the other side of the island with an anchorage where the locals moor their trading vessels."

"Yes, I vaguely remember seeing something there when we passed through the Grenadines years ago," the mate replied.

"We have to get over there and find some sort of boat that we can commandeer to get us out of here. Do you think everyone is fit enough to make the hike across? I wouldn't think it's more than a mile or two."

"Everyone is suffering from cuts and bruises but no one is incapacitated. When do you want to start?"

"There's no point in spending any more time on this deserted beach than we have to," the captain surmised. "We might as well start by hauling the life raft up there into the scrub so it's out of sight. Then we should hike over to the other side of the island and see what we can find."

After disposing of the clumsy rubber raft, the men limped their way along the beach until they found a small path winding inland. In the moonlight, they followed the track as it meandered through the thick dry scrub, leading them gradually up the hill to the top of the ridge. This part of the island was actually quite narrow, with not much more than a quarter of a mile separating the Atlantic side to the east from its western Caribbean shore. From where they stood, they looked to the southwest over a broad, semi-protected bay. Near the shoreline, silhouettes of a handful of local sailing craft floated in the silver reflection of the bright moonlight. In single file, they walked down the hill towards the anchorage.

The track was little more than a goat trail, and several times they had to ease their way through the scrub, but eventually they emerged onto a worn footpath that led towards the island's only settlement, which consisted of a small group of simple houses scattered over a flat area of grass-covered land a few yards behind the tree-lined beach. Quietly finding their way to the sandy bayside, they looked out over the water at the half-dozen sloops riding at anchor. Huddling together, they now began to discuss their options.

"Looking at our choices doesn't fill me with the greatest of confidence, I must admit," Albrecht said. "What exactly can we achieve from here? What is our goal? If we leave this island, where do we go and what are our chances of getting home without being captured?"

"Our ultimate goal would be to somehow get onto another U-boat, wouldn't it?" Weiss asked. "But how do we do that? We have no radio, we have no boat and we have no way of letting anyone know that we are even alive."

"If we could get to Martinique, perhaps we could turn ourselves in there," Pobanz suggested. "Exactly how we would do that I have no idea, but it would be better than staying here and being captured by the British."

There was a long silence. Then the captain spoke. "Maybe there is a way out of this after all. Jost, you are right. The only way for us to escape the Caribbean is on another U-boat. And where is the one place we know our comrades will be stopping?" Albrecht asked, looking from one man to the other. "That's right – Tintamarre! So what we need is a boat to get us there! Now, from what I see out there on the water, there doesn't seem to be anything substantial enough to carry all of us that distance, but I think I do know of a place where we could find one that would. I think you know where I am talking about, don't you Mr Weiss?"

The first mate smiled as he nodded. "Petite Silhouette," was all he said.

Nils took the binoculars out of his bag and examined the anchored vessels. Most were simple open fishing boats, none of which looked anywhere near big enough to carry his shipwrecked crew.

There was, however, one larger sloop that could possibly take them all. Examining the vessel more closely, Albrecht could see a small dinghy tied astern.

"Men, that big sloop is the one we must target," he said, as the binoculars were passed around. "First we need to find something to get us out there." Walking along the moonlit shore, they came to a stand of coconut trees with a few small rowboats hauled up underneath them. "Right, who is volunteering to row me out there?" Jaeger and Hassler, the youngest of the survivors, stepped forward.

The most seaworthy craft was chosen and quietly dragged down to the water's edge. "The three of us will go out there first and then come back for the rest of you," Albrecht said. It took a few minutes to get organised with the oars, but eventually they were pulling the boat across the choppy bay towards the large sloop the captain had earmarked earlier. "That small dinghy trailing astern indicates someone must be sleeping aboard," Albrecht whispered, "so keep it quiet." Drawing up to the sloop's wide, heart-shaped transom, Jaeger jumped up on deck with the tattered bow line, and after shipping the oars the others lightly followed, tying the small boat astern. The anchorage was not a calm one. The sloop rocked and rolled on its mooring. The long main boom creaked and groaned as it slammed from side to side against the main sheet. Just at that moment, as the three men stood in the stern of the boat trying to get their bearings, a voice could be heard emanating from the shadowy companionway of the small deckhouse, followed by the movement of the dark shape of a man climbing up on deck. "Eh, eh...wha' de hell is dis' a-tall?"

For the first time he could remember, Nils Albrecht was at a loss as to what to say. He had never been in a situation where it was necessary to commandeer a boat from someone. But then the gravity of the situation returned, and he remembered exactly why he was there.

"My name is Kapitanleutnant Nils Albrecht of the Greater German Reich, and I am here to requisition your vessel," he said in his best English, drawing the revolver from out of his waist. "I want to assure you that we are not here to hurt you, so you need not be afraid. However, I am armed, as you can see, and I will use my weapon if necessary. Do you understand?"

"What de ass I seein' here a-tall? T'ree white men come like jumbies from out o' de watah an' dey tellin' me dey is takin' me vessel? I's an ol' mon, an' I seen a ting or two in dis life, but me never seen nothin' like dis," the man muttered, as much to himself as to the strangers before him. "Well le' me tell you somethin', Missa German whatever you is – my name is George Paris an' I is de Master a dis vessel, an' she ain't goin' nowhere without my say so, gun or no gun. So tell me Cap, what is it exactly you does want from a poor-ass man like me?"

In the darkness, a smile crossed the German captain's lips. He liked this fellow and his straightforward attitude. "Well, Captain Paris, I will be honest with you. I was the officer in charge of German U-boat 112 destroyed by Allied warplanes yesterday, and I was lucky enough to get some of my crew ashore on your island after it sank. I am therefore in need of your vessel here to transport my men to a place where I can arrange for their safe passage home. Do I make myself clear?"

"So let me get dis straight. You fellas is from one o' dese underwater warships dat I been hearin' 'bout dat has come all de way over here 'cross de wide ocean to cause confusion in de Caribbean? You come here to kill we hard workin' men who never did nothin' to provoke you, who don't know nothin 'bout your war, who only out on de hard ocean tryin' to make a crust to feed dey family, and now you an' your boys is more or less shipwrecked here on my island, and you does wan' to take all dat I have in the world to save yo' desperate ass...is dat de story?" he asked, crossing his arms and leaning back onto the cabin top.

"The fact is, Captain Paris, we are at war, where unfortunately the norms of civilised society don't apply. I need to look after my men, and so like it or not, I'm going to take your vessel, with or without your assistance," Albrecht firmly answered.

The old West Indian pondered the situation for a few moments. "Well I can see dat I is in no position to negotiate – you is holdin' de gun an' I ain't. Where is it exactly dat you want to go? I ain't know where Germany even be!"

"I appreciate your candour, sir. The balance of my crew is waiting for us on the beach. Once we pick them up, I would like to leave for the island of Petite Silhouette. Is there any problem with that?"

Captain Paris smiled, his white teeth flashing through the darkness of the night. "Man, dat ain't no problem a-tall! Petite Silhouette is jus' up de road a piece – jus' 'round de corner. I t'ought you was goin to say Jamaica or some such far-away place!"

Nils Albrecht returned the smile. "Captain Paris, if you and your vessel can get us to that island we will be more than satisfied. And one more question – how much water do you have aboard? I have a terribly thirsty crew ashore there."

"Don't worry, Cap! One ting we has aboard is plenty o' sweet watah. So I suppose we should get tings ready. Le' me go forward and shake up me crew. You don't need to worry none 'bout explainin' much to he. Young Punkin is a good-natured soul, but de poor boy was born deaf an' mute. He's handy on a boat though, and don't be fooled, he is brighter dan you t'ink. Oh, and one mo' ting. It lookin' like we goin' to be shipmates fo' a spell, so you can drop de 'Cap'n Paris' business. Here in de Cays, most everyone does call me Garfish, or jus' 'Fish' fo' short." And so saying, the wiry captain dropped down the forward scuttle and a few moments later was followed up on deck by his solitary, sleepy crewmember.

Jaeger was ordered to row ashore for the others, and not long afterwards he was back with the balance of the crew.

The breeze was fresh and steady, and without so much as a sound, the two West Indians went to work raising the sloop's big gaff mainsail. Albrecht crouched aft near the tiller, secretly appreciating the fact that they were not attempting to perform this manoeuvre on their own. Once the sail was set, the agile skipper moved to the mainsheet. "I'm letting go dis small boat you all borrowed," he said over his shoulder. "It belongs to a friend of mine an' it's his pride an' joy. It should wash up on de beach all right, but I'm sure he'll wonder how de hell it got dere when he finds it in de mornin'."

With the canvas mainsail now slatting back and forth, Punkin began hauling on the anchor line, and as he did, several of the younger Germans went forward to help. Once the anchor broke free and was hoisted up on deck, Punkin sprung to the jib halyard and hauled away. Within moments it was made fast, the flapping jib sheet was pulled off, and they were sailing. Both men moved about the boat with well-practiced precision, each knowing exactly what had to be done.

Garfish settled down at the tiller and studied the trim of the sails. They were beginning to find a rhythm, and the sloop was sailing nicely as they worked their way up the lee side of the island. "This seems to be a handy little craft, Captain. What type of work do you do with her?" Albrecht asked.

"De *Juanita?* Man she's built like a wall-house. She was built by the McLains over in Windward Carriacou, an' she's sailed all t'rough dese islands 'tween Grenada and St. Vincent. She's done a fair few trips up nort' fo' 'bubs' as well. I've carried loads of cement up here to de Cays from Grenada dat schooners would t'ink twice 'bout, an' caught more fish than I could ever count, so don't frighten Cap. We should be in Port Victoria sometime around midday tomorrow."

"And 'bubs'? What exactly do you mean by that, sir?"

"'Bubs'? You know bubal…contraband…duty free alcohol an' cigarettes?"

"Of course, of course," Nils replied with a knowing nod.

Moving to the windward rigging, he cast his eye over the deck of the island sloop covered with his crew. "Well I have to admit I never in my wildest dreams would have thought that we would be making our return trip to the Fatherland on a craft such as this. What about you, Mr Weiss?"

"The world's greatest clairvoyant would have had trouble predicting this, sir," the mate replied with a shake of his head.

The sloop sailed north away from Cannouan, leaving behind the souls of lost comrades and the ship that had been their home for close to three years. In the light of the new morning sun, the captain was seeing his crew as if for the first time, for now they were not merely a face and rank performing a job under the auspices of military order, but living and breathing souls who were sharing a totally new and different experience together. Some, like stubborn Kreigal the dour engineer, were visibly uncomfortable and obviously out of their element. Others, especially the younger ones, seemed to be enjoying the experience. Jaeger and Hassler could not contain their exuberance, clearly revelling in the feeling of being such a part of the wind and waves. As Albrecht moved amongst his men, he came to the conclusion that whether they were comfortable in this situation or not, at least their minds were being distracted from the horrors of the past few days and months. And they were still alive.

Looking back towards the tiller, he was surprised to see the person steering the boat was not the wizened West Indian in the straw sombrero that had been there from the start, but instead was young Hans Jaeger. Garfish was sitting with his back to the bulwark, watching as the German carefully steered the sloop to windward. Then, as if distracted by a sixth sense, the old man sprung to the stern and started hauling in the fishing line they had been towing since early morning. A big fish had been hooked and was dragging in the wake behind the boat. "Hey white boy, gi' me a luff!" he yelled from the taffrail to the helmsman. Jaeger turned and looked aft in bewilderment, flustered with the order and clearly unsure what to do. "Come on now, head up before we lose dis kingfish – she's a real beauty!" he yelled over his shoulder as he hauled in the fishing line.

Punkin suddenly appeared next to Jaeger, and gently took his hands off the tiller and pushed the helm down, carefully easing the sloop up into the wind. The sails began to flap and their forward motion slowed to almost a standstill; the thin black man all arms and elbows as he rhythmically pulled in the handline, Punkin artfully slowing the vessel without putting her about as she now hobby-horsed in the lumpy swell. There was excitement all around. Heads were craned and comments made as the fish was pulled in. Then, just at the right moment, Punkin left the helm. Reaching into the bulwark, he unhooked a gaff. Leaning over the rail, he deftly hooked the big fish through its gills, and together the two West Indians hauled the fish aboard.

The big silver and black kingfish shivered and shook, beating its tail on the green-painted deck until the skipper reached into the rail behind the mainsheet and grabbed a little billy club, and with one accurately aimed blow, sent the fish into its death throes. It vibrated violently for a few moments, before its inevitable death.

"Man, dis is one nice fish, you hear?" Paris said, more to himself than anyone else in particular. In the meantime, Punkin had returned to the tiller and after setting the sloop back on course, handed the boat back over to Jaeger.

After several hours of heading north, the sloop was put about onto port tack. Albrecht and his mate Weiss gazed over the scattering of islands around them, reminiscing about the days they ran the *Kate* along a very similar course.

"Dat small island just over us we does call 'Rammay', Cap," old Paris said, squatting on the deck and pointing out with his calloused hands the islands sitting to windward of them. "De next one is Isle e Cat and de big one behind is Bequia."

"You might find this hard to believe, 'Fish, but before the war, my mate Mr Weiss and I spent several years hauling cargo through the Caribbean on a small freighter called the *Kate*. In our travels, we met a schooner captain who you might know by the name of Jack McLeod, which led us to visit his island of Petite Silhouette many times. As a matter of fact, we even spent two weeks inside the reef at the Tobago Cays helping him salvage his schooner, which had been thrown ashore during a hurricane. And what a job that was!"

At this George Paris became quiet, looking back and forth between the two German officers. "So you fellahs has been here befo'," he finally stated. "And it was you who had de steamboat dat dragged de ol' *Roulette* off a de beach an' towed her back to Petite Silhouette?" Nodding his head, the realisation began to dawn on the weathered seaman. "So you-all knew about what you might find on Cannouan, and you does know what you'll find at Petite Silhouette! Now I is startin' to see how dis whole damn story beginnin' to make sense."

"What an operation that was!" remembered Weiss. "That crew we carried down from Port Victoria were some hard-working fellows! They surely knew what they were doing."

"Well dat story is like a legend now through dese islands," Paris agreed. "Most people would have gone off and lef' dat vessel fo' dead, an' de bones o' her would be dere rottenin' in de sands still. But not ol' Jack McLeod! Dat is one hard white man, you hear!"

"There was another man who stood out. He was his wife's father, as I recall. I don't exactly remember his name."

"Dat would be O'Neil deVilliars... dat's another giant of a man. 'Tween he an' Cap'n McLeod, they could lif' up de world if dey had to." Garfish paused and closely contemplated the two German officers, silently lost in thought. "So you is de one..." Finally he mumbled a few words to himself, sucked his teeth and shook his head in exasperation.

"What is it Captain Paris? Is something bothering you, something you don't understand?"

"Understand? Man, dey's plenty o' tings dat me can't work out! Like how it is a Cap'n like you, who knows an' lives by de rules o' de sea, an' one minute do what he can to help a brother in distress, turn tings aroun' an' do jus' de opposite? It's like de whole damn world gone contrary!"

Nils Albrecht could do nothing but avert his gaze of the perplexed West Indian. What could he say that would help him comprehend?

And so the sloop sailed on. Across the windward horizon lay the blue outline of Mustique, further to the south the high peak of Mount Majestic and their destination, Petite Silhouette. It was close to midday when Nils Albrecht sought out Captain Paris, who was now at the helm.

"It's my feeling, Captain, that it may not be the best of ideas for us to sail into Port Victoria in broad daylight with a boatload of German sailors on deck. Obviously we want to attract as little attention to ourselves as possible. Somehow we must delay our entrance until later tonight. Is there anywhere we could anchor for a few hours and perhaps prepare one of the fish you have caught? My men haven't eaten much in the last thirty-six hours."

Garfish studied the German captain. "Well it's never a good idea to enter a port in broad daylight wit' contraband on board – you is only axin' fo' trouble. I suppose we could haul up yonder under Savan and anchor fo' a spell, yes. We could den go ashore an' cook up de couple o' fish we caught and sail over once its night. I could use some food meself. Dem johnny-cakes we had fo' breakfast done gone longtime."

Reunion

The *Juanita* cleared Fish Rocks and silently sailed into Frigate Bay. It was getting on towards midnight when the gaff sloop ghosted through the calm at the head of the bay towards the cluster of working vessels moored off the beach of Port Victoria. The town was peacefully sleeping; a handful of flickering lights the only sign of life ashore. After finding what they were looking for, the *Juanita* dropped her sails and glided in alongside the schooner *Roulette*. "So far so good," whispered Albrecht to Weiss as they sprung over the bulwarks on to the deck, quickly followed by the others as they tied the sloop alongside.

"Secure our two guests in the cabin aft, Mr Weiss," he whispered as he took a cursory glance about. "Get the lads to have a good look over the ship. I'm going ashore. Jaeger, Hassler, I want you two to come with me." Climbing back aboard the sloop, they were just about to descend into the dinghy when the sound of muffled shouts came from aboard the schooner. Out of the corner of his eye Albrecht caught sight of a fleeting shadow; the next moment he turned to see a teenaged boy practically run into the mate's arms. The youngster put up a struggle trying to escape, but was finally subdued.

"What is your name, boy?" the captain asked firmly.

No answer.

"Again...your name!"

Finally the boy replied. "Henry McLeod," he mumbled.

"What are you doing aboard?"

"I'm de watch keeper," the boy shyly answered.

"Are you alone aboard? Is there anyone else?" the captain demanded.

"No sir...dey ain't no one else. It's me alone aboard."

"Take him back and hold him with the others," he ordered, and the boy was taken away. "That should make things a little easier,"

Albrecht said to himself as they climbed into the *Juanita's* rowboat and pulled it ashore.

The three men hauled the dinghy up onto the sand before sliding through the shadows of the tall coconut trees and onto the adjacent road. For Albrecht, just being ashore brought the memories rushing back of the many pleasant days he had enjoyed in the little harbour while passing through the islands on his freighter, not to mention the several weeks spent working with his friend and his crew while salvaging his schooner. He recalled the many times he had visited the McLeod household, and as they stepped onto the path leading up the hill it was as if he had been there only yesterday, when he was treated just like part of the family. Reaching the top of the track, a dog began to bark as they hesitantly approached the house. Nils Albrecht slowly stepped up onto the veranda, with Jaeger and Hassler a pace or two behind. The watchdog had done his job, because a moment later he was standing face to face with Captain Jack McLeod.

"Can I help you blokes?" he firmly inquired.

The two men were a pace or two apart, their faces lost in shadow. "Sorry to disturb you at this uncivilised hour, Jack. Unfortunately, I didn't have much of an option. I'm sure you remember me. It's Nils Albrecht, former captain of the motor vessel *Kate*."

Jack stood bare-backed in the darkness. The barking dog had stirred him out of a peaceful dream, and now he was confronting three strangers on his front porch in the middle of the night. It took him a few moments to comprehend the meaning. "Nils Albrecht from the *Kate*? Well I'll be buggered! What the hell are you doing here?"

"I guess you could say I'm caught between a rock and a hard spot, much like you were once upon a time in the Tobago Cays. It's been a few years since we last met, and I'm sorry it must be like this. Given a choice, I would rather have had this reunion in more pleasant circumstances. Never the less, I am now a Kapitanleutnant in the German Navy, here on what can only be described as official business."

"I've got to admit, you've caught me with all sails aback, mate. You're one of the last persons on earth I would've expected to be standing here at this hour of the morning. All the same, it's good to see you," he said, extending his hand.

Albrecht accepted the offer, and the two men shook hands. "It's unfortunate that things are as they are. The world is a far different place these days. Still, it doesn't stop me from remembering the good times we had in the past."

"Yes, those were good days in truth. But listen, we can't just stand out here chatting in the dark. We'll wake up the kids. Let's go sit in the galley where we can talk."

Nils followed Jack down the stairs into the dark little cookhouse, leaving the two sailors standing watch outside. A kerosene lamp was lit and they each took a seat.

The two men sat facing each other across the kitchen table in awkward silence. "So, Nils, what's going on? You don't wake a man up in the middle of the night just to say g'day," Jack finally said, slouching into the back of his chair.

"Yes, I'm sorry about that, but like I said it couldn't be helped. It is an adverse set of circumstances that have brought me here. Until two days ago I was the captain of a U-boat, when it was unfortunately shot out from beneath me. Nine of us were lucky enough to get ashore on Cannouan. I don't hold out much hope for the rest of my crew...they are all more than likely dead. Last night I commandeered a local sloop and directed its captain to bring us here. To be truthful Jack, I don't have many options. It's only because I've been to your island before and have nowhere else to turn that I'm sitting here right now."

"I'm not sure I know what to say. It is not every night a German U-boat captain comes knocking at my door."

"I completely understand what you must be thinking. And as an old friend, I sincerely apologise for what I'm about to tell you, but as an officer in the Kriegsmarine I'm compelled by duty to look after my men and do all I can to get them home. Jack, I'm not here to ask a favour. It is imperative I get my men north as quickly as possible. To put it bluntly, I need your schooner. And I want you to accompany us as our pilot."

Jack McLeod sat up and took a deep breath. He stared across the table into the eyes of a man he knew to have been honest, decent, trustworthy and true to his word. He also knew him to be very determined. "Tell me Nils – what will you do if I say no?" he finally replied. "What if I say that as much as I would like to help a friend in need, I draw the line at assisting the German Navy? Then what is your plan? Are you going to hog-tie me and carry me aboard anyway, or put a gun to my head and threaten to kill me?"

Albrecht reached under his jacket and took out the revolver tucked into his waist. Placing it carefully on the table, he leaned back in his chair and crossed his arms. "Jack, I didn't come up here expecting you would offer to help me out just for old times' sake. But I'm afraid you will be walking down the hill and coming with us, just as I have asked. I did come here with the hope we could work this problem out like old friends and come to an arrangement that will make the best of a bad situation. What I'm offering you is this – if you agree to accompany us north, once we have safely reached our destination and disembarked, you will be free to bring your schooner home. For all intents and purposes you will be our prisoner until then, but I will make sure that in the end you will be allowed to leave. You have my word on it. I am afraid this is the best proposal I can make."

Jack rubbed his shoulder wound, the scar from the bullet he took still showing a livid red. He absentmindedly clenched and re-clenched his left hand, as if testing the strength of his arm. "And what if I say no? What if I just tell you to bugger off – friend or no friend?"

Albrecht shook his head and took a deep breath as he casually picked up the revolver. "I was hoping we could work this out like gentlemen and I wouldn't have to resort to threats, but in reality you leave me no choice," he replied. "Look at it from my side. I'm a desperate man with nowhere else to go. So you will come with us, and I won't have to force you at gunpoint or threaten you in any other way. I know this because we are holding your son on board, and he will be sailing north with us."

Jack quickly jumped to his feet as the importance of what he had just heard sunk in. "So you're using my son a bargaining chip, you Nazi son-of-a-bitch! What other depths are you willing to stoop to?"

"Stop right there, Captain McLeod!" Albrecht firmly said as he pushed his chair back and stood up, levelling the pistol at Jack's chest. "There will be no more conversation! I don't like the situation any more than you do, but it is just the way it is. The boy did us a big favour by being on board and we caught him, simple as that. We are going now, and you are coming with us."

The two men stared at each other for the longest of moments. "I really don't have any choice, do I?" Jack finally remarked. "Do I have time to get dressed, or are you going to frog march me away half naked?"

"Of course, but quietly. I would naturally prefer you didn't mention any of this to Jasmine. I hope you don't mind if I accompany you – just in case."

Leaving the cookhouse, Jack climbed the few steps to the porch and walked quietly to his bedroom with Albrecht just behind. He entered the dark room, leaving the German standing discretely in the shadows outside of the doorway. Jasmine half opened her eyes. "What's going on? Who are you talking to?" she sleepily asked.

Glancing out the door, he then looked back at his wife. "I forgot to tell you. I'm going up to the bush with a couple of the boys. Just tell Iverson, will you? I'll see you later."

"Okay then," she replied dreamily, turning over as she drifted back off to sleep.

After quickly putting on his khaki work trousers and shirt, he took one last long look at his wife before slipping out to join the others. "I just need to grab my hat and put out the light," he said. Entering the cookhouse he leaned over and blew out the lamp, while at the same time removing from his pocket a piece of chalk used for marking out timbers in the boatyard. While deliberately fumbling in the dark, he slowly found his hat hanging on its nail by the door, below which he quickly sketched a swastika and below it a cross with an 'N' at the top.

"Who is Iverson, Jack?" Albrecht asked as they started down the hill.

"Oh, he's just a shipwright I have working for me."

"Funny, I don't remember the name."

"No, I don't think you would have met him."

The only thought on Jack's mind as he walked down the hill concerned the two boys who he knew to be sleeping aboard the schooner. What would the Germans do with them? Surely they wouldn't want to take them along? But the boys would know too much to be simply put ashore. The dilemma had him worried. As he walked across the decks of the little sloop and climbed over the bulwarks of the *Roulette*, Jack was anxious to know what the outcome would be.

"So, Captain, my men are holding our young stowaway in your cabin. I presume you would like to see him?" Albrecht asked.

Jack's heart skipped a beat as he went aft and dropped down the companionway steps. There, sitting on the floor along with the two crew members of the *Juanita*, was his son Henry. "Are you okay, me boy?" he asked, bending over to look at him.

"Yes Papa, don't frighten. Dey just caught me as I was tryin' to slip away." Looking up at his father he slightly shook his head and rolled his eyes. "I'm sorry, but I wasn't fast enough. Errol's a lot faster dan me." he muttered.

Standing up, Jack understood the meaning of his son's coded words.

"So this is Henry, is it Jack?" Albrecht asked from behind. "It's remarkable how quickly they grow up. I remember him when he was just a small boy."

"Yes, I'm afraid it is," Jack replied, swinging around to face the German. "But I don't see any reason for him to go with us. There's no point in putting a youngster like this in harm's way. I'm asking you as a gentleman to allow me to put my son ashore."

The German captain contemplated the question as he looked from father to son. "I'm afraid not," he exhaled, shaking his head. "As much as I would like to leave him behind, he simply knows too much. The alarm would be raised before we were out of the harbour. He will have to come with us, along with the other two sailors here. I'm sorry, but my hands are tied. Now are there any other preparations we have to make before leaving?"

"I suppose not. What's happening with the sloop alongside?"

"The sloop belongs to Captain Paris here, with whom I presume you are acquainted? I have been considering the options about what to do with this craft, and I've decided to leave it here. I of

327

course cannot allow the crew to stay, so they will come with us. I could simply tow it out to sea and cast it loose, but there is no reason at this point to ruin a man's livelihood. This fellow has been good to us. I would hope he can return here with you and carry on with his life after all of this is over. It will certainly give your people on the island food for thought in the morning. In fact, I'm sure it will assume the proportions of quite a mystery, with you and your schooner replaced by an unknown sloop. My old friend Squally the sailmaker will have plenty to talk about under the trees when morning comes! I'd love to be here to listen to all of the different theories," Albrecht smiled.

"You don't know the half of it, mate," Jack said under his breath.

"Let's get underway then, shall we, Captain?" Albrecht said, motioning his prisoners onto the deck. The mooring lines were shifted over to the *Juanita*, the engine was started, and the big schooner backed away from the beach and slowly motored out of the harbour. With one hand on the wheel, Jack took a last look ashore before turning his attention back to the task at hand. After rounding Fish Rocks, the captain gave up the helm to his counterpart and went forward to supervise the raising of the skiff on to the deck and then the hoisting of the sails. Once the sails were set, Jack returned aft to the wheel. "Do you mind me asking now where we're going so I can plot a course?" he asked. "Or is it top secret information?"

"I think that is more than a reasonable request, Captain. We are bound for St. Martin, so you can set your sails accordingly."

And so the sheets were eased and the schooner *Roulette* headed north, and as they broad reached towards Isle de Quatre and Bequia, Jack took one last look astern at his island as it faded into the distance, determined he and his son would somehow return to see their home and family once again.

Kidnapped

Henry was fast asleep in the fo'c'sle when the noise of footsteps and low voices on deck roused him. He and his cousin Errol were aboard the *Roulette* as night time 'watch keepers', a job they always looked forward to whenever the schooner was in port. There was rarely much for them to do but occasionally pump out the bilge with the cast iron deck pump and keep an eye on the mooring lines, and for this they would receive a few pennies from the captain. But for two young boys, it was great sport to be in charge of such a vessel, even if it were tied to the coconut trees. Tonight, however, would be a different night – a night they would never forget.

Henry stirred and listened for a moment to the whispers coming from topside. Rolling out of his bunk, he carefully climbed the rungs of the ladder, and peaking over the scuttle coaming scanned the moonlit deck. What he saw were a handful of strange-looking white men crouching low and murmuring in subdued voices amongst themselves. One of them was carrying what looked to be a gun strapped over his shoulder. Climbing back down the ladder his heart was racing. "Errol!" he whispered, shaking his partner. "Wake up! Wake up you blasted loggerhead!"

"What de…"

"Shhhhh! Listen! Dere's white strangers on deck an' dey has guns! Have a look up de ladder, but be careful!"

Errol climbed up and glanced over the sill, then came down quickly. "What do we do?" he breathed.

"We can't let dem find we fo' a start," said Henry, "an den we has to get ashore an' tell Papa."

"How we goin' do dat, Henry? Dem white men does have guns!"

Just then there were voices at the top of the scuttle, and then the hatch slide was being pushed forward. Henry grabbed Errol and they dodged into the darkness. At the forward end of the crew's quarters, half of a bulkhead separated the eight bunks from the chain locker that took up the forward end of the vessel. The two boys jumped over the bulkhead quick as a flash and laid down flat atop the anchor chain. Footsteps were heard coming down the ladder, and then voices in a strange language. Henry looked towards Errol in the pitch darkness and tried not to breathe. There were a few knocks and taps on wood, a laugh, and a few words in a strange tongue before the two men ascended the ladder again. Still the boys lay flat, not moving a muscle until Henry slowly gathered enough courage to peek over the bulkhead. They were gone. Carefully climbing out of the locker, the boys crept back to the ladder, and side-by-side climbed to the top. On deck, at the starboard rigging, a knot of men gathered. On the port side, two others stood with their eyes searching keenly ashore. A couple of men moved aft and descended into the cabin. "It looks like dese men is movin' aboard," whispered Henry. "If we stay here dey'll catch we an' who knows what dey'll do den!"

"So what we goin' fo' do? If we run, dey'll shoot we for sure."

Henry was quiet for a few moments, lost in thought. "Okay Errol – everyt'ing's goin' to be up to you. I'm goin' to do somethin' a bit crazy, an' when I do, you must slip out o' this hatch flatter than a green-bellied lizard an' crawl forward, you hear? When de time's right, you ease yourself over de rail an' slide down de bobstay. Den you must swim ashore an' dodge across de beach and get up to de house quick smart an' tell Papa what's happenin'. You understand?"

"Yes, but wha' you goin' fo' do?" Errol asked, the whites of his eyes big as saucers in the night.

"You don't trouble wit' me, you just do what I say, you hear? Now you ready?"

Henry took a last glance at his cousin and then slipped out of the hatch. Once on deck he began to run aft, where he was immediately spotted by the strangers. Stopping in his tracks, he turned to his left and jumped over the rail onto the sloop alongside. Errol watched as a group of the men grabbed hold of him as he attempted to leap overboard. It was then he made his move. Scrambling out of the hatch he crawled forward, and hiding in the shadows waited for the right moment to slip over the bows. As Henry was hauled aft and taken below, he took his chance. The boy quickly climbed over the bulwarks, slid down the bobstay and eased himself into the water, but before he could swim for shore he heard voices, and to his horror observed three of the strangers land on shore. As he bobbed in the water under the schooner's bow, he caught sight of the men as they crossed the beach and disappeared into the trees. When he was sure they were gone, he silently paddled the few yards to shore and darted across the sand behind them.

Under the cover of the coconut trees Errol stole through the shadows, following the shapes of the men ahead as they made directly for the path leading to Henry's house. At the top of the track he heard Dingo bark, and then muffled voices coming from the house above. Hiding under some bushes, he laid flat and waited. After what seemed an eternity, he finally saw the light extinguished in the kitchen above him, and holding his breath, glimpsed the shapes of four men move past him to the road below. "Dat was Henry's papa wit' dem strangers!" whispered Errol to himself. Quietly following, he waited until the men left the road for the beach and then dodged after them. Hiding behind a fishing boat he saw Henry's father help shove down a beached dinghy and go aboard the *Roulette*.

Wha' do I do now, Henry? Errol silently asked his absent partner.

Jus' wait an' see wha' happen; dat's all you can do, a voice inside his head whispered back.

Errol knelt in the shadow of the fishing boat and watched the *Roulette* slowly motor out of the harbour. The young boy's shoulders slumped. "What should you do now, Errol?" he asked himself out loud. "I should tell someone – but who?"

And then the answer came to him. "What 'bout Granpa O'Neil? He'd know what fo' do! He knows everything 'bout everything!"

Errol sprinted across the sand and onto Bay Road. He dashed passed the almond trees and the wharf and tore through town, ran into the boat yard and then up the hill, charged through the front gate, and to the yapping of Benjie the dog pounded on O'Neil's front door.

"Uncle O'Neil! Uncle O'Neil! Quick – open de door!" he yelled. "De *Roulette*! It's de *Roulette*! She gone!"

Finally the tall shape of O'Neil could be seen standing aside the open door. "Errol, is dat you? What is it boy? Come inside, come inside," he said, as he motioned him through the door. "Slow down man, slow down an' tell me wha' happen."

The boy blurted out his story as O'Neil sat in his favourite chair and listened intently, every now and then asking a question. When Errol was finished, he sat quietly back and slowly shook his head. "So now it's Germans in de harbour? What de hell I hearin' here a-tall!"

O'Neil slowly stood, straightening out his long, sinewy frame, and walked through the front door. Hands on hips, he stood for a few moments lost in thought, Errol patiently by his side and quietly looking up to him for direction. In the boatyard before him, the nearly completed schooner caught the eerie light of the setting moon as the black silhouettes of coconut fronds waved gently in the moonlight. "Okay, I want you to wait for me here while I get dressed. We does have some work to do."

Striding along Bay Road, O'Neil walked with purpose, the boy having to jog to keep up with him. Stopping, he took him by the shoulders and looked him in the eye. "Errol, I want you to run ahead and wake up your Tanti Jasmine. Don't mention anything 'bout wha' happen – I'll talk to her and explain things myself. Tell her I'll be there shortly, and ask her to light de fire an' put on de kettle. Once you done dat, I want you to run on and wake Clancy, and get him to come quick smart to her house, you hear? Tell him whatever you want, but jus' make sure he does come quick. Now go on…"

O'Neil walked on. Reaching the spot where the *Roulette* had been moored, he went to the water's edge and pondered what was there. In her place was a small Cays sloop – a 'Kopai', as they were called – which he thought he recognised. Continuing on, he arrived at a neat and tidy house set just off the road. Walking to the door he knocked firmly until it was finally answered by the large figure of Zepheryn Burroughs, his kindly face etched by sleep. "O'Neil, it's you. Man, wha' happenin'? Is de church on fire?"

"No man, it ain't de church. It's Jack an' de *Roulette*! As wild as it sounds, I think dey has been taken by Germans, and young Henry along wit' dem! Errol did see it all happen and came an' tol' me. De boy wasn't just dreamin'…de vessel's done gone in truth. Get dressed as quick as you can and meet me up at Jack's house. I got Clancy's comin', an' all o' we must decide what to do."

As he reached the house, Jasmine was there to meet him. "What's goin' on, Papa? Errol woke me and all he would say was dat you were coming and to make some tea! Why is Errol here without Henry? Dey's somethin' happenin' an' it don't seem right!"

O'Neil gently took his daughter by the arm and led her inside the kitchen. "It's alright, girl. Let's make some tea and I'll tell you what I know."

While the kettle boiled, O'Neil related Errol's story. Once he had finished, Jasmine sat down at the table and put her head in her hands. "What de hell kind o' story is dis a-tall? What would German's want wit' de likes o' we? An' why take me son? Jack's a man dat can take care of himself, but Henry? He's just a boy!"

"It's a terrible thing dat has happened, Jasmine, but you must give Henry credit," O'Neil said, taking hold of his daughter's hand. "Dat wasn't just brave – it was real smart what he did. You got to be proud of him."

Jasmine stood and went to the stove. O'Neil watched his daughter take a deep breath and straighten her shoulders. "Once Jack is dere, I know dey'll be right. He won't let anything happen to he son. They'll be right, I jus' know it."

The sound of low voices drifted up the footpath. Out of the darkness appeared the young face of Clancy deVilliars, followed by the stoic, older head of Zepheryn Burroughs. Jasmine was busy at the coal pot frying salt fish fritters on a cast iron skillet. "You fellahs want tea, it's there in de pot," she said seriously. "Come on in now, Errol – don't be shy. You're a part of all o' this too, isn't it?"

The three men sat at the table and were joined by the bashful boy. Once again, O'Neil related Errol's story. Jasmine placed a heaping plate of the fried fritters in the middle of the table and then sat down. "De clue to dis mystery," continued O'Neil, "is what Jack wrote on de wall behind all-you." The two men turned around and examined the chalked hieroglyphs sketched near the doorway. "Dem tings mean anything to all you?"

"Well it looks to me de cross with de 'N' must be a compass pointin' nort'," said Clancy after a few moments.

"Yes, and de bent-up sign is a symbol of de Nazis, isn't it?" added Zepheryn, turning back to face O'Neil.

A long silence drifted through the room.

"Okay, let's try an' work dis puzzle out," O'Neil continued. "A boatload o' Germans turns up in de harbour in de middle of de night. Three o' dem make straight fo' de house an' wake up Jack, den force him aboard an' sail off wit' he an' young Henry. We know it's a fact 'cause Errol saw it happen."

"But why Jack an' de *Roulette*? And how would dey even know 'bout de house an' how to find it?" Jasmine asked.

"Errol, you saw 'em come up here. Did they wander around like blind men in de dark lookin' befo' findin' de place, or were they certain sure where they were goin'?"

"No, Uncle O'Neil. It's like dey knew from de start where fo' go. They made straight fo' de track like dey been here yesterday."

A silence permeated the room. "Germans in de harbour an' dey does know where fo' go? Man, me never even met a German in me life – except…" They all looked at each other at the same time.

"Nils Albrecht, de man wit' de steamboat dat pulled de *Roulette* off in de Cays!" exclaimed Zepheryn. "Remember? He would know de boat, de island, and Jack and where he lives! Could it've been him?"

"It must o' been him! Who else would even have an idea where to go? Sounds like dat German come here like a man-o'-war bird flyin' home to roost!"

"I know he was at the house many times fo' meals when all-you was rebuilding the *Roulette*," Jasmine said. "He and Jack used to spend hours of an evening at the chessboard. He was a real gentleman, very thoughtful and polite."

"So what de hell he doin here after all dat time?" queried Zepheryn.

"Must be sailin' fo' de German navy now. Errol said dey was wearin' uniform."

"Den why would he need Jack an' de *Roulette*?" persisted the mate.

"We know dey came on de ol' Kopai moored where de vessel was. I had a look earlier, an' she's everything like Garfish Paris' sloop, *Juanita*. Dem Germans must o' come ashore somewhere in de Cays an' made him bring 'em here," reckoned O'Neil. "We know de Yankees is huntin' submarines wit plane and boat. Most likely their vessel got bombed an' was sunk. Somehow de survivors get ashore, an' since Nils been here befo' on de *Kate* an' knows 'bout Jack, he forces George to bring 'em here. If dey needs a vessel to get away on, none could be better than de *Roulette*."

"But where to? From Jack's clue it must be north, but where?" asked Jasmine.

"It can't be Martinique or Guadeloupe because de Americans have dem places sealed off tight as a drum wit' their blockade. Nothin' dere's gettin' in or out," Clancy said.

"Well, it's a wide ocean and we'd only be guessin' as to dem German's bad intentions. Us sittin' here tryin' to figure out where dey bound to is nothin' more than a waste o' time. What we do know is de vessel's done gone an' she's most likely headin' north. De question is, what we goin' fo' do 'bout it?"

At this point Jasmine spoke up. "I just remembered something! I was half asleep when Jack left an' I didn't think about it 'til now. I asked him where he was goin' and he said he was goin' to de bush. Den he said somethin' strange. He said 'tell Iverson'."

"He must o' meant fo' we to contact Harry Iverson! If anyone would know what to do, it would be him. It's a good idea, but how de hell we goin' to get in touch wit' he?" O'Neil asked.

"What about dat Navy man in Barbados who de Cap'n said he been dealin' wit'?" Zepheryn asked. "What's he name? Lawrence?

I t'ink Josh Samuels would know how to get on to him. An' we know Harry has a radio on he yacht, so to me de best thing would be to go to Barbados and see Samuels."

"An' den what? Just leave Jack and Henry and his vessel to de mercy of dem Germans?" asked O'Neil. "No man, we does have fo go an' see what we can do to help. So dat's de plan. We start now and get a crew together, and we take de *Theodora* and sail fo' Barbados. We leave as soon as we can. We deliver de message, and find out wha' happenin'. Den if we must sail somewhere to de north, it would be a fast trip. From Barbados we'd be sailing to windward of all a de islands so we'd have de clear straight breeze."

"What about we take de *Antipodes*?" Zeph suggested. "You never know, dat whaleboat sure been handy in de past."

"Good idea Zeph, we'll put her on deck. What about de vessel, Clancy? She ready to sail?"

"She's alongside de wharf wit' a half a load o' cement in for St. Vincent, but dat could be good. It will gi' she plenty o' ballast. We can t'row sail 'pon she."

"Okay. So Zeph, you organise de crew. You know de ones. Young Errol here can help you. Me an' Clancy will start getting de vessel ready. All right, let's go! Time's a-wasting!"

O'Neil turned to his daughter as they stood to leave. "What's it dat Australian husband o' yours would say? 'She'll be right'? We'll find dem girl, don't frighten."

The Chase

In the early hours of the morning, a crowd began to gather on the wharf alongside the schooner *Theodora D*. It didn't take long for word to spread around the island, and as the morning grew so did the crowd, much to O'Neil's annoyance. For him, the quicker they could get away the better, and the last thing he wanted was the distraction of answering questions. Squally soon was there, the unique timbre of his voice rising above the general murmuring of the crowd.

"Man, Squally's got ammunition to carry on wit' fo' weeks," Kingsford said to Bull with a smile as they went about their business of getting the boat ready to sail.

Bull chuckled. "What! Man dis is what you does call news! Ain't nothin' like dis ever happen on de island befo', and he goin' to make de most of it. Dem ol' men's ears will be ringin' under de trees fo weeks!"

Clancy walked out of the government offices alongside Inspector Ballentyne, who had hurriedly issued him a clearance for Barbados. "This is a most unusual turn of events, I must say," the inspector said. "I will write a report and send it off to St. Vincent, but I would think this whole matter will be resolved before it ever reaches the proper authority. This is when it would be helpful to have a wireless transmitter on the island. Perhaps this might spur the government into giving us one."

"I wouldn't hold your breath, sir. As you know, we just another small island to dem. Nothing ever happens here."

"No, just minor invasions by the German Navy," he retorted as they reached the wharf. Pushing through the curious crowd, they reached the awaiting schooner. "Good luck, Captain deVilliars," the policeman said, shaking the young skipper's hand. "I'm sure I can speak for the whole island when I say all of our thoughts will be with you."

Clancy jumped aboard, and the mooring lines were all let go. Using her two spring lines the engineless schooner was walked astern, and as she drifted away from the wharf, the staysail was hoisted and steerageway found. The foresail was raised next and she began to pick up speed, and turning to the west headed out of the harbour. On the wharf the knot of people remained, silently watching as the vessel gybed around Fish Rocks and began to hoist the mainsail. Just then, the portly figure of Aubrey Kincaid could be seen making his way onto the wharf, waddling as quickly as his short legs and walking stick would take him. In due course he fetched up alongside the uniformed inspector. "I say, Ballentyne, is it true what they say? Jerry has actually made off with McLeod and his schooner?" he asked incredulously.

"I am afraid so, sir. You never would have thought it would come to this, would you?"

"I suppose it wouldn't hurt to break out the hunting rifles then, eh what? No telling what we could be in for next!"

The inspector smiled at the vision of the old planter defending the island from a German invasion with his antique pair of shooting rifles. "I would sincerely hope it would never be come to that, Aubrey," he said.

Jasmine McLeod stood on the veranda with her youngest son in her arms and her twin daughters entwined around her legs as she watched the *Theodora* slip behind Gunnery Point and disappear from view. "Where's Henry gone, Momma?" one of the little girls asked.

"He gone aboard de vessel with your Daddy," she answered vacantly.

"Are they coming home soon?" inquired the other twin, looking up with her dark brown eyes.

Jasmine looked down with a smile at her daughters. "They'll be home jus' now," she said. "Your Grandpa and Uncle Clancy gone to make sure o' dat."

It took the *Theodora D* twenty-two hours to sail the ninety-four windward miles to Barbados. Although Clancy was officially the captain, everyone knew it was his father O'Neil in charge. He drove the vessel hard. In his days of sailing schooners, O'Neil had been to Barbados more times than he could count. Not only did he know the exact compass bearing, he knew the fluctuations of the wind, where a slight variance of a few degrees one way or the other would be to their advantage or detriment. He knew exactly what phase of the moon they were in, and could read the current by observing its movement on the surface of the water and by how the seabirds were working. And he was meticulous about how he set the sails. For those twenty-two hours, the crew never stopped trimming one sheet or another. He had them tack twelve times.

"Ah, boy, dis is what you call schooner sailin' we," Kingsford said to Gilbert as he took his stint at the wheel. "When you take a vessel like dis wit' a solid foundation, and you does load her down well wit' ballast, well man, don't be afraid to throw sail 'pon she! Let me axe you, what exactly is our course?"

"Nor'-east b' east," Gilbert answered.

"Correct! An' where be de wind?"

"East nor' east…right on de nose," he again replied.

"Right again! And is anyting 'bout dat goin' to hold we back? No's de answer! And is wave, wind, sea or tide goin' to keep we from where we goin'? No again! Because one t'ing you does know about Uncle O'Neil is he don't frighten fo' nuttin' on land or sea. Man, he an' Cap'n Jack did come out a de same mould! When dey does say east's de course, well it's east we bound!"

Joshua Samuels was traditionally at work by the stroke of eight, and this morning was no exception. As he entered his outer office, battered briefcase in hand, he was surprised to find O'Neil deVilliars and his youngest son waiting patiently for him. "Well this is truly a sight for sore eyes!" the shipping agent exclaimed, pumping his old friend's hand. "I never thought I'd see the day when O'Neil deVilliars would be back in my office! I thought you had given up the sailorizing and were spending the rest of your days building vessels. It must really be something special that brings you here! What was it Clancy, did you bring him along just for old times' sake?"

"It's good to see you Josh, but I didn't come here this time for sport," O'Neil said grimly. "A problem has come up an' we need you to do something for us."

"Yes, yes – come inside and tell me what this is all about."

A few minutes later, the well-connected agent was on the telephone to Naval Command and the wheels were set in motion. Samuels set up an immediate meeting with Commander Lawrence, and the two sailors were ushered straight into his office upon their arrival at Government House. He was most interested in the report of what transpired at Petite Silhouette, and was impressed by the initiative these islanders had shown in getting the information to him as quickly as they had. As the three men discussed the details of the situation, a radio call was put out for Harry Iverson, and it was discovered he had just sailed into Antigua that morning. After a couple of hours of negotiation, it was decided that the *Theodora D* should sail immediately for English Harbour on the British island of Antigua, where they would meet with Iverson and draw up a plan of action. "Does Iverson have any notion of where these Germans might be heading?" O'Neil asked Lawrence, when he returned to his office following the radio conversation.

"I think he must have an idea, otherwise he wouldn't have asked for you to sail for Antigua. Now gentlemen, I understand your concern, and I realise you want to help, but in the end this is a military matter. If it wasn't for your track record during the operation in Martinique, I would have simply thanked you for your information and then advised you to sail back home, but Commander Iverson is insistent you rendezvous with him. The Commander obviously feels there's a role for you in all of this, so I'll go along with his request. I'd like to emphasise that you'll be operating completely under his authority, so what he says goes. I understand that time is of the essence, so if you have no more questions then I wish you good luck."

The two men walked quickly through the busy Bridgetown streets, and as they jumped over the bulwarks onto the schooner's deck, O'Neil gave the order to cast off and get underway. Zepheryn and the rest of the crew had anticipated this and had the sails unstopped and ready to hoist, so within a matter of minutes the lines were let go, and in the fluky calms of the Carenage Basin the *Theodora D* made sail and eased her way out of the harbour and into the open Caribbean Sea. The island of Antigua lay approximately 275 miles to the northwest. "T'row every piece of rag on she boys! We got no time to waste," O'Neil ordered, and so with topsails and fisherman staysail set they pulled out of the lee of Barbados, and with a solid tradewind blowing across their beam, reached away north.

The *Vagabond* lay quietly moored in the well protected and secluded anchorage of English Harbour on Antigua's south coast. It was mid-morning and all was quiet aboard the yacht as she sat stern to the cobblestone quay of the abandoned ruins of Nelson's Dockyard, the yacht's four sailors still exhausted from their overnight sail from the French island of Desirade. Harry Iverson and his crew had all been under a fair amount of pressure of late, and were looking forward to a few days of respite.

Their most recent operation had begun several months previously, across the channel from Guadeloupe in the quiet anchorage of Prince Rupert Bay, Dominica. It didn't take Gregoire Deslisle long to make contact with the leaders of the close to two thousand Guadeloupian refugees who had risked their lives escaping south across the rough and treacherous Dominica Channel, in what for the most part were simple, open fishing boats. This exodus was called "La Dissidence", and it was a direct result of the openly racist and dictatorial policies of the pro-Nazi Vichy administration that had been running the big French island for the past three years. Cracks were beginning to appear in the façade of this fascist government, and the *Vagabond* made several smuggling runs to the nearby Iles des Saintes, which were used as a jumping off point for first Gregoire and then Rabbit to blend into the thick of the mounting unrest on the main island of Guadeloupe, with the objective of hastening the demise of the regime.

The culmination of their work was the risky midnight pick-up the previous night, when the two agents were delivered by a fisherman to the waiting yacht as she lay hove to in the lee of the rugged island of Desirade, located off the northeast corner of Guadeloupe. As the *Vagabond* sailed north that night towards the island of Antigua, Harry was given a brief rundown of the situation on the strike-torn island.

"Guadeloupe is at a crossroads at the moment, with the present ruling elite clinging to power and the masses praying for change," said Gregoire as the yacht lifted over the rolling Atlantic swell. "As in Martinique, the government has become nothing more than a dictatorship supported by the military, with brutality and repression increasing daily. The man who's pulling the strings is Admiral Robert's henchman Admiral Rouyer, who set up Guadeloupe's version of the Sécurité Nationale, which the people have lovingly named 'the Gestapo'. Over time, general elections have been suspended, public assembly outlawed, and almost all of the island's thirty-two elected mayors have been replaced by sympathetic stooges. So many workers have left the island, they can't find people to cut the sugarcane or work the land. Food and fresh provisions are being rationed. People are hungry. And you know the saying – 'a hungry man is an angry man'. There is a very strong underground resistance as a result of all this, and we found plenty of support for Les Maquis Caraïbes."

"How long before the island reaches tipping point?" Harry asked as he ducked an eruption of white water cascading over the bow.

"I believe the end is near. It could be a month or two – it could even be days. When this regime falls, it will come down like a house of cards. Even the police and the military are starting to look over their shoulders. I would have stayed on but for another close call with the Gestapo. There are still many informers who'd be well-rewarded for being a part of my capture, so I listened to Rabbit and kept to our plan and reluctantly left."

"And what about you Carlisle? Besides trying to keep Gregoire here out of trouble, did you stumble upon anything of interest?"

"Well now you mention it, dere's one ting I picked up dat I think you'll find real curious. You remember a while ago, Jack told we 'bout a little coaster he'd seen actin' a bit strange around St. Barths, an' we figured it was most likely de same one we saw in Martinique? I saw she alongside in Pointe-a-Pitre, and more than once. She was loadin' fresh provisions and water. When I asked around I found she was runnin' between Guadeloupe an' Phillipsburg a couple o' times a month. From what I saw, de locals wasn't too happy 'bout it either. Because of all de shortages, people strugglin' to find food to eat, but dis ship loadin' provisions by de truckload. An' dey is gettin' protection from high up, too. De day I watched, there were armed navy guards protectin' de cargo as it was bein' loaded 'board de ship."

"You don't say? And where, I wonder, could all of those provisions and water be going?" Harry asked. "A poor, sparsely populated island like St. Martin? Interesting…"

The radio call from Barbados had found Harry sitting at the chart table re-writing his notes while the details were still fresh in his mind. "No rest for the weary," he said to himself after finishing his long conversation with Commander Lawrence.

Leaning back in his seat, he lit up a cigarette and gazed out of the hatch at the blue sky above, turning the mysterious disappearance of Jack and the *Roulette* over and over in his mind. It had been a knee-jerk reaction to plan the rendezvous with the Petite Silhouette schooner in Antigua. Harry really had no concrete evidence as to where the Germans would be going, but after what Rabbit had told him, he had a gut feeling St. Martin held the key. A plan had begun to form in his mind, and he knew things had to move quickly.

Lawrence had made a call to the local British commander on Antigua, who had arranged for someone to pick him up in a couple of hours. At exactly 01:00 a military vehicle pulled to a halt astern of the solitary yacht moored to the quay, and Sergeant-Major Derek Hightower introduced himself to Iverson as he stepped ashore to meet him. "Deuce of a place to get to over here, Commander," the Sergeant-Major said as he climbed in next to his guest in the back seat of the olive green jeep. "A boat could be moored here for weeks without anyone noticing."

"It's one of our favourite anchorages in all the Caribbean, but it is lonely," Harry answered. "The only guests we have ever entertained are the ghosts of Nelson's Navy! I'm surprised the powers that be haven't seen fit to utilise the facilities here at English Harbour. You wouldn't think it would take much to make the place usable again."

The sergeant shrugged his shoulders. "What you say makes sense, but we're dug in with the Yanks on the other side of the island, so this place just sits here deserted. One day someone may do something with it, I should think."

The jeep bumped across the dry, barren island for close to an hour before they passed through a gated security checkpoint into the small military compound. "Welcome to the home of the Leeward Island Defence Regiment," the Sergeant-Major said as they alighted from the vehicle. "As you can see, our presence here is slightly overshadowed by our American neighbours." Standing in front of the old plantation manor house with the strong easterly breeze in his face, Harry watched the activities below with interest. Alongside stood the Sergeant-Major, hands clasped loosely behind his back. From this vantage point, a handful of Navy seaplanes could be seen landing and manoeuvring on the broad waters of the bay spread out below them. On the north side of the harbour, on the top of a flat peninsula jutting out into the Atlantic Ocean, trucks and graders and other vehicles could be observed busily constructing a long runway.

"All this looks quite impressive," said Harry. "This is the first time I've been out here. It's quite remarkable to think the Yanks have built all of this in less than two years."

"I suppose when you throw enough men and money at something you can make anything happen," Hightower responded. "I will give them credit, though. I've been told two years ago what you see before you was nothing but a disused sugar plantation on one side and mangrove swamp on the other, with a shallow harbour full of reefs in between. Now the Navy is sending out flights of flying boats, and the Army has nearly completed their own runway. A shipping channel has been dredged, and observation towers constructed. I suppose some would argue the four million dollars it cost them was money well spent."

"And you, Sergeant? Have you been posted out here long?"

"I have been in Antigua for about six months now. I was at the evacuation of Dunkirk, and then saw action in North Africa and Crete, where I fought with Laycock's 7th Commandos. After the regiment was disbanded in Egypt following the fall of Crete, I was transferred out here to train up the Leeward Island Defence Regiment. Unfortunately, there isn't quite the amount of action here as there was over there."

"There could be worse places in the world to be stationed, I would imagine."

"I suppose that's one way to look at it, sir."

The door behind them opened and the gangly frame of a British officer approached the two men. "And you must be Commander Iverson! Colonel Clairmonte Foulkes, at your service," the officer smiled, hand outstretched. "Thank you Sergeant, that will be all."

Inside the confines of the Colonel's office, the two men quickly got down to business. "Firstly, Commander Iverson, I think we should discuss the latest communiqué I received this morning. After speaking with Commander Lawrence in Barbados, I was contacted by a Lieutenant-Commander Blackwell from our Caribbean Defence Command in Trinidad, who arranged this meeting. He has asked me to facilitate any requests you might have. So how can I assist?"

"Thank you for getting onto all of this so promptly, and sending your man to collect me. There has been a development that needs immediate attention, and your assistance will be crucial in dealing with it. I believe Lt. Commander Blackwell has asked you to set up a meeting with a Captain Swan, who is in command of US Naval Air operations here?"

"Yes sir; that has all been arranged. We will in fact be joining Captain Swan for lunch."

"Good. Briefly, this is the situation…" And so over the next fifteen minutes, Harry related what he knew of Jack's disappearance to the British officer.

The driver eased the staff car over the potholed road before pulling up alongside an airy, open building with wide verandas built off the beach in a picturesque little cove on the northeast side of the island. There were hammocks strung between the coconut trees, and several deck chairs lined the sugar-white sand.

"This looks more like a resort than an officer's watering hole," Harry said.

"Yes, these Americans don't do anything by half measure."

The two men stood on the wide veranda, quietly admiring the view. Moments later, a military staff car arrived, and they were soon joined by a middle aged naval officer who exuded the casual air of rank only the Americans could express.

"Good afternoon, Colonel Foulkes," the officer said with a brief salute.

"And good day to you too, Captain. May I introduce Commander Harry Iverson?"

"Captain Jake Swan. Pleased to make you acquaintance," he said, shaking hands firmly. "Shall we take a seat? The food in this place is great, but they sure as heck don't know about doing anything in a hurry. I've got a pre-flight briefing at seventeen hundred that I've got to be back for, so let's get started, shall we?"

While they waited for their meals, Captain Swan broached the subject that had brought them together in the first place. "This morning, Colonel Foulkes informed me that his superiors in Trinidad requested this meeting, and I later received the go-ahead from HQ in Puerto Rico to honour the Colonel's request. All I've been told is that you're working with British Naval Intelligence and that I should listen to what you have to say. So tell me, Commander, what's all of this about?"

"What I'm about to tell you has come about over the past thirty-six hours or so, and I'm just trying to fit the pieces together myself. For over a year and a half now, I have been working closely with a civilian from down the islands by the name of Jack McLeod, an Australian who has been running cargo through these islands for years. Over time Captain McLeod has proved himself to be quite valuable to the Allied cause. It seems he and his schooner disappeared from his home island of Petite Silhouette the other night, and indications are that they were hijacked."

"Hijacked? That's different. Do you have any idea who's behind it?"

"The evidence points to a crew of Germans submariners. We don't have all the details, but somehow these men appeared on the island in the middle of the night and at gunpoint dragged our man and his schooner away, destination unknown. Trinidad did some checking with your people and found a flight of Mariners out of Chaguaramas reported the sinking of an enemy submarine to windward of the lower Grenadines just two days previous to this incident. We feel these men are survivors from this U-boat who somehow found their way to the island."

"Well that's a hell-of-a story, Iverson!" Captain Swan exclaimed. "Do you have any idea where they could be headed?"

"McLeod left behind a clue indicating they are heading north. Everything else is speculation. It would be virtually impossible for them to enter French waters without being stopped, so that should rule Martinique and Guadeloupe out. And obviously they can't land on any British or US territories. It would therefore be logical to assume these Germans only hope of rescue would be to somehow find their way aboard another U-boat. The logistics of doing this would be difficult, if not impossible, to organise. How would they make contact? The only way would be if they had outside help. Our theory is they may have a connection here in the Leeward Islands, and this could be where they are headed."

"There are close to a dozen islands in the Leewards, Commander. Do you have anything a little more specific?"

"Over the past year and a half, Naval Intelligence has received unsubstantiated reports of possible German activity centred on the Dutch side of the island of St. Martin. It is only by piecing these fragments together that we have arrived at this theory. There is an Austrian shipping agent in Phillipsburg who has come to our attention, as well as a small freighter that doesn't seem to fit the normal profile. Unfortunately, our limited resources have not allowed us to take the time to verify these claims. But at face value, this island may be the only safe haven for a boatload of desperate enemy survivors. One side is Vichy French, the other ruled by a country now in the hands of Nazi Germany."

"Maybe, but I do know the other Dutch islands of Curacao, Bonaire and Aruba have been heavily reinforced by the US Army. St. Martin may not have been, but there are American contractors there at the moment doing the survey work for an Army air strip. I would think a crew of German sailors landing there would attract a considerable amount of attention."

"I agree. But it could go beyond that. What if there was a German agent there who could make contact with a U-boat, and he could arrange for one to turn up and collect these sailors? And what if we could somehow determine where and when this pick-up would be. Wouldn't this be of interest to the US Navy?"

"Of course it would. But that's a lot of ifs, isn't it Commander? When and ifs aren't my business. Let's get down to brass tacks. What exactly would you like me to do?"

"Time is of the essence. Your flyers are running daily missions from here, and I was hoping you might be able to give us a hand to locate this vessel."

"Okay – let's see if I got it straight. You're telling me a local trading vessel has gone missing, and the theory is that it might have been stolen by what could have been Germans. You're pretty sure it's heading north, but otherwise the only other idea you have as to where it might be going derives from a few rumours you haven't had enough time to check out properly in the first place. And out of the thousands of square miles of water and hundreds of islands in the Caribbean, you're guessing this mystery ship is bound for the general area of St. Martin. Listen, Commander, no disrespect intended, but my flyers have a huge area to cover. Tell me why I should send them off looking for a needle in a haystack."

The waiters appeared and began to clear the table. Harry lit a cigarette, leaned back into his chair, and waited until they were done. "I can't really argue with your succinct summation, Captain. And putting aside the fact this man is a friend of mine and I'd like to somehow assist him, I'll tell you why you should be interested. If my gut feeling is correct, and these men are enemy sailors and they do have a contact in these islands, then there is the distinct possibility a U-boat will arrive in these waters within the next few days to collect them. I believe this remarkable set of circumstances has presented us with a chance we must not waste. If we can

348

discover where this rendezvous is to take place, and can deduce exactly when it will be, then we will have in our hands a golden opportunity to not only save this man, but also disrupt and destroy a vital link in the German supply chain. Because if I am right, there is a network up there that could well be providing U-boats with much-needed supplies – a network that may have been operating right under our noses for more than a year."

"I'll be truthful with you, Commander Iverson. I've got one squadron of Mariners here at present, and one of Catalinas. My boys are flying their butts off. They're covering an area the size of a small European country every day. My crews are putting in more than one hundred hours of flight time a week. We don't have the resources to start changing our grid pattern for the sake of hunches or theories. Now that's not to say we won't keep a lookout for your boy and his schooner. If we do happen to see anything, we'll let Colonel Foulkes here know about it. And if you do come up with something a bit more concrete than an educated guess or a gut feeling, I'll be most interested to hear about it. So unless there is something else, gentlemen, I'll have to excuse myself. But don't let me rush you. You should try the key-lime pie. It's fantastic!"

Harry Iverson sat with Colonel Foulkes drinking coffee. "Well that didn't go over too well, did it?"

"No, I suppose not," agreed Foulkes. "If you can't rely on help from these fellows, then what are you going to do?"

"I'm going to have to press on regardless. Hopefully I can get the proof Swan requires. The first step is to somehow find McLeod and his schooner. There's no time to waste, and we must use whatever resources we have available. Now, Colonel Foulkes, your Sergeant-Major Hightower impressed me as quite a handy sort of chap. There seems to be a bit more to him than meets the eye. He gave me a brief description of his background. Dunkirk, Egypt, Crete…not your normal résumé for a run-of-the-mill drill instructor."

"Hightower has an impeccable record. He still resents the fact that Laycock and his commandos were thrown to the wind, and that he probably could do more with his talents than simply training recruits in this out-of-the-way backwater. I think he was taking his frustrations out the other night when he took on six Yanks in a bar and sent them all packing. Why do you ask? Do you see a role in all of this for him?"

"I liked the fellow the moment I met him, and I'm going to need all the help I can get. Do you think you would miss him for a week or two?"

"Tell me what you are thinking, Commander."

"I think we should order some more coffee."

Their discussions went on late into the afternoon. Harry didn't arrive back on board his yacht until well after dark.

The flight of Mariners took off into the sunrise. Hightower had been alongside the *Vagabond* with his jeep well before first light, and now as the sun edged over the eastern horizon Harry Iverson watched one after another of the flying boats power into the wind, skip over the waters of the bay and build up speed until they finally lifted off, reflecting glints from the morning sun off of their silver wings as they banked away to the north. Finishing his cigarette, he flicked the butt out of the open window and turned to face Colonel Foulkes as he rushed in, his aide stepping out and closing the door behind him.

"Sorry to keep you waiting, old man, but quite a lot to organise at such short notice. Sit down, sit down," the officer said as he moved in hastily behind his desk. "Good news – Hightower and the ordinance we spoke about yesterday have been organised. He is sorting out the details as we speak. Unfortunately our Sergeant-Major feels that none of the recruits he has been training are anywhere near ready enough to be of any help if things get hot, so I'm afraid that is about as good as I can do as far as manpower goes. As you can see, this is hardly a burgeoning military garrison brimming with war-hardened veterans we have here, but at least you will have one very good man you can rely on."

"One good man is far better than a dozen who don't know what they're doing," Harry said. "Now, I believe we should take this time while Hightower is getting his equipment sorted to work out our radio schedule and other details. If this situation develops as I think it might, you will serve as an invaluable link in communications between me and Captain Swan."

When the *Theodora D* sailed through the heads and into the outer anchorage of English Harbour on the island of Antigua it was early afternoon, the schooner having covered the two hundred and seventy-odd miles from Barbados in a little over twenty-seven hours. Rabbit was on deck and saw the sails of the big schooner break through the entrance, and after jumping into the tender, rowed quickly across the empty waters of the bay to meet them. One by one, the sails were lowered and the schooner's speed subsided, until she swung head to the wind and her anchor splashed into the water of the outer harbour, when Rabbit came alongside and climbed on board.

"So Rabbit, tell me what's happenin'," O'Neil said, turning to speak to the barebacked Bajan with the sun-browned skin and blond hair only after he was satisfied the anchor was well and truly set.

"Well, since Cap'n Harry got dat wireless call yesterday he's been as busy as a Philadelphia lawyer," Rabbit answered from beneath his straw sombrero. "He was ashore most o' yesterday an' was gone by first light dis mornin'. He tol' me to keep a good lookout for all-o'-you and den tell you to get some rest when you can because we'll most likely be sailing sometime later dis evening."

As the men talked, Rabbit's keen blue eyes watched the quick-working crew coil down the ropes and furl the sails. A shout rang out from the galley.

"Food on!" called Jono.

"Okay, time fo' eat. Dat was some solid sailin' we done last night, an' I sure all o' dem boys could use a proper feed. What 'bout you Carlisle? You like some pelau? You lookin' like you could afford puttin' some meat on your bones."

"Man, I ain't sayin' no to one o' Jono's pelau's! It's a long time since me had some proper chicken an' rice!"

Intrigue in the Islands

The skiff pushed off from the darkened ruins of the deserted dockyard and rowed silently across the calm, twilight waters towards the outer anchorage of English Harbour. After shipping the oars and gliding alongside the *Theodora D*, the occupants passed up two heavy duffel bags before clambering over the high bulwarks themselves. High on the hillside above, the last flicker of sunset faded from the old stone walls of Nelson's observation post, known as Shirley Heights, as a knot of men gathered on the stern deck of the grey cargo schooner anchored far below. O'Neil and his crew were joined by Harry, Rabbit and Gregoire, and everyone was introduced to the schooner's latest crew member, Sergeant-Major Dereck Hightower.

"First of all let me compliment you and your crew, O'Neil, for getting here as quickly as you have," Harry began. "You must have set a record between Barbados and Antigua!"

"Mon, you t'ink it easy?" muttered Kingsford. "De man threw every piece o' canvas aboard 'pon she an' was still callin fo' more! Dat's what you call boar hog sailin' in truth, mon!"

"We all know why we are here this evening," Iverson continued after the laughter died down, "and we are facing quite a challenge indeed. Let me start with what we know to be the facts. Three nights ago, Jack McLeod, his son and his schooner were forced to sail from the island of Petite Silhouette at gunpoint. We are almost certain that these men were German sailors, and more than likely the survivors from a U-boat sunk by American forces two days previously. It is O'Neil's theory they are being led by Nils Albrecht, a man who would have extensive knowledge of these waters after spending years navigating his own cargo ship through the islands before the war. Because of a hieroglyph left behind by Jack, we are assuming they have sailed north. This is about all we can say we truly know. From here on, we must venture into the murky waters of speculation. Many months ago, Jack himself informed me of his concerns of enemy activities in the area around St. Barths and St. Martin. Over time, further evidence has come to light reinforcing the theory that U-boats could be secretly being resupplied somewhere around St. Martin. It is therefore my contention these German sailors have sailed for this area with the hope of being picked up by a passing U-boat. I believe the *Roulette* will be found somewhere around those islands. Where exactly, I am not sure. Luckily, we have a man here from St. Barths who knows the surrounding islands well. If you were rendezvousing with a U-boat, Gregoire, which spot would you choose?" Harry asked.

"There are several small, isolated islands with half-decent anchorages that would be suitable for a U-boat to approach. To the north of Anguilla are Sombrero and Dog Islands, then there is Tintamarre to the east of St. Martin, and closer to St. Barths, Ile de Fourchue. If your hunch is correct and these U-boats are being resupplied at a base somewhere near St. Martin, then it would be from one of these islands."

Harry took a pull of his cigarette and pondered what Gregoire had said. "Unfortunately we don't have the luxury of time to explore all of these places individually. From Sombrero to St. Barths is a large area to cover. And if the rendezvous is to take place sometime within the next few days, then Jack and the *Roulette* are more than likely anchored somewhere nearby. The first thing we must do is find her. Hiding a one hundred foot schooner containing a boatload of shipwrecked German sailors would be no easy task. The question is, where do we start looking? Any ideas, Gregoire?"

"If indeed there is German activity around those islands, someone will have heard or seen something. There are people I know in St. Barths as well as Marigot in St. Martin who would be well worth approaching. In Gustavia there is Antoine Degras. He is a good friend of mine and can be trusted. Antoine and his family have been in business for generations and know everyone around those islands. If there is a whisper of a rumour circulating, he will have heard it. I suggest O'Neil and his crew sail for St. Barths, and once there contact Antoine. I can sail with the *Vagabond* and we can make for Marigot, where I know people and have some good connections. We could then all meet again in Gustavia twenty four hours from now and see what we've come up with."

After due consideration, Gregoire's plan was accepted. An hour later, the two vessels slipped through the heads and made sail for their respective destinations.

The first rays of the rising sun bounced off of the slab of stone the locals called Pain de Sucre, the shadow of the sails of the *Theodora D* stealing their golden reflexion as she passed to windward of the big round rock, reaching in the last quarter of a mile for the island of St. Barths after sailing through the night from Antigua. As the schooner shot through the passage between Les Gros Islets and Les Petits Saints into the amphitheatre of the outer anchorage, her sails started to come down, flapping lazily in the light morning breeze. Rounding up under her mainsail, she slowly glided to a stop, the water under her spoon bow erupting into shards of crystal as the anchor was let go from the cat head, the metallic rattle of chain through hawse pipe echoing around the quiet bay.

With the anchor down and set, the life boat was hoisted off the deck and lowered into the water. "It's a long time since I been to St. Barths, Zeph. You know de place better than me," O'Neil said to the mate as they stood together on the foredeck, the morning sun reflecting off their faces. "Why don't you go ashore wit' Clancy an' Dawson and see what you can find out. I might go in a bit later on."

The port was quiet as the skiff was rowed into the calm inner harbour, with only a small sloop alongside the wharf waiting to load rum. On the opposite shore, the *Lady Luck* was moored stern to, her white paint, varnished teak and polished chrome gleaming in the morning sun. Once alongside, Clancy stepped ashore and disappeared into the whitewashed house of the Port Captain.

"Cap'n Gastonay hasn't seen or heard anything of de *Roulette*, Uncle Zeph," he said as he hopped back into the boat several minutes later. "He says it's well over a year since he's seen Cap'n Jack. We need to visit Antoine Degras."

They touched the skiff up on the gravely shore where several fishing boats were hauled up. Dawson remained with the boat while the others walked the few yards into town. Striding across the cobblestone street, they rounded the corner and entered the Degras' chandlery. Antoine Degras sat on a stool counting out galvanised shackles. "Good morning, boys! Good to see you!" he said, standing to greet the two sailors. "I didn't notice the *Roulette* in the harbour this mornin'. You just sail in?"

Zepheryn stared at their friend for a long serious moment. "We didn't really sail up on de *Roulette* – we came north on de *Theodora D.* Cap'n Jack's lookin' like he could be in some serious trouble an' dat's why we here."

The smile evaporated from Antoine's face. "Trouble? What kind of trouble?"

"It's a little bit tricky. Is dere somewhere quiet where we can have a word?" Zeph asked.

"Sure, we can go upstairs."

They followed Antoine up a flight of stairs to his apartment above the chandlery, where an elderly woman was busy cleaning. Antoine joked with her in the local dialect and she replied in kind before turning and shyly smiling towards the visitors. "This is my mother," he said. "She's always asking me why I'm not married. She says I'm too old to be looked after. I tell her she must be patient."

"'Nothin' comes before its time' is how we does put it down home," Zepheryn said with a grin.

After a little more light-hearted conversation with his mother, she left the room and they took a seat at a simple, round wooden table. "So tell me what's happening, boys?"

Zeph pushed his flat cap onto the back of his head, leaned forward in his chair and told Antoine the story of the *Roulette's* mysterious disappearance. "Gregoire Deslisle advised us to come an' see you. He says to say hello."

"Gregoire Deslisle! I haven't seen him for years!"

"He mentioned he hadn't been home in a while. He's over in Marigot at de moment, but you most likely will see him soon.

Anyway, we're thinking de Cap'n and his vessel are somewhere about dis area. We think dese Germans will be tryin' to somehow make contact with a U-boat, and dat once dey does meet up, Jack an' he son's lives won't be worth half a shilling. We reckon we don't have much time to work it all out, but what's most important is we find dem befo' any get-together takes place. De long an' short of it is dat we could use your help," he finished.

"Since Jack was last on the island, I've been taking note of some of the activities taking place around here. I've been listening to the whispers – this is a small island and there are no secrets. I'm certain Martin Lefèvre and the Irishman O'Loughlin have some sort of business going on, and a small coasting freighter that's been drifting around these waters for the past year or so could be tied up with them as well. The rumour is that they are selling alcohol and cigarettes to passing submarines. This would take some organising if it were true, as you could well imagine. My cousin Luc Gastonay works on O'Loughlin's motor boat. I'm sure he knows more than he's letting on. Give me a little time and I'll make some inquiries."

"Right…well listen man, we jus' wanted to let you know what de hell's goin' on. We're here to make sure de skipper and he son get out o' dis in one piece."

"Don't worry boys. I'll do whatever I can to help."

The whitewashed village of Marigot sat tranquilly below the green hills of French St. Martin. The *Vagabond* rolled lightly to the swell that wrapped around the point and into the open roadstead. Besides two old schooners at anchor, the harbour was deserted. As Gregoire helped Rabbit lift the dinghy off the deck into the water, a small motor vessel spewing black smoke let go from the wharf and began to motor out of the harbour, the roar from its loud diesel echoing off the surrounding hills. "That's the mail boat to St. Barths," Gregoire said, as the crew all watched the rust-streaked boat head around the point and turn east up the channel. "It doesn't look like the maintenance program has improved any since I last saw her!"

Leaning into the hatchway, Harry called down to his wife below deck. "Val, I think it would be a good idea if we got moving. We're going to get some rain soon," he said.

Harry pulled the companionway hatch shut as his wife emerged into the cockpit. "I'm sorry if I was taking too long darling, but we have been sailing all night and I can't go ashore looking like a Cornish fisherman!" Rabbit and Gregoire stood at the stern of the neat double-ender, smiling to each other as the dinghy was hauled alongside.

"I know dear! I don't like to rush you but just look at those dark clouds to windward. It would surely be better to get into town before that lot sets in, wouldn't you think?"

Rabbit rowed the four of them ashore. Jumping out as they touched the sand, they quickly hauled the varnished clinker tender high up under the broad-leaved seagrape trees lining the picturesque bayside. "We can separate here," Gregoire said. "I have an old friend who owns a general store in the heart of Marigot who knows everything that's happening on this side of the island. I'll go and have a word with him and see if he has heard anything. Near the markets just off the main square there are some food shacks. I'll meet you there as soon as I can."

A narrow alleyway between two waterside buildings led onto the main street of the village. Gregoire disappeared around a corner as the others continued on towards the centre of town. As they did so, the first drops of rain began to fall. Darting down the street, they found the busy marketplace, where they ducked into a bamboo shack just as the rain began to pelt down in earnest. They found seats at a table and silently watched the squall sweep across the harbour. Outside, the rain poured off the corrugated iron roofs in sheets. The morning shoppers that filled the markets rushed for cover, looking for whatever shelter they could find.

Rabbit spoke quickly in patois to the proprietor, a large, caramel-coloured woman wearing a red, yellow and black headscarf and a similarly colourful dress. She cackled a gold-toothed giggle at whatever it was he said before bringing them a plate of freshly baked coconut breads and three glasses of mauby – a sweet drink made from sugar cane and the bark of a special tree.

They ate and drank in silence, watching the rain tumble down outside.

As quickly as it had come the rain stopped, as if a celestial tap had been turned off. Rabbit went to the doorway and peered outside. "I think I might take a walk down to de fishmarkets, Skip," he said. "You never know what one o' dem fishermen might've seen."

Val also decided to take advantage of the break in the weather and went off with Rabbit to the markets to do her shopping, leaving Harry at the table waiting for Gregoire to return.

Harry sat quietly smoking a cigarette and looking out over the harbour when Gregoire entered the little shop. "Any luck, old man?" he asked.

"Maybe yes and maybe no," he replied as he took a seat. "My friend Baptiste was busy with a couple of labourers unloading his truck when I arrived, but he took a few minutes to speak with me. He has known Captain McLeod for years, and was concerned to hear of his disappearance. He hasn't seen the *Roulette* for a long time, but when I mentioned the word U-boat his ears pricked up. He told me to come back in an hour when he could talk. There have been some things in the last couple of months he has seen and heard, and he was anxious to discuss them, especially if it helps get Jack to safety."

As the two men pondered this development, they were joined again by Rabbit. "I t'ink we might be in luck, Skip," he said in a low tone as he sat down. "I was down talkin' to some fishermen yonder and I asked if any o' dem had seen a large, green schooner anchored up anywhere in de area over de last couple o' days. None o' dem had seen anything. I was just about to give up when I heard someone speakin' English. It turns out dis fella's from Anguilla," Rabbit said, nodding his head towards the low flat island off in the distance. "De man said he was pulling he fishpots off some shoals to de north of Anguilla just dis mornin' when he noticed a vessel moored to leeward o' de cays out dere. I asked if it was a quiet sort of place, an' he said yes, it was only a couple o' de boys from Sandy Ground dat sets pots an' dives conchs out dere."

"That's good news indeed, Carlisle! It sounds very promising. This could be just the breakthrough we've been looking for! Did you ask him what he thought they were doing?"

"De fellow say he thought it was strange for a vessel to be anchored out yonder. Thought maybe they was poachin' turtles. Said sometimes poachers can be dangerous an' he didn't really want to get dat close," Rabbit shrugged.

The table fell silent. Harry passed around his packet of cigarettes and struck a match, lighting up the others before his own. He took a deep pull and stared out the window.

"It also sounds like your friend Baptiste might have some information for us as well, Gregoire. If you did spend the day here looking into things, could you somehow get back to St. Barths tomorrow on your own?"

Gregoire turned and said a few words to the proprietor. "She says the mail boat runs to St. Barths every day but Sunday."

"Right then chaps, this is what we'll do," Harry said. "Carlisle, Val and I will leave now and sail out towards this place and see if we can get close enough to deduce whether this vessel is indeed the *Roulette*. From there, we can sail on to St. Barths."

"Yes, and that will give me a chance to spend some time with Baptiste and look into things here. I can then catch the mail boat in the morning, which would put me in Gustavia by tomorrow afternoon," Gregoire added.

"Jolly good. Hopefully by then we will have enough information to see where we stand and work out a course of action."

They left the little harbourside shack and went off in different directions. After finding Val they walked quickly back to the dinghy, with Harry deep in thought. No one said a word as Rabbit rowed back to the boat, and as soon as they were alongside and made fast Harry went below to his navigation table and took a look at a chart of the area. Taking out his dividers, he measured the distance from Marigot across the channel and around the western end of Anguilla, and then out to what were labelled on the chart as the 'Prickly Pear Cays'. "It looks to be about sixteen miles from here to these cays the fisherman was talking about, which seem to be two small islands with a large reef on the north-east side. What do you think, Carlisle? It is well off the beaten track."

"Yes, dey does look just like de man said. From how he described it, I t'ink dey'd be anchored somewhere here on de nort' side o' de two cays and in behind de reef," he said, pointing out the spot on the chart with his finger. "It does look to be a good place to hide out in truth."

"If it is actually the *Roulette* out there, the last thing we want to do is scare them off. The trick will be to approach the place without attracting too much attention. How we do that will be a challenge."

Harry led the crew back up on deck and they quickly prepared the *Vagabond* to sail. The anchor was raised, the sails were set, and soon they were running down the channel towards the low, flat island of Anguilla.

The *Vagabond* rounded the sandy cay at the western extremity of Anguilla and set out for the two small islands to the north. As they sailed across the broad, sheltered waters separating them from the main island, Harry and Rabbit discussed strategies.

"How do you think we should approach this, old chap?" Harry asked. "From here the islands look quite low, so there is no real hope of sneaking up on anyone. The last thing we want to do is get too close and alert them to our intentions. I'd assume they would have lookouts posted, possibly on the island itself, and they would most likely be a little bit jumpy."

"If a vessel is there, de main thing is to make sure dat it's de *Roulette*, isn't it? Why don't we haul off de sheets and poke up to windward, and once we're up over de cays see what we can see? From de spreaders I'll be able to tell if it's Jack's vessel or not. I'd know she from miles away."

"And how, Mr Haynes, would you be able to tell the difference between her and any other island schooner?" Val asked.

"Easy. De *Roulette* – being a Gloucesterman – carries a fore topmast, so if it carries one, de chances are good it's her.

Schooners from Bequia, Carriacou, Anguilla an' de rest are all bald-headed on de foremast. We should be able to see dat from miles away."

"Right you are then! Let's trim these sheets. Val, would you like to take the helm?" The sails were set to the new course, and as the gaff yawl heeled to the breeze, Harry went below to take another look at the chart. Several miles to weather of them a broad, shallow reef ran in a northerly direction before curling back to meet the easterly tip of Anguilla. Between this reef and the shore was an expanse of deep water. Their present course would carry them to windward of the two small islands before they would intersect this reef and be forced to tack, which should be sufficient enough distance to allow them to identify the anchored schooner – if one was there.

To the east, the sea was a deep, indigo blue. Whitecaps flashed across its windblown surface. A scattering of high clouds drifted across the sky. The bow wave surged off to leeward. Breakers ahead in the distance suggested the shallows of the far-reaching reef. The sun, canting slightly to the west, had the two small islands to leeward shimmering like a mirage, while casting a reflection of sparkling diamonds across the surface of the sea. Slowly the dark shape of an anchored schooner began to emerge from behind the sandy spit that formed the point of the closest of the cays. Rabbit grabbed hold of two halyards alongside the main mast, and hand over hand climbed swiftly to the hounds. Standing on the spreaders, he gazed off to the west. As Val guided the yacht to windward, Harry steadied himself alongside the mizzen mast and studied the vessel through his binoculars. For several minutes no one moved from their positions, until the spell was broken by Rabbit, who grabbed hold of the halyards and slid back down to the deck.

"No use carrying on any further, Cap," he said. "We've got what we come for. Dat's de *Roulette*, certain sure."

"I'd have to agree with you, old man. She looks everything like her to me," Harry said with a smile. "What a relief! We've found the *Roulette!* Well done everyone!"

The order was given to tack, Val pushed the tiller over and the yacht went about. The sheets were eased, and soon they were sailing a reciprocal course back in the direction from which they had come.

"So what is the next step?" Val asked.

"As much as I would like to stay close and keep an eye on her, we don't have much choice but to press on for St. Barths and meet up with O'Neil and his crew," Harry said as he cupped his hands and lit a cigarette. "Now we know where the *Roulette* is. The next thing is to find out where she's going."

The *Vagabond* left the two cays behind, and with the white limestone cliffs of Anguilla to port, soon rounded the sandy west end and set off across the channel for St. Martin and the island of St. Barths that lay beyond.

The portly merchant looked up from behind the wooden counter as Gregoire walked through the door below the sign which read Baptiste et Fils ~ Épicerie. Turning to his wife he said a few words, and then motioned for Gregoire to follow. Baptiste held up a hinged leaf at the end of the counter, and then led his visitor through the gloomy storeroom filled with dry goods and out the back door into a small courtyard. They sat down at a circular wrought iron table that lay basking in the sun. "Since your earlier visit this morning, I've been doing some thinking, my friend," the shopkeeper said. "All of a sudden a few things started to add up. You, of course, are acquainted with Louis Grimaud?

"Naturally. He is one of the biggest landholders on the French side of St. Martin. His family runs a business similar to your own."

"That's right. Louis and I went to school together in Guadeloupe, and I suppose it would be fair to say we have never been the closest of friends. Now, everyone on the island is feeling the effects of this war, and we are used to putting up with shortages, but until recently I doubt if I ever sold Grimaud more than a tin of sardines. Yet on several occasions in the past year he has been into my shop and bought large amounts of foodstuffs, things that in the normal run of events he would never purchase from me. And it is not just me. He has been seen buying what he can from other competitors as well. I asked him once if he was feeding an army, and he looked at me and laughed."

"That sounds curious," Gregoire said. "What could he be doing with all of those stores?"

"One only wonders. But that's not the end of it. There is a shipping agent from the Dutch side by the name of Wolfgang Kruger. He is an Austrian, an ex-merchant seaman who appeared on the Dutch side about the time of the royal proclamation that made Phillipsburg a free port back in '38. He's not the most popular man on the island, to put it mildly. Not known for his social graces, we could say. He runs the docks over there, and is the Netherlands Oil Company's main agent. Basically, all oil imported from the refineries on Curacao bound for this and adjacent islands is controlled by Kruger's agency. Since his arrival here, this man has rarely been seen in Marigot, yet more than once over the last few months I have spotted him having lunch with Louis Grimaud around the corner at Chez Benoit. What sort of business could these two pirates have in common, I could only imagine."

Gregoire contemplated what his friend had just told him. "Of course, there could be a simple explanation, but obviously there is some sort of connection. How well is your truck running, Roger? Is it up to making a trip over to Phillipsburg? I wouldn't mind having a look at what's happening out on the docks at Pointe Blanche."

"The truck's running fine, my friend. Give me five minutes and we can be off..."

Roger Baptiste's ancient truck slowly wound its way along the potholed Marigot to Phillipsburg road. Bordered by tall shade trees, the road bisected a green pastureland dotted with cattle. Rising above them to the east ran a ridge of high hills; to their right, the broad Simpsonbai Lagoon glittered in the late morning sun. They passed an unobtrusive sign informing them they had crossed onto the Dutch side of the island, and after snaking through the village of Kool Baai, the road led them up into the dry hills.

It was slow going as the dirt road zig-zagged across the island. Finally it began to descend towards the town of Phillipsburg, which sat on a narrow strip of land dividing a large, landlocked salt pond from the sea. Situated behind a crescent-shaped beach at the head of Groot Baai, the town was not much more than two dusty roads lined with houses.

They passed through the shady town and turned towards the wharf located below the prominent white cliffs of Pointe Blanche. The truck was now bouncing down a sandy track that paralleled the beach to their right. A few open fishing sloops were hauled up under the scattered coconut trees along the bayside. Out on the turquoise water, several schooners lay idly at anchor, swinging to the easterly breeze as it whipped down off the dry brown hills and out to sea. Because shallow sandbars filled Groot Baai, broad, heavily built, flat bottomed sailing lighters were used to haul goods between the cargo vessels anchored out in the deeper water and the wharf ashore.

Roger Baptiste pulled up and parked in the shade of a coconut tree. Getting out of the truck, they walked over to the edge of the rundown wharf, where several lighters were tied up alongside. Barebacked stevedores loaded bags of salt from a rusty lorry onto one of the rugged open sailing barges. "That's the ship we're looking for," Gregoire said, nodding towards a freighter floating several hundred yards offshore. It was the same black coaster he had last seen alongside the docks in Pointe-a-Pitre, Guadeloupe. "She looks like she's well loaded, too. She's right down on her marks."

Lounging in the shade of a ragged tarpaulin, the crew aboard one of the lighters were eating their lunch. Gregoire noted which man was the captain and endeavoured to catch his eye. "Excuse me, Skip," he called down into the boat, "I wonder if you could tell me something?"

The captain put down his plate of rice and fish and walked over to the rail, squinting up into the sun. "Yes, mon, what can I do for you?"

"I'm expecting some freight from Guadeloupe and I was wondering if it might be aboard that freighter out there," Gregoire said. "Has she just arrived?"

"No mon, me doubt if it would be 'board dat vessel. We just finish loadin' she wit drums o' fuel oil. Most likely she'll be gone in de next day or two."

"Fuel oil? That's interesting. Where do you think she'd be taking it?"

"Dem say dey haulin' it to Saba and 'Statia, but mon, me don' know what kind o' engines dey'd have on dem small islands to burn so much fuel. De amount o' oil we put aboard dat vessel over de las' few months, dey must be drinkin' it over dere like watah!"

"All the oil aboard that ship and I'm struggling to find fuel to light my lamp! Just one last thing Skip – would you know who her agent is?"

"Dey's only one agent around dese docks. Kruger's he name. Dat shack over yonder's his office, but I t'ink he gone somewhere wit' a partner o' his from de French side. He might be back later."

"Okay Cap, much obliged. I'll have to check again this afternoon." Gregoire waved and they walked to the truck. Baptiste started the engine and they headed back towards Marigot.

"Well that was a handy little tid-bit of information. It's no wonder we're rationing fuel here on St. Martin," Baptiste said. "It seems like most of it is going somewhere else."

"Yes, and that somewhere is what we want to find out…"

It was after sunset by the time the *Vagabond* tacked into the outer anchorage of Gustavia. The afternoon breeze had eased off with the setting of the sun, and now the yacht was gliding across the calm, deep violet surface of the bay, lifting to the zephyrs that drifted off the land and meandered over the water in dark lines. After one final tack, her jib and main were lowered and she slowly coasted to a stop, dropping her anchor off of the beach that bordered the eastern side of the harbour. When it was dark, two figures slipped like shadows into her dinghy and rowed silently across to the anchored schooner *Theodora D*.

"Good evening, gentlemen," Harry called up to the shadowy shapes leaning over the bulwarks. "Permission to come aboard!"

"Come up man, come on aboard," was the call from above, and they scrambled up the wooden boarding ladder which hung over the side. O'Neil deVilliars met the two visitors at the head of his apprehensive looking crew. "So wha' happen' Captain Harry? Anything to report?" he queried.

"It has been a most productive day, I must say," the Englishman responded cheerily. "We have discovered where the *Roulette* is anchored, among other things."

"Well dat is good news! Let's go below an' hear all 'bout it. Dawson, nip down an light de lamps gi' we," O'Neil said as he led the way towards the companionway aft.

"Good evening, Sergeant Hightower. How are you enjoying your stint at sea?" Harry asked, joining the hardened soldier as they followed O'Neil aft.

"It's been an education, that's for certain sir," he replied with a shake of the head. "The fish-head soup for breakfast was a first for me, I must admit."

The crew made themselves comfortable around a table set up in the middle of the captain's cabin. "Right, gentlemen," Harry said. "It has been an informative day, so let's get started. The first and most important part of our business is that we located the *Roulette*. Carlisle here picked up a tip from an Anguillan fisherman on the docks in Marigot, and when we followed it up, we discovered the vessel was indeed anchored out behind the reef at Prickly Pear Cays, a few miles to the north of Anguilla. We didn't get too close, but we are sure it was her."

"Dat's good news, man! Now we know where Jack an' dem is, what we goin' to do to get dem off o' de boat?" O'Neil asked.

"I'm afraid it won't be that easy. We know the Germans are well-armed, and where they are located offers no opportunity to approach them without being seen. I don't really believe they will remain anchored there for too much longer, however, because when you think about it, there's not much future for them out there. In my view, they most likely are simply waiting for something to happen. We have no idea when that could be, but hopefully we have a day or two in which to prepare. Gregoire has stayed on in Marigot to chase down some information and will come across on tomorrow's mail boat. I think it is important to hear what he has to say before we make any plans. Did you discover anything here today that might be of help?"

"Yes man, we had a good chat with Antoine Degras," Zepheryn said. "He's certain sure dat Jack's old partner Sean O'Loughlin is up to somethin'. Martin Lefèvre looks to be in wit' him as well. Antoine said he's seen de *Lady Luck* movin in an' out o' de harbour at odd hours o' de night. De quiet whisper around de place is dat dey's movin' bubal onto submarines, but it's not something people want to say real loud, if you get my meaning. He said he was goin' to check into it an' let we know more tomorrow."

"Lefèvre's main business is alcohol and cigarettes, isn't it?" O'Neil asked. "I know it was he who Jack used to deal with befo' dey had a fallin' out."

"That is an interesting conclusion, isn't it gentlemen? So this old Irish bootlegger and his partner might be taking advantage of U-boats appearing in the area to sell them some local product. But we still are only seeing part of the picture. Where would they deliver their goods? Surely not at those cays where the *Roulette* is anchored – they are far too treacherous a location for a submarine to approach, especially at night. And how would they know when a U-boat is in the area? Somehow they would have to have a way to communicate with them. There is still a lot we need to know before we can fill in all the blanks," Harry concluded.

The room fell silent. Finally it was Rabbit who spoke up. "You know, me an' Sean O'Loughlin go way back. I've known dat ol' smuggler fo' donkey's years, since my bootlegging days on de east coast o' de States. We used to offload our hooch onto his ol' rumrunner de *Vamoose*. I know he an' Cap'n McLeod was good friends in dem days too. It might be worth a stroll out to he house to say hello. Maybe put a bit o' pressure on him to see which way he turns. If he does know what's goin' on and is in as deep as we t'ink, he might lead us straight to de Cap'n."

"I think that's a jolly good idea, Carlisle," said Harry. "In the meantime, I think it might pay us to take a look at two of the possible locations near here that Gregoire mentioned while we have a chance to do so. The whaleboat shouldn't attract much attention. Why don't we send it out and have a good snoop around Fourchue and Tintamarre and see if we can't uncover some sort of sign? I'm of the firm conviction that one of these places will prove to be the spot we're looking for. And if you go along, Hightower, it will give you a good chance to reconnoitre the lay of the land."

"Dat's a good idea, man," allowed O'Neil. "Clancy and some o' de boys could run down to Fourchue in de *Antipodes* to have a look around, an' den on to Tintamarre. In de long run, it could be well worth de effort."

"In the meantime, I'll get on to our American friends in Antigua. Now that we know where the *Roulette* is, maybe they can keep an eye on her for us from the air," added Harry.

Search for a Sign

Early the following morning the whaleboat was rigged, and with Clancy at the helm, a crew of five pushed off for Ile de Fourchue, five miles away to the north. An hour later, they entered the anchorage of that rocky, barren island. Except for the seabirds it was completely deserted. After sailing to the top of the bay, they touched ashore, hauled the boat onto the black sand beach and made the sails up. "Why don't we split up and see if we can discover any evidence of Jerry paying the island a visit," Hightower suggested before finding a trail and making for the highest part of the island.

"This is an impressive spot," said Hightower once they had reached the top of the ridge. "It is perfectly protected and very isolated. It seems like an ideal location for a U-boat to anchor unnoticed."

"Yes, de anchorage is good, but look at all dem rocks an' shoals around de place," Clancy said, pointing out all the surf-fringed hazards which encircled the island. "If you knew where you was goin' den it would be alright, but fo' a stranger who's never been here to enter dis place in de dark o' de night wouldn't be easy."

"No...I see what you mean. It would be a perfect spot for an ambush, too. I think if a sub did come in here, we could make it quite uncomfortable for him," Hightower said, looking at the four high peaks and scattered boulders that ringed the circular bay. Putting the binoculars to his eyes, he looked away to the north. "So if that is the Dutch side of St. Martin, then the long and flat island off the end of it must be Tintamarre."

"Yes, man – dat is Tintamarre in truth."

For close to an hour, Hightower and Clancy worked their way along the ridgeline, gleaning as much information as they could while Kingsford, Earl, Gilbert and Dawson searched the bayside for clues. "I've seen enough from up here," the sergeant said at last. "Let's go find out if the lads have discovered anything before we shove off for Tintamarre."

Scrambling back down the rocky trail, they reached the boat as the others made their way back from opposite ends of the bay. "Anything to report, gentlemen?" Hightower asked.

"Man, we didn't see nothin' but driftwood an' crabs," answered Kingsford.

"If Germans is doin' business inside o' here, dey ain't comin' 'shore far as I can see," agreed Gilbert.

"Right then, lads. Let's push off and see what Tintamarre might tell us." The island was roughly ten miles away. It took a little less than two hours for the *Antipodes* to reach across the channel to get there. As they approached the island, they picked out a shallow barrier reef with breaking waves that paralleled the southern shore. Behind the line of surf, they could see deeper water inside. An entrance into this lagoon was spotted and noted. Passing around the rocky south-westerly point, they sailed into a broad, half-moon bay bordered by a wide, pink sand beach. Clancy sailed the whaleboat in close to the deserted shore until they reached the northern end, where they hauled the boat up. Knee-high surf lapped on the sand. The crew tied up the sails and walked slowly up the beach towards the trees behind.

"Someone's been usein' dis place, an' it don't look like no fishermen," shouted Gilbert. He had found the charcoal remains of a campfire set against a bluff of sandstone. Old wine bottles lay scattered around the campsite. The others walked over to meet him.

Hightower bent down and picked up one of many spent shell casings that littered the sand. "Mauser seven millimetres," he said, turning the cartridge over in his fingers. "Standard issue for Kriegsmarine officers. Someone's been having target practice."

"Man, dis here's a party spot in truth," noted Kingsford, picking up a couple of empty rum bottles.

"I'd like to get on top of that hill over there," Hightower said. On the north side of the bay stood a bluff of red tinged rocks, perhaps one hundred feet high. Walking along a narrow footpath that wound through the briar and manchineel trees bordering the beach, they reached the northern end, and then tracked inland around to the backside of the hill. Here they found a gradual incline leading to the top of the hillock. This spot proved to be the highest point on the island, commanding a view of the protected anchorage and beach below, as well as most of the flat, scrub-covered island running out to the east. The ruins of some old buildings could be seen, as well as the outlines of dried up gardens and cotton fields.

"This is the place lads, no doubt about it. There's been some traffic in this bay. The evidence is plain to see," Hightower said. "Look – down there you can see a spot just off the beach where a big fire has been lit. That must be what they use as a beacon to guide the submarines in. This spot up here is where we would want to set up shop. We should have a look at the rest of this place and familiarize ourselves with it. I think we'll be coming back here in the very near future."

And so the small group wound down the hill and spent the next few hours taking a good look around. Sergeant Hightower's mind was racing. He looked at the islanders accompanying him. They were resilient, and they were practical. They were good sailors, and he didn't doubt their courage. But they were not soldiers, and they had never heard gunfire. They had never seen men die in the heat of battle. He knew he was on his own here, and he had to come up with a plan that made the best use of the resources he had at hand, without putting any lives unnecessarily at risk.

During the sail back to St. Barths, he began to put together the foundations of a plan in his head. As he sat on the rail of the whaleboat as it lifted over the Atlantic swell, watching Earl and Dawson and Kingsford and Gilbert trim the sails and Clancy steer the open boat over, around and through the large ocean waves, he knew he had the makings of a good team.

By the time they tied up alongside, he had a good idea of what they had to do.

Following their traditional morning swim, Sean O'Loughlin and his wife Mercedes wandered back up the steep drive leading to their 'maison' overlooking Baie Saint-Jean, joking and laughing as they climbed up the hill. As the pair reached the top of the rise and started across the flat towards the house the playfulness stopped. There was someone sitting at the bottom of the steps, and he stood as they drew near. He removed his straw hat, and with his blond hair, sun-browned skin and blue eyes, the fellow had all the resemblance of a St. Barths local, except there was something different that caught Sean's eye, something that made him think he knew this man from another place, another time. As they reached within a few paces of the stairs, Albert the gardener came rushing around from the side of the house, worry etched across his black face. "I am sorry, Monsieur, but this man says he is here to see you. I tell him we are not taking on help but he is not listening and won't go away!" Obviously flustered, Albert turned towards the stranger, and raising his arms in exasperation rattled off something in patois, which was returned with a smile.

"It's alright, Albert. Thank you for doing your job, but you can relax," O'Loughlin said, a sly grin of recognition gradually appearing as he faced his visitor. "It's been quite a number of years, and we both were much younger then, but I do believe I know this fellow. It's been a long time, Rabbit. It's good to see that you are still alive and well."

"And it's good to see you, Sean," was the reply as the two men silently locked eyes.

"Excuse me," Mercedes interrupted, "but I think I'll go have my shower." After a belated introduction she jogged quickly up the stairs, leaving the two men alone.

"So if it isn't Rabbit Haynes, standing there like a virtual ghost of my distant past!"

"Well it ain't no jumbie, Sean, it's meself. As far as I can recollect, de las' time I saw you was on a cold November's day out on Vineyard Sound, when I was lucky enough to offload my rum ahead of a big Nor'easter dat broke apart dat 'three mile' bootleg fleet. I turned and ran south fo' Nassau, and heard later dat you'd sold de *Vamoose* and moved on to Florida or Cuba or Mexico – no one knew for sure exactly where. And now here we are, meetin' up in St. Barths of all places."

"If you say that was the last time we met then I won't doubt it. You always did have an excellent memory. But as good as it is to see you, something says you didn't come all the way out here to the far side of this lonely island just for old times' sake. So tell me, Mr Haynes, what I can do for you."

"You're right 'bout dat, mon. It's not joke I makin'. De reason I'm here is dat a good friend of ours is in trouble an' I been asked to try an' help get him out of it. I sailed up here wit' some boys from Petite Silhouette. De long an' short of it is Jack McLeod an de *Roulette* has disappeared. Dis story sounds crazy, but we does think Jack an' he vessel been hijacked by some shipwrecked German submariners. Dey disappeared a few nights ago from Petite Silhouette, and we don't know where dey gone. I had de idea dat maybe you might be able to gi' we a hand to find him."

"That's an intriguing story, to say the least. Sounds like the old boy has found himself in a bit of a bind. I'm not quite sure what I can do to help, but I'd surely like to do what I can. Perhaps you'd like to join us for breakfast, after which we can discuss the situation in more detail," he said.

Odette, the couple's gregarious Guadeloupian cook, had set out her usual breakfast of assorted fruits, French pastries, coffee and tea on the veranda overlooking the bay. Rabbit politely joined the couple at the table, charming Mercedes in Spanish with tales of his days and nights in Havana. O'Loughlin looked on with amusement, happy to see his wife entertained by his charismatic old acquaintance. "Why have you waited so long to come to St. Barths, Carlisle? It is exciting people like you that we need here to liven up the place, wouldn't you agree, Sean?"

"Be careful what you wish for, my dear," O'Loughlin replied. "I've seen this man in action and he sets a pace few mortals can keep up with. But now I'm afraid you'll have to excuse us, darlin'. Rabbit and I have a little bit of business to discuss." And despite Mercedes' half-hearted attempts to prolong their conversation, the two men pried themselves away from the table and made their way to the Irishman's simple study.

"You've certainly got a tiger by the tail wit' dat one, Sean," Rabbit commented as the heavy wooden door swung closed behind them.

"She's a real live wire, and that's a fact," agreed the Irishman. "So now tell me, what is this about Jack?"

"Well it just so happened dat Jack went to bed one night and de nex' day he and his schooner were gone. I was on the island at de time, an' de boys asked me to gi' dem a hand to try an' find out what happened and track him down. De only clue was dat a couple o' young boys saw what we think were Germans go aboard with him dat night an' den sail away north. All we could figure was dat dey came off a U-boat."

"This is a pretty wild story, Rabbit. Naturally I'd like to help. What is it you think I could do?"

"We both know dat de Caribbean is a big place, but somethin' made we think he might be somewhere 'rond here. Den I remembered hearing you had a plane, an' I thought dat since you an' Jack was ol' friends maybe you wouldn't mind goin' up to see if you could spot him somewhere about de place. We know it's only a shot in de dark, but I didn't have anywhere else to turn."

O'Loughlin looked across the table at the Bajan, shaking his head. "I'm sorry, but I'm having a problem with one of my engines at the moment, and I'm waiting on some spare parts to come from the States. They should be here any day now. Once I've done the repair then I'd be only too glad to help. Jack sounds like he's in a hell of a bind. What actually made you think he might be around these parts?"

"Oh, it's only a few rumours dat we did hear about de place; you know how things does float 'round tru dese islands. We did hear a story down south dat U-boats been seen takin' supplies on board somewhere 'round St Barths. But dat's nothin' more than idle gossip a Kopai from down Carriacou way did gi' we. I'm sure dat if dere was anything to dem stories you'd be de man to know about it."

Again the Irishman shook his head. "I'm sorry I can't help you. I've heard nothing of the kind taking place around here. But then Mercedes and I are living far off the beaten track. I don't really have my finger on the pulse like I used to," O'Loughlin said as he stood, slowly making his way towards the door. "I wish you boys good luck. Jack is a dear friend. I sure hope you find him. If I do hear of something, I'll try and let you know. Once the plane is up and running again I'd be more than happy to go up and have a look around. And of course, if my motorboat the *Lady Luck* can be of assistance, then by all means let me know. Other than that, I don't think there's much I can do to help."

"Yes man, de *Lady Luck*. You never know. She might come in handy in truth. If we does hear of anything we might jus' gi' you a shout."

The two old friends shook hands. The meeting was over.

Heatwaves shimmered off of the old stone wharf. The red rooves of Gustavia baked in the hot sun as the brown hills, dry as tinder, waited patiently for the coming of the rainy season. A scattering of people stood idly by, squeezed against white walls in search of midday shade. Complaining of the heat and lack of rain, they quietly gossiped amongst themselves in their daily wait for the St. Martin mail boat. In the distance, black smoke funnelled into the blue Caribbean sky, and soon the battered ferry materialised against the backdrop of rocky islets and sapphire sea. Gradually it grew in size, its white bow wave becoming more and more distinct. Drifting out from their enclaves, the islanders ambled towards the wharf's edge to meet the rust-streaked vessel as it slowed and berthed alongside. Once made fast, a burst of activity commenced. Boxes and crates and baskets of produce were passed ashore and hauled away, a few passengers disembarked while others climbed aboard. Several cows and goats were led from the foredeck across a steel ramp and herded away down the dock.

In the midst of this activity, the ship's captain, a bad tempered, red-faced man wearing an open khaki jacket with epaulets stood near the gangway handing out notes and messages to a clutch of individuals surrounding him. This was the mainstay of the daily communication network between the two French ports. One of these people who anxiously awaited a hand-delivered message from Marigot was the sharply dressed Martin Lefèvre. The captain called his name; he unceremoniously grabbed his envelope and made his way down the gangplank. This unremarkable transaction was casually observed by Gregoire Deslisle, who had boarded the ferry that morning in Marigot. He watched Lefèvre push his way through the small crowd, and once ashore pause long enough to quickly read the note before hurrying off into town.

Gregoire had not been home in over five years, and though he tried not to admit it to himself, he was excited. He also knew the nature of his fellow islanders, and so was prepared for their welcoming. As he walked down the gangway, he caught the eye of many an old acquaintance or relative, only to be acknowledged with a typically solemn nod or simple good day, as if he had seen them only yesterday. Some people did say a word or two, or utter a humorous comment along with a quick smile, but for the most part his homecoming was subdued at best. For this, Gregoire was secretly pleased. He had other things on his mind. Leaving the wharf, he kept one eye on the quickly walking Lefèvre, who didn't go far before climbing into his sparkling maroon Peugeot. Standing on the corner, he watched the automobile drive quickly down the street before accelerating up the hill, heading for the other side of the island. He seemed to be in a hurry, and Gregoire had a good idea where he was going.

I can see how the system works now, he said to himself. Before their departure from Marigot earlier that morning, Gregoire had seen the note delivered to the ferry captain. The message had been handed over by Louis Grimaud.

Crossing the street, he entered Le Corsaire, his father's rum shop. Thierry Deslisle was quietly wiping down the wooden countertop when he looked up and saw his son. His greeting was far from subdued as he came around the bar and hugged him, and despite a broad smile, there was a tear in his eye. Afterwards they went into the courtyard behind, and following a shout upstairs his mother came rushing down, and this time the tears flowed freely. Other family members appeared. His sisters laughed and joked with him. They sat down, and everyone asked questions. His mother brought food. Yet as much as he tried to show enthusiasm for his homecoming, he was distracted. And his grey haired father took notice. Finally the two were left alone.

"I've heard a few stories lately from down the islands. We've even received a letter not long ago from Auntie Adèle in Martinique. Her words were rather guarded, but she hinted in a round-about way you were somehow involved in the 'La Dissidence'. Could this be true?"

"I have many tales to tell, Papa, starting with my trip to Guiana from Frenchtown. We could sit here for hours. As to Auntie Adèle's story, well yes, there is some truth to it. But I honestly don't have the time at the moment to go into it all. What I can tell you is I need some advice and a bit of help. There is something that's going to happen within the next day or two, and people's lives will be at risk. It all centres around our old friend Jack McLeod and his schooner *Roulette*…"

The house faced on to the inner harbour of Gustavia. Its shingles were bleached grey with age, its red iron roof rusted in places, the paint from its shutters old and flaking. Antoine and his brothers now used what was in days long past the Degras' family home as a boathouse for storing their traps, nets and other fishing paraphilia. A few feet away, the surface of the harbour was smooth as glass, reflecting a scattering of lamplights at this late hour of the night. Inside, a kerosene lantern burned brightly, and a small gathering sat patiently waiting for the arrival of one more person.

"Sorry I'm late, gentlemen, but I had some last minute business to attend to," said Harry as he walked in, pulling up a wooden wine crate for a seat. "So tell me, what do we know?"

"Well, Harry, it seems each of us has attacked this problem from different directions but have come up with the same answer," began Gregoire. "I'm not sure of all the details, but one thing is certain – everything starts with Wolfgang Kruger. Yesterday I went down to the wharf at Pointe Blanche and located the freighter we saw in Guadeloupe. I'm certain she is loaded with drums of oil, and this fellow Kruger is the agent. My contact in Marigot confirmed he has on several occasions noticed this man in the company of another businessman from the French side by the name of Louis Grimaud, who I believe contacted Martin Lefèvre today with a note sent over on the mail boat. I soon discovered that upon receiving this note Martin drove straight over to see Sean O'Loughlin. The whole operation seems very well organised. I came away from Marigot with the firm conviction something is going to happen very soon, and what the others here have to say only reinforces that assumption. All indications point to tomorrow night being the night. Antoine, you tell Harry what you found out today."

"My cousin Luc, who is O'Loughlin's deckhand, was reluctant to say anything at first, but when I twisted his arm he admitted they would be loading the *Lady Luck* tomorrow night, and they only loaded on the night a delivery was made. On these nights he only helps stock the boat. He doesn't sail with her. It is only O'Loughlin and Lefèvre who make the trip, so he doesn't know exactly where it is they go."

"I walked out to Saint-Jean today an' spoke wit' Sean," Rabbit said. "I told him a spiced-up version of de story, an' axed if he could use his plane to look fo' de *Roulette*. He wasn't too interested, said she was broken down. Now we find out he's makin' a move tomorrow night. Dat tells me somethin'. I was on de way back to town when I saw dat fellow Lefèvre go past in he fancy car, an' man, he was makin' some speed."

"So at least we know dat de Irishman loadin' some bubal tomorrow night. The question is, where's he goin' wit' it?" O'Neil asked. "Its dat what we really need to know."

"From what I saw today, I believe there is no doubt Tintamarre is where everything happens. This is a Mauser shell casing," Sergeant Hightower said, passing around the copper cylinder, "and there are plenty more where that came from. This weapon is standard issue to German officers. There is plenty of other evidence to suggest U-boats have used the island for a rendezvous point, and presumably more than once."

"I don't want to throw a spanner in the works," said Harry, "but I just received some information this evening over the wireless from our friends in Antigua that a schooner fitting the description of the *Roulette* was seen sailing north today towards the island of Sombrero. Could it be we're wrong, and Sombrero is really where they're headed? "

Silence descended over the small room. It was Gregoire who spoke first. "Let's look at what we know. We understand why Kruger, O'Loughlin and Lefèvre are in this, but why would Louis

<hr />
379

Grimaud be involved if he didn't have some sort of stake in the deal? Then it dawned on me. The only reason I can see for him being included in this convoluted operation is that he in fact is the owner of Tintamarre. Otherwise, what is he bringing to the operation?"

"That makes a lot of sense," said Antoine. "Kruger masterminds it and supplies the oil and the freighter, Martin Lefèvre makes his profit on the alcohol and the Irishman gets his cut for using his speedboat to deliver it. Why would Grimaud be involved if not for Tintamarre?"

"But why would dey be making for Sombrero if Tintamarre is really where they need to go?" asked O'Neil.

"Maybe somethin' made dem leave de cays before dey wanted to," offered Rabbit. "Maybe dey's just wastin' sail befo' de time."

Again there was a pause as everyone pondered these thoughts. "Right then, gentlemen. It seems to me we have to make a choice. We can't be in two places at once. I believe we must make an educated guess, commit to it, and jolly well hope we are right! I don't need to mention the consequences if we are wrong. Which will it be – Sombrero or Tintamarre?"

"Well nothin's guarantee even if we right!" said O'Neil. "But if you want my vote, I say Tintamarre."

The rest of the room unanimously agreed.

"That's it then, lads! Tintamarre it is, and I pray we are right. Now let's get down to the details. We are now committed to the time and place. The question is, how exactly are we going to safely remove McLeod and his son with the scant resources we have at hand?"

"First of all, Commander, we need your friends at the US air station in Antigua to get on board with us," advised Sergeant Hightower. "Then we need to set ourselves up on the island. I have put together a plan, but we will need the Yanks help to have any possibility of succeeding. The few of us against a heavily armed U-boat and crew wouldn't stand much of a chance. We do have the element of surprise on our side, which we must make the most of. When we leave here tonight we must have a rock solid plan, and each of us must know exactly what we're doing."

The conversations went on late into the night. When they broke up, everyone knew what had to be done. They only hoped their calculations would prove them to be right.

Six Days

"It's a few years well since I spent time 'board a schooner de size o' dis," George Paris said, as the *Roulette* sailed out from under the calm in the lee of St. Vincent. The sea was alive with whitecaps as the breeze whipped around the north end of the island. Flying fish broke out of the bow wave as the schooner lifted to the new swell. Garfish turned the wheel as Jack sat on the lazorette hatch next to him gazing off to leeward, when a cry came from aloft. "Blows!" shouted Henry as he stood excitedly on the trestletrees, one arm extended as he held on to the rigging with his spare hand. Suddenly a humpback whale broke through the surface, breaching close under their lee, spray and foam streaming off the leviathan as it soared from out of the depths before crashing back into the sea. It was the first of several as a big pod of whales entertained the crew of the schooner for close to an hour. It was a sight Jack had seen many times, but for the young German submariners it was obviously a phenomenon they had never witnessed, and they joined Henry in responding with childlike glee.

"Look at them," Jack said, shaking his head. "They're nothing more than big kids."

"Yes man, it makes you wonder what de hell dey doin' way out here on de wild ocean so many miles from home," the old West Indian replied.

"They're here doing greedy men's bidding, is what," Jack responded. "It's the story of the world isn't it? It's the blood of the innocent that greases the wheels of ruthless ambition."

"You not far wrong wit' dat, Cap. Dat dere says it all."

Twenty-four hours later, the *Roulette* was sailing under reduced canvas in the midst of the Leeward Islands. After passing well to the west of Martinique, their course had taken them below the towering peaks of Dominica and Guadeloupe, to leeward of the lush volcanic mountain of Montserrat, and then to windward of Nevis and the green hills of St. Kitts. Now the purple outline of St. Barths floated above them to the east, and beyond sprawled the island of St. Martin. It was late afternoon, and the schooner was jogging along under staysail and mainsail alone. It was Albrecht's plan to enter the anchorage at Phillipsburg under the cover of darkness. He had to locate Wolfgang Kruger, and with no radio there was no other way than to physically go in and find him. So now they were slowly heading in a northerly direction, wasting time as they waited for the coming of night.

The sun disappeared behind the solitary cone of Saba and nightfall was not far behind. Still the *Roulette* coasted along. "There is no advantage in us arriving early. If Phillipsburg is anything like it was when I was there last on the *Kate,* everyone will have retired by ten o'clock," Albrecht said. "We should plan on dropping the anchor just before midnight." And with German precision, that is exactly what they did.

Groot Baai spread out before them, the pungent smell of the landlocked salt pond situated behind the town drifting across the water with the wind. A scattering of schooners and lighters swung to their anchors in front of them. Standing on the foredeck, the two captains looked across the water towards the beach that even on such a dark night shone brightly through the gloom, behind which perched the village of Phillipsburg, the odd light burning in a window being the only sign of life. "What's next, Nils? How are you going to pull this off without arousing suspicion?" Jack asked.

"I'm afraid I can't really disclose that to you, my friend. I'm going to ask the four of you to step down into the forecastle, and stay there until I get back. This is for your own good. If my contacts here knew you were aware of their identities, your life wouldn't be worth anything. So if you please, gentlemen?" Albrecht motioned for Henry and the others to be brought forward where they all were escorted down the ladder into the dark forepeak.

Walking aft, Albrecht gave the orders and the ship's lifeboat was hoisted over the bulwarks. "Keep a good watch over our friends, will you, Jost?" the German captain ordered. "I'm going to visit our one-eyed associate Kapitan Marstrom over on the *Tor* and hope to God that we can work something out over the next couple of hours."

"Will do. Good luck, sir," the mate replied.

Weiss stood at the rail and watched as two young sailors rowed Albrecht across the water to the black coaster. It was several hours before he returned. "Good news, Skipper?" Weiss asked as he climbed back aboard.

"Things went about as well as could be expected. Kruger wasn't very happy about being dragged out of bed at this hour, but in the end radio contact was made with Lorient and a meeting was set up for Saturday night."

"And where are we to go until then?"

"Marstrom advised us to sail a couple of hours north and anchor off a small group of remote islands called the Prickly Pear Cays. He has scouted all of these out-of-the-way places and assured me no one will bother us there, at least not for a few days. He says these cays are only visited occasionally by local fishermen."

"And do you think Captain McLeod is familiar with this place?"

"Mr Weiss, you are talking about Jack McLeod! I don't think there is an island, reef or rock anywhere in these islands he doesn't know about!"

Before first light, the anchor was hoisted and the *Roulette* sailed quietly out of Groot Baai; a few hours later she nosed her way in behind the small pair of islands identified on the chart as the Prickly Pear Cays. Jack climbed up the ratlines to the foremast hounds and shouted instructions to Garfish at the helm as he guided the vessel in, watching the dark blue of the deep water gradually lighten in hue as the bottom shoaled up towards the shallow reef to windward. Swinging his eyes to the south, Jack examined the two nearby islets that were separated by a narrow channel. The easternmost of these two cays was flat, covered with grass and thick scrub, and skirted by a beach that ran three-quarters of the way around it. From his vantage point Jack could see the low, flat island of Anguilla several miles away, behind which stood the distant peaks of the French side of St. Martin.

Finally the schooner settled over a white sandy patch devoid of coral that Jack knew would be good holding ground, and so shouted down the order to drop the anchor. "This sure looks like a nice spot, doesn't it, Henry?" he said to his son, who had followed his father up the ratlines to the trestletrees. "It's too bad we're here in such a difficult situation."

"Dis reminds me of de time you took we down to de Tobago Cays. I loved it dat time. When we get home can we go again?" Henry asked, looking up at his father.

"Absolutely. It's the first thing we'll do when all of this is over. We'll get your momma, sisters and brother aboard, and we'll sail down and spend a week in the Cays. We'll live on conches and lobster and turtle, and soak ourselves in the shallows, have fires and roast fish on the beach. How does that sound?"

The boy broke into a big smile. "I can't wait!" Then for some reason the boyish grin evaporated from his face and he looked off towards the distant horizon.

"What is it Henry? Something on your mind, mate?"

The easterly breeze rattled through the rigging. From the height of sixty feet they silently gazed over the blue sea, the islands, the whitecaps, the many colours of the reef, the seabirds gliding past. From this vantage point the world looked different; pristine, untouched, devoid of any sign of man. "What's goin' to happen, Papa? Dese men talk funny but I like dem, 'specially my friend Hans. Are dey goin' to be alright?"

Jack turned his face towards the wind and thought for a moment. "I won't lie to you, son. The truth is, I don't know what's going to happen," he finally responded. "I hope they'll be able to go their way and we can go ours, but only time will tell. All I can say is that I'll do all I can to make that happen."

The boy looked away again. "I don't understand why dere would ever be a war. Maybe I will when I get older."

Jack reached around the masthead and put his big calloused hand on his sons shoulder. "I'll give you a hint me boy – I don't understand it either. And I never will."

During the solitary night-time hours at the wheel as he drove his schooner north, Jack tried to gather his thoughts. Somehow the fates had conspired to put him in a situation that had no obvious solution. His wounding in Martinique had affected him greatly. At first it had made him think about how lucky he was to be alive. The bullet had done some serious damage, but an inch one way or another could have led to a much different outcome. It could have pierced his lung, or a main artery, or even hit his spine. But it didn't, and though it was a slow and painful recovery, he had survived. He came out of the experience feeling weary, like the bullet might have taken the last few ounces of his invincibility along with it. It scared him, too. It reminded him of his own mortality, that he was not in fact the master of his own fate. It was like the natural flow of his life had been interrupted. He couldn't sleep. His restless, broken nights were like torture as he lay wide-eyed waiting for the dawn. The world had lost its beauty, and for the first time in as long as he could remember he wearily rose each day to a dark world of uncertainty.

"Man, wha' happen Jack?" O'Neil said to him one day. "It's like dat bullet did take 'way all o' you' spirit. De hand is gettin' better, but it's like your soul done lost its strength. I seen dis happen in men befo'. It can lead a man straight to de rumshop. An when dat happen it can be a hard road back. I know it ain't none o' my business, but as a sailin' man you should know dat behind every calm dere's breeze. You jus' have to be patient an' wait fo' it to reach."

And then Nils Albrecht appeared, materializing like a spectre out of the darkness. It was like a bucket of cold water thrown into the face of a drunken man. He had no choice but to stop feeling sorry for himself, wake up, and respond to the situation.

What had him most concerned was the safety of his son, so during the few moments when they were alone, he told Henry that when the time came he would have to be ready to save himself. "There'll be no argument, mate," he had said. "When I tell you to go you get yourself overboard and swim for the nearest shore. I don't want you concerning yourself with me or my welfare. Once I know you're safe, my chances of making it through this will be much better. Do you understand me, Henry? I need you to promise me that when I say go, there'll be no hesitation."

The boy had reluctantly agreed to his father's order. Still, whenever the occasion arose, Jack would ask his son the same question. "When I say go, Henry, what are you going to do?"

"I'm going to go, Papa," the boy would obediently answer.

"Damn right you will."

Jack had also been able to find time alone with George Paris to convince him that in the long run it would be better for him and Punkin to follow his lead. "You don't have fo' frighten for me, Cap'n Jack. I's too old to try and make some sort of heroic excape. Dey does call me Garfish, but put me in de watah an' I'll sink quicker den a ballast stone. Me can't swim," the Grenadian had said. "The more I t'ink about it, de more I feel dat if we get back to de Cays in one piece I'll jus' be happy to let Punkin run me vessel whiles I get back home to Sauteurs and work me garden, smoke me pipe an' take tings a bit more on de easy side."

As each hour at anchor passed, the tension and nervousness of the situation slowly grew. Because they had stopped moving, the feeling persisted that they were nothing more than sitting ducks, just waiting for a military vessel to appear around the point at any minute. Lookouts were posted on the island and aloft, and watches were kept through the night.

The West Indians aboard weren't bothered by the situation, though, and in fact made the most of it. The area was teeming with life, and it didn't take George, Punkin and Henry long to get their fishing lines rigged up and over the side. Soon they were pulling red snapper, grouper and other rock fish onto the deck. Garfish had also taken over the role as cook, providing good, solid food from out of the galley.

Close to noon on their second day in the Cays Jack noticed a set of sails break out from behind the eastern end of the sandy islet to windward. Although well over a mile away, it only took moments for his experienced eye to recognize the configuration of the craft's rig. There was only one gaff yawl he knew of that sailed the waters of the Eastern Caribbean. It had to be the *Vagabond*. When after only a short while the boat turned and ran off towards where it had come from, it simply reaffirmed this notion. *Harry's in the area, and it looks like he's spotted us!* he thought excitedly. This was an immediate boost to his spirits. If Harry was here, then surely something was about to happen. When it did, Jack knew he must be ready.

And still the tradewinds blew, and rainsqualls made up and tumbled down and carried away to leeward, and the anchor chain banged and clanked as the vessel swung and surged to the swell and breeze, and time seemed almost to stand still as they all waited for Saturday to roll around.

It was late at night, and Jack had risen from his bunk where he had been restlessly tossing and turning. Climbing up on deck, he sat down on the wheelbox and breathed in the cool salt air. Overhead, the Milky Way painted a glittering swath from horizon to horizon out of a cloudless sky. From forward, the figure of Nils Albrecht emerged out of the gloom, silently joining him next to the wheel. Nils finally broke the spell. "It's a beautiful night, isn't it? You'd never know there was a war going on somewhere."

"Yes mate, it's a beautiful night indeed, just like last night was. And you can be certain those stars will rise and set exactly when and where they're supposed to tomorrow and the day after that and so on until the end of time, just like you can be equally certain men will continue working out better ways to kill each other."

"I have to agree with you there," Albrecht sighed. "My countrymen have become quite adept at it, I must admit."

"Well they're not the only ones. You can see why someone like Garfish would be confused," Jack said. "What we see around us is his universe. I'm sure he could never understand why anyone would put all that time, effort and money into building something as awe-inspiring as a submarine, only to come all that distance with the sole objective of wreaking havoc on people who have done them no harm and are simply doing what they can to exist."

"It has taken me some time, I suppose, but I'm slowly coming around to his way of thinking. Not that it matters much. The zealots that are controlling my fate are hell-bent on achieving what they set out to do, no matter the cost. I don't like my chances. I might have been fortunate to survive this latest confrontation, but I'm conscious of the fact that I probably won't be so lucky next time. The odds are stacked against me and getting worse by the day."

"Tell me Nils, how'd you get caught up in this mess anyway?"

"I returned to Hamburg with the *Kate* a few years before the war started. Life in the coasting trade those days was hard. Freights were low, if you could find one, and Europe was in the midst of a terrible depression. The Kriegsmarine was on a recruitment drive and officers from the merchant marine were being heavily targeted. My ship was going broke, and I was offered a commission as a submariner. In the end I couldn't refuse. I was never too comfortable with the concept of National Socialism, but I have to admit even I was blinded by the patriotic fervour sweeping across the Fatherland. And then the war started, and my first mission to the North Atlantic quickly brought me back down to earth. When this drive into the Caribbean came about, they looked at my past and sent me out here in the first wave. I'm sure you heard of the attacks in Port-of-Spain and Castries? They were my handiwork."

"That's funny," Jack remarked. "Then it was you I passed in the Bocas the night of the first attack. Imagine – you and I were crossing tacks as far back as that! I've got to say, it was quite a daring effort. But then I had a hunch that whoever it was behind those raids had been here before."

"Yes, well it was all too easy back then. At first it just seemed like some sort of sport. A numbers game built around tonnage sunk – the highest number wins. And of course there is always the consideration that you have been sent out to do a job, so you want to do it to the best of your ability. No thought about the innocent lives you are taking. Then something happened that brought home the reality of it all. It was not far from here, just south of Nevis.

Early one morning, an island schooner was spotted sailing north. I had another officer on board who happened to outrank me, and although it was against my wishes he insisted we must do our duty and sink the enemy, no matter who it was. To this day, I remember the look in those men's eyes when they realized what was going to happen to them! But what could I do? I'm an officer in the Kreigsmarine. I have no other option but to follow orders, and will continue to do so until I am either dead or the war is over. That's my reality. That's my fate." The silence of the night ascended over the two captains' conversation. Finally Jack rose and stretched and moved to the hatchway.

"Because we were once friends, I can truthfully say that I'm sorry for you. I understand what it is you're going through because I've been there myself. I try and find some sort of reasoning behind all of this, some kind of deeper meaning, but I can't. The only answer I can come up with is that we are simply pawns caught up in someone else's game, condemned to be pushed into moves that a greater force is making. In the end, we can only try and make the best from a limited number of choices. Anyway, enough of this. It's all a bit too much to think about. I'm going to put my head down and see if I can get some sleep."

"I've enjoyed the chat, Jack. It reminds me of the old days on your veranda."

"It's been good. Maybe we'll have a chance to continue the conversation when all of this is over."

"You never know, my friend…you never know."

The following morning, half of the crew was occupied fishing off the stern while several others sat in the shade under an awning set up amidships. Jack had pulled out his old chess set, and he and Nils were involved in a tight game when a shout rang out in German from the trestle trees. Albrecht and his men immediately went to the port rail. To the northeast, not a mile away, was the shape of a sail moving in their direction.

As it grew near, it could be seen it was not a large vessel. It was painted Admiralty grey, and was flying the red duster astern. It had a local look about it; a single mast with a gaff sail set. The jib was down and the vessel was motor sailing into the wind. Albrecht gave the order for his men to duck below into the captain's cabin. The sailors quickly armed themselves and waited. "It's up to you, Jack, to make sure these fellows continue on their way. If they come alongside, they won't be going any further," warned the German captain.

The vessel continued on its course towards them. By now Jack could tell it was not much more than forty feet long. Garfish, Henry and Punkin continued to fish off of the back of the schooner. The boat steered towards their stern, and as it got closer slowed its speed. Gliding slowly behind the *Roulette,* several men stood on the afterdeck behind the wheel house, gazing in curiosity. Jack raised a hand in welcome but was met with expressionless black stares. Then the vessel slid past, and Jack understood. Across the stern was written *Sombrero Light I,* and below, *Road Bay.* Moments later the vessel picked up speed and soon was motoring through the passage between the cays. "It's the Sombrero lighthouse supply boat," Jack said simply to Albrecht, who now stood next to him. "It looks like they're based over in Road Bay, Anguilla."

Silently they watched the boat disappear. Moments later Albrecht turned and in brisk German shouted orders to his men. They immediately began to pack their things away. "I don't like the feel of this, Captain McLeod. Anguilla is a British island. There is no telling who those fellows might talk to once they get back. Please make your vessel ready to sail immediately."

Jack shrugged his shoulders. "Will do, Herr Kapitan. Could I ask where we'll be sailing for?"

"We will sail for Sombrero Island. At least we know the supply boat has gone in the opposite direction. We need to kill some time. I think we've been here long enough."

The vessel was quickly made ready to sail, and within the hour her anchor was raised. The *Roulette* slowly motored out of the anchorage, and as she did so the German crew stood on deck and gazed astern, as if to say goodbye. The Prickly Pear Cays had been a lucky find, a place of tranquil respite, and now it was being returned to the birds and the fish and the turtles. As they motored past the bleak western cay, the boobies, shags and gulls rose up in squawking protest. The vessel was brought head to wind, the sails were hoisted, and as they set off north the crew took one last, sombre gaze. The seabirds circled and darted and fed, the waves crashed over the reef, the eternal wind continued blow, and the cays reverted to their solitary, wild timelessness.

Several hours later, near sunset, the sound of an airplane could be heard. It came from the south, passing well to the east, maintaining its altitude and distance from them. Aboard the schooner, all eyes were locked on to the distant shape as it eventually banked away to the west, its black silhouette superimposed against the crimson sunset as it headed back in the direction from which it came.

"PBY Catalina," was all Nils Albrecht said. He went below to take another look at the chart. It was near dark when he returned to the deck. The Sombrero light flashed on the distant horizon. "I will now tell you our final destination, Captain," Albrecht said, joining Jack at the wheel. "We need to be anchored at the island of Tintamarre by sunset tomorrow. I trust you can regulate our speed and distance to get us there at that time."

The *Roulette* spent the balance of the night and the following day sailing different courses and speeds, doing their best to while away the time. As the hours passed, so the tension aboard increased, and though a constant lookout was kept, there were no more sightings of military aircraft. Finally, in the afternoon of their sixth day together, the schooner rounded the desolate end of Dog Island and turned southeast, and as they did so, a dramatic change came over the nine German sailors aboard. They knew where they were going. The reality of what they would soon be facing had re-entered their consciousness. The time had come. It was back to the all-encompassing life of fear, death and destruction once again.

End Game

The whaleboat sailed out from under the protection of the four barren hills of Ile de Fourchue and struck out into the channel as the sun rose. O'Neil planned to land early in the day on Tintamarre, hoping to be set up before anyone else arrived. Two hours later, they approached the offshore reef that ran along the southern side of the island, and the crew were on the lookout for the entrance into the lagoon that they had spotted the day before. Standing on the bowseat, Kingsford guided O'Neil through a cut in the reef into the deeper water behind. Sailing parallel to the shore, the whaleboat skipped over the translucent waters of the choppy lagoon, the dark shapes of coral heads standing out against the white sandy bottom. One hundred yards away to starboard, the snowy foam of breaking waves streaked over the shallow brown of the reef, before dissipating into the deeper water inside.

At the eastern end of the lagoon they found an isolated landing spot between two rocky spits where the boat would be obscured from vision. The crew hauled up onto the sand and struck the rig. After laying the mast and sails inside, they made everything ready for a quick departure.

"Alright boys, let's go have a look at dis place," O'Neil said as he led his small band off of the beach. Barefoot, his brow shaded beneath his ever-present straw hat and armed with his razor sharp cutlass, O'Neil set off with the same determination he used to face any challenge, whether it was harpooning a whale, cutting wood in the bush or salvaging a schooner. Others ran just to keep up with him. It was no wonder his fellow islanders called him 'Zeus'.

The whaleboat crew followed a small track leading from the lagoon to the anchorage on the lee side of the island. Carefully creeping through the scrubby trees, they squatted and observed the beach before them. It was deserted. On the north side of the bay, they spotted the bluff of red-tinged rocks that Hightower had described. They followed the path behind the beach, then climbed to the top of the hill, where they made themselves at home in the shade of a couple of big, bushy tea trees. "Dis is a good spot, man," O'Neil commented as he looked out over the bay. "From up here we can spy de whole o' de island."

After clearing some space with his cutlass, O'Neil slowly unwound his tall frame and sat down, leaning back against the stout tree trunk. "What time is it Clancy?" he asked as he gazed across the water towards the shore of nearby St. Martin through the binoculars.

"Just after nine."

"I'm guessing dat if dese Frenchmen comin' over here like Cap'n Harry think, dey should reach sometime between twelve an' three. Me no know where dey's comin' from, but I doubt dey'd bring a boat all de way from Marigot. I'd think it more likely dey'd keep one somewhere nearby...just over yonder behind dem reefs looks promising. Harry said dere's a little village on dis side o' St. Martin dey does call Cul-de-Sac, so maybe dat's where dey comin' from. We got time. I'll keep a look-out while you boys get to work. All o' you know what fo' do."

Clancy, Earl, Gilbert, Kingsford, Bull and Dawson wound their way back down the hill. The small group spent the morning examining the cove from one end to the other, reaffirming what they had seen the day before. It would be important. They would have to be able to know how to get back to the safety of the whaleboat in an emergency, and they would have to be able to do it in the darkness of the night.

The midday sun beat down on the six sailors as they returned to the lookout after their exploration of the island. Upon reaching the shady top, they wiped the sweat from their dusty brows and took hearty gulps of water from the canteen as it was passed around. O'Neil still sat with his back to the tree, binoculars hanging from around his neck. "So, everything set?" he asked his son, lifting the glasses up to his eyes yet again.

"Yes, mon – we found what we lookin' fo'. An' we worked out a way to get back to de boat from here dat keeps us away from de beach if we need to. So now I guess all we can do is sit back an' wait."

"Okay den, why don't you all get something to eat and den find a place to rest yourselves. You boys didn't get much sleep las' night, and I have a feelin' it's goin' to be a long day."

It was close to four o'clock when O'Neil stirred up the crew. "Here we go boys. Ting's on de move! It looks like de first o' dem 'bout to arrive!" After a few moments, he passed the glasses over to Clancy, who had slid quickly alongside of him. Looking into the late afternoon sun as it reflected brightly onto the water from over the high peaks of St. Martin, he picked out the splashing bow wave of a small motorboat against the shaded hillside behind.

"Yes man, I see him now. Looks like he came out o' dat bay over yonder, just like you thought he might," Clancy said, handing the glasses back to his father.

It wasn't long afterwards when Kingsford's low whistle was heard from his perch on the north side of the bluff behind them. The others excitedly crept around to see a schooner skirting the rocky northern extremities of St. Martin, its dark silhouette embossed against the silver gleam of the afternoon sun on the water. "It's de *Roulette* breakin' 'round de point!" exclaimed Gilbert.

"Yes, dey looks to be maybe a half hour away. It's like everything startin' to happen at once! Dat little motorboat will be here shortly, too," O'Neil said. "I suppose we should get ourselves ready. Bull, Gilbert, Earl – you fellas know what to do. Best you get moving now before dey get any closer."

Throwing a military issue canvas bag over his shoulder, Bull led Gilbert and Earl down the hill to the sandy track that ran behind the beach. Jogging through the shady trees, the trio reached the far end of the bay. Here Earl split away towards the whaleboat, while Gilbert and Bull moved out onto the rocky southern point, where amongst the boulders and cashee trees they had previously located a nook overlooking the crescent shaped beach. Settling in, they made themselves as comfortable as possible, knowing they had several hours to wait before they would be called into action.

Earl splashed his way along the edge of the lagoon to where the *Antipodes* was hauled up. Climbing into the whaleboat, he removed from out of the stern locker an important piece of equipment common to all Grenadines whaleboats – a mirror. During the whaling season, this was how the whalermen communicated with each other. Perched high on the hills of Petite Silhouette and Mustique, spotters would direct the men in the boats towards the spouting and breaching whales by the use of coded flashes. Earl knew Harry would be anxiously waiting for the signal from his perch high on the ridge of Ile de Fourchue, so he hurried to catch the last of the sun's rays before it disappeared behind the nearby hills of St. Martin. Ascending to the top of a rocky knoll, he flashed his signal, angling the mirror so as to redirect the sun's rays towards the waiting Englishman over ten miles away. He didn't have to wait long for a reply – a bright flash soon answering back from the top of the distant island. Earl sent back an acknowledgment before returning to the *Antipodes*. Once it was dark, it would be his job to re-rig the boat and make her ready for a quick departure.

On top of the bluff on Tintamarre, four sets of eyes stared intently towards the distant peaks of Fourchue. "Dere's de flash! Harry's seen we sign," O'Neil exclaimed with a tone of relief. "It looks like Earl got he signal off just in time."

Soon the methodical popping of a single-cylinder diesel could be heard from the small boat powering in below them. As it drew near, the shapes of three men could be seen standing inside the open wooden motorboat. The two thin, black figures in the bow sported the typical broad straw hats with pointed crowns worn by French island fishermen. Lying low on the top of the hill, they watched as the helmsman threw an anchor over the stern, while the two men forward jumped into the waist-deep water and ran a bowline ashore. Once the launch was made fast, they began offloading a variety of items out of the bow of the boat, the two crewmen under constant harangue from the big bellied captain. When the boat had been emptied the men disappeared into the interior of the island, only to reappear onto the beach at random intervals with firewood and dry coconut fronds. "Well it sure looks like dey knows what dey have fo' do," Clancy whispered. "It's not de first time dey been t'rough all o' dis, dat's fo' sure."

Long shadows spread across the bay as the *Roulette* motored into the anchorage. The anchor was let go, and the schooner drifted back with the wind and swung to her hook. An undercurrent of excitement ran through the group on top of the hill as Jack and Henry and the other two West Indians were identified moving about on deck just below them.

Seabirds skimmed low over the water in silence, and slowly day turned towards night.

To the west the opaque sliver of a new moon fleetingly appeared through breaks in fast moving clouds. Darkness rushed down from the east, and with it came more wind, whistling across the tops of the island's forgotten cotton stalks and rustling the dry trees. A black squall full of rain followed soon after; short blasts of windblown bullets sweeping down from the open Atlantic, passing overhead and then careening away helter skelter to leeward like a banshee. "Moon down squall," commented O'Neil after its passing, the teardrops left in its wake dropping from the tea tree's fluttering leaves.

"Yes man, an' dere's more where dat came from," agreed Kingsford. "Change o' moon, change o' weather."

Below, tucked into a nook between the rocks, a small fire was burning with the three Frenchmen gathered around it. "Looks like dey's roastin' some fish," Clancy observed.

"Yes, and dey has de rum bottle out as well," said O'Neil, passing the binoculars on.

It was after ten when the men rose, stretched and moved away from the fire, disappearing into the darkness of the island's interior. One of them carried what looked to be a large light. "Must not be long now, boys. Looks like dey movin' into position," whispered Clancy.

On top of the hill, the watchers lay still. Time slowly passed. Below, the fire burned down to embers, the black curtain of night obscuring all detail. Ten minutes passed with nothing happening. Fifteen minutes and the anchorage was completely obscured, as if it were covered with a cloak. And then, from out of the murky reaches of the channel to the south came a bright burst of light; a pinpoint of rhythmic flashing. A simultaneous whisper of acknowledgment passed between the men. "Blows!" muttered O'Neil in the language of the old whalermen. "Stand by your peak and throat! It's all happenin' now!"

The flashing light out to sea was answered from the south point of the island. "And there's the answer! I sure hope Gilbert an' Bull is well hid! Dem Frenchmen might step on dey toes when dey passin'!" Kingsford commentated.

Minutes slowly slipped by. The wind chased the last embers of the small bayside fire into the air. Suddenly a massive blaze appeared on the beach – a bonfire touched off by the small boat's captain. As the beacon blazed towards the sky, another fire appeared across the water on the hillside on St. Martin. "So dere's de second range marker," observed Clancy. "Dat's how dey line de sub up." Peering over the edge, the four men anxiously waited for the U-boat to appear. They watched as more dry branches were tossed on top of the blaze. And still there was no sign of the submarine.

The bonfires continued to be stoked. And then they heard it – the gradually deepening drone of diesel engines. Slowly the silhouette of the rectangular conning tower of the German U-boat materialized out of the murky distance as it crept into the bay. Partially illuminated by the flickering firelight, they watched the submarine ominously motor towards shore, until with an audible grinding noise the long, black torpedo of a ship could be heard running itself aground onto the bottom of the bay. Moments later, the range light ashore was extinguished, as was the one on St. Martin. Far-off German voices began to echo through the night.

From each end of the bay, unseen eyes nervously watched on. "Well, Mr German, we's ready," O'Neil half-whispered under his breath. 'It's up to all-you to make de next move."

From off in the distance the faint sound of a different engine could be heard, and as it drew closer, the stroke of a large two-cylinder diesel was soon recognized. Through the wandering flash of the U-boat's searchlight, the outline of a small freighter could be seen entering the bay, the noise growing gradually louder until once alongside the starboard side of the submarine the engine was put into reverse, mooring lines were thrown across and the ship was secured amidships.

Rabbit Haynes and Gregoire Deslisle lounged in the doorway of the ruins of an old stone warehouse near the water's edge in Gustavia harbour. Headlights swept around the corner and Sean O'Loughlin's convertible bounced down the road, pulling up and parking astern of the *Lady Luck*. They watched from the shadows as the aging but still athletic Irishman extracted himself from behind the wheel and closed the door behind him.

Walking to the water's edge, he climbed into the dinghy and pulled himself the few yards out to the stern of the launch and scrambled aboard. Moments later another set of headlights swung around the corner and a lorry rumbled up, turning as it reached the waiting yacht so the open bed backed towards the water. O'Loughlin adjusted the lines until the stern of the boat was hanging only a few yards from shore.

Two men climbed out of the cab and walked around to the back of the truck, joining two others who stood up on the bed. Little was said as a line was formed and the cargo was quickly unloaded, one box after another being silently passed onto the waiting motor boat. The last case was handed aboard, the men jumped into the back of the truck, the driver quietly closed his door, the engine was restarted and the lorry spun to its left and drove off into the night.

As the truck disappeared around the corner, Rabbit and Gregoire moved quickly across the road and jumped aboard the *Lady Luck*. O'Loughlin and Lefèvre spun around to challenge the two intruders, a puzzled look of surprise spread across their faces. "You can have the night off tonight, Martin," Gregoire said in the local patois. "We'll be Sean's crew tonight."

As he began to open his mouth in protest, Rabbit removed an Enfield revolver from his waist and levelled it at him. "We're not askin' you to go, Monsieur Lefèvre…we're tellin' you. Now get yo' ass ashore," he ordered.

Lefèvre did not have to be told again. He jumped ashore and quickly made his way down the road, briefly stopping at the corner for one last look before he was lost from sight.

"So what's goin' on here Rabbit? Am I being hijacked?" O'Loughlin demanded.

"It's nothin' so serious, mon. Me an' Gregoire are here to try an' get Jack out o' dis mess o' trouble dat he's found himself in, an' now, like it or not, you is part of it too. So all you have fo' do is drive your vessel. You jus' do what you normally do, an' we'll tell you de rest."

The Irishman cast his eye over his two visitors. "Gregoire Deslisle? Thierry's son?" Gregoire nodded. "I've heard a few stories about you. And Rabbit?" O'Loughlin shook his head and smiled. "Just like old times."

"Yes, well we does have we own bit o' history. And for some reason, dere's usually firearms and alcohol involved."

The engines were started, the mooring lines dropped off and the *Lady Luck* motored slowly out of the calm inner harbour. "I should have known something was up the moment I saw you out at the house. Still, I'm impressed with your resourcefulness. How did you know I'd turn up tonight? And what if I didn't?"

"All dem questions will be answered befo' de night is through, don't frighten. Now, dere's one more ting we must do before we go. We need to stop alongside o' dat schooner over yonder." O'Loughlin cast a suspicious eye at Rabbit, but did as he was told.

Shadowy figures on deck were waiting by the rail to take the lines as the launch pulled up next to the high, grey topsides of the schooner. As the crew held the ropes, a heavy green duffle bag was passed over the bulwarks, followed by the tall figure of a man who sprung down nimbly onto the deck. Rabbit carried the bag through the open side door and into the wheelhouse, introducing the newcomer. "Sean, meet Sergeant-Major Dereck Hightower of His Majesty's Leeward Island Regiment. He'll be riding along with us tonight as well."

Sean O'Loughlin pulled a cigarette packet out of his shirt pocket and passed it around as he examined his newest guest and his belongings. "I wonder what other surprises you might have in store for me tonight. I'm guessing it isn't just a change of clothes you've brought in that bag, Sergeant?"

"You don't need fo' worry 'bout about dat, Sean," Rabbit confided. They motored unhurriedly away from the schooner. "You just need to do what we tell you. As I said before, everything will come clear in de end."

Leaving the outer anchorage, Sean O'Loughlin pushed the throttles down and the *Lady Luck* picked up speed. Clearing away from the calm lee of the land, they bounced across the small passage towards Ile de Fourchue. Passing in close to the rocky shore, the island's four peaks loomed dark and menacing above them to starboard. Soon they left the island behind and were crashing out into the open channel. "Not much of a night for yachting," O'Loughlin yelled over the hum of the engines as the motorboat launched through the white foam of an oncoming wave.

"She's a bleak an' stormy night in truth," Rabbit agreed as the boat shuddered through yet another big roller. "Bad weather goin' to be de least of our worries tonight, though," he muttered under his breath.

On board the *Roulette,* the entry of the U-boat was observed by all with great interest, if for different reasons. "Well there you go, fellas," Jack said as he stood with arms crossed alongside the German captain and mate, "I've fulfilled my side of the bargain at least. I don't see your crew jumping up and down with joy, though. Maybe they were hoping your ride wasn't going to turn up after all. I guess you can't blame them. It's not like you blokes are about to set off on a luxury cruise, is it?"

The fire burning ashore cast an eerie light over the water, reflecting from the barrels of the submarine's deck guns and superstructure, creating a nightmarish image as the big, black shadow slowly slipped into the bay. "No Jack, you are right. My men and I have all seen about as much action as any submariner would ever hope to see. We've been bombed and strafed and shot at from every angle. We've crash dived more times than we could count, dodged depth charges and reached depths far beyond our designed limits. We've witnessed comrades blown to bits and seen our ship destroyed, been cast adrift and still lived to tell the tale. No, we're fully aware of what we're facing the moment we step aboard that U-boat. Wouldn't you agree Mr Weiss?"

"Not much I can add, sir," answered the battle-hardened sailor. "Our lives are in the hands of the gods. It's as simple as that."

The fire beacon was reduced to glowing embers, and except for the faint hum of the U-boat's generators there was little sign of life ashore or on the water. It was Albrecht who decided it was time to move. "Captain McLeod, I will require the use of your life boat in a moment. I need to go aboard and make myself known to my fellow commander and explain our situation to him. I'll get two of my men to row me across. Weiss, get the men ready."

"Yes, well don't forget to mention our little arrangement, will you? I'll just be happy when this is all over with and we can go our separate ways – not that I haven't enjoyed your company."

Standing at the rail, Jack put his arm around his son's shoulders as they watched the skiff push off and row away towards the black beast that was now occupying the centre of the bay. "Man, dat ting look everything like some sort o' creature dat spring up to de surface from outta de depths to eat mankind alive," Garfish murmured. "Punkin askin' me what de hell it is, but I ain't have no signs to explain! I told him it's a vessel lives under de sea, but he don' believe me."

"But what did dey really build it for, Papa? It doesn't look to me like it could haul much cargo," Henry observed.

"Cargo? Man dat ting fully loaded but it ain't wit' rice or cement," old Paris stated. "It looks to me like dat vessel built to drogue one ting alone, an' dat ting be death!"

They were joined now by Weiss, in company with a sailor toting a machinegun under his arm. The group once again became quiet. Jack took a prolonged sidelong look, and at length broke the silence. "It looks like the holiday is officially over," he said, staring at the man's weapon.

"I don't know which holiday it is you are talking about," Weiss replied.

Moments later the sound of another ship entering the bay reached them, and not long afterwards they watched the *Tor* tie up alongside of the U-boat. "Well it looks like the fuel barge is here," Weiss observed.

As they gazed across the water, there was plenty of activity aboard the sub. Not long afterwards the skiff hove back into view, this time with two added passengers. Nils Albrecht climbed the boarding ladder followed by two uniformed and well-armed sailors. "Sorry Jack, I was given no choice. These men are to stay on board with you until we are ready to go. You and your crew will be asked to go down below and stay there until we leave. Kapitan Becker wanted to have you manacled, or at least secured, but I managed to persuade him otherwise. Now, it's time I get my men moving so we can finally take leave of your generous hospitality. It's always the same with unwanted guests, isn't it? They never seem to know when it's time to go!"

Jack and the others sat around the captain's mess table in the light of a hurricane lamp, listening to feet scuffling on deck as the castaways left the ship. The doors at the top of the steps swung open, the companionway hatch squeaked as it slid forward, and Kapitanleutnant Nils Albrecht descended the stairs, his face showing in the lamplight none of the relaxed features the last week aboard had bestowed upon it. "Listen Jack – I must keep it brief. I'm not going to lie to you. This is a difficult situation. There is no benefit to the Kriegsmarine, my colleague Kapitan Becker, or our other associates over there to see you go free. They are determined to eliminate any knowledge of this operation escaping here tonight. I don't know how I'm going to do it yet, but I gave you my word to you and I am going to keep it. If it's the last thing I do, I will make sure you all get out of this safely. Be patient, and trust me."

Nils Albrecht nodded one last time and left the cabin, closing the hatch and doors behind him.

"Right, now we have to get you blokes out of here," Jack whispered. "You have to get ashore as soon as you can. I'm sure our friend Cap'n Albrecht has his heart in the right place, but I don't trust the rest of them over there. We have to figure out a way the three of you can get overboard and swim ashore."

"Well Cap, I t'ink I did mention it befo', but I have a problem wit' dat plan. I can swim 'bout as good as a conch shell," explained Garfish. "Punkin can swim, but not me, so I'd rather take me chances aboard here wit' you. It looks like it'll be you and me against de whole o' de German navy, Skip."

"What about you, Papa? What're you goin' fo' do?" asked Henry.

"I'm not sure what I'll be doing, mate, but the time has come for you to get ashore and get out of harm's way. Now, I reckon you two boys can squeeze through the lazorette from here and climb out the back hatch. What I need to do is attract the guard's attention while you slip out, so this is how we'll do it. " Jack explained his plan to the others, and they stood and made ready to go. The two young boys stripped down to their shorts. Jack gave his son a hug while Garfish used sign language to make sure Punkin understood exactly what was happening. "Everything's going to be okay, Henry. I don't want you to worry about me – understand? You just get ashore, take cover and look after yourself and Punkin. Remember the plan and take your chance when you can."

At the aft end of the cabin, there was a small doorway cut through the bulkhead allowing access to the lazorette. Jack watched as the two boys disappeared into the dark storage area, imagining them climbing across the piles of rope, spare blocks and rigging as they made their way to the hatch that opened up onto the deck aft of the wheelbox. Pausing at the bottom of the companionway, he looked at George and nodded. Climbing to the top of the ladder, he opened the hatch slightly and pushed the doors open, and facing aft looked into the eyes of the armed sailor he knew would be posted there.

"Halt!" the German shouted, threatening Jack with his machinegun.

"Okay, okay," he smiled, raising his hands in the air. "Don't shoot mate. I just need to take a piss. You know my friend...pissen?" And slowly lowering his hands, he indicated what his intentions were. Over the German's shoulder Jack could see the lid of the hatch crack open ever so slightly.

"Nein!" the sailor answered, followed by verbal threats in German and more intimidation with the gun, the gist of which was for Jack to go back down below deck. He could see more time would be needed, so taking no for an answer was not an option. "Listen, mien froinde, I need to piss and you can shoot me if you want but I'm going to walk to that rail and urinate!" Jack pushed past the guard and walked to the waist-high bulwark, and unbuttoning his fly, proceeded to pass water over the side. Looking over his shoulder he could see the guard watching him closely, but more importantly, in the darkness behind he vaguely made out the spidery shapes of the two boys as they slipped out of the hatch onto the deck. Making the most of this distraction Jack took his time as he finalised this call of nature. Slowly zipping up his fly he caught the fleeting shadow of a figure slide over the bulwark. As he descended the stairs he noted that neither guard aft or forward had noticed a thing. *Good on ya, boys,* he said to himself. Having his son off of the boat took a great load off of his mind. "Looks like they made it overboard, 'Fish," he said as he sat back down at the table.

"Well dat is one less ting fo' worry we, isn't it, Cap," Garfish stated, leaning back into his chair. "So what do you suppose dey is goin' to do wit' all o' we?"

"That's a damn good question. I'd rather not wait to find out. I think we've got to give the boys a few minutes to get ashore and then we've got to try something ourselves."

Henry lifted up the lid of the lazorette hatch ever so slightly and peered out through the gap. First he could hear his father in a loud conversation with the armed guard, and then he could see him move to the starboard rail. This was their chance. Carefully sliding the cover back, he made just enough room to hoist himself out, and keeping low, lay quickly down on the deck. Punkin followed right behind. Silently closing the lid, he could see his father doing his utmost to maintain the charade. Finding the end of the coiled mainsheet on the deck next to him, he tied a bowline and looped it over the quarter bits, then lowered enough of the sheet over the rail to reach the water. He took a deep breath. It was time to go. In one motion, he rolled over the bulwark, and holding on to the rope, lowered himself hand-over-hand until he slipped silently into the water. Treading water he looked up and watched the dark figure of his companion slide down the rope and ease into the sea next to him.

The night was dark; the sea was even darker. Small wavelets slapped past the high topsides of the schooner as she slowly rolled to the side-on swell. Hanging on to the rope, the two boys got their bearings. Henry was nervous. He had never been swimming at night in water this deep before. He could feel his heart pounding inside of his chest, but he knew he had to go. Tapping Punkin on the shoulder, he held up is hand showing three fingers, then two, and finally one. Letting go of the rope he held his breath and submerging beneath the surface swam as far from the vessel as he could. Finally he could go no more and came up for air as quietly as possible. Moments later Punkin broke through the surface and Henry drifted over to meet him. Now they began to paddle as carefully as they could towards the rocky point his father had pointed out earlier. The wind was strong and the small waves slapped over their heads, but they slowly made progress, attempting to make as little disturbance on the surface as possible. It was an unnerving feeling, swimming through the murky water, but soon he could hear the wash of waves on rocks and knew they were getting near the shore. The bluff loomed overhead; the shoreline was now well defined. Spotting a small break in the rocks, Henry swam for it, and then his feet felt the sandy bottom and the next thing he knew they were wading ashore.

In the young boys' eyes, the shoreline before them looked treacherous and forbidding. They were scared. An eerie glow emanated from the small fire on the beach only a hundred yards away, and they were afraid they might be seen. The cliff face loomed over them as Henry, crouching low, led Punkin up into the shadows of a sharp jumble of rocks, where they ducked out of sight. Shivering in the cool wind, the boys' teeth chattered as they squeezed together, the ghostly shapes of the schooner and submarine floating before them like nightmarish phantoms in the night. His father told him to get ashore, hide amongst the rocks and wait, and he had no intention of doing otherwise.

Then the shape of a figure suddenly appeared out of the darkness before them, ducking around the rocky point.

"Henry – hey Henry!" a voice whispered.

The boy's heart jumped. He knew the voice! "Over here, Dawson! Over here!" he excitedly whispered back.

"Man we saw splashin' in de watah and t'ought it was two turtles before you two ran 'shore," Dawson uttered as he crept up to meet them. "Come now – follow me. Keep low an' keep to de shadows til we 'round de point. You can axe questions later."

The two boys did as they were told. A few minutes later they were lying down next to Henry's grandfather on the top of the hill. "I'm glad you made it Henry, but dere's no time to explain," O'Neil said after giving the boy a pat on the back. "I jus' want you to keep your head down an' follow orders. No matter what happens here tonight, you got to be brave. You understand?"

The boy nodded an affirmative. "Yes, Grampa, I'll be brave."

The *Lady Luck* roared into the anchorage, her twin Sterling petrol engines announcing her arrival. Slowing to a stop, she tied up alongside of the steel freighter, which was now busy pumping fuel oil into the submarine's tanks. Rabbit worked the fore deck, Gregoire the stern as they passed over the mooring lines, playing the part of O'Loughlin's crew. Once his lines were secured, the Irishman stepped out on deck. Looking up, he acknowledged the freighter's captain, who stood out on the wing deck of his wheelhouse with his hands on the railing. "Good evening Marstrom," O'Loughlin shouted. "We have a wee bit of cargo for our friends over there. Are they ready for it yet?"

The one-eyed skipper surveyed the waiting rumrunner for a moment before replying. "I'll get Kruger. He's next door having a word with the captain," he called back. "Come aboard."

Rabbit wandered aft with Gregoire and entered the wheelhouse. Hightower stood at the bottom of the steps that led to the dim forward cabin. "Right – I'm going to go over and meet with this lot next door," O'Loughlin said. "They usually send some sailors over to help unload the cargo, so needless to say, Mr Hightower, you will need to keep out of harm's way until that operation is finished. The forward head should be fine. I don't think anyone will want to join you in there. While I'm next door I'll see what I can find out about Jack."

O'Loughlin slipped out on deck and vaulted over the rail of the neighbouring freighter. Climbing up the steel deck ladder, he crossed through the vessel's darkened wheelhouse and joined the *Tor's* captain, who stood on the portside wing deck overseeing the pumping operations. On board the U-boat, Kruger could be seen to be involved in a volatile conversation with several German officers. Beyond the bridge of the submarine, the lofty spars of the *Roulette* could just be seen. "What is going on over there?" the Irishman inquired, nodding towards the knot of arguing Germans. "It looks as though our friend Kruger isn't too happy with something. And what's the story with the schooner? It's strange a vessel like that would happen to be anchored here tonight, isn't it?"

Marstrom turned his head slightly, examining O'Loughlin with his one good eye, and then turned his gaze back on to the U-boat. "The schooner is why Kruger is here tonight," Marstrom finally said. "It seems the crew from a sunken U-boat were brought here from down south aboard it. Now he wants the schooner and her crew destroyed."

At that moment, Kruger turned to see O'Loughlin watching him. On the bridge of the U-boat words were spoken, an order was given and a handful of German sailors climbed across onto the deck of the freighter. "There are your men, O'Loughlin!" the agent shouted. "Send over your cargo!"

The Irishman climbed down the ladder to the deck and led the sailors back to his boat. Soon cases of wine, rum, whiskey and cigarettes were being passed hand-to-hand from the *Lady Luck* across to the U-boat. Finally the last case was delivered, and O'Loughlin joined Marstrom once again, this time to witness Kruger awkwardly climbing back aboard the freighter. Puffing hard, the overweight Austrian climbed the steps to the wheelhouse. Upon arrival, the bootlegger handed the agent a folded piece of paper. "My bill, Herr Kruger," he said.

"Ya, ya – it's all taken care of. Just wait a moment and the money will be here. They'll be paying us in French Francs, so just be patient. One of their sailors will be bringing them across any minute."

"It's not that I don't trust you Kruger," O'Loughlin stated, "but including this one, you owe us for three shipments. Don't worry, you say. This is the German Reich we are dealing with, you say. One day they will rule the world and you are worried about a few bottles of wine, you say. Lefèvre swore you told him the money would be here tonight, and I'm not taking another raincheck."

"Don't get yourself all worked up, O'Loughlin! We've got plenty of time tonight. The captain is sending his men ashore to stretch their legs and relax with a drink or two. They've been aboard that sardine tin for over sixty days without a break. We'll be in for some fireworks later when they use that schooner over there for target practice," Kruger laughed.

"What is that vessel doing here anyway?" O'Loughlin queried.

"Oh some submariners nicked it after their own sub was sunk. They got the captain to bring them here, telling him he could go free once they'd boarded another sub. Stupid bastard! As if we can let him go after seeing what we're doing here! If he leaves here alive, the whole Caribbean would know our story by morning, and we would all be finished. I have enough trouble keeping things quiet as it is, and now that the Americans are on St. Martin, I need to be twice as careful."

"So how is it looking for future work, Kruger? What are the Germans telling you?"

"Well to be truthful," the shifty agent confided, "things don't really look to be going too well for the Kriegsmarine at the moment. According to my latest information, this could be the last ship we deal with here for quite some time. The captain was telling me about the problems they are facing both here and in Europe. Between you and me, I'm seriously thinking about starting up a new enterprise. As you know, the Americans are going to be building an airstrip here, and where there are Americans there are dollar bills. I think some good money could be made supplying them with certain - shall we say - products? As you would know, women are scarce here on St. Martin, but the Dominican Republic is not too far away, and I'm told the women there are not only beautiful, but would love the idea of earning Yankee dollars. All I need is a good, fast boat like yours to run over and bring a few back. If you are interested, perhaps we could discuss business."

Sean O'Loughlin stared at the greedy agent, fascinated with how quickly the man's loyalties could change. "Sounds interesting, Kruger," he finally said. "One of these days I'll come over to Phillipsburg and we can talk about it."

Two German sailors came on board, and one was carrying a briefcase. They followed Marstrom into the wheelhouse. "I look forward to it. But that's for later. Now, I think we need to count out this cash."

Last Lap

The bright silver glint from the distant mirror shook Harry from his stupor. Although he and Val had been waiting atop the peak at Ile de Fourchue since early morning, when the signal finally came it was almost a surprise. It had been a long, hot day; a day when anticipation and uncertainty made each moment drag incrementally forward, as if time were towing a sea anchor. The *Vagabond* had sailed out of Gustavia harbour not long after the *Antipodes* that morning, the whaleboat's white rectangular sail floating on the blue horizon ahead as they made for their separate destinations. After anchoring in the deserted bay and climbing to the top of the hill, they had shared the duty of watching distant Tintamarre through their binoculars. There now was a feeling of relief knowing their assumptions made during the previous days had proven to be correct. Harry took up his own mirror and flashed his reply. Then he lit a cigarette. "There is the first part of the riddle answered," exhaled Harry, as he finally relaxed in the shade of a smooth round boulder. "We know the *Roulette* has been moved and is moored there, which is a very strong indication that something is about to happen. Unfortunately, our work up here is not done yet."

"What do you expect will happen next?" Val asked.

"What we need now is for Jerry to play his part and show his hand. Before we call Antigua, we need to know that a U-boat has entered the bay, and I wouldn't expect that to happen until well after sunset. If all goes well, we should pick up some sort of sign from up here some time before midnight. If we haven't seen anything by then, we'll have to resort to our fall-back plan, but I'm hoping it won't come to that." Harry wearily stood and put the glasses back up to his eyes, scanning the horizon for any sign of life. "And just to make the situation a little bit more challenging, it looks like we are about to get some foul weather." As they gazed out towards the windward horizon, the rising breeze could be felt on their faces, and dark clouds and rain could be seen moving quickly towards them.

"I think we could use a thermos of strong, hot coffee and a little something to eat, don't you?" Val suggested as she donned her rain coat. "It looks like we're in for a wild night." After leaning over and giving her husband a peck on the cheek, she started down the hill towards the bay and their anchored yacht. "I won't be long, dear," she said.

Darkness fell, and with it came the heavy squalls. And still Harry Iverson and his wife stood resolutely on, waiting for the last part of the puzzle to fall into place. Finally, as the clock moved towards midnight, they saw what they were waiting for; a coded flashing from a ship at sea, answered by a light from the southwest end of the island. "That's it! And none too soon, I might add. I was starting to think our German friends just might not turn up after all," exclaimed Harry. "Let's pack up and get moving. We have a radio call to make. I just hope these Yanks honour their promise and do what they said they would do. We don't want to even consider the consequences if they don't!"

Harry and Val carefully made their way back down to the bayside, launched the dinghy and rowed back to the boat. Once on board, Harry went straight to the chart table, set up his radio and made the call he had been waiting all day to make. After receiving a reply, he started the engine, and with Val at the helm, went onto the foredeck and pulled up the anchor. A few moments later, the yacht was motoring out of the bay, and under shortened sail entered the blustery channel.

In the squally conditions visibility was not ideal, which made for a nerve-racking little crossing, but an hour and a half later the *Vagabond* sailed in to leeward of the island of Tintamarre. The light caused by a fire burning ashore revealed the faint silhouettes of the three smaller craft moored each side of the monster submarine. Harry looked at his watch. They were early. They had no choice but to hove-to and wait.

Nils Albrecht leaned over the U-boat railing, lost in thought. The last of the fuel transfer was taking place and it was his job to oversee it. Earlier, he had encouraged Kapitan Becker to take advantage of his presence to go ashore with his men and stretch their legs. The ship's engineers had begun to wind up the refuelling operation. In another half hour, the U-boat's crew would be returning from the beach. If he was going to do anything to keep up his end of the bargain with Jack, it had to be now. Weiss wandered over and leaned onto the rail next to him.

"What did you find out, Jost?" Albrecht asked.

"I just finished speaking to Becker's chief engineer. From what he understands, the idea is to set some charges aboard the schooner and detonate them just before their departure. Kruger has made sure McLeod and the others do not survive the night."

"Just as I thought. It's time for me to move. Go find Klausterman and Jaeger for me, will you please? Have them meet me on the foredeck straight away. I'm going back aboard the schooner. You're in charge here until I return."

"Are you sure you want to do this sir? I don't imagine what you propose will go over too well back at Kriegsmarine HQ."

"War or no war, there are some things that still need to be honoured. Thanks for your concern, Jost, but I've made up my mind. Now get to it – we don't have much time."

"Aye, aye, sir," the mate replied with a casual salute. As Albrecht skipped down the stairs to the foredeck, he heard the mate shout the names of the two sailors. Moments later, they joined him at the rail.

"Let's go, gentlemen. We're going over to relieve the two guards on board the *Roulette*. I'm sure they would enjoy some exercise." The three men jumped into the schooner's skiff and Jaeger rowed them across. "Stay at the oars, son," Albrecht ordered as he climbed aboard. "I want you to take these men ashore and then come straight back, and when you do, come along the port side."

Once on deck, the captain relieved the two guards of their weapons. "Thank you, men. We'll take it from here. You may go and join the others ashore. Jaeger will row you in." The two guards reluctantly accepted their orders and climbed down into the boat. Jaeger pushed off and slowly pulled the boat towards the beach.

Albrecht led the way aft, and as they reached the cabin doors he turned to face his engineer. "What happens here tonight is strictly between you and me, Stefan. Do you understand?"

"You can depend on me, sir."

Nodding gravely, Albrecht opened the cabin doors. "Wait here," he said before disappearing down the steps.

"What time is it, Clancy?" O'Neil asked, as he peered through the binoculars.

"Ten minutes to two."

As he spoke, the two large petrol engines aboard the *Lady Luck* could be heard starting up.

"Stand by boys – dat sound means dere's not long to go."

At the other end of the bay, Gilbert and Bull anxiously waited to initiate their own part in the plan. "Dere's de first sign," Gilbert whispered as they heard the sleek rumrunner fire up its engines and motor slowly out of the cove. "It won't be long now."

The German Kapitanleutnant descended the steps into the aft cabin. Garfish sat at the table, his serious face reflected in the glow of a kerosene hurricane lamp. "Where is Jack?" Albrecht asked, raising the gun as he reached the bottom of the ladder.

"Right here, Nils," was the reply, as an arm strongly grasped him around the neck from behind, a rigging knife held at his throat. "Just relax and give me the gun, mate. Don't force me to do something I don't want to do."

"I think it is you who should relax, Jack. I have come here to uphold my end of the bargain. Klausterman is standing just above you, and any false move and we'll both probably be dead. I have sent the two guards ashore, and as soon as your boat returns you will be free to go. I advise you not to do anything rash, my friend."

Jack looked over his shoulder to see the muzzle of a machine gun pointing at him from out of the darkness. Slowly he relaxed his grip. Albrecht turned around to face him. "Sorry, Nils. I didn't think it was going to be you. I needed to try something. Unfortunately we're running out of options."

"I would be disappointed if you hadn't, to tell you the truth. But now you have no choice but to trust me." Albrecht stepped back and looked around the cabin. "Where are the young boys?" he asked.

"I'm not really sure, mate. Haven't seen them in a while. Maybe they escaped."

"I don't know how you pulled it off my friend, but in the circumstances, I'm very glad you did. Perhaps you'll be able to tell me all about it one day. Anyway, there isn't much time, and I'm going to need your help. It has been impressed upon Kapitan Becker that we are to leave no witnesses. Their plan is to send some men over to plant some explosives aboard and deal with you at the same time. To avoid all of that we need to act first, which unfortunately means I will not be able to save your schooner. Destroying it is a necessary part of the diversion. We must be quick about it because my colleague Korvettenkapitan Becker will be returning back to his vessel within minutes."

"So what is it you need us to do?" Jack asked.

"First I would like Captain Paris to take those three spare lamps over there and light them."

Garfish pushed himself away from the table and went to where the spare hurricane lamps were hanging. A few moments later the cabin was bathed in light.

"The better we do this, the more chance we have in actually getting away with it. Now where do you keep the spare fuel for your lamps?" Nils asked.

"There is a steel can in the galley house, just inside the door."

"Good." Nils called up to Klausterman and ordered him to retrieve it. Moments later the engineer returned and passed the steel container down the steps.

"Now open this and pour half its contents on the floor." Jack did as he was told, and Albrecht passed the can back up on deck, along with a hurricane lamp. "Here, Stefan. Take this can and empty its contents in the forepeak. And use this lamp to ignite it."

The sound of the skiff bumping against the port topsides could be heard inside the cabin. "It sounds as if Jaeger has returned. Let's go up on deck."

"I can't say I'm happy about you torching my schooner, Nils," Jack said as they stood at the bottom of the companionway. "I suppose there isn't any other way?"

"I can't think of one without getting myself court marshalled or even shot. Unfortunately there are two of us who need to get through this quite difficult situation. Now, I have been to Tintamarre before and know how the system here works. Those local men ashore won't leave until our U-boat departs. They have to look after the range lights that will guide the ship out of the anchorage. I'm sure I don't have to spell it out, but their boat will be your ticket off the island." Albrecht then handed Jack his service revolver. "You can take my hand gun. It isn't loaded, but they won't know that."

"You seem to have covered every angle. I suppose when you think about it there is symmetry in all of this."

"Symmetry? What exactly do you mean?"

"Well you saved my vessel once. I guess it makes sense you are the one who destroys it."

"You are a shipbuilder, Jack. I believe you have the resources to build another. Now let's give moving – there's not much time left. I'm going to send you ashore with Jaeger. He can drop you over amongst those rocks at the point. Once on the island, you should be alright. Now get in the skiff. And good luck to both of you," Nils Albrecht said, holding out his hand.

"Thanks. You are indeed a man of your word, and I won't forget it," Jack said, shaking hands. The two men then climbed up the companionway, slipped over the rail and dropped into the boat. They pushed off and the young German rowed them ashore.

416

Jack and Garfish had just stepped ashore and were ducking towards the rocks when they heard the whistle. "Over here Skip!" Dawson called. Turning, they ran towards the sound.

"Dawson! What the hell are you doing here? Did you see Henry?" Jack whispered.

"Dere's a few of us here, man. Henry an' de nex' boy are fine. Dey's wit' de others up on top o' dis bluff. Follow me." Dawson led them around the point. Crouching low, they wound their way between the rocks and climbed to the top of the hill, where they crept up and knelt near the others.

Henry quickly crawled over and hugged his father. "It's okay mate – we made it," Jack sighed.

"Sorry, but there ain't no time fo' dat now, Jack," O'Neil whispered over his shoulder. "All hell is 'bout to break loose here and we has to be on our toes! You'll want to lie down and take cover."

"Right-o," he replied as he rubbed his boy on the head before crawling up next to O'Neil where he could overlook the scene below. "So what's happening?"

"Well there ain't much time to explain, we is on de final countdown. We just need to keep we heads down an' hope Harry has done he work."

Moments later a light flashed three times from out of the black void to leeward of the bay. "There's Harry's signal!" said Clancy. "Stand by for action!" Rising up to one knee, he lifted a flare gun in the air and fired. The trail of an orange phosphorescent rocket arched high up over the bay, reached its apex and then began to slowly descend, throwing the whole of the anchorage into an unnatural, infrared glow.

Moments later, Gilbert fired a flare from the opposite end of the bay, and now the three ships were lit up brightly beneath the two burning orbs. From their vantage point on top of the hill, they could see the German sailors on the beach all freeze and look skyward. On board the submarine, the few silhouetted figures did the same, as if momentarily stunned in the nightmarish luminosity. On board the *Tor,* Marstrom and Kruger both turned their heads to the heavens, and the young sailor Jaeger stopped mid stroke in the skiff on his way back to the schooner, puzzled as to what was happening.

The schooner *Roulette* was ablaze. Nils Albrecht emerged from the smoke-filled aft cabin to the illumination of the flares overhead, and simultaneously Stefan Klausterman reached the deck after setting fire to the fo'c'sle. Picking up his weapon, the big engineer walked slowly aft, his head cocked as he gazed into the sky. Distracted by the confusion, neither Albrecht nor Klausterman took much notice of the approaching motorboat until it was right alongside. It was only then that they noticed the olive-clad man in a beret rise up to one knee on the cabin top of the *Lady Luck*, a Sten submachine gun pointed directly at them. There was a frozen moment when Kapitanleutnant Nils Albrecht locked on to the eyes of Sergeant-Major Derek Hightower. At that moment, he knew all was lost.

And then the night erupted as the first aircraft swept in to view, coming in low out of the western darkness, guns blazing.

The bursts from the Sten were short, direct and accurate. Smoke and flames began to climb out of the schooner's open hatchway. Nils Albrecht staggered backward as the bullets ripped into him, their force knocking him down the steps into the burning cabin. He was dead as he hit the floor. Before Klausterman could lower his weapon he too took the full brunt of Hightower's sub-machinegun, the eerie day-glow light of the burning flares that hung overhead highlighting his awkward pirouette as he spun and collapsed onto the deck. In an instant, the soldier sprang over the bulwark and onto the schooner, where he charged down the steps into the strengthening inferno, followed by Rabbit and Gregoire. Jumping over the prostrate form of the German captain they rushed into the cabin, calling Jack's name, only to be thwarted by the intense heat and flames. "It's no good! We're too late!" shouted Hightower. "There's nothing we can do!" Rabbit tried to push past but was grabbed by Hightower. "If he's in there, he's gone! It's no use – come on!" And after one last hesitant look, Rabbit and Gregoire scrambled back up the steps on to the deck, where they heard one more burst of gunfire from down below. "There would be nothing worse than burning to death, no matter

---

418

who you are," the soldier explained as he brushed past the others. "We should check to see if anyone's forward."

In the midst of bombs, machinegun fire and the roar of attacking planes, the men rushed forward. Gregoire tried to enter the forepeak but was again knocked back by the flames. Shouting Jack's name, he received no reply. Returning to the cargo hatch, he found Rabbit climbing back on deck from out of the hold equally disappointed. "Hightower was right, man. We's too late. I think we better get de hell out o' here. Dere's nothin' we can do now." Turning towards the rail, they saw the commando kneeling next to Klausterman, his hand on his throat checking for a pulse from the fallen German sailor. Slowly standing, he solemnly and deliberately pointed his gun at his body and pulled the trigger. Then he reached down and grabbed the engineer under the arms and dragged him aft, where he was tumbled down the steps next to his captain.

The men jumped back aboard the *Lady Luck*. Rabbit pushed the bow away from the burning schooner.

"Where's Jack?" queried O'Loughlin, spinning the wheel as the three men entered the wheelhouse.

"He won't be coming wit us, I'm afraid. We're too late," Rabbit answered. The Irishman pushed the throttle down and the *Lady Luck* accelerated out of the anchorage.

It had only taken a moment for the sailors on the submarine to realize the significance of the flares, and they were rushing to the deck guns as the first plane dove into the bay from the west, the twin .50 calibre Browning machine guns blasting away from the nose turret as the Mariner 'Flying Boat' screamed in from astern, the bullets chopping through the water and up the deck before the bombs whistled past, bursting at the water's edge and blowing several bodies high into the air. On the beach, it was chaos as the ship's crew rushed into the churning sea, struggling to return to the U-boat before it was too late.

As the gunners frantically manned the deck guns, the second Mariner hove into view, its two 1,700hp engines shrieking as it streaked in at close to two hundred miles an hour. Columns of water shot high into the night as bombs and bullets exploded all around the U-boat. On the conning tower, Weiss had quickly grasped control. The submarine's emergency hooter was blaring rhythmically. The two main engines were started, and the crew was rushing to battle stations as they desperately attempted to regroup. By the time the third Mariner banked in to attack, the anti-aircraft guns were ready and began returning fire. The freighter *Tor* was finally getting underway when the third bomber dropped its payload, and as one shell detonated and blew a gaping hole into the long sterndeck of the U-boat the other smashed in just forward of the coaster's main hatch. Marstrom swung his wheel hard to starboard as the empty fuel drums on deck of the ship burst into flames. Pushing his slow-turning diesel engine up to full revolutions, he accelerated and the blazing ship slowly crept out of the anchorage.

On the beach, the German officers were screaming at their men to get back aboard, hysterically ordering them to get to their stations. The first set of flares slowly dissipated in intensity, but as they did two more replaced them in the sky. The fourth Mariner now attacked just as pellets of rain began to descend out of the night sky. The wind whipped over the flat island, a harbinger of the squall to come, and though the flares still burned in the sky, the targeted submarine slowly became obscured by the driving rain. On board the U-boat, wounded men were being dragged out of the water and shunted down below. In the surreal glow, rainwater streamed off the men's faces as they desperately struggled to get the crew back aboard and their ship under way. In the midst of this confusion and devastation, Grimaud's little launch could be seen disappearing into the rain-swept night.

Weiss rushed to the rail and peered through the squall towards the burning schooner. He watched as Jaeger rowed back alongside and climbed aboard, running up the steps and on to the bridge. "Where is Kapitan Albrecht? Where is Klausterman?" he shouted as he grabbed the passing boy.

"They are dead! Someone came off of that motorboat firing a machinegun! There was nothing I could do, sir!" the boy screamed back.

A hand grabbed the mate's shoulder and spun him around. "We need to go! Now!" Becker shouted into Weiss's face, his eyes bulging in panic.

"Are there any more men on the beach, sir?" Weiss yelled back.

"I don't give a damn! We need to save the ship and use this cloud cover while we can! Now let's get the hell out of here!"

The squall hit with a vengeance. The rain was horizontal; the wind whipped across the island and out into the bay. As the storm continued to blow down from the heavens, the damaged U-boat backed out of the anchorage and swung her bow south. The rain came down in torrents, obscuring the entire anchorage from view. Finally the squall passed, and when the last wisps of wind and rain had floated away over St. Martin, all that could be seen in the Bay of Tintamarre was the burning hulk of the schooner *Roulette*.

From the top of the hill, the men slowly rose and watched in a sort of stupefied awe, not really sure if what they were seeing was real. To the southeast of the island, the battle continued as the warplanes pursued their stricken prey. Tracer bullets slashed through the brutal blackness of the night; sounds of the battle drifted down on the wind like distant thunder. In the channel, the *Tor*, now well ablaze, was gradually drifting westward.

The group of men watched on in silence as a fireball ripped across the sky when one of the planes was hit. Banking away, the crashing Mariner canted towards the island, a flaming missile streaking towards them, skimming low over the lagoon before slamming into the island. The sound of crunching and twisting metal accompanied the towering explosion as over fifty thousand pounds of aluminium and steel loaded with fuel, bombs and ammunition hit the earth, cartwheeling across the dry centre of the island and disintegrating into pieces before its mutilated carcass came to a rest. Within moments, the flames began to take hold of the dry scrub, and soon the interior of the island was well alight.

"I think it would be a good idea we get back to the whaleboat," O'Neil said matter-of-factly. "Dere ain't nothin' we can do to help anyone who's aboard what's left o' dat; dey's all gone to meet dey maker. Wit' all dem dry cotton stocks it won't take long before dis whole damn island will be up in flames."

The group quickly picked up their gear and headed down the hill. As they did, the burning schooner broke free of her moorings and began to drift sideways out of the bay.

"De man post must o' done burn clean away," O'Neil said as the men all stopped to watch the flaming wreck in the grip of the stiff tradewind drift off into the night.

On the track they met Bull and Gilbert who were ecstatic to see Jack and Henry alive, both having thought they had not survived the burning *Roulette*. "When you all came back along the beach, did you see any survivors?" Jack asked.

"No, man; you don't want to go down dere a-tall," Bull answered solemnly. "Dere ain't nothin' left but pieces o' people floatin' in de tide, an' it didn't take dem sharks too long to find 'em neither."

Together they all jogged silently back to the waiting whaleboat, which Earl had rigged and ready to go. "Man I glad to see all o' you! I had no idea what was goin' on yonder. Dat crashin' plane had me duckin' fo' cover! Man, dat was close!" Pushing off into the lagoon, they used the oars to carefully pick their way out through the narrow entrance, and once free set off into the wind-torn night towards St. Barths.

On the windward horizon, they watched the firefight as the battle drew to a close, the doomed submarine soon to be condemned to the bottom of the Atlantic Ocean, another in the long line of U-boats to be simply described as 'lost with all hands'. Astern, the island of Tintamarre was on fire, the towering red flames glowing in the darkness.

The schooner *Theodora D* left for home the following afternoon. The *Vagabond* sailed for Antigua at the same time. The unpleasant day was dark and squally; the sea grey and filled with whitecaps. A smoky haze obscured the island of St. Martin as Tintamarre burned. Normally they might have waited a day or two for better weather, but after a grim but relief-filled reunion aboard the schooner that morning, it was suggested by Antoine that they leave before anyone started asking questions. Tintamarre was a French territory, after all, and an act of war had taken place. There would most certainly be ramifications.

The mood aboard the schooner was sombre. There was much for the crew to process, and Jack tried to spend as much time as he could with his son. He knew Henry was struggling to come to terms with what he had seen. During his time aboard with the German sailors, he had come to be quite close to several of them, and his father knew he would be trying to comprehend the meaning of their deaths. Try as he may, however, he could get little out of him. Henry spent an inordinate amount of time aloft, sitting on the foremast trestletrees, silently passing his time with Punkin. The crew did what they could to try and coax the teenager out of his funk, but it was hard to get him to crack a smile, even for Kingsford.

"I'm worried about Henry, O'Neil. I don't like him keeping everything to himself," Jack said one afternoon, as they sat with Garfish in the sten of the vessel. "I wish I could get him to just talk to me."

"What – you want de boy to be somethin' different than yourself? Wit you an' Jasmine's blood running t'rough he veins, he be as hard-headed as dey come! What we saw de other day was frightenin' in truth, but we all have to learn to deal wit' it in we own way. All de talk in de worl' ain't goin' to rectify dat," O'Neil replied. "De boy comin' of age, mon. It's a hard lesson, but it's one he must learn."

"I does agree wit dat, Skip. Life ain't easy a-tall, an' all o' we has to find dat out one way or de other," Garfish added, as he stood to check the fishing line.

As for Jack, his thoughts kept returning to Nils Albrecht. The vision of his friend's last moment on earth would be imprinted in his memory forever. Words such as duty and honour and obligation continually demanded to be defined. Watches came and went, and islands slipped slowly by. But the images of that fateful night on Tintamarre remained. If anyone warranted a memorial, if a tribute should ever be bestowed on the selfless actions of a man, Nils Albrecht was deserving of that commendation. And yet he would vanish from this world without acknowledgment or accolade. In the end, Jack finally reasoned, we all turn to dust and are forgotten. Words count for nothing. It was only a man's actions that held any meaning. Doing the right thing was all that really mattered in life.

And so the schooner sailed south, and each day slowly passed. At times they were frustratingly becalmed under the high mountains to windward, and at times they had all of the breeze they wanted. But gradually the weather improved, until the morning three days later when they hauled off around Ile de Quatre and sighted the beckoning peak of Mount Majestic on the distant horizon. It was only then that the crew's hearts joyfully lifted. They were all truly thankful to be home.

Petite Silhouette

The *Theodora D* was met by an anxious crowd alongside the wharf at Port Victoria. And although there was a great feeling of relief when her crew stepped ashore unscathed, there was also an undercurrent of confusion and puzzled curiosity as to what actually happened to this weary-looking group of sailors over the past fortnight. After the initial emotion had passed, the questions came thick and fast. Were they really Germans who had sailed off with Jack and Henry? Where was the *Roulette*? How was Garfish and the *Juanita* involved in all of this? And most of all, what really happened 'up north'?

In the end, it was O'Neil who took control of the situation. Standing on the schooner's bulwarks with one hand grasping the main rigging, he quickly silenced the crowd. "Quiet down all you an' listen!" he shouted over the murmuring mob. When silence finally descended over the wharf, he continued. "We know all you is curious to know what really happen' during de las' couple o' weeks, an' when you does hear de stories you'll t'ink it's joke we tellin'. But don' frighten, most all of it will be true. For now, though, you must be patient. Let dese boys get some rest an' catch hold o' demselves. Take it easy. You'll hear all about it soon enough!"

Jasmine was in the garden when she caught the first glimpse of the schooner's sails as they broke out from under Gunnery Point. Calling to Little to keep an eye on the children, she ran to the wharf and was the first aboard once the vessel was made fast. "Papa tol' me she'll be right, an' when he says somethin' it usually happens dat way," she said as she hugged her two boys. "Even so you fellahs had us all worried sick. Last time it was bullet wound. You have fo' stop all o' dis, Jackson McLeod. Can't you see I'm getting' grey hairs already?"

For Jack it was an indescribable feeling to be home, like the silence after the passing of a hurricane. The pent up feelings of tenseness and anxiety and worry for the safety of his son in particular were finally released, and all he looked forward to were a few nights of uninterrupted sleep.

True to O'Neil's words, it didn't take long for the story to come out as it spread like wildfire from one end of the island to the other. From under the trees of the harbour to the rumshops of Le Moulin, to even the Sunday sermon, it was the only topic of conversation for days on end.

As for Garfish and Punkin, Jack and O'Neil made sure they were not forgotten in all the excitement, making them feel like honorary citizens of the island. It was O'Neil who encouraged him to heave his vessel out, and several members of the *Roulette's* old crew gave Garfish a hand with the cleaning and repainting. Squally contributed by 'overhauling' his sails, and after being reprovisioned by the village shopkeepers the *Juanita* set sail for the Cays.

Over the next weeks, Jack went about making preparations for the building of his new schooner. He finalised the dimensions of the vessel he had always had in mind, and began construction of the half-model which he would use to define her shape. Slowly the events which took place on Tintamarre receded from his thoughts. Then one day he received a letter postmarked Trinidad. Tearing open the envelope, he opened it and read:

Port-of-Spain, Trinidad
June 20, 1943

Dear Jack,

I hope this letter finds you well, and that you and your family are adjusting to life without the 'Roulette'. I thought I should drop you this line to inform you that for the time being at least, I have been moved 'upstairs' and will be

426

taking over a new position in New York. I will be working for the same employer, but in a position of greater responsibility. Val and I will be laying up the yacht here in Trinidad, and as you West Indians would say, 'if God spare Life' hope to return to her after this dreadful war and continue our life aboard her. I look forward to resuming our discussions of 'Cryptozoology' and other interesting topics sometime in the near future.

Your Friend,
Harry

A scorching sun burned out of the clear western sky, its white-hot heat boring into the boatyard as it hung suspended over Gunnery Point. Another work day was winding to an end. "Man, dat sun hot like fire we," Uncle Llewellyn said, as he straightened himself up and wiped his brow. With his axe in one hand and his adze in another, he wearily made his way towards the tool shed. "Dese tired ol' bones is beggin' fo' a sea-bath. I bent up like a crab-hook!"

"Dere's some heat passin' today in trut'," agreed Cuthbert. "It goin' be a long walk back to La Moulin, dat's fo' sure."

Llewellyn sucked his teeth. "Man, I been tellin' you long time to move up here to de harbour. Livin' over yonder's like livin' on de backside o' de worl'."

Jack smiled as he sat back and listened to the familiar chitchat. Finally he stood and collected his own tools amongst the pile of wood chips surrounding him. His khaki workshirt was drenched with sweat. "That sea-bath sounds pretty good to me, Uncle Lew. I'm bloody knackered. I think I'll be heading straight for the water myself."

Joining the other workmen, Jack made his way towards the tool shed. But something made him stop. It was a sound, a far-off distant drone that made him halt in his tracks. One by one, the workmen in the yard fell silent. Even the old women collecting woodchips straightened up and listened. As the sound grew closer, everyone in the boatyard slowly lifted their head towards the sky.

And then the airplane appeared from over the northern ridges of the island. It swept in low over Frigate Bay, flying parallel to the white sands of Grande Plage, the noise from its twin engines echoing around the harbour. At South End, the plane pulled up and banked to the west, where it continued to circle until it made another low run in, passing directly over the main wharf and the heart of Port Victoria itself. With Bristol Hill looming directly in its path, the plane banked hard left, arching to the north, before it swung back towards the setting sun once again. Somewhere out over Savan Island, it made one last turn, and after straightening came skimming in low, finally touching down just inside Gunnery point and Fish Rocks. Once in the water, the flying boat motored slowly in towards the main wharf.

"Well I'll be stuffed," Jack muttered.

"Who de hell you t'ink it could be?" O'Neil asked as he wandered up next to him.

Jack shook his head in disbelief. "It's Sean O'Loughlin, that's who it is!" Walking up to the main wharf, Jack edged his way through the crowd until he came to the end of the jetty, where a weathered old sailor was busy tying off a mooring line. O'Loughlin was on the forward deck of the plane, adjusting the rope's length. Finally satisfied, he made the line fast. Looking up, he spotted Jack on the wharf watching him.

"You sure know how to make an appearance, don't you, Sean?"

"Well I always said I wanted to drop in and see you, now, didn't I? You wouldn't perhaps have some sort of dinghy would you, boy-o? Mercedes and I would love to come ashore!"

"Alright mate – I'll be out in a tick!" Pausing for a moment, Jack stood and watched as O'Loughlin disappeared down through a hatch in the foredeck of the plane. The two big propellers perched on top of the wing over the central fuselage had come to a stop. The plane swung slowly from side to side in the wind.

Walking up the beach, Jack pushed down a small punt and rowed out to the plane. Dodging in under one of the wing floats he came up alongside the main hull, which had its side door open waiting for him.

"Welcome aboard! I hope you have time for a glass of the ol' bubbly!"

"Welcome to Petite Silhouette! It's good to see that you two finally made it," Jack said as he climbed aboard.

"Good to be here, Jack. Cheers," the Irishman said, handing him a flute of chilled Champagne.

"So nice to see you again, Captain McLeod," Mercedes said, as they touched glasses. Her jet-black hair was tied loosely back; she wore an aviator's jumpsuit which matched O'Loughlin's. "To Petite Silhouette!" she toasted.

Jack took a drink and then had a long look around. They sat at a finely polished mahogany table. The interior was immaculately finished, the joinery exquisite. Through a doorway in the bulkhead, he could see what looked like a master bedroom. "This really is as you described, Sean. She really is a 'flying yacht'. So tell me, what brings you to Petite Silhouette?"

"Well, you know how things go – nothing stays the same forever. After our little episode out on Tintamarre, things started to get a bit hot around St. Martin. The Yanks already had a bit of a presence there with construction starting on their airport, but after Tintamarre some serious questions were being asked. Gunther Marstrom somehow managed to beach the *Tor* over at Simpson Baai, and no one has heard of him or his crew since. Kruger himself was eventually arrested as he tried to sneak off to Anguilla. It's too bad the bastard wasn't barbequed aboard the *Tor*, but that's how it goes. At any rate, I didn't see Kruger as the type to keep his mouth shut for very long. His French partners would be safe – they have too many important people in their pockets. For us it was going to be different. I could see the writing on the wall as far as our life in St. Barths was concerned. A bunch of bureaucrats arrived from Guadeloupe and began to snoop around. Of course they didn't get anything out of the locals, but I had the feeling that it would only be a matter of time before my activities came to their attention. Lefèvre made me an offer on my house and the *Lady Luck* that I couldn't really refuse. I knew I had to get my plane out of St. Martin before the authorities put two and two together, so I agreed to Lefèvre's terms and made what in military terms would be described as an 'orderly retreat'."

"Unfortunately we had to leave some lovely things behind, but we still have our lives and our freedom. Those are the most important things," Mercedes said.

"I appreciate exactly what you are saying. Speaking of leaving things behind – did you ever hear what became of the *Roulette*?"

"As a matter of fact I did," Sean replied. "It seems that what was left of her eventually drifted on to the reefs of St. Martin, where she broke up. I heard that Grimaud ended up salvaging a few burned-up bits and pieces. It must have hurt you tremendously to see your schooner come to such an inglorious end."

"The *Roulette* was a great vessel. But she had a good run. Forty years is a lot more than most Gloucestermen would ever be expected to survive. So now I've been forced to make a start on my next schooner. That's how it goes. And it seems that you two are in the same boat. You've had to leave St. Barths behind and look to start anew. What's next, if you don't mind me asking?"

"South America has always been a fascination of ours. We'll have a look at Venezuela, then perhaps Colombia. There is always the Amazon and Brazil. We might get to Argentina, or maybe even as far south as Chile. This plane can land almost anywhere. It's a hell-of-a big continent down there, so who knows?"

"It all sounds like quite an adventure, mate. You must send me a postcard every now and then and let me know what's happening."

"We'll make sure we keep in touch, boy-o."

"Now Jack, maybe you can answer a question for me," Mercedes said. "Whatever happened to that charming fellow from Barbados? What did you call him darling – was it Rabbit? He seemed like a lot of fun. I wish we could've seen more of him."

"Rabbit? Oh he's the real definition of a rolling stone, that's for sure. He went back to his wife in Barbados only to find that she had spent all his money and taken up with another man. He had a little fishing sloop there, so he took off with his oldest son and sailed for the Cays. He stopped in here for a few days on his way south. Rabbit said he was going fishing, but I wouldn't be surprised if he doesn't get back to what he knows best – smuggling rum!"

"Well I'm really excited that we're going to finally get a chance to meet your wife and see this beautiful island of yours that I've heard so much about."

"Absolutely! If you'd like we can go ashore now. You'll need to bring your ship's papers with you, Sean. Our good constable asked if you could stop by and attend to formalities. I'm not sure how he's going to clear an airplane in. That should be interesting."

"Oh, it shouldn't be a problem. I'll just tell him she's simply a yacht, only of the airborne type."

The six o'clock chimes rang across the harbour as Jack sat on the veranda with his morning cup of cocoa-tea. Since his return home he had lost himself in the construction of his new schooner, and the memories of the events at Tintamarre had begun to slowly recede. O'Loughlin's visit brought it all rushing back to him.

The seaplane hung on a mooring in the bay below. *A sign of the times,* Jack said to himself. Most of the people of Petite Silhouette had never seen an airplane before yesterday. He was sure it was something they wouldn't soon forget. And he was certain it would inevitably happen again. It was as if the pages of history had turned to a new chapter, just as the sinking of the *Roulette* represented the end of the last one.

As these and other thoughts sailed through Jack's mind, the sound of engines echoed through the harbour. He could see Sean O'Loughlin appear on the foredeck attending to the mooring line. The noise had awakened the children, and they all rushed out to sit with their father. Jack watched the silhouette of his old friend disappear back through the deck hatch, wondering if it would be the last time he would ever see him. With his sleepy daughters on his lap and Henry playing with his youngest son at his feet, he observed the plane slowly turn as it taxied for its take-off. The propellers increased their revolutions, the craft picked up speed, and accelerating downwind it began to skip over the wavelets until it slowly became airborne, the morning sun reflecting off of her wings as she lifted into the western sky.

The plane banked leisurely to port. Silently they observed the silver shape shrink into the distance until it finally disappeared into a bank of clouds to the southwest. "Well dat was exciting, wasn't it kids?" Jasmine finally said. "Come now – let's get some breakfast. It's time all o' you got ready fo' school."

The twins moaned as they slipped off his lap. Henry slowly staggered to his feet, handing the toddler to his father before wandering back into the house. The boy squirmed playfully in his arms.

A new day was starting.

He put his son down, stood and stretched. Lost in thought, Jack watched a flock of white seabirds wheel low over the windblown surface of the indigo bay. He was home and alive and exactly where he wanted to be. He'd better get moving. There was a schooner in the boatyard waiting to be built. Reaching down, he took the little boy's hand in his own. "Come on, mate. Let's go see if we can find you some tucker."

The End

Epilogue

By July of 1943, the German assault on the Caribbean was all but over. As in all other theatres of World War II, German industry could not keep up with the incredible pace set by the Allies, especially the United States. Never again would the U-boats come close to the damage they inflicted on Caribbean shipping as in the year of 1942, when 336 ships and over 1.5 million tons of shipping was officially confirmed sunk. Official records of schooners lost to submarine activity only tell a part of the story; their destruction would for the most part be passed down by word of mouth through island lore.

The German U-boat expedition into the waters of the West Indies inadvertently caused a far greater effect on the islands than just a military reaction to a strategic threat. The rapid deployment of US forces in the Caribbean with the associated construction of military facilities that accompanied it led to a massive development of the basic infrastructure of the major islands of the West Indies. When the war ended in 1945, military airstrips on the islands of Antigua, St. Lucia, St. Martin, and Trinidad, among others, formed the foundations for the commercial airports that quickly followed. This paved the way for the gradual increase of tourism that snowballed into the multi-billion dollar industry it is today. Another consequence of this instant growth was the dissemination of contemporary trades and skills, which in turn gave the islands the tools to develop their new, self-reliant economies.

In the matter of a few short years, World War II dragged the West Indies away from the colonial plantocracy of its past into independence and amalgamation with the modern world. The islands were changed forever.

Glossary of Nautical & West Indian Terms

AB: Stands for Able-Bodied Seaman.

Aback: When the wind strikes the leeward (back) side of the sail.

Aft: Towards or at the rear of a ship.

Afterdeck: The part of a ship's deck past amidships toward the stern.

Aloft: Up the mast, above the deck.

Alongside: To berth next to a wharf or other vessel.

Arrowroot: Starch extracted from the root of the plant, Maranta arundinacea.

ASDIC: Underwater detection device used by Allied forces in WWII.

Astern: Behind or at the back of a vessel; to move in a backward direction.

Athwartships: Across the vessel; from one side to the other.

Bald-headed Schooner: A schooner without a fore topmast.

Ballast stones: Rocks used as a weight to increase the stability of a vessel.

Beam: Breadth of a vessel at its widest point; deck support athwartships.

Beat: To sail to windward close-hauled.

Bilge: The lowest compartment on a ship below the waterline,

Bill of Lading: A contract that covers the specific terms agreed to by a shipper.

Bobstay: A wire or chain used to support the bowsprit of a ship.

Bollard: A short vertical post on a ship or a quay, principally for mooring.

Boom: A spar which supports the foot of sail.

Bowsprit: A spar extending forward over the bow of a vessel.

Brestline: Diagonal mooring line used alongside; retards movement fore and aft

Broff: A simple broth usually made from fish.

Bubal: Local slang for contraband, especially alcoh. ol and cigarette.

Bulkhead: An athwartships partition within the hull of a ship.

Bull jowl: Traditional sauté made with salt fish, tomato, onion and hot pepper.

Bulwarks: The part of a ship's side that is above the deck.

Bumboat: A small boat used to ferry supplies to ships moored away from the shore.

Cable's length: A nautical unit of measure equal to one tenth of a nautical mile.

Calabash: A hard-shelled gourd that when dried can be cut to make a bailer.

Careen: To expose one side of the ship's hull below the water line for maintenance.

Cathead: Wooden beam located on the bow used to support the ship's anchor.

Centreboard: Wooden board lowered through a boat's bottom to reduce leeway.

Centrecase: A wooden box which houses a boats centreboard.

Clewed out: A sail pulled out to the end of a gaff, boom or yard.

Close hauled: Sailing as close as possible to the wind.

Close reach: Sailing with the wind slightly forward of the beam.

Coal-pot: Cooking device with a raised iron bowl and a central grid. Uses charcoal.

Cocoa-tea: Drink made from chocolate, sugar, hot water and thickened with flour.

Companionway: The access to the main cabin.

Conch: Large shelled sea snail that forms a staple part of the West Indian diet.

Coo-coo: A heavy bread-like porridge made from ground corn meal.

Dead reckoning: Navigation using previous position, boatspeed and heading.

Donkey engine: A deck engine or winch on freight vessels used to hoist cargo.

Double-ender: A vessel with a stern similar to the bow, like a canoe.

Downhaul: Line or tackle used to put downward pressure on a sail or spar.

Downwind: To leeward, running before the wind.

Fathom: Nautical unit equal to six feet used for measuring the depth of water.

Fender: A bumper used when mooring alongside a wharf or vessel.

Fisherman's staysail: A rectangular sail set between the two masts of a schooner.

Flying jib: The outer jib or third headsail set on a schooner. Also called a jib tops'l.

Fo'c'sle: The forecastle, a structure in the bow of a vessel where the crew is housed,

Foremast: The forward mast on a schooner.

Forepeak: The forward area of a sailing vessel below the deck.

Fore rigging: The wire attached to the chainplates that supports the foremast.

Foresail, (fores'l): A fore and aft sail set behind the foremast on a schooner.

Forestay: Rigging wire between the foremast head and the end of the bowsprit.

Full astern: On a motor vessel, to go backwards at full speed.

Gaff: A spar to which the head of a four-sided sail is attached.

Gaff jaws: A wooden yoke-like apparatus attaching the gaff to the mast.

Galleyhouse: Cooking area on a working vessel usually found aft of the foremast.

Gloucesterman: Fishing schooner built in Gloucester, Mass., famous for speed.

Gudgeons: Metal brackets which form the hinging mechanism on a boat's rudder.

Gunnel (gunwale): The upper edge of the side of a vessel or boat.

Gybe: To change from one tack to the other with the wind from astern.

Half-model: A scaled model of a vessel used to construct the full-scale version.

Halyard: The line on a mast used for hoisting a sail.

Hardening up: To tighten the sheets so a boat can sail closer to the wind.

Head: The toilet area of a ship or yacht.

Head (of a sail): The uppermost corner of a sail.

Headsails: The sails set before the most forward mast, otherwise known as jibs.

Heave out: To careen a vessel for repairs or maintenance.

Heave-to: To stop the boat by coming head to wind and backing the headsail.

Heeled: When a boat is inclined by the action of the wind or sea.

Hounds: The area on a mast where the spreaders attach.

Hove-to: See heave-to.

Inboard: Within the hull or toward the centre of a vessel.

Jack Iron: Especially strong rum made from the dregs of the fermentation barrel.

Jib: A triangular sail set before the foremast.

Johnny-cakes: Bread made from flour and water usually fried in a pan with oil.

Keel: The structural backbone of a vessel located at its deepest part.

Knockabout: A sailing vessel that does not carry a bowsprit.

Kopai: Local slang for a sailor or sailing vessel from the southern Grenadines.

Lazorette: The after section of a vessel usually used for storage.

Lazy jacks: Lines which help control the mainsail when reefing or furling.

Lee shore: A shore lying to leeward of a ship constituting a danger in a storm.

Leeward: The direction away from which the wind is blowing.

Light (de jib): To slack out the jib sheet, then pull it in again.

Lift : A beneficial change in wind direction when sailing to windward.

Luff: The leading edge of a sail.

Luff: To sail too close to the wind; to make a sail shake.

Main boom: The spar to which the foot of the mainsail is attached.

Mainmast: In a two masted schooner rig, the aftermost and tallest mast.

Main rigging: The wire attached to the chainplates that supports the main mast.

Mainsheet: Sheet used to control the mainsail.

Mainsail (mains'l): Fore and aft sail attached to the mainmast of a schooner.

Main thwart: A seat which runs laterally (athwartships) across a small boat.

Make fast: To secure a line or sheet.

Manila Rope: Rope made from Manila hemp.

Mannish watah: A soup or broff made from goat or conch said to imbibe virility.

Man post: A beam fit through the fore deck to which the anchor rope is made fast.

Masthead: The top of a mast.

METOX: A receiver installed in U-boats tuned to pick up enemy radar.

'Midships: The part of a ship midway between bow and stern (from amidships).

'Midships' hold: The middle cargo compartment of a cargo vessel.

Mooring line: A rope used to hold a boat in place.

Oakum: Loosely twisted hemp fibre impregnated with tar used for caulking seams.

Oarpins: Pair of pegs through which an oar passes when rowing.

Obeah: Caribbean folk magic, sorcery, and religious practices of African origin.

Oilskins: Waterproof gear worn by sailors for protection against bad weather.

On the wind: Sailing close hauled.

Outboard: The direction away from the centre of a ship.

Outhaul: Line or tackle used to pull a sail out to its fullest extent.

Peak halyard: Rope used to hoist the outside end of a gaff sail.

Pelau: Meal of chicken and rice when both are cooked together in the same pot.

Pintles: The hinging mechanism on a rudder which incorporates a pin.

Port side: Facing forward, the left side of a boat.

Port tack: Sailing with the wind coming from the port side of the boat.

Quarter bits: Posts set in each corner of the sterndeck used for making ropes fast.

Ratlines: Rope or wood tied between the shrouds used for climbing aloft.

Rhum de l'Alize': Translates from French to Rum of the Tradewinds.

Rig: General term for spars, sails and rigging.

Rig: Describes type of vessel (i.e. schooner, sloop, yawl etc.).

Running rigging: Ropes that set and adjust the sails.

Sails aback: When the wind strikes the leeward side of a sail.

Sail palm: Leather handpiece that helps push a needle through a sail.

Schooner: Sailing vessel with two or more masts rigged fore and aft.

Sheave: The grooved wheel a rope passes over when going through a block.

Sheer: The top edge of the side of a vessel.

Sheets: Ropes used for adjusting the set of a sail.

Shrouds: The wire rigging that supports the masts athwartships.

Skiff: A small boat.

Sloop: Sailing boat with one mast.

Sprit: A spar that crosses a four-sided sail to support the peak.

Squall: A rainstorm of short duration usually with strong wind.

Standing Rigging: Fixed wires which support the masts.

Starboard: When facing forward the right side of a vessel.

Starboard tack: Sailing with the wind coming from the starboard side.

Stem: Structural part which forms the bow of a boat.

Stem Staysail, stays'l: A jib that attaches to the top of the stem.

Stern: The aftermost part of a boat.

Tack: To change a boat's direction by steering through the wind. Go about.

Tack: The lower forward corner of a sail.

Tacked down: To make fast the tack of a sail.

Tail: The free end of a sheet that is not dead ended (attached) to a block.

Tern Schooner: A fore and aft rigged vessel with three masts.

Trim: To adjust a sail so that it sets to the direction of the wind.

Trim: The attitude or balance of a vessel in the water.

Throat: The part of a gaff that is closest to the mast.

Topsail: A triangular sail set above a gaff on a fore and aft rigged vessel.

Topsides: The side of a boat between the waterline and the deck.

To weather: To windward. Also, to sail to windward of a given point.

Trade winds: The prevailing pattern of easterly winds found in the tropics.

Transom: The surface that forms the stern of a vessel.

Trestle Trees: Athwartships members, which support both rigging and topmast.

Upwind: In the direction from which the wind is blowing.

Whaleboat: A double-ended boat of 26 feet traditionally used for hunting whales.

Windward: The direction upwind from the point of reference.

Wing on wing: Sailing downwind with the mainsail and jib set on opposite sides.

Whelk: Marine gastropod snail found in temperate waters.

Wheel box: Structure which houses the ship's wheel on traditional vessels.

Weather tide: Current which is running against the direction of the wind.

Yawl: A vessel rigged with two masts, the smallest set aft of the rudder post.

Schooner

Roulette

DESIGNED BY BB CROWNINSHIELD NA

Length over all ~ 113'-9"
Beam ~ 23'-10"
Draught ~ 12'-1"
Originally Built as HARMONY by Oxner & Story
Essex, Mass., 1903

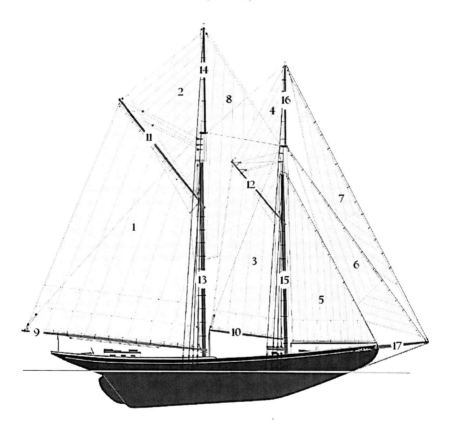

1 Mainsail	7 Flying Jib	13 Main Mast
2 Main Topsail	8 Fisherman Staysail	14 Main Topmast
3 Foresail	9 Main Boom	15 Foremast
4 Fore Topsail	10 Fore Boom	16 Fore Topmast
5 Stem Staysail	11 Main Gaff	17 Bowsprit
6 Jib	12 Fore Gaff	

For more information about this Book and its Author, go to
www.tradewindpublishing.com

CPSIA information can be obtained
at www.ICGtesting.com
Printed in the USA
FSOW01n0454170816
23308FS